PRAISE FOR BETH K. VOGT

"Vogt is paving a way for herself in the world of women's fiction. The Thatcher sisters deal with real issues and, despite their trials, find love and friendship in the midst. The ending of *Moments We Forget* will leave readers delighted."

RACHEL HAUCK, *NEW YORK TIMES* BESTSELLING AUTHOR

"In *Moments We Forget*, Vogt again proves she's a master at peeling back the layers while gently navigating the dynamics of faith, family, and sisterhood. This book challenges the tough, the real, and the exquisite journey that is the life we live—shining a spotlight on the hope we cling to when all points don't line up the way we'd first planned. I was at once encouraged and soon blown away by this book!"

KRISTY CAMBRON, BESTSELLING AUTHOR OF *THE LOST CASTLE* AND *THE BUTTERFLY AND THE VIOLIN*

"Delightful to spend time with the Thatcher sisters once again! Jillian shares her vulnerability and growth in completely relatable ways. We feel like part of the family and cheer as Jillian, Johanna, and Payton find their way back to each other."

KATHERINE REAY, BESTSELLING AUTHOR OF *THE AUSTEN ESCAPE* AND *A PORTRAIT OF EMILY PRICE*

"In *Moments We Forget*, Beth Vogt tackles the topics of childlessness, infidelity, and faith, weaving them with sensitivity and grace into a gripping novel that's impossible to put down. Fans of family dramas won't want to miss this one!"

CARLA LAUREANO, RITA AWARD–WINNING AUTHOR OF *BRUNCH AT BITTERSWEET CAFÉ*

"With deftness of pen and intuitive sensitivity to such tender issues as family tension, sibling conflict, and infertility, Beth Vogt brings yet another beautiful story of redemption in the midst of pain to her readers. An emotional, captivating continuation of the Thatcher sisters' story, sure to satisfy readers longing for this sequel. Bravo!"

AMY SORRELLS, AWARD-WINNING AUTHOR OF *BEFORE I SAW YOU* AND *LEAD ME HOME*

"It's rare when a second novel in a series surpasses the first, but *Moments We Forget* is just such a book. This continuing story of the Thatcher sisters is rich in emotion as the sisters explore issues of family and faith, find healing for troubled relationships, and forge exciting new ones. I can't wait for the next novel in the series!"

DEBORAH RANEY, AUTHOR OF THE CHANDLER SISTERS NOVELS AND *A VOW TO CHERISH*

"What a delight to catch up with the Thatcher sisters in this second installment of Beth Vogt's series. I so appreciate the authenticity of the way the Thatcher family is portrayed and I especially enjoyed getting a little more insight into oldest sister, Johanna. Handled with grace and threaded with poignancy, *Moments We Forget* weaves through the many layers of relationships to get to the heart of what it means to be a family."

MELISSA TAGG, AWARD-WINNING AUTHOR OF THE WALKER FAMILY SERIES AND THE ENCHANTED CHRISTMAS COLLECTION

"Beth Vogt is a writer who sees deeply into people and relationships, and that insight translates beautifully into her novels."

CARA PUTNAM, AWARD-WINNING AUTHOR OF *SHADOWED BY GRACE* AND *BEYOND JUSTICE*

"*Moments We Forget* is a beautiful exploration of the often-complicated and messy relationships between sisters. Vogt skillfully weaves a tale infused with tender truth-filled moments, gentle grace, and the hope and healing found through faith."

CATHERINE WEST, AUTHOR OF *WHERE HOPE BEGINS*

"Written with her characteristic depth, Vogt's *Moments We Forget* explores the sometimes-unpleasant realities of the world, but still manages to leave the reader with beautiful hope. By the end, the characters were friends. I wanted to sit beside them, cry with them, and wrap my arms around them as they wrestled through questions everyone must ask at some point in life. Vogt's books have always belonged at the top of my must-read list, and *Moments We Forget* is no exception."

LINDSAY HARREL, AUTHOR OF *THE SECRETS OF PAPER AND INK*

"Beth Vogt writes with honest warmth, with a true understanding of her characters. What excellent weaving of stories. I never want to stop reading her novels!"

HANNAH ALEXANDER, AUTHOR OF THE HALLOWED HALLS SERIES

"With her latest book, *Moments We Forget*, author Beth K. Vogt has put me in a dilemma. The story is so compelling that I want to devour it in one setting. Yet it's so incredibly well written I want to savor every word. Vogt is truly a master storyteller and now every book is automatically on the top of my must-read list."

EDIE MELSON, DIRECTOR OF THE BLUE RIDGE MOUNTAINS CHRISTIAN WRITERS CONFERENCE

"With tenderness and skill, Beth Vogt examines the price of secrets, the weight of tragic loss, and the soul-deep poison of things left unsaid."

LISA WINGATE, *NEW YORK TIMES* BESTSELLING AUTHOR OF *BEFORE WE WERE YOURS*, ON *THINGS I NEVER TOLD YOU*

"Once again Vogt's beautiful writing captures the struggles and hopes of her broken characters, this time with a cast of sisters who find themselves forced to confront their pasts, their fears, and the healing power of forgiveness. Powerful, moving, and redemptive. Everything I hope for in a Beth Vogt novel."

SUSAN MAY WARREN, *USA TODAY* BESTSELLING, CHRISTY AWARD–WINNING AUTHOR, ON *THINGS I NEVER TOLD YOU*

"Questions, regrets, and memories hang over all our lives. *Things I Never Told You* authentically explores past and present hurts in a way that will take readers deeper into the heart. Beth's story will give real hope to anyone struggling with fractured relationships."

CHRIS FABRY, CHRISTY AWARD–WINNING AUTHOR OF *DOGWOOD* AND *THE PROMISE OF JESSE WOODS*

BETH K. VOGT

Moments We Forget

Tyndale House Publishers, Inc.
Carol Stream, Illinois

a
Thatcher
Sisters novel

Visit Tyndale online at www.tyndale.com.

Visit Beth K. Vogt's website at www.bethvogt.com.

TYNDALE and Tyndale's quill logo are registered trademarks of Tyndale House Publishers, Inc.

Moments We Forget

Designed by Julie Chen

Edited by Sarah Mason Rische

Published in association with the literary agency of Books & Such Literary Management, 52 Mission Circle, Suite 122, PMB 170, Santa Rosa, CA 95409.

Moments We Forget is a work of fiction. Where real people, events, establishments, organizations, or locales appear, they are used fictitiously. All other elements of the novel are drawn from the author's imagination.

For information about special discounts for bulk purchases, please contact Tyndale House Publishers at csresponse@tyndale.com, or call 1-800-323-9400.

Library of Congress Cataloging-in-Publication Data
Names: Vogt, Beth K., author.
Title: Moments we forget / Beth K. Vogt.
Description: Carol Stream, Illinois : Tyndale House Publishers, Inc., [2019] | Series: A Thatcher sisters novel
Identifiers: LCCN 2018047778| ISBN 9781496427281 (hc) | ISBN 9781496427298 (sc)
Subjects: LCSH: Sisters—Fiction. | Domestic fiction.
Classification: LCC PS3622.O362 M66 2019 | DDC 813/.6—dc23 LC record available at https://lccn.loc.gov/2018047778

Printed in the United States of America

25	24	23	22	21	20	19
7	6	5	4	3	2	1

"A sister is both your mirror—and your opposite."
ELIZABETH FISHEL (1950-) JOURNALIST & AUTHOR

Moments We Forget *is dedicated to all sisters who struggle in their relationships with one another. Who fight to find their place between "me" and "us." No sister relationship is perfect. And some sister relationships are bound in pain. But even then, there can still be love.*

I HAD HALF AN HOUR, no more than that, to get my life in order so my sisters would never suspect how unprepared I was for this morning.

I kicked the back door shut, dumping the plastic grocery bags onto the kitchen counter, easing the ache in my arms. If Johanna were hosting this morning, she'd have something homemade baking in her oven, the appealing aroma filling her immaculate kitchen.

Well, one thing was for certain—I was not Johanna.

Winston's frantic barks sounded from upstairs. Seconds later, he was scampering around my feet, his sudden appearance meaning I'd forgotten to lock him in his kennel. Again.

"Bad dog." A halfhearted reprimand. "You're not supposed to be down here."

I pulled items from the plastic bags. *Please don't let me have forgotten anything during my mad dash through the grocery store.*

Cream for Johanna's and my coffee—although she was going to have to make do with my Keurig coffeemaker, not French press.

A small box of sugar so Payton could enjoy her coffee with the preferred three heaping spoonfuls per cup.

A premade fruit salad.

Blueberry muffins.

Keurig pods.

Nothing fancy. But at least I wouldn't look like a complete failure.

I suppose to a casual observer, Johanna, Payton, and I—the three remaining Thatcher sisters—appeared successful. And yet, while we might claim certain professional and romantic achievements, we still struggled to find our way as sisters.

At times Pepper's words—the ones Payton had shared with Johanna and me several months ago—seemed more of a taunt than an encouragement.

"Sometimes you just have to forget all the other stuff and remember we're sisters."

Shouldn't a role you acquired at birth be simple? Something you learned to do, along with walking and talking and navigating adolescence?

But then Pepper's death at sixteen splintered our already-precarious bonds.

I selected three mugs from a kitchen cupboard. This was no time to try to unravel the complicated dynamics between me, Johanna, and Payton—not when they'd be here any minute. And not with so much riding on this morning.

It's funny how much hope people put into a cup of coffee.

Social media—Facebook and Instagram and Twitter and Pinterest and even millions of people's text messages around the world—overflow daily with memes and GIFs lauding the miracle qualities of coffee.

Coffee is the gasoline of life.

All I need is coffee and mascara.

Behind every successful person is a substantial amount of coffee.

I drink coffee for your protection.

Drink coffee and do good.

And now . . . now coffee would be the glue that bonded the three of us together.

Coffee and a book, if Payton's latest "we should do this!" idea succeeded.

Despite our determination to try to be better sisters—to overcome the damage to our relationships caused by Pepper's death . . . and secrets . . . and not knowing how to even relax with one another—it was all too easy to succumb to a lifetime of bad habits.

Of course, I knew my given position in the Thatcher sisters, volunteering to have our first Saturday morning book club meeting at my house. There were times I doubted that I'd ever get my "Is everybody happy?" theme song out of my head.

It didn't matter that I had a full-time job. That I battled unrelenting fatigue. That Geoff and I were starting renovations on our house next week. I laughed and brushed off their multiple "We can do this, Jillian," offers with light-hearted responses of "I'm good. Really. This isn't a problem at all."

And then I'd resorted to a last-minute trip to the grocery store for premade options for this morning's breakfast.

"A girl has to do what a girl has to do" was fast becoming my mantra. Only I was doing less and less and hoping to get by.

Winston scratched at the back door leading from the kitchen to the yard, distracting me from my musings on the power of caffeine mixed with a heavy dose of self-doubt.

I bent down and ruffled his white ears before opening the door. "Sorry to leave you sitting there."

He ran off along the chain-link fence, barking at a squirrel or a bird. No, wait. That was our next-door neighbor, Gianna, out with her toddler.

"Good morning. Sorry about the barking." I stepped outside, snapping my fingers. "Hush, Winston!"

"It doesn't ever bother us." Her daughter knelt, reaching through the fence. "Oh, don't do that, Avery!"

I grabbed Winston's collar, tugging him back beside me. "He won't bite, but he is a nonstop licker."

"We've talked about getting a dog, but right now my hands are full trying to keep up with a two-year-old."

"I can imagine. But she's a cute handful." I checked my watch. Almost nine o'clock. Johanna and Payton would be here anytime now. "I'm sorry. I need to go. My sisters are coming over this morning."

"How fun. I wish I had a sister." Gianna took Avery's hand, helping her stand and brushing off the knees of her jeans. "And I need to try and tire this one out so she'll take a nap for me later."

"Good luck with that."

She tossed a wave over her shoulder. "See you later. Come on, Avery."

I released Winston. "Gianna—"

"Yes?"

"I did mention Geoff and I are renovating our kitchen, right?"

My neighbor kept a firm grip on her daughter's hand, despite Avery's attempts to squirm loose. "I noticed the huge dumpster in your driveway—a pretty big clue— and you also said you were thinking about it earlier this summer."

"I guess that thing is hard to miss." Winston sniffed around my feet. "I just wanted to warn you there'll be workmen around during the day, but most of the noise will be inside the house. A friend is acting as our project manager, and he knows all the workers."

"Great. Thanks for letting me know."

A knock at the front door as I entered the house signaled the arrival of one sister—most likely Johanna, who was always early.

She greeted me with a quick hug, setting her leather purse and her book on the small oak table Geoff and I kept by the front door. At least she'd brought her copy of the book we'd chosen. The question was, had she read it?

"Good to see you, Joey. How are you?"

"Tired." Johanna slipped off her leather sandals, looking trim in black capris and a red flowing top with cutout shoulders. "Between my work and Beckett's schedule at the Air Force Academy, life's crazy."

"Still, it must be nice having him in the same state at least."

"He might as well have kept his original assignment in Alabama. The superintendent at the academy keeps him so busy dealing with speeches and briefings and I don't know what else, we barely see each other."

"But you see him more than you did when he lived in another state, right?" And not seeing each other was the norm for Beckett and Johanna.

"I'm not keeping track of hours and minutes."

"One thing I know is you and Beckett can do this. You've managed a long-distance relationship for years, which means you can manage crazy hours with both of you living in the same town. I remember how excited you both were the weekend he drove into the Springs."

"You're right, Jilly. I'm still getting used to this new phase. It was so sudden."

"Why don't you go make a cup of coffee? I apologize that it's from a plastic pod and not your preferred French press. But I do have cream . . ." Had I taken the time to put it in the fridge? Payton pulled up in front of the house as I started to close the door. "I'll wait here for Payton."

"Sounds good." My oldest sister disappeared in a light cloud of her Coco perfume.

Payton released her long auburn hair from its ponytail as she half ran up the sidewalk. "Hey!"

"No need to run—you're not late."

"I lost track of time." She shook her head, strands falling around her shoulders.

"Well, come on in." We shared a quick hug. "Do you want coffee or water?"

"Both sound great. I'm dehydrated and undercaffeinated—a bad combination, especially if I want to get along with Johanna this morning."

"Don't start." I resisted the urge to shake my finger at Payton.

"It was a joke."

In the kitchen, Johanna had arranged the fresh-from-a-plastic-container muffins onto a plate. The premade fruit salad now sat on the counter in a white ceramic bowl.

"Thanks." I retrieved a serving spoon from the drawer. "I could have done that."

"I figured I would make myself useful while I waited for my coffee." She gave Payton a slow once-over. "Did you just come from the gym?"

"Technically, yes, but I was coaching, not working out. I met one of my JV girls for a private lesson. She wanted to work on blocking." She raised both hands, waving aside her explanation. "Sorry if you're offended, big sister. I couldn't shower if I wanted to be here close to on time."

Johanna hadn't commented on my casual attire of relaxed

jeans and a navy-blue Broncos T-shirt—a well-loved gift from Dad. But Johanna and Payton would find something to bicker about even if they'd taken a vow of silence. And me? I would always be the designated driver of the emotional vehicle that carried our merry little trio.

"You look fine, Payton. This is a book club, not a formal affair. Grab yourself some coffee and I'll get your water." I retrieved a glass from the closest cupboard. "I thought I could walk you both through the kitchen—tell you about our renovation plans—before we sit down and talk about the book. Zach was here last night, finalizing everything."

There was no overlooking how Payton's eyes lit up at the mention of Zach. Maybe someday soon she'd share more about their relationship. For now, she maintained a "just friends" demeanor and kept all details to herself. Of course, even friendship with the man she once blamed for Pepper's death would be considered progress by a lot of people.

"I still don't understand why our family—and Payton in particular—is so chummy with Zach Gaines."

Payton stiffened at Johanna's comment.

"Zach helped us select these beautiful white cabinets—" I spoke up, hoping if I kept talking, I could divert the brewing tension—"that he'll custom design and install for us. A few will have inset glass. They'll work so well with the counter-tops we picked out. The counters are made from pressed paper, if you can believe that."

"Pressed paper?" Johanna's brow furrowed as if I'd sug-gested we were using blue-lined notebook paper for our kitchen counters.

"It's a new green alternative. We selected a pewter color. Between enlarging the window over the sink and knocking out the wall between the kitchen and the dining room, everything is going to feel so open and light."

Payton finished chugging her glass of water, ignoring Johanna's glare. "Zach told me that he also agreed to be the project manager."

"Geoff asked him about that when we first started discussing renovating the kitchen. What with Geoff taking on some extra projects at work and me being gone at the bank, we figured we needed someone to oversee the renovation. Zach talked with his boss, who agreed to a four-day workweek for him in the office and one day from home." My explanation was more for Johanna's benefit than Payton's, who I'm certain already knew this. "Geoff and I have so much more peace of mind, knowing Zach is going to make certain everything stays on track."

"What else are you planning?"

Before I spoke, I prepped Payton's coffee, silently counting off three sugars. "We picked out dark wood floors last weekend. And I finally decided to splurge on a waterfall counter for the island. I also asked Zach to check on replacing the back door with French doors."

"Those will be expensive." Johanna found plates and silverware, obviously ready to eat.

"Yes, but my bonus was bigger than we expected, and Geoff had been saving for this before we got married. Besides, we want to do the kitchen right and not have any regrets later."

Johanna offered both of us plates. "You've been watching too many home makeover shows."

My big sister was not going to talk me out of my fun—or convince me to be more economical. Geoff and I knew what we were doing. And it wasn't as if we'd spent a lot of money on a lavish wedding.

"We're considering this renovation a belated wedding gift to ourselves." I added cubes of cantaloupe, honeydew, and watermelon to my plate. "We're both ready to have this curling laminate pulled up. The old, worn cabinets torn out."

Geoff and I were looking ahead—not back over our shoulders at everything that had overtaken us during the past year after my breast cancer diagnosis and treatment.

"Why don't we each get something to eat, refresh our coffee if we need to, and go sit in the living room so we can talk about the book?" Winston scratched at the back door again. "I'll let Winston inside and put him in his kennel."

Payton selected a muffin, pausing to take the plate that Johanna held out to her. "Oh, don't do that. He won't be a bother."

"Right." I couldn't help but laugh. "We all have food. You know he'll wander around begging."

"We won't feed him, will we, Johanna?"

Johanna sniffed. "I'm not the one who sneaks food to that dog."

"I'll behave."

"You're as bad as Dad when it comes to Winston."

In a few moments, we were all settled—Johanna and I on

the couch and Payton in Geoff's favorite oversize chair, with Winston sitting at attention at her feet.

Payton made a display of ignoring Winston's whines. "So what did you all think of the first chapter?"

"I don't like the idea of having to read a biography. I feel like I'm back in college."

Payton groaned. "Johanna, you said that about the classics Jillian suggested—and this was the one book we all agreed on. Besides, I'm the one back in college."

"I just think we should have looked at more options."

"We made the decision to read this book." Payton held up her copy. "We all bought it. It's done."

Before I could decide if I was going to jump in and referee this early, my phone pinged with a text message.

"This might be Geoff checking with me while he's finishing up at the gym. He probably wants to see if we need anything at the store." I angled the phone where it sat on the coffee table, ready to silence it. But instead of Geoff's familiar face, Mom's name appeared.

How are you feeling today? You've looked so tired lately that I was worried, but then Johanna explained that it's a common side effect of the medication you're on.

What?

I gripped my phone, rereading the message, ignoring the fact that Johanna and Payton were both watching me. "Johanna, you're talking to Mom about my medication?"

"What do you mean?" Johanna sipped her coffee, eyeing me over the rim of her cup.

Before I could answer, there was another ping.

And I can understand if you're also upset that you can't get pregnant while you're on Tamoxifen.

No. I pressed my lips together, struggling to think of what to say—how to respond to Mom's text. To what Johanna had done.

If the first text was bothersome, the second one was as if Johanna had invited herself and all of the family—Payton, our parents—to my various doctors' appointments. She might as well have included Beckett and Zach Gaines in the group, too.

"You told Mom that I can't get pregnant?"

Johanna's facial expression didn't change as she took another sip of her not-French-press coffee before replying. "What are you talking about?"

"I'm talking about these two texts from Mom." I held up my phone. "She says you explained how my medication is making me tired. And told her that I can't get pregnant while I'm on Tamoxifen."

"Oh, that. We were talking . . . I can't remember when. And she said she was worried about you." Johanna nibbled on a cube of watermelon. "I took the time to explain things to her so she would understand what was going on."

"Why would you do that?"

"Because she was worried about you." Johanna spoke slowly, as if I needed her to enunciate so I would be able to understand. "I just told her things everybody knows. Fatigue is a common side effect of that medication—"

"Everybody knows?" My voice was getting louder, but I didn't seem to have any control over it. "Does everybody know I can't get pregnant? Did you post it on a billboard along I-25?"

"Now you're being ridiculous, Jill." My sister dismissed my questions with a shake of her head. "People know you can't get pregnant while you're on Tamoxifen."

"You know, Johanna." Payton spoke up. "*You* know."

"Of course I know. I'm a pharmacist."

"That's exactly my point." Payton was in full-on offensive mode now. "You had no right to talk to Mom. Will you just admit you invaded Jillian's privacy?"

It was as if I could see my words, Johanna's words, and now Payton's words swirling around me like a verbal tornado, the strength of it already threatening to pull me apart. Johanna leaned back. Payton leaned forward. Both of them ignorant of the increasing danger.

"I shouldn't have said anything." I tossed the statement like a white flag. "Can we just talk about the book?"

Payton twisted to look at me. "Are you kidding me? Of course you had to say something. Johanna never should have talked to Mom without asking you if it was okay first."

"You're both overreacting." With a wave of her hand, Johanna dismissed both Payton and me. "Mom asked a few questions. I answered them."

"You, of all people, know about HIPAA and patient privacy, Johanna."

Johanna gritted her teeth. "We're family, Payton."

"Family takes care of each other. Family respects each other. You never have our backs."

"It's nice to know how you really feel."

"It is how I feel. It's how Jillian feels, too."

And now I was being dragged into Johanna and Payton's fight.

"Don't speak for me, Payton."

Payton's eyes widened. Then she crossed her arms. "Fine. Speak for yourself."

"I would, if I thought anyone was listening."

At last I had my sisters' attention.

Being with Johanna and Payton was like competing with athletes when you knew they played dirty—and wanted to win at any cost.

Silence.

No one was saying anything. And none of us had been listening to each other, either.

"Did you have something to say, Jillian?" Payton's voice was quieter, but there was an edge to it, an unspoken challenge.

No matter what I said, one of my sisters would not be satisfied.

Better to focus on the original reason we were together.

"What I wanted to do today was have coffee and talk about a book." I glanced at my phone again. Set it aside. Maybe I could let Johanna know how I felt about all this . . . just say it and be done with it. "Not find out Johanna had talked to Mom about my private life."

"I don't understand why you're making such a big deal about this, Jillian. You would have told Mom eventually."

"Maybe. Okay, yes, I probably would have talked to Mom—but that's the whole point." I focused on Johanna, hoping she would understand. "*I* would have told her. Not you. Me."

How did Payton and Johanna spend so much of their lives arguing with one another? Listening to them disagreeing, pushing and pulling for the chance to occupy the right position, always exhausted me. The rare occasion I stood up to Johanna wore me out within minutes. And now, with everything else going on, I might as well be trying to stand up for myself while running on an out-of-control treadmill.

"I don't understand why you can't see I was only trying to help. Mom was worried and I gave her the information she needed so she would be calmer."

"It wasn't your place—" Payton stepped back into the conversation.

Johanna immediately turned on her. "I was talking to Jill—"

Confronting Johanna had been a bad idea. I was the peacemaker, not the one who challenged her. That was Payton's role.

"To get through this first book club meeting, are we going to need to pretend we're back in elementary school and read our books in silence?"

My attempt at humor failed. Whatever fragile truce we'd declared the past few months seemed to rip apart.

"I think—" Johanna stood—"I'll just call it for today."

I scrambled to my feet, causing Winston to jump up from where he was resting in front of the fireplace. "Johanna, don't leave."

"Obviously my attempts to help Mom are being

misinterpreted. And I didn't come here to be attacked or to join a . . . a reading circle."

And with that, Johanna collected her book and her purse and stalked toward the front door. Winston scampered around her feet, impeding her getaway.

I covered my face with my hands, the slam of the door echoing in my head. "I shouldn't have said anything."

"Don't be silly." Payton sounded as if she wanted to laugh. "Of course you should have."

"But now Johanna's upset . . ."

"She wants you to think she's upset. She's made a scene and walked out, and she hopes you'll call her later and apologize. That way she doesn't have to say she's sorry."

"What?" I peered at Payton over my hands.

"Think about it. Has it ever occurred to you that Johanna likes to be upset? That she uses it to keep us in our place?" Payton offered me a smile. "Whatever you do, don't call and apologize. You didn't do anything wrong."

"But I—"

"You didn't do anything wrong." Payton slipped Winston a bite of blueberry muffin. "And I bet you that Johanna will still be here tomorrow with everyone else to prep for the renovation."

⌒

Colorado Springs knew how to do Septembers.

The trees in our neighborhood were hinting at autumn with leaves changing to brilliant yellows and oranges and reds, even as the temperatures remained warm, but not in the "why is it still so hot?" range. September was like an anticipated visit with a pleasant friend who stopped by once a year and never overstayed their welcome.

I looped my arm through Geoff's, my head just brushing his shoulder. His verbal command released Winston from a heel to walk in front of us.

"He's doing well at obeying you when we're out on a walk."

"Better. He's doing better." His eyes shielded by both his glasses and the brim of the baseball cap that tamed his unruly brown hair, Geoff tugged on the leash to remind Winston that he wasn't his own boss. "If he wasn't on this leash, he'd take off running for no reason at all."

"It's such a nice afternoon. Although I do look forward to seeing snow on the Peak again."

"Well, it's shown up in August before, so it's not impossible to happen anytime now." Geoff adjusted his long-legged stride to my slower pace. He probably wasn't even aware he'd developed the habit during the past months. "I just realized you never told me how the book club went this morning."

"We may have had our first and last Saturday book club . . ."

"Oh, come on. What could go so wrong?"

"Well, Johanna walked out in a huff."

Geoff chuckled. "What did she and Payton argue about this time?"

"They didn't argue . . . well, they did. But it started off with me and Johanna arguing. . . ."

"You . . . argued with Johanna." Now Geoff had the nerve

to laugh—his familiar full-on head-thrown-back burst of laughter that caused Winston to glance back at him. "I'm supposed to believe that?"

I pulled away from Geoff. "I know, right? What would you say if I told you I snapped at Payton, too?"

"I would most definitely not believe that."

"It was a mess."

"I can see why you said it may be your first and last Saturday book club. The three of you couldn't even discuss a book together?"

"It had nothing to do with the book."

"What was the problem then?"

"I found out Johanna talked to Mom—without my permission—about my medication and the side effects. About the fact I can't get pregnant until I'm off the Tamoxifen."

"Okay."

Geoff might as well have said, *"Is that all?"*

"Why aren't you upset about that?"

He shifted the brim of his baseball cap. "I didn't realize you expected me to get upset—"

"Geoff, that's personal information!"

"Johanna told your mom, not a stranger."

"Why are you taking her side?"

"Whoa." Geoff stopped on the sidewalk, turning to face me and bringing Winston to an abrupt halt. "No taking sides here—and if I was, I would be on your side. Just processing things out loud, which I will stop doing immediately because it's not helping either of us."

I leaned closer to him, resting my head against his chest.

"I'm sorry. I didn't realize how much it still bothered me. It didn't help that I was tired and nervous about not having done enough to make things nice for the book club."

"I'm sure Johanna and Payton were happy with what you had—"

"I told them about the kitchen renovation, and Johanna questioned all our choices. How much money we're spending. And then we'd barely started talking about the book—and Jo was complaining *again*—and Mom texted, which is how I found out she knew about my not being able to get pregnant."

Geoff slipped his arm around my waist, easing me forward, and started walking again.

"Maybe we should have said something up front to everyone, back when we decided to freeze my eggs. But it's a little late to rethink our decision to keep that private, right?"

Geoff didn't respond—keeping quiet like he often did when we talked about my cancer and especially when we talked about the reality that I might struggle getting pregnant. Always so careful not to upset me.

A few more moments of silence and then, "We'll figure it out together—like we always do."

"Was I wrong?"

"Wrong?"

"To get upset about Johanna telling Mom?"

Geoff stopped again. His eyes warmed as he leaned closer, his kiss gentle. "You know I will always be on your side, Jill."

I closed my eyes, allowing the moment to lengthen.

Forgetting we were on a walk, until Geoff jerked away as Winston pulled on the leash.

"Sorry." He gave me a slow wink.

"It's okay." I faced forward as Geoff allowed Winston to tug him along. "So tell me, what's going on with you?"

"Work got interesting yesterday."

"When is cybersecurity not interesting?"

"True. But yesterday my boss asked me to consider speaking at a conference on ethics in cybersecurity."

"Ethics?"

"Yes." Geoff ducked under a low-hanging tree branch, filled with leaves turning a bright orange. "There are different ways to approach the issue, so I need to figure out if I want to do it and, if so, what they're looking for."

"*They* being?"

"My bosses. The conference is in Denver early next spring."

"This sounds like a great opportunity."

"It'd be different. I'm used to doing my work, coming home—maybe *attending* a conference. I've never even thought about speaking at one."

"You'd be great at it."

"Thanks for the vote of confidence."

"How soon do you have to let them know?"

"They mentioned it yesterday. I said we'd talk again next week."

"I know you need to think about it some more, but my vote is yes."

He paused long enough to press a quick kiss on the top of my head. "And thanks for that."

This was a chance to support my husband, an opportunity to turn the spotlight off me, my cancer, and put it onto Geoff. Onto something positive. This speaking opportunity was an indicator that things were better. Not perfect, but better.

We were passing Gianna's house—almost home. "I reminded Gianna about the kitchen renovation when we were talking earlier today."

"Why?"

"Because workers will be around. Cars and trucks parked in front of our house—possibly in front of her house. I just thought it was the neighborly thing to do."

"Right. I hadn't thought about how the renovation might affect the neighbors—I mean, beyond the fact that they have to look at that dumpster."

"Avery, her little girl, loves Winston, but Gianna says she has her hands full with a two-year-old."

"I can only imagine."

"What would you want?"

"What?"

"Would you want to start our family with a son or daughter?"

Geoff adjusted his glasses. "I hadn't really thought about it."

"No preference for a boy or girl?"

"No . . . no preference." Geoff stopped by the gate leading into the backyard and handed me Winston's leash. "Here, take him on inside. I'll go get the mail."

"We can get the mail . . ."

He jogged away with a quick wave. "I'll be waiting at the front door."

"Okay. Fine."

That was a bit abrupt. But it gave me the chance to appreciate my husband as he jogged around to the front of the house . . . a moment to daydream about the day we'd go for a walk with our son or daughter. Of course, I'd learned not to think too far ahead, but it was good to allow myself to dream again, if only for a few moments.

The Thatcher sisters were together two days in a row—a rare event now that we were all adults. And a risky one, given the interpersonal fiasco during our first-ever book club meeting.

Also risky considering how I had listened to Payton's recommendation and hadn't called and apologized to Johanna.

Hadn't made things all better.

Of course, when Geoff and I talked more Saturday night, he'd agreed with Payton, telling me not to call Johanna—and not to worry so much. So it was two against one opposing me about contacting my older sister. Instead, to resist temptation, Geoff and I had watched a movie, and then I'd gone to bed early and slept late.

It wasn't all an escape—sleep was survival nowadays.

Now my house seemed to overflow with people moving between the main floor, the upstairs, and the basement. The cupboards in the soon-to-be-renovated kitchen stood open, half-empty. Mom faced the fridge, either setting the contents onto what little counter space we had, adding them to a pot of soup simmering on the stove, or throwing them into a big black trash bag. Payton and Zach, who'd come later than everyone else because they'd probably attended church, wrapped and stacked plates and bowls in a large blue plastic bin. They didn't mention where they'd been and no one asked because Thatchers didn't "do" God—but Payton seemed to be curious, thanks to Zach's faith. Johanna staked out her own corner and analyzed my spice rack, tossing outdated square tins and glass bottles into the trash.

"Where's Winston? Who let him out of his kennel? Winston?" I stood at the bottom of the stairs that led up to our bedrooms. "Did someone put him in the backyard?"

"Yes. Dad has him outside." Mom leaned around the fridge door. "If you're not careful, he's going to steal that dog one day."

With my mischievous dog found, all I had to remember was what I'd been doing before I realized Winston wasn't in his kennel.

"Did you find those other plastic containers?" Payton closed an empty cupboard door.

"Right! I left them upstairs."

"I'll get them." Geoff gave me a quick kiss in passing. Zach offered to carry down more storage bins and followed behind him.

"I thought I'd done more to get ready for demo day." I pressed both hands to my face. "But what with Geoff and I both working . . ."

"We'll get it done." Payton came and stood next to me, offering me a side hug. "This is a great time to clean house, no pun intended. Mom will wipe down the fridge for whoever is picking it up later. Zach promised to make a run to the thrift store with the giveaway box. Johanna's going crazy checking dates on all your spices and canned goods, so you'll be all set when you're restocking your brand-new kitchen."

We all observed the invisible boundary lines, first set up by Johanna dragging the trash can over to the counter and turning her back on everyone. Enough distance so there was no discernible friction—and no real conversation, either.

But working together was better than arguing.

"Jill, the fridge is empty and the veggie soup is simmering. Your dad wants to take Winston for a walk." As I moved away from the stairs, Mom nodded to where Dad now waited by the front door, Winston prancing around his feet on the end of his leash. "Is it okay if I go with them?"

"Go. Relax. Tackling the fridge was a huge job."

"When we get back, we'll run to the store and get bread to have with the soup."

"You don't have to do that."

"Soup is always better with bread. I'll grab something for dessert, too."

And it would make Mom happy to feed everyone today and to know Geoff and I would have leftovers tomorrow.

Geoff stopped beside me. "All the storage containers go in the basement until after the renovation, right?"

"Yes. We just need to make sure they're labeled."

Johanna spoke up from her corner of the kitchen, still facing the spice rack. "Dishes, glassware, and utensils are labeled with blue duct tape. Food items are labeled with yellow duct tape. Pots and pans—silver. Other cookware items—white."

"Okay." I guessed that rapid-fire announcement counted as talking to me. Sort of.

"You mentioned you were using a small fridge during the reno, so I made up a box of items for you and Geoff." She still hadn't looked at me. "Keurig, paper plates, bowls, cups, napkins, plasticware."

I tried to keep up with all she'd said. Colors. The items she'd put in the box. Where had she said she'd put it?

"Did you tell Geoff?"

"No." Johanna tossed a quick glance over her shoulder. "Do you want me to?"

"No. It's fine. I just wondered."

I would act like I was following along. It was what I did more and more these days—struggle to follow along. Pretend.

Johanna tilted her head, watching me as if she detected my confusion. I needed to choose to ignore one or the other—the confusion all around me or the confusion swirling inside me. And I needed to remember it was okay to forget things every once in a while. Everybody did that.

"Where's the number of the guy who's coming to pick up the fridge?"

Geoff. Back with another question.

"Didn't I give it to you when we were talking last night?"

"No. You said you'd give it to me today. I want to call him and confirm when he's coming over."

"Oh. Right." I scrambled to separate today from the details of yesterday and something that happened several weeks ago. "We posted the fridge on craigslist, right?"

Geoff had grabbed a bottle of water off the counter and

gulped half of it down while waiting for me to answer. "We were going to. But then you said that one of Harper's neighbors bought it to use in his garage."

"Right. Right."

Now if only Geoff would keep feeding me clues—bits of information that would help me remember where I'd left that phone number.

"I think his name was . . . Rick . . . or maybe Ron."

"Do you want to call Harper and ask her?"

That would be easier. But I had written the information down. It wasn't like I could call my best friend every time I forgot something. "Let me find the number. I know I have it."

Ten minutes later, after searching the messages on my Facebook page, my texts, and my voice mails, as well as a pile of papers on my bedroom dresser, I found the information Geoff needed. It was like playing a virtual game of Memory with my brain, flipping over different things to find the matching details and put together the question and answer I needed. *No . . . no . . . no . . . yes!* And behind me, I left a pile of papers strewn across our bed, which I'd have to deal with later.

What would be the next question that would cause me more mental muddle?

Dinner was a welcome respite from a day of nonstop activity. And we didn't use any of the paper products Johanna had brought, thanks to Mom picking some up at the store, along with the bread, butter, a half gallon of ice cream, and a tiny container of vegan Häagen-Dazs for Payton.

A lull in the conversation as we all sat around the dining room table seemed like the appropriate time to thank everyone for their help.

"I hope you all know how much Geoff and I appreciate everything you've done to help us get ready for tomorrow." I was careful to scan the table, making eye contact with no one specific for longer than half a second, if that.

"Beckett's sorry he got called into work." Johanna still didn't quite look at me when she spoke, but at least it seemed that comment wasn't meant for the group at large.

"We understand work trumps packing up our kitchen." Johanna offered me a glimpse of a smile. "Thanks."

"I'll check with the guys one last time." Zach spoke to Geoff. "Make sure they'll be here bright and early."

"I hope not too early. I know you're not sleeping well, Jillian. . . ." Mom's voice trailed off as she traded a look with my older sister. "I mean, Johanna mentioned . . ."

And now glances were exchanged between Mom and Johanna. Payton and me. Mom and me. An awkward game of visual avoidance.

Somebody had to say something.

Fine.

"I know you and Johanna have talked about my . . . my health, Mom. But I . . . I would prefer you didn't."

Now not only was I taking Payton's advice and not apologizing to Johanna, but I was correcting her and Mom. At the same time. In front of everyone.

What little soup I'd eaten threatened to rise back up my throat. I tried to swallow, massaging my collarbone.

"I wasn't trying to talk about you behind your back." Mom's voice wavered.

"I understand that." Johanna's heated stare seemed to scorch my face. "But Johanna shouldn't have discussed the side effects of my medication and . . . and the fact that I can't get pregnant while I'm on Tamoxifen without talking to me about it first."

I could almost hear Payton cheering me on from the sidelines, adding an invisible cartwheel just for fun.

"But why didn't you tell me?"

Mom's question, weighted down with the unspoken words *after all, I'm your mother,* silenced me for a moment . . . and then backed me into a corner.

"I'm sorry, Mom." The words whooshed out of me like helium from a deflating balloon. "Maybe I should have talked to you sooner. . . . If I had, I could have avoided all this."

And with that simple apology, all was as it should be in the Thatcher family again. I'd assumed my expected place, which so often included an apology of some sort. And Johanna and Payton were once again at odds—with me in the middle.

"Oh, Jill, I understand." Mom's smile encompassed my mistake with instantaneous forgiveness. "You were trying to do what you thought was best."

And I'd made a mistake.

Now that I'd admitted it, everything was better—the world was right when I was wrong.

It looked as if Payton was going to say something, but Zach gave a quick, almost-imperceptible shake of his head. She pursed her lips and exhaled . . . and said nothing.

I waited for Johanna to step in. Maybe follow my lead with her own apology.

"I'm sorry this was even a topic of discussion again." She stood, gathering her bowl and napkin. "I explained yesterday that all I was doing was answering Mom's questions—not attempting to invade anyone's privacy."

Not quite the apology I'd hoped for.

"Johanna, don't try to make it sound like what you did was right." Payton jumped past Zach's restraint.

"We're family. And like it or not, we are all affected by the fact that you had breast cancer, Jillian. I, for one, would rather talk about things. Not hide things."

Oh, there were so many things our family didn't talk about.

How Pepper's death had affected Payton. How it had affected all of us. How Johanna had read Payton's journal and that led to the decision to send Payton away for medical help when she was sixteen . . . We chose silence over words again and again.

My sister's words slammed against me, scattering what was left of any defense I'd tried to muster. I wasn't hiding when I decided not to discuss every little medical detail with my family . . . I was trying to deal with my life. One day, one reality, at a time.

If anything, I should have started and finished with the apology. I knew the routine and shouldn't have deviated from it. What good had it done?

My family was horrible at respecting boundaries. And apparently the temporary cease-fire between the Thatcher sisters was at an end.

2

I COULD FIX THIS.

Given a moment—one single, uninterrupted moment—I could fix this.

First I needed to figure out what was wrong. Why my boss was standing in my office asking, "Where were you?" as if he were my father and I were some delinquent fifteen-year-old daughter sneaking into the house after curfew.

"Jillian, why didn't you answer my phone calls? My texts?"

"I was at lunch—" I searched my purse—"and I didn't get any calls or texts."

I ransacked the depths of my canvas tote bag. ChapStick. A metal tin of peppermint Altoids. An almost-empty package of tissues. My car keys. Two tubes of lipstick. My wallet. Half a movie ticket. An endless assortment of crumpled receipts. One of Winston's chew toys.

Oh, that would impress my boss.

Where had I left my phone?

Harper, my ever-reliable friend, slipped around me, deposited the bag containing my leftover lunch on my cluttered desk, and began opening and closing various drawers, finally producing my cell phone. "Here it is."

Mr. Hampton remained facing me.

"I'm so sorry. I left it . . ." The words stalled in my throat. No sense in stating the obvious. "What did you need me to do?"

"Where's the closing package for the Spencers? Everyone's waiting at Ascent Title—they were supposed to close on their new house forty-five minutes ago."

I stepped forward even as heat coursed through my body. "I e-mailed that to the title company right before I left—"

"They never received it. They sent you several e-mails. Called your office. Your cell. And now they're calling me."

As if on cue, both my cell and office phones rang, the sound traveling up my spine and lodging in the base of my brain. "I—I'll handle this."

"Do that. Please." My boss pivoted like a soldier on guard duty and left without another word.

"What can I do?" The shrill rings of competing phones almost drowned out Harper's question.

"Nothing." I took my cell and muted it as I eased into the chair behind my desk. "This is my problem."

"Are you sure—?"

"Harper!" I stopped. Modulated my voice down from panic mode. "Just let me do this, please."

"Sorry. Tell me if you need anything."

As Harper disappeared with an encouraging thumbs-up and a smile lighting her brown eyes, I answered my phone. "Jillian Hennessey. How can I help you?"

"Jillian, where's the blasted paperwork for the Spencer closing?" The familiar voice of one of the loan officers over at Ascent Title seared my ear. I scrambled to remember his name. Joe? Joseph? Jonas?

Jonah.

"I e-mailed it to you an hour ago, Jonah." I powered up my computer.

"Never got it."

"That's impossible." I wouldn't deny being forgetful, but I knew I'd sent that paperwork. I could even have Harper vouch for me—if I hadn't just banished her from my office—because I'd asked her to wait while I finished up. "Did you check your spam folder?"

"I've checked everyone's in-box and everyone's spam folder. It's not in this office." Jonah almost spat the words at me. "I've got two angry parents in my conference room. Their three kids are hyped up on soda and cookies and have used all of my computer paper to color on. My receptionist had to take their dog—their very large German shepherd—for a walk to get it out of our storage room! Did I mention my receptionist is allergic to dogs?"

As Jonah talked, I scrolled through the e-mails in my Sent

folder. And there! There was the Ascent Title e-mail with the attached closing package. I switched to my in-box . . . only to find the e-mail returned as undeliverable.

I'd sent the package to an old, outdated e-mail address.

A groan welled up from deep within me and escaped through the phone.

"What? What did you do?"

"I was right . . . and I was wrong." Even as my brain wanted to shut down, as my throat tightened, I knew I had to be professional and own my mistake. And then fix it. "I accidently clicked on the wrong e-mail address. Then I left for an early lunch and forgot my cell phone. Which is why I didn't respond sooner."

Within seconds, I'd corrected my error and resent the information, but only after double-checking the e-mail address. "The package is on its way to you. I'm so sorry, Jonah. Really, really sorry."

"I don't have time for apologies, Jillian. But you owe me." With a click, the line went dead.

I dropped the phone onto my desk, collapsing with my forehead pressed against my crossed arms. How stupid could I be? Not that I'd be asking that question out loud to give anyone the chance to volunteer an answer.

Too many mistakes. Too many things left undone at the end of the day that were then waiting for me when I came to work each morning. Too many days that started off with me determined to do better, to accomplish everything I needed to do, to catch up . . . and by midday, fatigue overtook my best intentions, confusion befuddled my brain, and anxiety strangled my confidence.

An hour later, Harper tiptoed into my office. Her exaggerated wide-eyed glance left and right, tossing her black hair against her shoulders, was almost enough to make me laugh out loud. Almost. "All clear?"

"Yes. Crisis dealt with." I leaned forward, resting my head in my palms. "I assume Mr. Hampton is in his office, letting me handle anything else that comes up."

"What happened?" Harper settled into one of the blue cloth chairs in front of my desk.

"Before that, I need to say I'm sorry for snapping at you earlier."

"Forget it. You were stressed." Harper waved away my apology. "Now tell me."

"You heard what happened. The closing package went missing—"

"How?"

"You saw me send it before we left, but I somehow clicked on the wrong e-mail address."

"Everyone's done that."

I ran my fingers through my short hair. "Yes, everyone does that. But I used to be so punctual and now . . . now I'm not. Everything . . . everything takes longer. Getting ready for work. Doing work. I don't remember things like I used to . . ."

"You need to give yourself a little time. We just passed the one-year anniversary of your diagnosis, Jillian. You're barely past your treatment. What happened earlier was an honest mistake."

"It was me—making another mistake." I jabbed my index finger into my solar plexus. "I come in late. I leave early." With every word I said, I added to my ever-growing list of faults. "And this week has been even worse, what with the kitchen renovation being delayed—not that it's my fault."

"Wait—what? The workers never showed up?"

"I've been so busy, I haven't had time to think about it. They're finally coming tomorrow—on a Saturday. They've promised Zach that they're finished with the other house project and that they'll start demoing our kitchen tomorrow."

"You're only five days behind. It could get—"

"Don't say it, Harper." I wanted to plug my ears with my fingers like a little girl but shook my head instead. "I've watched plenty of home renovation TV shows. I made the mistake of doing a search online of kitchen renovation horror stories. I know it could get worse. Just don't say it, okay?"

The faint spicy scent of roasted chicken and grilled peppers and onions tickled my nose. Why did I smell fajitas? Wait—there, on the corner of my desk, sat my abandoned white-paper sack of lunch leftovers. Perfect. With one swift move, I tossed them into the wastebasket beside my feet.

"What are you doing? I thought you were taking those home for dinner tonight."

"I never put them in the fridge."

"They're fine, Jill. And you hardly ate anything at lunch."

"No, thank you. My appetite is off."

A shadow filled the doorway of my office as Mr. Hampton

appeared again, his glance skimming past Harper to me. "Jillian, could we talk in my office?"

I half rose, wiping my palms against the material of my linen pants. "Now, sir?"

"I don't want to interrupt." His glance ricocheted between Harper and me. "Fifteen minutes is fine."

As he disappeared, I collapsed into my chair, causing it to roll backward. "Well, that's just perfect."

"What?"

"He probably thinks we were sitting here wasting time talking about the latest story on the British royals."

"I seriously doubt the man even knows William and Kate, much less Harry and Meghan, exist. And I work here, too. We could have been talking business."

I repositioned my chair. "What am I going to do, Harper?"

"Do? You're going to go talk to Hampton. It'll be fine."

"But he came by and we were just sitting here . . ."

"Exactly." Harper stood, motioning me to my feet. "We were talking, not playing cards or surfing the Internet, looking at clothes or vacation spots. Stop imagining the worst."

Harper ushered me out of my office with a pat on the back and one of her trademark positive thoughts. "Mark Twain said this—'I've had a lot of worries in my life, most of which never happened.'"

Despite her encouragement, today was almost as bad as the day I'd gotten the biopsy results. When I knew I had breast cancer but didn't know how bad it was.

No. Nothing . . . *nothing* would ever be as awful as that day. Cancer had snuck up on me the night of my engagement party as soundlessly as my footsteps along the carpeted hall-way between the bank's offices.

Cancer had ravaged my health. Undermined my future. I'd almost allowed it to destroy my relationship with Geoff, except he'd ignored my "You can't love me" protests and proved me wrong.

Now was not the time to remember all of this. I needed to be calm. Unemotional. Not to assume anything and overreact.

Mr. Hampton welcomed me into his office with a nod, indicating I should sit in one of the faux leather chairs positioned side by side in front of his desk. He looked as neat and put together at four o'clock as he had when he'd arrived at seven thirty—his customary start of the day. Dark suit. Light-colored dress shirt. Patterned tie. Shaved head. And the menthol aroma of some sort of aftershave lingered in the room.

An abstract print in blue, yellow, and orange hung on the wall behind his desk, and a small window allowed some natural light in. A low bookshelf contained an orderly array of binders and books, and several family photos placed just so indicated that yes, Mr. Hampton was a family man, too.

My boss cleared his throat, but before he could say anything, I rushed ahead. "Mr. Hampton, I wanted to apologize again for what happened. I accidentally clicked on an out-dated e-mail address—"

"Thank you, Jillian." Mr. Hampton folded his hands on top of his desk. "I understand. And I hope you know that you've been an excellent employee."

He paused, his words putting me on alert. I shifted in my seat, maintaining both eye contact and silence.

Mr. Hampton cleared his throat. "I also want you to know my decision is not based solely on what happened earlier today."

"Your decision?"

"Yes. Jillian, I'm sorry, but your position here at the bank is terminated."

I swallowed, my mouth dry. "You're firing me?"

"Again, I'm sorry." My boss rubbed his palm against his bald head. "We both know you've had a challenging time with your workload the past few months. And it's not that I'm not sympathetic. I am. Things just aren't getting done in a timely or thorough manner. Your job here is a full-time position but, what with you coming in late and leaving early, you're still keeping part-time hours."

What was I supposed to say? He might as well have listened in on my earlier conversation with Harper.

"It was understandable when you were originally diagnosed with cancer—with the expectation that you would eventually get back to your normal work schedule. And I know that you made every effort to maintain your hours and workload. What happened with the closing today is merely another indicator of your inability to keep up with the demands of your job." He shuffled some papers on his desk. "I've talked with some of the management team, and they agree there are extenuating circumstances here. Confidentially, there are also some changes being set in place for the company."

I tried to keep up with what he was saying. "Changes?"

"Nothing I can discuss openly at this time, except to say there will be some downsizing in the months to come. The banking industry is more and more about digital interfacing. In light of all of this, Jillian, we'd like to offer you a decent severance package." He lifted a slim manila folder from his desk. "You can look this over, discuss the details with your husband if you'd like to, and let me know if it meets your approval."

I was being shown the exit in the nicest way possible— and also being asked if that was okay with me.

My fingers trembling, my first attempt to take the folder failed. I couldn't even get fired without messing it up.

What was I supposed to say? *Thank you*?

"We'll talk on Monday. Is that all right with you?" Mr. Hampton saved me from trying to figure out the appropriate words.

"Yes, sir."

Whatever was in the folder, I was as good as fired. It wasn't like I would turn down the offer. The only thing I had to figure out was how to tell Geoff. But right now I needed to stay calm. Somehow be appreciative . . . although all my job training never prepared me to thank my boss for firing me.

I needed to pretend I was some award-winning actress playing the part of a gracious woman who smiled though her heart was breaking. Discover the technique for talking while fighting back tears. My gaze made it as far as the bridge of Mr. Hampton's nose. I smiled, hoping the action stopped my lips from quivering. Stood. Shook his hand. Heard my thank-you collide with his.

One more thing lost to cancer.

My best friend did not take no for an answer.

It didn't matter how many different ways I tried to decline her impromptu suggestion for a Girls' Night. Harper was having none of it.

"I know Geoff's working late, so there's no rush for you to go home." Harper tilted her head, one eyebrow raised, giving me her "I mean business" look. "We'll be sitting down—not working out at a gym, so it doesn't matter if you're tired."

"I just don't want to." I stood next to her car in the bank parking lot, the manila folder in one hand, my purse slung over my shoulder. My sunglasses hiding the fact that I'd spent five minutes in the ladies' restroom crying. Not that crying had done anything except ruin my makeup, what little I wore. But when your eyelashes are almost nonexistent thanks to chemo, mascara is a must.

"Which is exactly why we're going to do this. Besides, we got lucky. We've got reservations at The Melting Pot. Me. You. And a pot of chocolate fondue." Harper laughed, slipping on her sunglasses. "And no, I didn't intend for that to rhyme. See you there."

With that, she rolled up her car window and drove away. I debated whether I'd meet her or just go home, but Harper was right, this was a good idea—and she didn't even know how my day had ended. I didn't want to be alone with the memory of being fired on constant replay in my mind.

Thirty minutes later, we sat in a small booth for two,

sipping glasses of wine, while our waiter prepared the Flaming Turtle chocolate fondue, complete with milk chocolate, caramel, and pecans.

"I figured you needed this. I know you feel bad about the mix-up with the closing package." Harper raised her glass and nodded toward the silver pot of fondue. "Can't go wrong with warm, decadent chocolate, right?"

The waiter set a white china plate filled with sliced strawberries, bananas, marshmallows, and brownies on the table with the encouragement to enjoy. Harper speared a piece of fruit. "Dig in—and talk to me."

Tonight was like so many of our Girls' Nights. Necessary. Therapy. No matter what, Harper and I made time for each other.

"Remember back in college, when a Girls' Night meant popcorn and a movie?"

"Look at us now, all grown-up and indulging in fondue and a glass of wine."

There were other less subtle changes, too. I was a newlywed . . . and a breast cancer survivor. Harper would be divorced soon, facing the unwanted reality that her husband would marry his former high school girlfriend as soon as the divorce was final.

"If there's one thing I've learned in the last year, it's that life is uncertain."

Harper pierced a piece of brownie with her fondue fork and raised it like a torch. "Hear, hear."

I touched the tip of my fork to hers.

"No, you have to put something on it."

I added a strawberry and returned the fondue-food-fork salute. "The other thing I know is that I want to be more like you—my always-glass-half-full friend. And if someone's glass is empty, you find a way to fill it up for them."

"Eat your fruit. You're making me cry." Harper dunked the brownie into the fondue pot. "Was there any more fallout from the closing snafu this morning?"

Where to start?

"I, um, spent the afternoon apologizing. I sent e-mails to Jonah and his boss. And I asked for the Spencer family's new address so I could send them a fruit basket or something nice."

"Hey, if you really want to make good with the parents, send something for the kids. They'll love that. Not a fruit basket—no kid wants grapefruit and apples. Maybe a movie gift card?"

"Have I ever told you that you're brilliant, Harper?"

"Yeah. Many times." Harper selected a second piece of brownie. "Then you're all good."

There was no sense in delaying the truth, even if talking about it ruined our fun night out. "No, I'm not."

Harper paused with her fondue skewer in midair. "What's going on? Jonah send you a nasty e-mail? Ignore it."

I indulged in a bite of banana dipped in melted chocolate, but it seemed to get clogged in my throat. I grabbed my glass of ice water and took a sip. And another. Waved away Harper's look of concern.

"I'm okay. I just . . . I lost my job."

"They can't fire you!" Harper's fondue skewer clattered against the side of the pot.

"Yes, they can. And they don't have to give any reason why, either. Have you forgotten that Colorado is an at-will state?"

"But you're one of the bank's best employees—"

"No." I had to stop Harper's loyal defense. Best friend or not, she was wrong. "I'm not. Not since my diagnosis. Not since the chemo. The radiation. Mr. Hampton offered me a decent severance package. And I got my bonus . . . so this could be a lot worse."

Here I was trying to tell Harper all the reasons losing my job was acceptable. Almost to be expected. Maybe by the time I talked to Geoff, I would be able to pull this off with a smile. Convince him, too.

"You're not going to fight this?" Harper slumped back against the padded booth.

"What good would that do me?" I needed to remember I couldn't tell Harper everything because some of what Mr. Hampton told me was confidential. I selected a strawberry, dipping it in the fondue. "The truth is, my future is as muddy as the chocolate in this pot."

"Now that's appetizing." Harper's laugh was brief.

"Some days it feels like I lost myself the day I was diagnosed with cancer. . . . I'm like Gretel in that fairy tale. Trying to find my way out of the woods, but I didn't drop any breadcrumbs to lead me back home—back to the woman I was before all of this happened."

"It takes time, friend. Time." Harper reached across the

table and squeezed my hand. "You haven't told Geoff, have you?"

"No. It's not the kind of thing you mention in the middle of the day when your husband calls to check in, you know?"

"I would have to agree with you."

No need to tell her that I'd let Geoff's call go to voice mail. That would be admitting out loud that I was a coward. Even though Harper was my closest friend . . . even though she knew me at my best and my worst . . . I still didn't want to say it.

"I have to figure out how to tell him what happened. It's going to be a shock—and a bit of a jolt to our finances, especially since we're remodeling the kitchen."

The blended music of laughter between a man and a woman pulled my attention to a couple in a booth across from Harper and me. They were snuggled up close, the man's arm draped across the woman's shoulders. An assortment of colorful helium balloons floated above the booth, while a small bouquet of red roses decorated one corner of the table.

"Look at them. They're so young. So in love."

"Isn't it sweet?" Harper rested her chin on her upturned hand.

"I was going to say, 'They're so clueless.'"

Harper's eyes narrowed. "Why would you say something like that?"

"It's the truth. They obviously haven't hit any bumps in the road of life yet—but they will."

"When did you become such a cynic?"

"I'm not a cynic. I'm a realist."

"And what good does that kind of negative outlook do for you?"

"I'm dealing with real life. You of all people know that life happens. That love doesn't always mean happily ever after—"

Harper crossed her arms, leaning away from me. "Right. My husband cheated on me. I'm getting a divorce. But I am going to have a good life despite that."

"I'm sorry . . ."

Two apologies to Harper in one day. If I'd gone home, I would have at least kept it to one.

Harper shook her head, her black hair brushing her shoulders. "Forget it."

"Harper." I waited until she made eye contact. "I am sorry."

"I know. We're good." She shrugged. "Look, Trent wasn't who I thought he was. He's a cheater. I know that. You know that. But I can't stay angry with the guy because if I do, he wins. He's already ruined our marriage. I'm not going to let him ruin the rest of my life."

"Maybe I need to treat cancer like you treat Trent."

"What do you mean?"

"Cancer doesn't get to ruin the rest of my life—even if it's ruined my body . . . and my wedding plans . . . and now it's taken my job."

Harper's laughter lightened the mood. "I like the way you're talking."

"Yeah, because I sound like you."

"Well, you're trying to sound like me. It's gonna take some practice to get it right."

Now our laughter fused together—and I couldn't help but glance over and see the couple smiling as they watched us. Two best friends having a fun night out.

The laughter lingered in my mind as I returned home later that night, only to be dispersed by Winston's desperate cries from his crate upstairs.

"Oh, poor puppy!" I dropped my purse as I scrambled up to the second bedroom to let him out, bracing as he jumped up and then leading him down and through the should-have-been-dismantled kitchen. "Let's go outside."

Tomorrow. Zach had promised the workers would show up tomorrow and start taking the kitchen apart.

Change . . . change . . . change . . . and yet getting nowhere fast.

And Geoff wasn't even here so I could talk to him about how my life had fallen apart. Again.

It was after ten, and I was alone.

Scratching at the back door reminded me that no, I wasn't alone. Winston was here. I swooped him up into my arms, cradling him close as he nuzzled my neck.

"What do you think, Winston?" I scratched behind his ears. "What should I do? Is it time for the 'Attitude is a little thing that makes a big difference' quote?"

If talking to a dog wasn't ridiculous, quoting Winston Churchill to him certainly was—but then again, the British statesman was his namesake.

"No comment?" Winston snuck a quick lick across my face. "You up for a movie, then?"

I settled on the couch, Winston curling into my lap as I restarted *What's Up, Doc?* where I'd stopped it last night, right when Barbra Streisand told Ryan O'Neal to meet her under the table and then said, "Oh, my goodness! There goes my napkin!"

Maybe laughter was the best medicine.

If nothing else, the romantic comedy entertained my faithful furry companion and me while I waited for my husband to come home. Maybe by listening to some scripted witty repartee, I'd figure out how to tell Geoff that I was now unemployed.

3

JOHANNA BENT OVER and ran the brush through her hair, the ends falling to just past her shoulders when she stood back up. She tugged at the bottom of her white cotton top and checked her watch. She still had an hour before her Pilates class started.

The shower in the master bathroom stopped as she straightened the comforter on the bed, settling the pillows just so. By the time she'd retrieved two white china cups of French-press coffee—one black, one with real cream— Beckett was in her bedroom, his short hair still damp, wearing his blue uniform pants and buttoning up his starched blue shirt.

"Morning."

"I brought you coffee."

"Thank you." Beckett set his mug on her dresser, leaning in to kiss her neck, his just-showered scent teasing her. "Too bad we didn't talk about working out together today."

"Since you were up at 5:30 for a run and I'm going to a Pilates class, it probably wouldn't have worked out anyway."

"Your schedule is a bit more flexible than mine right now." He slipped his belt through the pant loops. Buckled it. "I've got to go into the office, do some final prep for the Corona meeting. Just a few weeks to go."

Johanna sipped her coffee, her nails tapping against the side of the cup. No barista, no matter how well trained, made coffee better than she did. "Which means we'll be seeing even less of each other than we are now."

"Like I said when I got reassigned to Colorado, I could have just moved in with you."

"And as I pointed out, there was no space here to accommodate your furniture and clothes and who knows what else on such short notice. And we certainly didn't have time to house hunt."

"But both of us living in the Springs does have its advantages." Beckett pulled her close, his kiss reminiscent of their time together last night.

Johanna allowed herself to rest in his arms. To enjoy this moment of closeness before they went their separate ways. "I suppose at some point I'll meet the superintendent and get a chance to say thank you—even if you're only here for a year."

Beckett released her, turning to the mirror over her dresser while he put on his tie, his grin reflected back at her. "Who knows? We could be married by the time I go to Alabama next year."

Here they were again, both living their lives single, but always coming back around to the question of when they were going to get married. Beckett mentioned it. She mentioned it. But they never settled on a date. A location. A time. Never determined just how, exactly, they were finally going to become Mr. and Mrs. Thatcher-Sager.

Beckett was handsome, the kind of man she'd always imagined marrying, with his dark hair and dark eyes and athletic build. But why did it seem as if she preferred dating him more than she wanted to marry him? She'd said yes to the engagement but could never get past that one "yes" to finalizing their commitment with an "I do."

Or was Beckett the one who always seemed to back away?

"How about if we talk dates once I get my promotion?" She came up behind him, slipping her arms around his waist. When he turned to face her, she stole another kiss that became a second and a third until she broke away with a laugh. "Enough. You have to go to work."

She moved to stand in the doorway, smoothing her hair back into place, while Beckett sat on the bed and put on his shoes.

"Any idea when the hospital administration is going to tell you that you've got the job for real?"

"It's been six months since they started looking for a new pharmacy director. Rumors are flying that they've made up their minds, so I'm expecting an official job offer any day now."

"And you'll take it?"

"What kind of question is that? Of course I'll take it. I deserve it." She led the way to the kitchen, talking over her shoulder, carrying their coffee cups. "But I also know what I'm worth, so I'm going to negotiate for a better salary and benefits package. And I'd like some say in who they choose to be my assistant."

"First a promotion. Then a wedding. Good planning."

Everything in proper order—that's the way she liked it. She'd get settled in her new job, and then she'd more easily convince Beckett to get stationed back in Colorado. To retire here in a few years. And his being stationed here now— seeing all the advantages of living in Colorado—would only help him make that decision.

He couldn't miss the beautiful view of the Front Range, of Pikes Peak, every day when he drove into work. And the weather—even now, the cool breeze blowing in from the open window in her living room was a reminder of how they'd slept with her window open last night, another advantage of Colorado living. Sure, she liked to travel, but she liked coming home. Liked telling people she was a Colorado native.

"Hey—how did that book club thing go with your sisters?" Beckett found one of the glass jars of overnight oats she'd made last night, thanking her when she handed him a spoon and napkin.

"It was fine, but I don't think it'll last." She sat beside him at the small kitchen bar. Of course Beckett would ask about the book club a week later. She was surprised he'd remembered it at all.

"Why not?"

"I said good-bye to assigned reading when I got my doctorate."

"Then why did you agree to do it?"

"Because Jillian and Payton wanted to give it a try. So I had to say yes, didn't I?"

"Johanna, you never do anything you don't want to do."

Beckett was right. She didn't.

"They want a reason to get together more often." Johanna sipped her coffee. "This was it. So I agreed."

"Are you saying you don't want to get together with your sisters more often?"

"Not to sit around and drink coffee and talk about a book I have to read, no."

"Okay. Why *would* you get together with your sisters?"

"What kind of question is that?"

Beckett shrugged, offering her a lazy grin. "It's a question, that's all. Are you going to answer it?"

"I get together with Jillian and Payton for family things. Birthdays. Holidays. Football games at my parents'."

"Required things, then."

"I guess so. Traditions. There's nothing wrong with that."

"I didn't say there was, Johanna."

Was Beckett analyzing her relationships with her sisters? Or was he just making conversation that she didn't really have time for? They so rarely talked about family—his family or her family. Or if they wanted to have a family—children—once they got married.

She wore his ring but didn't know a lot of specifics about Beckett. And they'd been together for eight years.

Not that she was worried. They were fine. And she was not a worrier. Maybe their relationship was different than some couples'. Different from Jillian and Geoff's. From Payton and Zach's—if they were even in a relationship. Why Payton would want a relationship with him, she'd never understand. She and Beckett had their own way of doing things—and it worked.

Beckett finished breakfast, offering her a quick kiss and a "Have fun at Pilates" as he left.

"You have fun at work."

He paused just outside the door. "Don't count on me for dinner. I'll text or call and let you know what's going on."

"That's fine. I understand."

"You always do. That's one reason why we're such a good team."

See. Even Beckett knew it.

"No pressure . . ." Johanna raised her right hand, palm upturned.

". . . and plenty of space." Beckett took her hand, pulling her close.

They both laughed at their little relationship motto. Kissed. Said good-bye again.

She and Beckett were like some couple in a romance movie. The perfect couple who had everything going for them and no problems to deal with because they got along so well. When something could have gone wrong, fate had intervened and brought Beckett to Colorado instead of separating them for another year.

Beckett looked trim, self-assured, as he got into his restored Datsun 280zx—not the most practical car for Colorado. There was something about a man in uniform she'd always liked.

"I'm Beckett Sager. And you're . . . ?"

"Not sure I'm going to tell you my name." Johanna waited to see what the man would say next.

"Fair enough. Play it safe when you first meet a man at Starbucks and you're from out of town."

"How do you know I don't live in Washington, DC?" They stepped forward with the line as customers placed their orders, their conversation blending with everyone else's, the background music, and the whir of blenders and coffee bean grinders.

"Because the first time I saw you here, you had a suitcase. I figure you're traveling, like I am." When she didn't respond, he chuckled. "You can at least tell me if I'm correct."

That wouldn't do any harm. "You're correct."

"And I'm TDY—that's military lingo for being on a business trip. I'm in the Air Force, stationed in Turkey."

"Turkey? Now that's interesting . . . but the uniform gave you away as far as being in the military."

"Yeah, I'm only a ten-minute missile flight from Syria, Russia, and Iraq. And I still don't know your name or what you do."

"Johanna—and yes, I'm attending a business conference."

He'd bought her coffee. Convinced her to have dinner with him that night. And they'd fallen into a long-distance relationship . . . and in love—love that had lasted eight years.

Johanna closed the front door. She'd been staring at Beckett's empty parking space. Despite such an innocuous beginning as meeting at a coffee shop while they were both out of town on business, they'd stayed together for longer than some couples stayed married. So why was she glad to see him leave this morning?

If she were being honest, there were days since Beckett had arrived when she'd wanted to call his boss and ask him why, why did he have to request Beckett for this assignment? Couldn't he have just left their lives alone? Let Beckett go to Alabama as they'd planned?

Was she so used to a long-distance relationship that she couldn't handle her fiancé in the same state—no, in the same city?

The possibility didn't bode well for their marriage. After the wedding, Beckett wouldn't just be spending the night at her house on occasion.

It was as if she'd gotten so used to Beckett being gone—being the Invisible Man, as Payton had once called him—that she didn't know how to adapt to him being here, face-to-face, up close and so personal all the time.

Johanna reached for her phone. Maybe Jillian could help her figure this all out.

No.

Her younger sister wouldn't understand. For all her struggles, she was thrilled to be married.

And Jill also wasn't so thrilled with her right now.

Besides, according to the time on her phone, she was going to be late to class if she didn't leave now.

She'd feel better once she worked out.

And once she got her promotion.

                —

Somebody was tearing my house apart—and, from the laughter woven through all the pounding against the backdrop of country music playing on a radio, they enjoyed destroying someone else's property.

Even as I buried my head beneath my pillow to escape the racket, the floor—and my bed—shook again. Okay. Time to give up on sleeping, get up, and go investigate.

"Geoff . . ." My pillow muffled my voice, but lifting it off my face revealed Geoff wouldn't be running to the rescue because his side of the bed was empty. That either meant my husband had not come home last night, which was highly unlikely no matter how busy he was with work, or that somehow I had slept through him kissing me hello last night and then kissing me good-bye this morning.

I shoved my pillow aside. Along with everything else, I was failing this whole newlywed thing, too. I dragged myself out of bed, changed from my pajamas into sweatpants and a long-sleeved T-shirt, brushed my teeth, and then ran my fingers through my hair. All the while, the banging, scraping, and laughter continued. Once outside my bedroom, Winston's yips and whines added another note to the noise until I released him from his kennel in the other bedroom.

Downstairs, Zach and a trio of workmen attacked the wall that separated the kitchen and the dining room. Armed with sledgehammers and crowbars, their faces obscured behind clear protective glasses, they were dismantling the outdated wooden cabinets that one of the previous owners had decided to paint a pale yellow—or as Geoff dubbed it, "dusty canary."

With a sharp bark, Winston alerted Zach to my presence, and he paused, wiping the back of his arm across his forehead, leaving behind a smear of dust. "Hey, Jillian. Sorry about the noise."

"No problem."

"Well, it's not even eight thirty, and we're off to a good start."

"Did Geoff let you in?"

"No. He was already gone when we got here. Which is why you gave me a key, remember?" He pulled a glove off one hand with his teeth, retrieving something from his back pocket. "I found this on one of the counters."

I scanned the note. "Looks like he's at CrossFit."

Zach rested his hands on the leather tool belt on his hips. "You okay, Jillian?"

"Hmmm? Sure. I'm fine. Even though I knew this was going to happen, it's still a bit of a shock to see the kitchen getting torn up like this."

"I can understand that." Zach grinned, shoving his protective eyewear onto his forehead. "But remember, all of this mess is the first step to getting your dream kitchen."

"Right. I'll keep telling myself that." I nodded to the other guys, who were taking a break, waiting for Zach and me to stop talking. "Well, obviously, I'm interrupting. I think I'll take Winston for a walk."

"Let me introduce you to the guys—you'll be seeing them again over the next few weeks."

"Sure. That'd be great."

After saying hello to the team and trying hard to act like I was remembering names I knew I'd forget, I made my way upstairs, the banging resuming behind me. Winston shook in my arms, licking my face.

"Sorry, Winnie. It's a lot of noise." I cuddled him close. "Want to go for a walk?"

At my words, Winston tried to wiggle out of my arms.

"I'll take that as a yes." Within minutes, I'd gathered his leash and slipped on a light jacket.

I could be the responsible one—even if all I was doing was taking a dog for a walk. Of course, it was early yet. The fatigue would find me soon enough.

A cloudless Colorado blue sky—one of my favorite things about living in my home state—and the bit of coolness lingering in the air made me thankful I'd worn my Windbreaker. Winston's steps doubled mine as he moved back and forth in front of me, sniffing the grass on both sides of the sidewalk. My slight headache receded as I left the workmen and the noise and the dust behind. For as long as the weather stayed nice, Winston and I would be enjoying multiple walks each day.

It wasn't odd to be home today because it was Saturday. Monday would be an adjustment. But even before I thought about being home during the week, I needed to tell Geoff that I'd lost my job. I should have told him already, but exhaustion ran my life and his work schedule ran his. It would be midmorning by the time he got home and showered, and he still wouldn't know I'd been fired.

"Geoff, I need to tell you something." I practiced the words out loud as I walked through the neighborhood, past other older-model homes like ours, allowing Winston to wander where he would on the leash.

No. That wouldn't work. I could see Geoff's reaction already. How he would go still. How his eyes would widen behind his glasses. How he would—just for a moment—stop breathing. Assuming I would say, "The cancer's back," telling him our worst nightmare had returned to haunt our waking and sleeping hours once again.

If I'd learned anything in the past year, it was to not beat around the bush, trying to figure out how to soften the verbal blow. To just say what needed to be said and deal with the fallout afterward.

"Geoff, I got fired yesterday."

There. That was the plain truth. Now what else could I say? My husband would ask why and how, and when he heard what happened, he'd come rushing to my defense.

I'd have to be ready for all those reactions.

"We'll be okay financially. I got a good severance package." I needed to remember to have the paperwork close at hand. "We have my bonus."

The last statement was true, but that money was allocated for the kitchen reno, not as an emergency fund in case—*when*—I got fired.

And I could look for work. But where? Who would hire

me when I would take the same mental and physical challenges to the next job?

Getting another job wasn't an option. The reality slammed against me, stealing my breath away.

Sure, I'd look good on paper. I had an excellent résumé. Years of experience. But as soon as a new employer saw me working . . . or struggling to work, day in, day out . . . well, there'd be no reason for my new boss to be as patient as Mr. Hampton had been.

I came to a stop at a street corner. Looked up, calling Winston to heel beside me, bending to ruffle his ears. "Good dog."

Now if I only knew where I was.

I closed my eyes. Opened them again as if a second glance would equal a magical second chance to recognize my surroundings. This moment . . . it was like so many moments in my day after day after days. The bewilderment would roll in, tangled up with fear, and the questions would start.

What was I doing?

What do I need to do next?

Who did I just talk to?

Do I have a meeting later today?

Winston whined, tugging at the leash, his face turned up at mine. *"Let's go."*

Instead, I turned around and headed back the way I'd come.

What a way to live—going backward. Retracing my steps, hoping to find my last familiar spot.

With every slow step, I regained my bearings. That house

with the bright-yellow door . . . I remembered that. That miniature stone wishing well in the front yard . . . I remembered that, too. Home was a bit farther away than I expected, but at least I knew where I was. When a car pulled alongside me and then slowed down, I picked up my pace, focusing on the sidewalk stretching out in front of me.

"Hey there, gorgeous. Can I give you a ride?"

Winston barked a greeting as my shoulders slumped.

Geoff.

"You scared me." I stopped, my reproof wiped away when I grinned at Geoff in his used Outback.

He leaned with one arm out the driver's side window. Offered me a smile—the smile I knew so well. "I went home and Zach said you went for a walk, so I decided to come looking for you. I'm surprised to see you this far from home."

"I lost track of time." Winston tugged on his leash, pulling me toward the car.

"You getting in?" Geoff eased the car over to the curb.

"Now that I know you're not some stranger, sure." I settled into the passenger seat, Winston in my lap. "Winnie needed a good long walk this morning."

"Looks like he got one." Geoff dodged Winston's attempts to lick him and kissed me. "Sorry I'm all sweaty. I was planning on taking him for a little run when I got back from the gym."

"You can probably skip that. I think I wore him out." I fastened my seat belt with a sharp metallic click. "Is it okay if we drive around for a bit? Especially if Zach and the crew are still there."

"I won't complain about the noise since it means they got started on the renovation. I can't wait to see our new kitchen."

"It'll be a while before that happens—at least a week longer than we planned." I rolled my window down halfway for Winston, who propped his paws up on the edge. "I was thinking we might have to make some adjustments. Maybe scale things back."

"Why?" Geoff slowed to a stop at a four-way intersection and glanced at me. "After all our discussions and decisions— now you want to make changes?"

Why was Geoff surprised? This was what we did best. Change.

A few clouds had appeared in what was once a clear blue sky. To the west, clouds also advanced over Pikes Peak, an almost-certain indicator we'd have rain this afternoon. Everyone in Colorado knew the saying: *If you don't like the weather, wait ten minutes.*

I just needed to tell him.

"I got fired, Geoff."

"You got fired . . . from your job?" Geoff stopped looking at the road to stare at me.

"Yes. Mr. Hampton is offering me a decent severance package—" maybe I should have waited until we were home so we had the paperwork—"but yes, he called me into his office yesterday and told me that I was terminated."

"And you're just telling me this now?"

"I was asleep when you got home last night. And you were gone when I woke up this morning . . . and that is not the point." I paused. Took a breath so I could lower my voice and stop stating the obvious. "We haven't had a chance to talk about it before now."

"What happened?"

"I made a mistake yesterday—"

"One mistake and you get fired?"

"It wasn't just that mistake." I stopped, not wanting to spend the entire conversation on the defensive. "We both know I haven't been doing my job, Geoff. I've never gone back to work full-time. I've tried, but I just don't have the energy. And I can't process things like I used to. I lose track of time. I lose track of papers. I'm anxious all the time about everything I'm not doing. I'm surprised Mr. Hampton didn't do something before now."

This wasn't Mr. Hampton's fault. I couldn't do my job at the bank anymore. Hadn't Geoff listened when I'd said all of this over and over again during the past months?

Winston twisted and stood on his back legs, nuzzling my neck and chin, trying to lick my face. Small canine comfort . . . but I'd take it.

There should be some relief that I'd told Geoff what had happened. But his reaction was creating distance between us, when all I wanted to do was ask him to pull over, to stop the car, to hold me and say, *"Everything's going to be okay, honey."*

We drove in silence the rest of the way home, pulling in front of the detached garage behind the house. Zach's truck was still parked outside, but the other workers' vehicles were gone. The silence grew between Geoff and me as we sat in the car.

At last, Geoff turned toward me. "Are you sure you don't want to fight for your job?"

"Yes." I rolled the window down completely, gulping in a few deep breaths of the fresh air. "I can't do the job anymore. I'd like to look over the severance package together."

"Okay. Can I shower first?"

"Sure. I'll make some breakfast." I rested my hand on top of my husband's where it sat on the steering wheel. "We'll figure this out. There's my bonus—although I know that's basically been spent. And I can . . . maybe look for something. Something part-time. Or I can work from home . . ."

"We'll be okay, Jilly." Geoff lifted my hand to his lips, pressing a brief kiss against my knuckles. "Compared to what we've been through, this is nothing."

Any thoughts of preparing a nice breakfast disappeared as I stepped out of the car, dodging the industrial-size blue dumpster sitting in our driveway and pulling Winston along with me. Inside, I lifted Winston into my arms as I faced the evidence of the workers' efforts. Where a wall once had been stood a gaping hole. All of the upper and lower cabinets were removed, along with most of the countertops.

"Hey, guys." Zach nodded.

"You're making good headway today."

"The crew likes demo day."

"That's obvious." Geoff rested his hands on his hips. "Taking a break?"

"I, um, needed to talk with you."

"Okay."

"We found a problem when we were tearing out the cabinets. Actually, two problems."

"No. Not this early on." My arms tightened around Winston.

"Yeah. These things happen. We can't do anything further until we deal with these two issues, so I sent the crew home."

"What's going on?" Geoff scanned the room as if he could figure things out himself.

Zach motioned to the space where our old fridge used to sit—and where the lower part of the wall was now missing. "Apparently there'd been a leak sometime in the past, and it'd been repaired. You can see the newer piece of drywall."

Geoff nodded. "Yeah. Maybe I noticed that when I moved in, but I didn't think much of it."

"I decided to check it out—that's why there's a section of the drywall removed."

"And?"

"I think there's a problem with your water pipes."

"The previous homeowners said they'd been replaced back in the nineties."

"Hearing that doesn't make me feel any better." Zach motioned to his iPad on the dining room table. "I did a little research while I waited for you, and this type of pipe—if it is the type of pipe I think it is—was used from the late seventies through the midnineties. If they're polybutylene, then we've most definitely got a problem."

"Because?"

"From what I read—I'm not a plumber—polybutylene

becomes brittle over time. Builders don't use it anymore. That's why we need to check."

"Okay." Geoff nodded. "You said there were possibly two problems."

"I also noticed mold along some of the lower framework behind the drywall. It doesn't look too bad to me, but I'm not a professional in that area, either. I know enough to know we need to have that looked at, too."

"So what do we do?" I spoke up, saving Geoff from asking the question.

"I already left messages with two guys I know. One deals with mold and the other is a plumber. I probably won't hear from them before Monday." Zach gathered his tool belt and gloves from the floor, along with his iPad. "I'll keep you posted. For now, you all have a good weekend."

"Thanks, Zach. You, too."

Geoff followed Zach to the front door. Thanked him again. Shut the door. Turned and stared at me. "It's going to be all right, honey." Geoff opened his arms, allowing me to step into his embrace, Winston between us.

"It's going to be expensive."

"We don't know how serious the problems are yet."

"With our luck, we'll probably have to level the house." My words were muffled against his damp T-shirt.

"Very funny." Geoff hugged me. "We shouldn't be surprised, right?"

"What do you mean?"

"Trouble comes in threes." Geoff forced a laugh. "We've hit our limit and it's not even noon on a Saturday."

"Oh yeah, right. Ha-ha."

"Come on, we've got to keep our sense of humor about all this." Geoff tried to step away. "I need a shower."

"I need another hug more than you need a shower."

His laughter rumbled in his chest. "How about I get a shower and then we go out for a celebratory breakfast?"

I leaned back so I could look into his eyes. "Just what exactly are we celebrating?"

"That we're in this together. Water pipes. Mold. Whatever."

"You're not sorry you married a woman who is always exhausted and unemployed—?"

Geoff stopped my words with a kiss, his lips warm, his touch reassuring. Winston licked his chin.

"Great." Geoff shoved him away. "That dog . . ."

"You gave him to me." I savored our closeness, in spite of Winston interrupting our kiss—and even in spite of the pileup of disasters this morning. Then I stepped away. "Go take a shower. I'll handle this little guy and grab a quick shower after you're done. And then you can take me to breakfast. *To celebrate*—and we'll look at the details of my severance package."

"Oh yeah. Looking forward to that."

I was, too—at least to having breakfast.

4

I APPRECIATED the familiar comfort of my parents' kitchen. Functional cabinets, smooth countertops, stainless steel appliances, the round table and matching chairs in the breakfast nook—all so ordinary and all so much more valued now that my own kitchen was partially gutted and awaiting assessments by both a plumber and a mold inspector.

And after being up all night, dozing on and off between kicking my blankets around and sweating through a pair of pajamas—yet another consequence of the Tamoxifen—the last thing I wanted to do was think about what Geoff and I were going to eat.

"Thanks for feeding us today, Mom." I leaned against the

counter as she sliced the rolls for the meatball subs, the room filled with the rich aroma of marinara sauce. "I didn't think about how much the remodel was going to inconvenience us. I mean, I thought I was prepared. But now we're dealing with the reality of a portable microwave and mini fridge in the dining room for the next couple of months. And eating takeout. Lots of takeout. Pizza. Chinese. Mexican. Repeat, repeat, repeat."

"You know you're welcome here for dinner anytime, Jillian. And I'll send you home with leftovers."

"I appreciate that too, but don't give us too much. There's not a whole lot of room in that fridge. Geoff's going to be surviving on peanut butter and honey sandwiches for a while."

"And you, too, I imagine."

"Mmm-hmm." Food wasn't as much of a concern for me. Months after finishing chemo, my appetite was still off. Not that I needed to give her another reason to worry by mentioning that.

My estimation of how long it would take to remodel the kitchen was as optimistic as my response to Mom was vague. There was so much to talk about—it was just a matter of picking which topic. And not surprisingly, I'd earned the unofficial title of "Bearer of Bad News" in the Thatcher family.

Postponing the inevitable, I focused on one of the "We're Married!" announcements Geoff and I'd sent out that was still posted on the front of my parents' refrigerator.

I removed the glossy photo from where it was held in

position by a magnet that detailed the Broncos schedule for last year. There we were, Mr. and Mrs. Geoff and Jillian Hennessey, inviting family and friends to the reception our parents had hosted several months after our secret marriage—you couldn't call it an elopement because we'd only run as far as a local judge's chambers. Me in the lavender chiffon dress I'd worn when we'd gotten married, and Geoff in a suit, his arms encircling me, our gazes locked, our smiles almost identical.

"I love that photo." Mom's voice was a gentle intrusion on my memory.

"Me, too."

"All in all, things worked out well."

"Yes, they did."

"Are you ever sorry you didn't have a traditional wedding?"

"No." I repositioned the photo onto the fridge. "No. There's been very little 'traditional' about this past year, wouldn't you agree?"

"True. But you and Geoff are doing fine."

Yes, well . . . there was no need to dispel that myth right at this moment.

"I'll go tell everyone lunch is ready."

"It's too bad Johanna couldn't join us. I can't imagine what came up at work."

I couldn't either, although I'd wager personal choice rather than a pharmaceutical emergency of some kind kept my older sister away from lunch today. Her "We're family!" tirade still echoed in my head. That, more than anything, had prompted the brief text to me: **Tell Mom and Dad I can't make it for lunch. Sorry. Work problems.** Having me deliver the message was a nice touch—a subtle reminder it was my fault she wasn't coming.

It was still a crowded table in the dining room, what with me and Geoff, Payton and Zach, and Mom and Dad, Winston tucked in his arms. The Crock-Pot filled with Dad's special meatballs was positioned in front of him, along with the platter of rolls and plates of provolone cheese and home-made sweet potato fries.

"Put that dog down while we're eating, Don." Mom's command was softened by a smile.

Dad slipped Winston a bite of cheese and set him down. Winston, moocher that he was, settled at Dad's feet, ready for the next stealth bite.

"Dad!" I shook my head.

"What? What?" Dad's innocent look was belied by yet another not-so-subtle sleight of hand, rewarding Winston with another nibble of cheese. "Tell us how the renovation is going."

I waited for Geoff to say something, but he reached for the plate of cheese. Zach busied himself ladling two scoops of meatballs onto a roll. Of course, it wasn't his story to tell. And as far as Zach knew, we had only one bit of news to share with everyone.

Geoff adjusted his glasses, which had slid down his nose a bit. Smiled. "Well, after a few days' delay, the team started demoing the kitchen yesterday. And that's when we ran into a couple of problems."

"Serious problems?" Dad's attention was now diverted from Winston's whines.

"If by serious you mean potentially expensive, yes."

Zach stepped in. "We discovered a leak in the wall where the fridge had been."

"Oh no." Mom paused passing the platter of fries to Payton.

"It looks like it may have been there before because that piece of drywall is newer than the others." Zach rubbed the back of his neck. "I'm frustrated because I should have noticed it sooner, but I didn't. When I removed the drywall, I found signs of an old leak in the pipe—and what looks like mold on the framework. I'm not sure the extent of the problem. We need to get that evaluated, of course. I've called a couple buddies of mine and I'm hoping to hear from them tomorrow—or early this week."

"Well, that's good."

"Fixing that could be pricey, but there's no sense worrying about it until we know what we're dealing with." Zach added two slices of cheese to his sub. "I also have a hunch we'll find old pipes, which means those are going to have to be replaced too."

"Just in the kitchen?" Dad ignored his lunch . . . and Winston's demands for food.

"If the pipe isn't up to code, Geoff and Jillian would have to redo the entire house."

The kitchen remodel was like all those times when I'd gone clothes shopping. I started out, my expectations high, knowing just what I wanted, how I wanted to look. I'd browse the racks, select a few items, encouraged by Mom's assurances that a top was my color. That a certain brand of jeans would fit.

And then, in the dressing room, disaster would strike when I was confronted with all the issues of my body. Short-waisted. Big-chested. Overweight.

Time to adjust my expectations to reality.

I welcomed the clasp of Geoff's hand, but he only gave my fingers a squeeze before letting them drop. His reassurance quick. Fleeting.

I never should have suggested we do the kitchen reno so soon after I finished radiation—even if Geoff had been talking about the project while we were dating. It seemed like a good idea at first—temporary, welcome confusion added to our lives. But now the costs were being tallied in my head—elusive, unknown numbers I tried to add up and balance with the bottom line in our bank account.

"Like Zach suggested, we'll wait and see what his friend says." Geoff offered a laugh. "I've been trying to think up a joke about a house demo all weekend, like Chip Gaines, you know? But I've got nothing. Maybe I should just take a good swing at the wall with a sledgehammer."

Zach held up a hand. "Not without supervision, man. We've got enough to worry about as it is."

Everyone's laughter seemed a bit forced, fading into silence. Dad took the opportunity to slip Winston a nibble of meatball, and I pretended like I didn't see it. When no one else spoke up, I figured that was my cue to deliver my news.

"Something else happened on Friday . . ." I paused as I became the center of attention, the concern in Mom's gaze unmistakable. I'd forgotten my own "tell them straight up" motto. "I lost my job."

Only Geoff and I were ready for my announcement because we'd had a day and a half to get used to the idea. Some. My words were a sucker punch, unfair to both my parents and to Payton and Zach.

Tears welled up in Mom's eyes. Once again I was making her cry. All humor left Dad's face. Payton gasped, and Zach reached for her hand in much the same way Geoff would have comforted me. But I was too caught up in my own unwanted moment of drama to try to decipher what was going on between my younger sister and the guy she was "just friends" with.

"What happened, Jilly?" Dad's use of my childhood nickname soothed my frayed nerves.

"It's a long story. To be honest, I haven't been able to keep up with my workload for quite some time. Since I had my mastectomy, really."

"Surely you explained that to your boss." Mom's words were short, her mouth tight.

"Yes. He's been understanding and patient. Everyone at work has been great." I found myself fighting to shoulder the burden of everyone's need for an explanation. "But there comes a time when I should be able to do my job again. And I can't."

"Then they should continue to be understanding—"

"I'm not sleeping well, Mom. I only manage to work part-time most days and I'm always concerned I'll make a mistake. I have a hard time tracking my tasks. I'm forgetting the details of things I've done for years. I heard about 'chemo brain' when I was first diagnosed. I just didn't think I'd deal with it."

Chemo brain. I'd said the words out loud. Another label to live with. How many undesirable labels would I have to carry in my life? The words weighed on my heart like the breast form I wore. Awkward. Unwelcome. There were times I forgot, but all too often I knew only one of my breasts was my own.

"I'm so sorry, Jillian." Payton's voice lured me out of the gray depths of my thoughts. "I know this is hard for you."

Her words, unsullied by false platitudes or suggestions of what to do, gave me room to breathe. To not have to pretend that I was okay. "I'm still trying to figure out what I'm going to do next. Geoff didn't find out until yesterday morning."

"She was asleep when I came in late Friday."

"And he was already at the gym when I woke up."

"Thanks to the team and me tearing their house apart."

"It's fine, Zach." I offered him what I hoped was a genuine smile. "At least we got to have the first book club get-together at the house there before the renovation started, right?"

"Right."

"The what?" My mother grasped for a chance to change the conversation.

"Johanna, Payton, and I are trying to read a book together." Even as I spoke the words, I heard echoes of the tension between the three of us from a week ago.

"That sounds like fun." Mom seemed eager for all the details.

Why tell her any differently?

"If we all agree to continue with the book we selected."

"What did you decide to read? A bestseller?"

"We chose a biography—but even that was a difficult category. Should we go with a historical figure or a contemporary one or a celebrity?"

"And?"

"Contemporary."

"And . . ."

"And what?"

"How did the first discussion go?"

I waited for Payton to step in, but she appeared ready for me to handle all of Mom's questions. "We got, um, a little sidetracked, didn't we, Payton?"

Not that I was going to tell Mom that we were interrupted by her texts.

"Yes . . . we did." My sister tossed me a wink. "I think we'll get better at sticking to the topic as time goes on, if Jillian has anything to say about it."

It was odd to feel aligned with Payton against Johanna. I was the peacekeeper. The one who stayed neutral when my two sisters argued—as they inevitably did. And if I was close to either of them, it was Johanna, who was only two years older than me.

But today . . . today I'd sit on the bench with Team Payton.

Johanna never could decide which she liked better. Being at the hospital during peak hours, when things were busy, the pace a bit frantic, but all the while knowing she and her staff were prepared? Or was it times like now, early morning, when the hospital was just coming back to life, and she was the first one to arrive, to get a head start on things? She already knew they'd be short-staffed in the outpatient pharmacy, thanks to a pharmacy technician calling in sick, but all other locations were fine.

She had a meeting later to talk about updating their procedure for restocking crash carts, but she'd been doing research and relished the challenge of improving the process. She'd also e-mailed several colleagues, asking how they were doing, putting out subtle feelers to see if they might be open to a job change—all potential candidates for the assistant director position.

She slipped on her white lab coat as she exited her office in the back of the main pharmacy, stopping as the hospital CEO approached, accompanied by a tall man she didn't recognize. With his tan and his lean build, he could be a runner—a runner who ignored the benefits of sunscreen.

"Good morning, Johanna." Dr. Lerner stopped just outside the pharmacy. "You're here early, I see."

She was always early, as Dr. Lerner was well aware. Her dedication to the job was one of the reasons she'd been selected as interim pharmacy director. "Yes, ma'am. How are you?"

"Doing well. I wanted to introduce you to Dr. Axton Miller. He's from Tucson."

"Good morning, Dr. Miller."

"It's nice to meet you, Dr. Thatcher."

Dr. Lerner paused, an almost-imperceptible pressing of her lips together before she continued. "Dr. Miller is interviewing for the pharmacy director position. He's a late applicant.

Highly qualified." The CEO reached a hand toward her. "As are you, Johanna. But after seeing his résumé, the administration felt we had to at least meet with Dr. Miller."

"Of course." Johanna fisted her hands in the pockets of her lab coat.

"I'm giving Dr. Miller a tour of the hospital and wanted him to see the various pharmacies before things got too busy." Her boss frowned as her phone rang, taking a moment to silence it. "I apologize, Axton. I thought I'd turned my phone off."

"No problem."

Axton? Dr. Lerner was on a first-name basis with this guy already? Johanna stepped forward. "Why don't I show Dr. Miller around?"

"I don't want to interfere with your morning, Johanna."

"As you already said, I'm here early. And there's no one more familiar with how everything is run." Her competition might as well realize what he was up against. If she needed to play tour guide, so be it.

"That's true. As I mentioned, Axton, Dr. Thatcher is our interim pharmacy director. She's done an excellent job, too." Dr. Lerner was already reaching for her phone again. "And I do need to take this call. Just come to my office when you're done here, Axton. Johanna will bring you back."

"I know the way."

Oh, he did, did he? Was this his first visit to the hospital? If anyone knew her way around Mount Columbia Medical Center, she did. She spent more time here than she did at home.

Dr. Axton Miller. His name sounded familiar—or did it? She was almost certain she hadn't met him before. And it was ridiculous to stand around here and try to figure out who he was. She needed to do what she'd been asked, return the guy to Dr. Lerner, and then get on with her workday.

"As I'm sure Dr. Lerner mentioned, Mount Columbia Medical Center is a three-hundred-bed hospital." Johanna opened the door to the outpatient pharmacy, stepping aside so Dr. Miller could go in first. "It's named after one of Colorado's fourteeners. We have a reputation of serving a more select population who is willing to travel for a higher quality and more comfortable level of care."

"So what you're saying is, the patient is less concerned about cost and more concerned about their care experience."

"You could say that." Whatever the man did, he had some knowledge of consumer-focused health care. "We have a main hospital pharmacy, as well as both inpatient and outpatient pharmacies, and both OR and same-day surgery pharmacies. This is our outpatient pharmacy." Johanna paused as Dr. Miller strolled through the area. "We're also in the planning phase to add an IV cancer clinic, which would require a cancer pharmacy."

"Yes, Dr. Lerner and I discussed that."

Of course they had. No doubt she'd touted the merits of the hospital, as well as discussed plans for the future—two of her favorite things to do—as part of a job interview.

"How long have you been the interim pharmacy director, Dr. Thatcher?"

"Six months."

"What are some of the challenges you face here?"

"There are no challenges." None that she wasn't handling—and none that she would discuss with him.

"Really?"

"No. Everyone knows what they're supposed to do, and they do it."

"I see." Dr. Miller turned to face her. "No concerns about medication nonadherence?"

Who did this guy think he was? Johanna resisted doing a double take. Did he believe she had insider information for him—her competition? Not that he could be any sort of serious contender for the job.

"Would you like to go see one of the inpatient pharmacy locations?"

"That would be fine."

They headed toward the elevators. "Are you and Dr. Lerner personal friends?"

"No."

That canceled out any sort of private connection between him and her boss. Maybe Dr. Lerner had mentored him at some point?

"How did you hear about the job opening, if you don't mind my asking?" Not that it mattered.

"I don't mind. A colleague told me about it." A glint of humor lit his eyes—one that remained the rest of the time they were together.

And his response told her nothing. Had Dr. Lerner contacted him? Or someone else here at the hospital? They were playing twenty questions, and he was an unwilling participant.

Half an hour later, she'd taken Dr. Miller to the various pharmacy locations, and now they rode the elevator in silence. What right did he have to come in here, disrupt her schedule, not to mention her direct route to a promotion, and then find something—or was it more than one thing?—humorous about their time together? Before she could continue questioning him, Dr. Lerner appeared in the hallway just outside the elevators.

"Dr. Miller, still with Dr. Thatcher?"

"Yes. We've had an excellent conversation."

Now the man was flat-out lying to Dr. Lerner.

"Well, if you're done here, I thought we could get some breakfast in the staff café. We can talk and see what kinds of questions you have about the job."

Maybe Johanna should volunteer to join them so they could discuss the job together—a little professional two-on-one. But it would be better to walk away and act as if the appearance of this man didn't concern her in the least. Because it didn't.

"Enjoy the rest of your visit."

"Thank you for the tour, Dr. Thatcher." The glint of humor in Miller's eyes had intensified, and a smile curved his lips.

"My pleasure, Dr. Miller."

As the two disappeared, laughter floated back down the hallway.

The joke was on her.

The first of her staff began to arrive, saying good morning. Johanna barely heard them. This was no time to panic, even if she had been aiding the enemy.

Let the administration interview someone else. Due process. It didn't change anything. She'd proven herself. Miller was an unknown—except for his résumé.

His résumé.

A few moments later, Johanna was in her office, in front of her computer, googling Dr. Axton Miller of Tucson, Arizona.

He'd graduated from Rutgers's PharmD program. A visiting professor to their dual PharmD/MD professor program. Participated in several humanitarian trips overseas. Nice touch.

And he'd started an off-site chemo program at the hospital in Arizona.

The words on the screen seemed to blur for a moment, causing Johanna to blink. Once. Twice.

"He's a late applicant. Highly qualified."

Dr. Lerner's endorsement of her rival burned like antiseptic poured on an open wound.

She knew why her boss was so impressed with Dr. Axton Miller. Dr. Lerner wasn't understating anything when she said he was highly qualified. The man was more qualified for the pharmacy director position than Johanna was.

ONE GOOD THING about not having a job—not that I was making a list—was that I wasn't missing work to be at my doctor's appointment. And it didn't matter that Dr. Sartwell was running a few minutes behind. I could wait . . . and wait . . . and wait.

Small comfort for a newly unemployed woman.

But any consolation in the midst of all the upheaval in my life was good. Of course, I'd be the one meeting the plumber at the house later today while he checked the kitchen pipes. And also meeting the person from the mold removal company, who would tell me how bad that issue was. After all, Geoff had a job—and I was thankful for that.

It only made sense that I met with people as needed during the renovation—not that we were hoping for any more issues to come up.

At least Dr. Sartwell and I were only talking today—no actual exam. Even so, her medical assistant had insisted on taking my blood pressure and temperature and weight. Funny how cancer and chemo and radiation made stepping on the scale the last thing I cared about.

Having to get weighed meant I was still alive.

For now, I'd sit. Relax. Not think about leaking pipes. Or mold. Anything happening outside this room? I didn't have to deal with it. Reality was, as a patient, not a medical provider, I couldn't handle any of it.

Every noise beyond the walls was muffled. Footsteps. Ringing phones. Voices. If I closed my eyes, the silence in the room surrounded me. Separated me from anything waiting for me. I could just be here. There was something comforting about the clean scent of ammonia that lingered in the room. I didn't have to think about the mistakes of the past week that left me unemployed. Or the unknowns that loomed ahead of me.

Tears threatened, the edges of my eyelids wet. Then I exhaled and accepted the moment. The quiet.

And found safety in the silence filling a doctor's exam room.

Dr. Sartwell entered with her usual gentle rap on the door, a "Good morning," and her easy smile. All familiar after so many months of diagnosis, treatment, and follow-up appointments. I acknowledged her apology for being late for my appointment, deciding not to explain that I'd enjoyed the extra moments of solitude.

"How are you doing today, Jillian?"

"I've been better." I wasn't being coy. Just honest. "Don't get me wrong. I've certainly been worse. But I've been better, too. I lost my job."

Dr. Sartwell stopped typing in her laptop. "What happened?"

"I can sum it up in two words. *Chemo brain*." Now the tears started flowing, my throat constricting. "Every day . . . I told myself I could do my job . . . that tomorrow . . . would be better . . ."

I paused, fighting for control. I wasn't going to break down and sob like a three-year-old on the verge of a tantrum. I twisted my fingers together, swallowed, willing myself to continue. To *adult*.

"I'm good at my job." A harsh laugh scraped raw against my throat. "Correction. I *used* to be good at my job. *BC*. Before Cancer. And before my mastectomy. Before chemo. Before radiation."

Before. Before. Before.

Dr. Sartwell placed a small box of tissues in front of me. I took one. Another. Wadded them together and pressed them against my eyes.

"I want my life back."

My life before I had to wear a prosthesis. Before I had to take Tamoxifen. Before I had night sweats and hot flashes. I was too young to feel menopausal—yet I wasn't even having periods. All the unspoken complaints clogged my throat but were evident in the tears that trailed down my face.

Cancer—and the cure—had wrecked my body. Not that I'd been the beautiful, smart, successful Thatcher sister, like Johanna. Or the beautiful, athletic, successful sister, like Payton—and like Pepper would have been. I was just Jillian.

I inhaled a shuddering breath. "I didn't come here to talk about this."

"It's important that you do, Jillian." Dr. Sartwell's eyes were kind behind her black cat's-eye glasses.

"It doesn't change anything. And I know I should be happy . . . thankful I'm alive. I want to be happy."

"Fine. You're happy to be alive. You made these decisions to beat cancer. But no one likes losing a job. No one likes dealing with chemo brain. Or the side effects of medication. And you shouldn't pretend to."

I mopped at my face with the remnants of the wadded tissues. "Stop being so understanding or I'll start crying again."

"That's a brand-new box of tissues."

Her words, her comforting smile, caused more tears. And somewhere inside, the pain eased. The weight shifted. Here I was, treating Dr. Sartwell like a virtual shoulder to cry on. But she didn't seem to mind. She wasn't looking at her watch. Wasn't telling me to snap out of it.

"You're here this morning so we can talk about things. See how you're doing. I'm sorry you lost your job, but a lot of women struggle with chemo brain after going through treatment. We talked about this."

"We did?"

"Yes—but we talked about a lot of things when you were first diagnosed. Treatment options, harvesting your eggs since you and Geoff wanted a family in the future, the timing of reconstructive surgery. It's a lot for anyone to remember."

"I just thought I'd be better by now."

"Jillian, you are better." Dr. Sartwell rested her hand on top of mine. Patted it in a motherly fashion. "And you will keep getting better. I'll have my medical assistant print up some resources to help with chemo brain. Simple things like carrying a notebook with you and writing down lists. And not multitasking. Research has shown that's not beneficial for anyone."

"Well, that's encouraging, I guess." I threw the wad of wet tissues in the wastebasket beside the desk. Grabbed a few more from the box. "I wasn't even planning on talking about that today."

"What did you want to talk about?"

"Reconstructive surgery?"

"You'll need a consult with a plastic surgeon. I can start the process by requesting that. What else?"

"Dealing with the side effects of Tamoxifen—the night sweats and hot flashes. The fact that my appetite is still off. My weight is down, but I know I'm supposed to be eating better than I am."

We turned our attention to the other topics for the remainder of my appointment. Dr. Sartwell's answers didn't fix any of my problems. Nothing changed. But at least I felt heard.

She was trained in medicine—to care for my physical

needs. As a family physician, she also was sensitive to my emotional needs. She knew about the scar left by my mastectomy. Probably knew that my weight had haunted me for years. But she didn't know everything about being . . . me.

"Like I said, Jillian, you're doing better than you think." Dr. Sartwell removed her glasses, letting them fall to the end of the silver chain so they rested against the front of her white coat. "How are you and Geoff?"

"We're fine. Busy. We decided to remodel our kitchen."

"That's a big undertaking." Dr. Sartwell stood, leading me to the door.

"Yes, well, it's good I'm not pregnant right now, isn't it? It's challenging enough keeping an eye on our dog while our kitchen is all torn up."

Even as I laughed, the words hit me. Cancer was controlling so many things in my life . . . and now it was delaying starting a family.

"Well, you could always adopt." A laugh accompanied Dr. Sartwell's words.

"Right." I stopped. Made eye contact with my family physician. "Wait . . . what?"

"You understand you can't get pregnant while you're on Tamoxifen, Jillian. But if you and Geoff don't want to wait five years to start a family, you could always look into adoption."

We said good-bye, but her words replayed over and over in my head as I left her office. Crossed the parking lot to my car. Drove home through traffic that was lighter than it had been during morning rush hour.

"If you and Geoff don't want to wait five years to start a family, you could always look into adoption."

Why did cancer have to dictate one more thing in my life? If Geoff and I waited until I was off Tamoxifen, I'd be thirty-eight before I could start trying to get pregnant. And despite harvesting my eggs, there was no guarantee we'd be successful.

Dr. Sartwell's offhand comment was brilliant. It was as if she'd handed me some sort of get-out-of-jail-free card. I could have a say in my life again. No more making decisions based on cancer. I would decide what I wanted . . . and when I wanted it.

⁓

I needed to stop daydreaming about taking control of my life again. Get out of my car and go into the house. People were waiting for me—especially since my appointment had run late. There was no forgetting when a plumber and a person from a mold removal company were evaluating your house, even if I had been struggling with keeping track of things for the past few months.

But why was Payton's car parked behind Zach's truck? Wait . . . what was I forgetting? *Think.* . . . Zach had volunteered to be here in case my doctor's appointment ran late, which it had. But had I asked Payton to be here, too?

It didn't matter. Zach and Payton weren't responsible for whatever was happening inside my house. I could either continue to sit outside in the temporary safety of my car . . . enjoy not knowing the reality of my kitchen renovation for a while longer . . . or I could go find out what had been discovered inside the walls of my house.

Like it or not, I was a grown-up.

Winston's barks greeted me as he tried to wriggle his way out of Payton's arms.

"I appreciate you being here, Zach." I set my purse on the table by the front door. "I'm sorry my appointment ran long. This is a fun surprise to see you, Payton."

"I didn't have classes this morning. So when Zach told me he was going to be here, I thought I'd drop by. I can't really do anything, but I did let Winston outside."

"Thanks." I retrieved my dog from her arms, accepting his frantic licks to my face. "Anything to report?"

"The inspector from the mold removal company showed up early." Zach motioned toward a few pieces of paperwork on the dining room table. "The good news is the problem doesn't look bad at all. It can be handled quickly, so we dodged a bullet on that one."

Zach paused—like the moment in a low-grade movie when the background music changes key and the camera zooms in closer on the main character. When footsteps sounded overhead, I almost laughed out loud.

"Why is someone walking around upstairs? The problem is in the kitchen." I tried to school my facial features in case the imaginary movie camera had focused on me. I'd play the calm lead in this scene, thank you very much. "Just tell me, Zach."

But before Zach could say anything, a tall man with a full head of salt-and-pepper hair and a beard to match stepped downstairs. He carried a metal clipboard and a flashlight and wore faded jeans, a flannel shirt over a white T-shirt, and well-worn work boots.

"I confirmed what I expected, Zach—"

"Hey, Allen." Zach nodded my way. "My friend Mrs. Hennessey is here."

"Call me Jillian. Please." If the guy was going to give me bad news, we might as well be on a first-name basis.

"Jillian, then." The man shook hands with me. "I'm Allen Thomas. Zach called me about your problem. I hope you don't mind me taking a look around upstairs."

"No. Although I'm not sure why you needed to."

"Zach mentioned the issue he found during the kitchen demo, and we were just following another hunch we had."

"We—you mean you and Zach?"

"Well, yes and no. You just missed Craig. He did the mold inspection—went ahead and checked upstairs, too. You've got a little mold in the shower area in your master bathroom, but nothing that can't be dealt with easily enough."

I tried to get my brain to process faster. Why hadn't I realized when Geoff and I decided to renovate the house that it would mean people I didn't know telling me things I didn't want to hear?

Winston wriggled in my arms, his small whimpers more frantic.

"Let me handle him for you." Payton smiled and took him from me, letting Winston outside before returning to stand beside Zach. Part of me wanted to excuse myself and escape with my dog into our backyard.

But that probably wasn't written in the scene.

"So that's it then—there was another area of mold?"

"No, ma'am." Allen exchanged glances with Zach. "Your pipes need to be replaced."

Even though dollar signs started multiplying in my head, I tried to act composed. "We were kind of expecting that—"

"And your electrical wiring, too." Zach's announcement upended my attempt to stay relaxed. Even as I tried to recover, I couldn't help but notice the interplay between Payton and Zach. How their hands touched for the briefest of moments as she supported him while he relayed the additional bad news.

Why was I so easily sidetracked by the possibility that Payton and Zach might be dating? I forced myself to refocus on Allen Thomas. Now was not the time to be thinking about potential romances.

"The wiring? We didn't have anyone come look at the wiring—did we?"

Allen spoke up again. "Your house is easily a hundred years old, ma'am."

"Ye-es, that's true. But wouldn't the house have passed an inspection when Geoff bought it?"

"It shouldn't have. Your house has aluminum wiring and two-pronged plugs. I'm no electrician, but I do know old wiring when I see it. And Zach was correct about your pipes being polybutylene. Like he said, those get brittle over time."

"All of them?"

"Yes, ma'am."

"I realize that was probably a stupid question . . ."

"It's fine, Jillian." Zach spoke up. "This is more than you were expecting."

Why hadn't I insisted Geoff stay home from work? My "I can handle it" assurance was collapsing under the weight of all this information.

"I'm just a little confused." I tried to gather my thoughts. "I'm sure when we got married . . . when we started talking about the kitchen redo, Geoff said the house was in good shape."

"You've got a nice little house here, ma'am. Good foundation. The roof looks fine, too—of course, I didn't look at it too closely on my way in. But things like electrical and plumbing in a house this old? You can't be too surprised when you have to replace 'em."

Well, I was surprised, despite Allen Thomas's take on the matter.

I could see words and numbers—calculations—scrawled on the paper on Allen's clipboard. On the dining room table was the bid from the mold restoration company. Even if it was only a small repair, it was still going to cost us money we hadn't planned on spending.

This was the worst time to be fired from my job.

"Like I said, I'm not an electrician, but you're looking at anywhere from four to eight thousand dollars—probably the larger amount. I have a friend I can call and see if he can get out here tomorrow or the next day." Allen offered me a white sheet of paper. "Here's my estimate for the plumbing work."

The ever-present mental fog seemed to thicken as Allen

spoke. Words were clogging my brain. Names and numbers . . . decisions to make . . . I couldn't process all this.

I didn't want to process all this.

"Jillian . . . Jillian, you okay?" Payton stepped closer.

I blinked. Once. Twice. I needed someone to tell me my lines. Give me a cue. Or else I needed to figure out how to ad-lib something. Finish the scene and get everyone out of the house.

"Plumbing. Sure. An estimate is . . . perfect." I took the paper from . . . what was his name? "And I'll look at the other stuff . . . talk about it with Geoff."

"Do you want me to call my friend?"

"Sure. Fine. Thank you."

All three of them were staring at me. Wasn't I saying the right things? "I'll talk to Geoff about everything you've told me. Wait to hear from the electrician. And then we'll . . . we'll go from there."

Go from there. That made sense, didn't it?

And the next time I saw Dr. Sartwell, I could tell her that I was adept in another way to deal with chemo brain.

Faking it.

6

I STEPPED INTO THE BACKYARD, closing the door on the mess that was my kitchen. Three days later, the area where the old refrigerator used to be was still exposed, the lower part of the drywall removed, revealing the mold problem that led to the plumbing problem that revealed an electrical problem, all against the backdrop of the demolished wall between the kitchen and the dining room.

My emotions were as torn up as the room I'd just exited. Any excitement about the renovation had been erased and replaced by estimates and endless dollar signs swirling around in my head. We needed to reevaluate our budget but couldn't do that until we had the final figures for the plumbing and electrical.

For a moment, I stood in the late September afternoon, trying to soak in the peacefulness of the neighborhood. Through Gianna's open window, I caught the sound of Avery's sweet giggle. Winston bounded about the yard. Weeks ago, I'd thought that maybe, just maybe, if we had any money left over in the kitchen reno budget, we could replace the chain-link fence, too.

I almost laughed out loud at that bit of wish-filled thinking. The more likely question was, what were we going to have to cut from our plans?

And right now, I needed to make a phone call. I could only hope Johanna would pick up on a Friday afternoon. If nothing else, I'd leave a message, asking her to call me back.

I tucked my phone under my ear, saying hello to Johanna when she answered on the second ring.

"Hi, Jill. How are you?"

"Pretty well."

"Uh-oh. That doesn't sound so good. What's wrong?"

That was Johanna—astute. No chitchat, just cut to the chase. But I preferred to back my way into the real reason I called.

"Well, besides the reno not getting started on time, we discovered some issues we've got to deal with."

"No surprise."

And no sympathy from my practical older sister, either. "True. I'm living in one of those TV shows I love to watch— and now I'm trying to stop myself from googling the endless assortment of kitchen renovation horror stories."

"Don't go looking for trouble."

I didn't need to do that—it had shown up on my doorstep, unpacked, and invited relatives of all sorts and sizes to come visit, too.

"What's going on?"

It didn't take long to update Johanna on all the house issues, especially when she only said, "There's more?" once and then remained silent while I told her everything with a final "And such is the joy of owning a one-hundred-year-old house."

Geoff and I should be good at the "do one thing and then do the next thing" routine. That's how we'd gotten through the months following my diagnosis. Only then, I'd let it drive us apart.

That wasn't happening this time.

Winston flopped down in a corner of the yard, panting, just waiting for the next reason to jump up and bark or run or do both. The dog had more energy than I did most days. I didn't have the ability to push Geoff away. And I didn't want to. Yes, I was tired. Discouraged. But I also knew what—who—I was thankful for.

"So there are problems you didn't know about, and the renovation is going to take longer than you planned. Surely Zach warned you about this."

"Yes, but I was kind of hoping we'd skip all of that and go straight to 'Ta-da! Here's your beautiful kitchen.'"

"Unrealistic. We can just hope it's not too expensive."

It was also unrealistic to expect sympathy from Johanna. That's not how my sister operated. Support came in the form of "Let me help you take your medicine. Swallow it quick and be done with it." With an occasional brief hug or smile . . . or donating her hair to Locks of Love in my name as a Christmas gift.

A sharp click interrupted, indicating one of us was getting another phone call. Maybe I should delay the rest of the conversation.

No. I wanted to finish this. Needed to finish it.

"Jill, Beckett's on the other line. Can I call you back?"

"No." My voice was louder than I'd expected. "No. I also called to tell you that I got fired last week."

And that was the worst way to tell my sister . . . but at least now she knew.

"What did you say?"

"I got fired. From my job at the bank."

"I know where you work, Jill." The click sounded again. "Let me put you on hold while I tell Beckett that I'll call him back."

Now I stood in silence—a silence that stretched longer and longer.

What was Johanna telling Beckett? Obviously something other than a brief "I'll call you back" message. Maybe more of a "Jillian lost her job and I'll call you back when I fix it" kind of message.

"You there?" Johanna's voice ended my guessing game.

"Yes, Johanna, still here."

"What happened?"

I'd anticipated Johanna wanting an explanation. Had practiced one. Now if only I could remember the short, sweet version.

"I've had a difficult time keeping up with things at work. I'm tired. I find it hard to multitask like I used to. You know what I mean . . ."

And there was Johanna's invitation to step in.

"Yes, those are all common complications after chemo and radiation—not to mention the medication you're on."

Her response was an echo of our recent argument, but I only wanted to deal with one thing at a time. I needed to be wise and choose my fights with my older sister. I preferred not to fight with her at all.

I swallowed back the desire to respond. "Exactly."

"When are you going to tell the rest of the family?"

Now that question I hadn't anticipated.

"Um . . . they already know."

"They already know? Mom and Dad? Payton? Even Zach Gaines, I suppose?"

There was no need for Johanna to list off the members of the family as if to remind me of whom I needed to talk to.

"Yes, they were all at Mom and Dad's last Sunday, so I told everyone then."

"You didn't tell everyone, Jillian. You didn't tell me."

"You weren't there, Johanna."

"I know I wasn't there, but you couldn't call me last Sunday? Text, maybe? Did you—oh, I don't know—lose my phone number or e-mail address?"

With every word she spoke, Johanna twisted our conversation more and more out of shape—from what had happened to me to some supposed offense against her. Her voice softened, going lower and lower, almost a whisper.

This was all wrong. Why was Johanna acting like the wounded party?

"I'm sorry, Jo—"

"At least you realize you owe me an apology."

"That . . . that wasn't an apology." I sucked in a breath.

"What do you mean by that, Jilly?"

"I mean . . . I am sorry you're upset. And yes, maybe I could have called you sooner." I wavered for a moment, knowing that what I said next was a turning point of some kind in my relationship with Johanna . . . possibly a point of no return. "But maybe . . . maybe you could understand that being fired is a bit of a shock? And that dealing with a renovation is hard enough without problems—even if I should have expected some? And you know I'm dealing with side effects of my medication because you're telling Mom all about them."

Words stumbled out of my mouth—a halting explanation ending with an accusation that fell into an abyss of silence that grew louder and louder.

For a moment, I wanted to declare victory. But that would be gloating. Immature. Besides, if I said anything else, I might unlock something even darker and hurl it at my sister.

"I know you need to call Beckett, so I'll let you do that. Good-bye, Johanna."

⌒

The mideighty temperatures were giving way to cooler evenings as the sun slipped behind Pikes Peak, but the warmth would return tomorrow, refusing to abdicate its seasonal position quite yet. Leaves were starting to drift down from tree limbs, dotting the grass with bursts of color.

"It's a perfect night to grill out." I carried the quartet of premade burgers I'd purchased at the grocery store out to the backyard. "All the better, since we don't have a working stove."

"We don't have a working kitchen. Period." Geoff accepted the paper plate from me. "But this is an improvement over takeout. Or peanut butter and honey sandwiches. Who knows? Maybe by the time the renovation is over, I'll be ready for some sort of barbecue championship—win us some cold hard cash."

"Right. Forget cybersecurity and take your grilling skills on the road. Maybe challenge Bobby Flay. But for now, we're eating together. At a normal time."

"It's okay to eat dinner without me during the week, Jillian." Geoff stood in front of his preferred method of grilling—a charcoal grill—waiting for the charcoal to heat up. He was a purist when it came to his burgers and steaks. No electric grill for him.

"I know. I'm not trying to make you feel guilty for working late."

After my talk yesterday with Johanna, the last thing I wanted was to be anywhere near guilt. I didn't want to be blamed for things or make someone else feel that way. And if anything, it should be the other way around. Geoff had a job. I didn't. His long hours might create some stress on our married life, but I'd known about Geoff's work hours before we got married. He wasn't causing financial problems by not having a job.

I should be cooking, not Geoff. I wasn't doing my fair share around the house.

More and more, my faults were piling up like some invisible block tower that would come crashing down, burying me beneath all my "I can'ts."

I needed to think about something else.

"Did you ever talk to your boss about that speaking opportunity?"

"What?" Geoff squinted his eyes against the smoke rising from the grill as he placed the hamburgers on with a soft sizzle of meat against metal. "Oh, that. Yes. I told him I wanted to do it. That still okay with you?"

I wrapped my arms around his waist, resting my head against his back. "I think it's fantastic. I'm so proud of you."

"I haven't done it yet."

"I know you'll do great."

"Thanks."

"Has Zach contacted you about the estimates for the plumbing or electrical jobs?"

"He called today and said he hopes to have them by early next week. Asked if I wanted him to go ahead and pull permits. I said yes."

"Okay."

Geoff twisted around to face me, removed his glasses, closing his eyes and pressing his fingertips against the bridge of his nose before saying anything else. "This is what I get for buying this house 'as is.'"

"I guess I didn't realize you did that." I rushed to soften my words. "Allen Thomas did say it's a nice little house."

"Except for the pipes and the wiring . . ."

"I love this neighborhood."

"And all this work will be great when we sell the house."

"Not that we're planning on doing that anytime soon." I backed toward the house. "What do you want to drink?"

"Tea sounds good."

I retrieved two bottles of unsweetened iced tea from the mini fridge, handing one to Geoff and keeping one for myself. He was adding salt and pepper to the hamburger patties. Maybe now was a good time to change the topic.

"Remember how I went to see Dr. Sartwell on Monday?" I twisted the metal cap off the tea.

"Yeah." Geoff faced me again. "You're okay, right? I thought you said everything was good."

"Yes. Everything is fine. Dr. Sartwell and I were just talking about things. Getting a consult for reconstructive surgery. The side effects of the Tamoxifen."

Even with my effort to sound calm, Geoff remained facing me, smoke billowing up behind him.

I knew our address. That we were renovating a one-hundred-year-old house near Memorial Park. But a year past my cancer diagnosis, Geoff and I still lived on the border of "what-if." What if my cancer came back? What if all the reassurances weren't enough to hold back something worse? What if my recovery . . . this rocky status of health . . . was only temporary?

I pressed the side of my clenched fist against my forehead as if doing so would force back the pressure building there.

I had a say in how things went in my life. That was what this conversation was all about.

"Something Dr. Sartwell said at the end of the appointment gave me an idea."

"What kind of idea?" Geoff took a moment to flip the burgers again.

"She reminded me that I can't get pregnant while I'm on the Tamoxifen."

"There's no chance we're forgetting that."

"But then she mentioned adopting."

Geoff stilled. "What?"

"She said if we didn't want to wait five years to start a family, we could always adopt." I tamped down the urge to hug myself. Rock back and forth. "I don't know why we didn't think about this before—"

"No." Geoff pushed his glasses back up in place. "No, I don't want to do that."

What? This was when my husband—my very understanding husband—was supposed to say, *"You're right. Why didn't we consider this sooner? It's a great idea. Definitely something worth talking about."*

But instead, Geoff said no—not once, but twice—acting as if I'd suggested we try to get pregnant right then, maybe not even bother waiting for the privacy of our bedroom. Geoff's voice had gone flat. Devoid of emotion. But he'd still said no, blocking me as efficiently as a left tackle on an offensive line. Shutting me out.

I took a slow sip of my tea, the liquid soothing the dryness in my throat as I composed my thoughts. This just-begun conversation was not over. "You don't want to do that? What is that supposed to mean?"

"It means I don't want to adopt." Geoff faced away from me, flipping the burgers again, his back rigid.

"Just like that, end of discussion?"

"What's there to discuss? You haven't talked about wanting to adopt before now." Geoff didn't even bother to face me again, causing me to strain to hear his words. "I don't want to adopt. It's not an option. Do we have buns?"

Do we have buns?

"Wait a minute." I positioned myself so he had to look at me, the smoke from the grill burning my eyes. "Geoff, just because we haven't talked about adoption before now doesn't mean it's not an option."

"What about the fact that I just told you I don't want to adopt?"

"Since when have you been against adoption?"

"I'm not against adoption—"

"Then explain why you won't even consider it."

"Look, I think it's great—for someone else. Not me."

Which meant not for me. Not for us. It was as if I was talking to a stranger with shuttered, cold eyes. Someone devoid of humor. Compassion.

My Geoff wouldn't shut me out like this with an unexplained, unemotional no.

"I thought we were having a conversation—"

"We are having a conversation, Jill."

"A conversation is when two people talk back and forth. When they listen to each other."

"I listened."

"You listened until I said the word *adopt*, and then you said no and that was the end of any real communication between us."

Silence.

"Geoff."

He crossed his arms. Stared at me. "What do you want me to say?"

"Tell me we can talk about the possibility of adopting."

Geoff pursed his lips. Swallowed, grimacing as if tasting something bitter. "I love you, Jilly. You know I do. But I can't tell you that. I . . . I've just never been one of those people who wanted to adopt. I don't think I could love someone else's kid, you know?" He shrugged, not quite meeting my eyes. "So there's no sense in talking about it. I'm sorry."

With every word he spoke, Geoff seemed to step farther away from me, although he never moved.

I hadn't realized how much the idea of adopting had become my own personal get-out-of-jail-free card, compliments of Dr. Sartwell. How much I wanted to be able to start a family when I wanted, rather than being on cancer's timetable.

And yes, I could hear the apology in Geoff's voice—both the spoken and unspoken one—because it clashed so loudly with the clear message that this topic was closed.

I pressed my lips together, almost choking on all the bottled-up words inside me. Stared at my husband. "Yes, we have buns. I must have left them in my car."

"What?"

"You asked if we had buns. We do. In my car." I took several steps back. "If you want them, you'll have to get them yourself. I—I'm not feeling hungry anymore."

I sounded childish, but I couldn't stop myself.

"Come on, Jill. Let's have dinner—"

"And talk about what? Work? Oh, that's right, I don't have a job. Adopting? That's a non-topic, too."

"Can't we just have a nice meal together?"

"Apparently not." Now I did wrap my arms around my waist, holding myself together. "I think I'll take Winston for a walk."

"I'll come with you."

"I wish you wouldn't." I motioned to the grill. "The burgers are burning."

I COULD GET USED TO the quiet . . . after all, that was normal. But I didn't want to.

I wanted to wake up because Winston was barking, alerting me to the sound of a truck rolling to a stop out front. I wanted my kitchen to resound with footsteps and hammering and drilling and scraping and men's voices and somebody's chosen radio station for the day . . . sounds indicating work had begun again.

I never thought I'd want people and noise in my house, but that would mean things were happening. Instead, everything remained at a standstill.

How ironic.

Progress was evading me in so many areas of my life. And it was all too costly.

I scooped food into Winston's bowl, popped a pod into the coffeemaker, and peered into the mini fridge, welcoming the tiniest bit of cool air on my face.

A couple of bagels. A tub of low-fat cream cheese. Leftover, overcooked hamburgers from Saturday night. . . .

I closed the fridge door and grabbed a banana from the basket on the dining room table.

"You all done, Winnie?" Coffee mug in hand, I opened the back door—which would probably remain a plain old door, rather than being transformed into classic French doors.

I rubbed sleep out of my eyes, feathering my still-short hair with my fingertips. Maybe I'd keep it this way, especially if it retained the wave that had appeared when my hair grew back in. And maybe one day I'd have decent eyelashes and eyebrows again.

Sometimes it was truly the simple things in life that made all the difference.

"Good morning, neighbor." Gianna's voice floated over from her yard, causing Winston to bound that direction.

"Morning. Sorry—"

"Winston is never a problem. Really. Avery enjoys him. And so long as you have a dog, I don't need to get her one."

"Oh, is that how it works?"

"That's how it works with a two-year-old, yes." Gianna met me at the fence, Avery crouching a few feet behind her, examining a dandelion in the yard. "How's the renovation going?"

Avery seemed fascinated with that simple yellow flower—a weed really. Her pudgy little fingers touched the bloom, and then she pulled it out of the ground, bringing it to Gianna, a smile lighting her blue eyes.

"For you, Mommy."

"Thank you, sweetie." Gianna took the tiny offering with a soft laugh as her daughter wandered off.

I tried to breathe against the tightness in my chest. To smile at the exchange. Make light of it. But Avery's innocent action showed me what Geoff was denying me with his abrupt *no* last night.

"Jillian?" Gianna reached across the fence and touched my arm. "You okay?"

"What? I'm sorry. . . . Did you say something?"

"I asked how the renovation was going."

"Oh . . . I . . . I missed that somehow." There was no explaining my lapse. "It's not going. We've had a trio of problems. A minor mold issue. And then we found out we needed new pipes and new wiring—for the entire house."

"Oh, wow." Gianna leaned against the fence. "That'll make my husband happy."

"Why would you say that?"

"He told me not to get any ideas about redoing our kitchen anytime soon. No keeping up with the Hennesseys."

"Nice to know my house problems will make your husband happy. We blew our budget pretty quickly."

"We're going for a walk. Want to join us?"

Avery had found a cluster of dandelions in a corner of the yard and was gathering a tiny bouquet of them for Gianna.

"That might be nice." Not that my neighbor knew I was lying to her. My phone rang in the pocket of my hoodie. "That's probably Geoff. . . . Maybe next time?"

"Sure." Gianna backed away with a small wave. "Come on, Avery. Let's go for a walk."

"Talk to you later." I turned away from the sight of mom and daughter heading out for their morning walk. A quick check of my phone confirmed it was Geoff. I was tempted to ignore the call, but that would be immature.

"Hello?"

"Jillian. Hi. I wanted to check on you."

"Outside with Winston."

"How are you feeling?"

"Fine. I've been up for a little while. I was talking to Gianna—"

"I don't want to interrupt . . ."

"It's fine. She's taking Avery for a walk."

A sigh sounded across the phone. "You're still angry, aren't you?"

I stopped just outside the closed back door. "I'm not angry."

"Then what are you?"

I couldn't . . . wouldn't toss out my usual excuses. *I'm tired. I'm having a hard time processing all of this . . .*

"I'm hurt."

"Hurt? Why?"

"Now that makes me angry." I cut off his response. "That's ridiculous, Geoff, and you know it. I'm hurt by our nonconversation Saturday night, when I wanted to talk

114

about adoption. And by how nothing else was ever said all weekend."

"What else was I supposed to say?"

"You could have asked me how I was feeling before now, when you're at work and I know you can't talk long. . . . Or maybe you could have told me what you were thinking or feeling . . ."

"But talking wouldn't change the result. Wouldn't have changed my mind."

"Maybe it would have changed how the weekend went. How this conversation is going. Maybe we wouldn't even be having this conversation."

"Or maybe the weekend would have been worse. Did you ever think of that?"

I leaned my head against the door. None of this was helping. If anything, we were only digging the line separating us deeper into the sand.

"Jillian."

I didn't respond. I used to love to listen to Geoff talk. I would close my eyes and get lost in the cadence of his voice. How he said my name. His laugh. Now all I wanted to do was say good-bye and have him go back to work.

I opened the back door, grabbing Winston's collar before he could run past me. "We'll talk later."

"Fine."

And for one of the first times since we'd gotten married . . . maybe the first time . . . we didn't say we loved each other before we hung up.

My cell rang as I headed inside, debating on showering

or crawling into bed, firing up my laptop, and watching a movie.

I grabbed my phone and spoke before he could say anything. "I love you—"

"Hey, Jillian . . . um, good morning?" Zach's hesitant greeting made me laugh.

Why hadn't I taken just a second to look at my phone to make sure it was Geoff before blurting out, "I love you"?

"I thought you were Geoff!"

"I figured." He chuckled. "Sorry. Just me."

"I'm so sorry."

"It's okay. How are you?"

"Other than embarrassing myself, I'm fine." I slumped back against the kitchen wall. "Can't complain. I mean, I could, but I decided to just enjoy the quiet house for now."

"Now it's my turn to apologize. I'm sorry about all this."

"It's not your fault Geoff bought an old house." I held on to Winston, who squirmed to be let down. No need to let our dog get injured and add a vet bill to our expenses.

"It is a good home, Jillian."

"And it will be all the nicer with new pipes and wiring, right?"

"Yes." Zach cleared his throat. "I wanted to let you know we're working on getting the permits processed. Once those are done, we can get back to work."

"Great."

"And you and Geoff—are you thinking about cutting costs at all? Changing anything?"

"I know we probably need to—I've already given up on

the French doors in my head—but we just haven't had the chance to talk about it yet."

"If you want, we can talk through some suggestions. I can't guarantee other things won't show up as we go along."

I settled on the couch, Winston in my lap. "Thanks for that bit of good news."

"Just trying to be realistic. You're still going to get your dream kitchen. We're just tweaking the dream a bit."

"Thanks."

"I'll keep you posted on everything. I won't be driving back down this week, though."

"I understand. Not much for you to do right now, is there?"

"Look, I understand you're probably feeling a little discouraged, but we'll get back on schedule. I promise. And I'm praying for you . . . and Geoff, too."

Was that some little code phrase Zach used instead of saying, "Have a nice day"?

No. He sounded too sincere for that. And knowing he was praying for me . . . for us . . . comforted me for some reason.

I carried Zach's words like a personal benediction throughout the morning, perhaps a bit more powerful than one of Harper's positive thoughts I still had taped to the mirror in the guest bedroom.

"I have a present for you." Harper marched into my apartment, her arms cradling a large glass jar topped with a bright-pink bow.

"What is this?" I shut the door, pivoting to find her only a few feet away.

"*Thoughts.*"

"*Thoughts?*" *I shifted the jar, examining the contents. It was filled more than halfway with strips of multicolored paper.*

"*Positive thoughts, to be exact.*" *Harper tapped the side of the jar.* "*Do you know how many hits you get if you google 'positive thoughts'? And Pinterest divides them into categories like work and life and women and health. You're lucky I'm not giving you two jars.*"

"*I wasn't expecting one.*"

"*You need these, Jill. I've been reading about cancer, and everybody says your mind-set makes a difference. So you read one of these a day, got it? Like a mental multivitamin.*"

"*How many strips of paper are in here?*"

"*I don't know . . . I just opened a Word document and started adding quotes. If you run out, let me know. I can add—*"

I shifted the jar to one arm and pulled Harper close, blinking back tears. "*You are the best friend . . . the absolute best friend . . .*"

"*And so are you. I told you that I didn't like cancer messing with you. I'm here for you, remember?*"

Every time I'd read one of the quotes, I'd taped it to the mirror over my bedroom dresser. When Geoff and I got married, he'd asked if I wanted to take all the strips of paper off, and I told him no. Absolutely not. He didn't argue, covering the mirror with a sheet.

He'd treated the mirror like a precious heirloom, transporting it in his car and placing it in a corner of our bedroom until we had time to hang it in the spare bedroom after we finished moving everything else over from my apartment.

I'd memorized some of the quotes, and a favorite by Helen Keller came to mind now.

"Although the world is full of suffering, it is full also of the overcoming of it."

The quote had seemed more appropriate—more needed—six months ago. A stalled kitchen redo was not true suffering. Inconvenient, yes, but not suffering. Not being able to get pregnant for five years? Geoff's aversion to adoption roadblocking my attempt to get around my inability to get pregnant? The possibility that I might not ever have children? That might be considered a type of suffering.

Now all I had to do was figure out the overcoming of it.

Johanna enjoyed being home—especially after the twice-a-month visits from the cleaning service she paid an exorbitant fee to. Surfaces dusted and sanitized, wood floors and carpeting swept and vacuumed, glass and mirrors polished, a faint scent of citrus lingering in the air. Order restored—not that she ever let anything get too messy.

Her living room was streamlined, with a sleek black sofa, two white chairs, and glass-and-metal side tables adorned with abstract metal lamps. Her small office, closed off with paned glass pocket doors, repeated the spare decor, with a glass-and-metal desk and a black leather chair positioned in front of minimalist bookshelves. She'd indulged in a bit of whimsy, arranging the books spine out by color, rather than by title or author.

She'd used Super White paint on her walls, creating a sense of being in a museum, aided by the various black-and-white photos displayed throughout the house. Some were Beckett's, some copies of favorites by photographer Toni Frissell. Maybe when she got her promotion, she'd celebrate by purchasing an original.

With Jillian and Payton coming over for round two of their book club, she'd added several fresh white orchid plants in the living room and dining room and even one in her study. The cleaning company knew to toss them once they died. She'd prepared two quiches last night—her favorite recipe and a vegan one for Payton. The aromas of cheese and onions and eggs filled her house, mingling with the scent of her preferred coffee, fresh ground and fresh brewed. No premeasured pods for her.

And she'd even read three chapters of the book. Skimmed was more like it, but she was ready not only to host, but to participate in any discussion Payton started—because that was Payton's responsibility, not hers.

She was also willing to forget her last conversation with Jillian. Fatigue was enough to make anyone unreasonable. And getting fired . . . well, she'd be understanding and not bring it up at all. Maybe for once Payton would play the buffer role between two Thatcher sisters, instead of Jillian.

Coffee, quiche, and surface conversation. A lot of sisters survived on this. Or less.

Johanna arranged cloth napkins, silverware, and spotless square glass plates on the dining room table. This was her role in the family—she managed things. Kept things orderly and under control. Of course, no one came right out and said, "Johanna, take care of things," but everyone knew that's what she excelled at.

Jillian was the peacemaker. Payton and Pepper? Their arrival had disturbed the family peace. But eventually they'd settled into their star status as the twins—attracting attention and earning the title of Double Trouble with their identical faces and their equally identical athletic ability. Well, not quite identical. Pepper had edged Payton out just a bit on the volleyball court.

Johanna straightened the tablecloth, smoothing a wrinkle and aligning the pieces of flatware. Order was a good thing. It kept frustration and disappointment at bay. And maybe one day her sisters would thank her. If they didn't . . . well, at least all was right with her world.

When a knock stopped her musings and summoned her to the door, Johanna was surprised to find not just one but both of her sisters standing together on her small front porch. "Did you ride together?"

Payton's brow furrowed as she shook her head. "Of course not. We just got here at the same time."

Why would the thought of her sisters driving together bother her? She and Payton weren't "besties." And she didn't have exclusive rights to a close relationship with Jillian, even if they were only two years apart and had always been closer, just like Payton and Pepper had been a matched set.

Jillian's hello and smile seemed natural enough, so maybe she'd forgotten their phone call from two weeks ago, too.

"Come on in. Let's eat while everything's hot."

As they settled around the table, Johanna served the quiche and poured coffee. "This quiche is vegan—tofu instead of eggs. And the sugar jar is right near you, Payton. I know how you like your coffee sweet. There's fresh cream for us, Jill."

"Thank you. You didn't have to go to the extra trouble—"

"No trouble." Johanna passed the other quiche to Jillian. "How are you two enjoying the book?"

"Has anyone actually read it?"

"Isn't that the plan? I read the first three chapters." She placed her napkin in her lap. "I don't recall setting a chapter goal for each time we meet. Maybe we should do that before we leave."

"I confess the book is on the table beside my bed—and that I'm stuck on the first chapter." Payton's smile held the hint of an apology. "I want to read it, but between classes and volleyball, it's just not happening."

"I'm not having any more success than Payton." Jillian seemed relieved at the confession. "You'd think with all my free time, I'd be reading all sorts of books. But magazines are more my speed right now. I start to read and doze off. I'm tired all the time."

"What's the update on the house? Zach told me the plan was to repipe first."

"They just finished putting in the new pipes this week." Jillian served herself a small portion of the nonvegan quiche.

"So next week the new crew will come in and start rewiring the house."

So much for trying to help Payton start a conversation about the book. It was as if Johanna was trying to lead and no one was following her. Why hadn't she remembered this whole book club thing wasn't her responsibility?

"So we're not going to talk about the book, then?"

Both of her sisters stared at her as if she'd declared she was going to *write* a book, instead of questioning their intention to talk about the biography they'd all agreed to read.

Jillian spoke first. "Maybe we could just relax and catch up with each other?"

"There's not too much to tell for me. Work is fine. Beckett's got this big annual conference this weekend. He'll be glad when it's over."

Jillian nodded and turned to Payton. "What about you?"

"Like I said, classes and coaching. I remember walking off the campus back when I graduated from college and thinking, 'I don't ever have to take another class'—and here I am, back in college to become a teacher, taking tests and writing papers with kids straight out of high school." She cut into the quiche without taking a bite. "I'm having fun coaching the JV team."

"Is your team winning?"

"We've won more than we've lost so far. I've got a great setter and a strong back row. Working on the block."

Johanna grimaced. "And she's talking like we understand all that volleyball terminology."

"Sorry."

"You're managing that while you're taking a full load of classes?"

"Don't have a choice. I don't want to be a college student forever."

"Is it weird, being back at your high school and coaching?" Jillian continued to act the part of the impromptu interviewer.

"It was at first. But I'm glad to help out. They weren't expecting their coach to go on bed rest for the last half of her pregnancy."

"So overall, you're glad."

"It's the right decision. Teaching high school English seems a long way off, but I'll get there."

"You look happier, Payton."

"Thanks. And Zach's told me that he likes being the project manager for your kitchen reno."

"I'm not sure he's telling you the truth there."

"He knew what he was getting into, Jill."

"Not everything, but I will say he's helped Geoff and me stay calm. And since we've had so many unexpected costs already, Zach's helping us figure where to cut so we don't completely blow our budget. We can't control the timeline, but we can try to scale back the costs."

It was like listening to casual acquaintances talking while enjoying good coffee and good food. All of this information could have been conveyed via texts, without any of them leaving their homes.

Payton looked tired.

Jillian looked tired.

Johanna was the only Thatcher sister who'd even gone to the trouble of putting on makeup.

"So, Jillian, have you looked for another job yet?"

Payton stared at her. "Johanna, were you even listening to Jillian?"

What was the attitude for—other than the fact that Payton always took an attitude with her?

"Of course I was listening—"

"—because if you had been, you'd have heard Jillian say she was tired all the time. Finding a job right now probably isn't her priority."

"I asked a reasonable question, Payton. And we are having a conversation, aren't we? One I can participate in? I thought if nothing else, Jillian might look for something part-time."

"Just because you think she should—"

"I didn't say she had to do anything—"

"Can we go back to coffee and quiche and talking about the book?" Jillian's voice rose just a bit louder than hers and Payton's. "Please?"

"I asked a legitimate question, Jilly."

"You're like a . . . a bulldog with a bone, you know that, Johanna?" Payton's china cup clattered in its saucer.

"Well, at least you didn't throw a volleyball analogy at me."

"All right! If I answer your legitimate question, can we please change the topic?" Jillian stared Johanna down until she nodded. "No. No, I'm not looking for a job right now. Not a full-time one. Not a part-time one."

"You didn't have to answer her, you know." Payton's words were mumbled around a bite of food.

"Oh, stop already!" Johanna sat ramrod straight.

"Both of you stop acting immature. We're adults, aren't we? Aren't we?"

Payton mumbled yes and Johanna offered a curt nod.

"What happened to remembering what Pepper said? 'Sometimes you just have to forget all the other stuff and remember we're sisters.'"

Payton's eyes welled with tears. "I'm sorry, Jill."

Johanna's lips tightened into a thin line. "It's a nice thought . . . but to be honest, I don't want Pepper's words thrown out to silence me every time I'm trying to have an honest, helpful conversation."

Jillian gasped. "Is that what you think I was doing?"

"Isn't it?"

Jillian pressed a hand to her mouth. Closed her eyes for a moment. "I'm sorry. I need to go."

"What's wrong?"

"What's wrong?" Jillian's voice pitched higher. "What's wrong is . . . maybe you're the one who's good at using words to silence people."

Payton reached for Jillian's hand as she pushed away from the table, rattling the water glasses and coffee cups. "It's okay . . ."

"I'm sorry, Payton. I'll talk to you later." Jillian gathered her purse and book and, without another word or a backward glance, walked out. The front door closed with a decisive click.

Johanna shook her head. "Well, Jillian is more exhausted than I realized. . . ."

"You think what just happened is about how tired she is?"

"You heard her. And no matter what you believe, I heard her, too—"

"Fine. We all know she's tired—although you seem to keep forgetting that. But if you were honest with yourself, you'd admit you've upset her. *Again.* Then you'd do something about it." Payton stood, picking up her book. "I need to get home and write a paper. Thanks for breakfast."

Had she just been put in her place by not one, but two of her little sisters?

As Johanna stood in her open doorway, Payton fast-walked to where Jillian sat in her car. When Payton knocked on the window, Jillian rolled it down. The two of them talked for a few moments before Payton leaned in and gave Jillian a hug. Neither of them acknowledged Johanna before driving off.

So much for the second book club session. All that had happened was she'd been reprimanded and then excluded by both of her sisters . . . and left with a bunch of food that would go to waste, including a tofu quiche.

PAYTON WASN'T SURE which was more exhausting—her non-stop former life as a party planner for Festivities, where she was at the beck and call of clients, or her now double life as a full-time student and part-time coach, with practices five days a week, mixed in with one or two games.

She leaned into her front door, using her shoulder to muscle her way into the foyer. With her double backpacks, she looked like one of the girls on her JV team. One backpack for her textbooks. Another for her volleyball gear. And just like her girls, she had homework to do after practice.

She abandoned the volleyball bag by the front door. Laundry would wait—but not too long if she wanted to avoid a rank odor when she unzipped that bag. The other one she dumped beside her couch—right next to her coffee table, the top inlayed with varied sizes and types of wood planks— so she could spread her dinner and laptop and books out later while she studied.

She'd never realized how much she needed a coffee table until the day early last summer when Zach showed up at her front door, a huge grin on his face, greeting her with a brief hello before taking her by the hands and dragging her out to his truck.

"What are you doing? I'm not dressed to go anywhere." Payton tried to pull away, to retreat inside so no one would see her in her old cutoff jean shorts, club volleyball T-shirt, and flip-flops, her hair piled on top of her head in a messy bun.

"We're just going to my truck." Laughter laced his words. "I have something to show you."

She stopped resisting, allowing him to lead her around to the back of the truck, where the tailgate was lowered to reveal something covered by a black tarp.

"Close your eyes."

"I can't see what it is anyway. And you want me to close my eyes?"

"Just do it, okay?"

"Fine." She scrunched her eyes shut. "There better not be an animal under there."

A swish of plastic and a brush of air against her skin signaled that Zach had removed the tarp. "Ta-da! You can look now."

Sitting in the back of the truck was a rustic square table in muted grays, whites, and blacks.

Payton gasped, reaching to touch the edge that had been sanded smooth. "Zach. This is beautiful. What is it?"

"It's a coffee table. Do you like it?"

"Of course I do. I love anything you make." She scrambled to climb into the truck.

"Whoa. Hold on there. What are you doing?" Zach wrapped his arms around her waist to hold her back.

"I'm trying to get a better look."

"Well, you can do that when it's in your house."

She stopped struggling. "In my house?"

"Yeah. I made it for you—if you want it."

"If I want it?" Payton twisted to face him, placing her hands on his shoulders. "It's gorgeous! I don't have a coffee table."

Zach's words were low in her ear. "I kinda noticed that."

"Thank you." She couldn't resist brushing his dark hair out of his eyes.

"You're welcome. My pleasure." Zach's eyes had warmed . . . and then he'd pulled away from her. Had he glimpsed the spark of longing in her eyes? "Let's get this in the house already."

If she wanted it. Of course she wanted the coffee table. She hardly ate in her breakfast nook anymore—not when she could sit on her couch and see the one-of-a-kind table Zach had designed just for her.

And be reminded to be careful about how much she wanted from him. How much she wanted for them.

Payton turned away. She couldn't think about that now. Not when she was this tired.

It didn't take long to undress and start a shower. Standing under the hot stream of water allowed her to rinse off all the details of the day. The faint echoes of the class lectures she'd attended. The blend of girls' voices and footsteps and balls hitting the court from practice. The noise of the grocery store from when she'd stopped to buy some basic necessities. Yogurt. Apples. Grapes. Salad. Bread.

Almost ready to face an evening of studying.

The ping of her cell phone broke through her thoughts. Probably Zach texting to see if she was home. As much as she wanted to talk to him, she wasn't going to rush these few, much-needed moments of relaxation.

After exiting the bathroom, wrapped in her robe, her hair pulled up in a towel, she tapped out a quick text.

Call you in five.

She braided her wet hair—a volleyball girl's go-to hairstyle—and put on a pair of gray sweatpants with a logo from the Colorado Crossroads tournament and a red Club Brio T-shirt. Then she settled on the couch with a bottled water and a packaged Southwest salad emptied into a large bowl and topped with the premade dressing. Zach was on speed dial and they were saying hello within seconds.

"I'm starved, so I'm going to be munching in your ear."

"That's okay. It's still nice to hear your voice. Tell me about your day."

"Same as usual. Classes. Coaching. I've got at least a hundred pages of reading to do. And that paper to start writing." She stabbed a fork into her salad. "Now tell me about your day."

"Same as usual here, too." Even the sound of Zach's voice talking about something as simple as his day was nice.

"Work. Got a new project to start evaluating. And I'm hoping to check on things at Jillian's tomorrow."

"Will you make the game tomorrow night?"

"Of course. You know how much I love high school volleyball."

"Uh-huh."

"I'm not missing any of your games, Payton. I'll be sitting in the stands, cheering for my favorite coach."

"Don't cheer for me. Cheer for the girls."

"I can't help it. The JV coach is my favorite."

"Cute. Very cute."

"Yeah, and she's cute, too."

Payton shoveled a huge bite of salad into her mouth. This was what all their conversations were like. Friendly—and a little bit more. She knew Zach liked her as more than a friend. And if she were honest, she'd admit she liked Zach as more than a friend, too. But they hadn't crossed that line. Not out loud, to one another, at least. They danced around it . . . got close . . . and then retreated. But in recent weeks, Zach's questions were more frequent.

"So what are you thinking about God, Payton?"

"Can I answer any questions for you?"

"What did you think of the pastor's sermon on salvation?"

She swallowed, forcing the strips of lettuce and cabbage down her throat. He meant well. Probably didn't even suspect that, at times, his words pushed her into a corner.

They were fine.

She was fine.

"So are we still on for Friday?"

"Friday?" Payton searched her mental calendar. "What's happening Friday?"

"We were planning on going to see a movie—"

"Oh no . . . I can't. The C, JV, and varsity teams are all doing a combined pasta dinner and game night. You know, a bonding thing. We have that all-day tournament on Saturday. We aren't going to be out late, but I have to go. All the coaches will be there."

"Sure. I get it. We just crossed wires on that one." A pause and then, "Church on Sunday still?"

"Of course church on Sunday. I'm looking forward to it. I'll meet you there."

They chatted for a while longer, Payton crunching salad in Zach's ear, before they said good night. The air always seemed to electrify between them during the last moments of their conversations, whether they were face-to-face or on the phone. Somewhere between their "good-byes" or "good nights" or "talk to you soons," other words lingered unspoken.

She'd told the truth when she'd agreed to go to church with him on Sunday. She wanted to go. In the past months, she'd gotten to know the people at Zach's church. The music was familiar, the words like "by His wounds we are healed" and "Immanuel, God with us" and "walking on water" no longer puzzling. The pastor's laid-back demeanor helped her relax, and at times his sermons made her laugh or touched a place deep inside her—a phenomenon she still didn't quite understand.

The one thing she was still trying to figure out was where

she stood with God. How to find her way to Him. Not just follow Zach or be pushed by him, but how to find her own path.

The ache in her chest was a combination of "have to" and "want to."

And it distanced her from the man she loved. The man she was in love with—but she only admitted that to herself.

She knew her good-bye sounded absentminded as if she'd already left the conversation. But she also knew Zach would overlook it, thinking she was tired. Which she was.

What he didn't know was that she wasn't studying. Wasn't writing her paper. She'd left her laptop and books in the living room and gone to her bedroom to remove the metal lockbox from the top shelf of her closet, where she kept it.

Correction. Not a lockbox—a *time capsule* she and Pepper had made and then hidden on their sixteenth birthday, determined to unbury it twenty years later.

And then Pepper's death had changed their plans. Changed so many things.

Maybe it was silly to still keep the box locked as if someone were going to come and steal it. Pilfer the contents. Who else would want what was inside? A collection of her and Pepper's team volleyball photos—varsity and club. A newspaper article about them that mentioned their nickname of Double Trouble. The handwritten lists of dreams they'd written when they were sixteen—the summer before Pepper had died.

And . . . the small diamond cross necklace Pepper had left for her—and that she hadn't discovered until a few months ago—along with her sister's note that said, *For when you know Jesus like I do.*

The unexpected gift Pepper had hidden in the time capsule was now tangled up with Payton's love for her sister and her love for Zach and all of her questions about God.

She didn't want to make a decision just to wear the necklace for Pepper.

She didn't want to make a decision just so she could be free to have a romantic relationship with Zach.

Believing—or not believing—in God should be simple. But it wasn't.

The weight of the delicate gold chain seemed to press against her fingertips, until she let it slip back into the metal lockbox. She started to close the lid, but then she retrieved the necklace and hung it on the corner of her mirror.

It's not that I don't believe in You, God. I do. I just don't know why I believe in You.

Was what little faith she had for Pepper? Was it for Zach? Faith had to be for her and God. Not them.

But she didn't want to disappoint either of them . . . and Pepper wasn't here anymore. Not even in her dreams.

This was all messed up. Like running and jumping again and again to check her vertical. *How high? How high?*

She wasn't doing it right.

The cross glinted in the overhead light. Those were real diamonds. How was she supposed to determine if her faith was genuine?

All she did know was that now, the way things were, the way she was, she couldn't have what . . . *who* . . . she wanted.

Waking up was a slow, pleasant process these days. A drifting up from deep slumber until I became conscious of light filtering into my bedroom, touching my closed eyelids. I stretched beneath the comforter and sheet, no longer afraid of the unwelcome pressure of my first thoughts. Months ago, the remembrance of cancer would shock all remnants of sleep from my body, even as I clutched the blankets closer and tried to recall one of the positive thoughts from Harper's glass jar. Then it was the remembering of loss—the loss of my breast. The loss of Geoff because my doubt and fears had shoved him away.

But almost a month after the fact, the recall of losing my job wasn't enough to disrupt my sleep. It was an unpleasant memory, but I no longer tried to shrug it off or push it away.

I'd gone to bed the night before, determined that if I fell asleep early enough—before Geoff got home—I'd get up before he left for work this morning.

But I hadn't.

And that realization jarred the contentment of the morning. His side of the bed was empty, the covers tossed back. I rolled over onto my side, pulling his pillow close and inhaling his scent, grasping a vague memory of him snuggling close and whispering, "I love you, Jilly," and me mumbling, "Love you, too," sometime late in the night.

We were okay. Busy, but okay. The attempted conversation about adoption had stood between us like a sentry, blocking me from going back to the way things were before

Geoff said no to adopting, while also stopping me from moving forward, to seeing some sort of compromise. But we'd found our way back to each other. There was an ache in my heart, a longing unfulfilled, but I was used to those. This was marriage, after all. Ups and downs. Arguments and making up. We'd have other arguments in the future, and we'd get past those, too.

As I continued to lie in bed, sleep crept back in. My eyelids were getting heavy and I pulled the comforter closer. Maybe I'd sleep a bit longer . . .

No.

I tossed the covers aside, the cool air causing me to shiver even as Winston's faint yip from the kennel in the other bedroom summoned me. Time to get up. I had things to do, even if the most pressing demand was our dog.

I'd established my new staying-at-home-because-I-don't-have-a-job routine. First, take care of Winston. Let him out. Let him in. Feed him. Repeat the out and in routine. And once he was happy, I could take care of myself.

I indulged in a longer-than-usual shower, hoping the guys wouldn't show up to work on rewiring the house before I was done, and then debated a few moments on what to wear. My closet had too much business wear and too few casual items, but the budget didn't allow for a shopping trip anytime soon. Dressy jeans and a short-sleeved blouse would have to suffice.

At least I accepted the way my body looked now . . . even the absence of one breast. I didn't like it, but I no longer turned my back on the mirror when I got dressed, before

I put on my breast form. If my husband could love me as I was, then I could at least face myself.

It was time to follow up on the reconstructive surgery consult Dr. Sartwell had ordered. That was my next step. When I'd first been diagnosed with cancer, I didn't realize how my life would fall apart and then become one long journey of trying to find my way again.

But no one was singing, "Follow the yellow brick road," and I was no Dorothy gifted with ruby-red slippers allowing me to click my heels and whisper, "There's no place like home."

No, I was the one looking for courage.

I held my blouse and bra in one hand, tracing the scar . . . *my* scar . . . with my fingertips before pressing my hand against the beating of my heart. What did they say? Courage didn't mean you weren't afraid.

The house was still as I pulled a makeshift breakfast from the mini fridge in the dining room. Milk for my bowl of cereal topped with slices of banana. Winston nipped around my heels, and I let him out into the backyard again with a "Go on and bark at the birds."

When someone knocked on the door, I expected the electrician, ready to continue rewiring the house. Carrying my bowl, I answered the door and found Zach waiting.

"Good morning." He offered me a small wave.

"Good morning. I'm surprised to see you here." I stepped back.

Zach remained on the front steps, his eyes scanning the area behind me. "Where's the team?"

"Not here yet."

"That's not good. I thought they'd be here."

"It's still early."

"Not that early." He pulled his phone out of his back pocket. "Let me text someone."

"You want some coffee?"

"No, thanks. I'm good."

Well, if Zach wasn't coming in, I guessed I could step outside and eat my breakfast standing on the steps.

After sending a message to rally the troops, Zach stuck his phone in his back pocket. "They got pulled onto another job that has to be finished today. They hope to be here this afternoon."

"That's fine." Not that I could complain . . . or finish the work myself.

"How are you doing with the renovation?"

"We're making progress, so I'm not complaining. And everyone has been nice. I don't worry about having them in the house, thanks to you and Allen Thomas approving them. I appreciate that, especially since I'm home all day now."

Zach leaned against the wrought-iron railing. "How are you adjusting to not working?"

"It's fine . . . I mean, right now the renovation is distracting me. And not having to fight through work is a relief. I'd been struggling during chemo and radiation. The last few months things had only gotten worse."

"Are you looking for a job?"

"No. Payton didn't say anything?"

"Should she have?"

"No, I guess not." I stirred my cereal. At least one of my sisters respected my privacy. Although telling Zach about my decision to stay home wasn't the same as telling him that I couldn't get pregnant. "It just doesn't make much sense to go job hunting, does it? I'd get hired and have the same problems. The reality is, I doubt I'd get a decent recommendation from my last job."

"I understand. It sounds like you're making the hard, right decision."

And that was all he said. No offering advice or trying to fix the situation. Or trying to fix me. He didn't go all spiritual on me and start talking about God or offering to pray, which would have made me uncomfortable, since I'd never prayed in my life. Not by myself or with anyone else.

Standing here, talking about what was going on in my life, it was like we were friends. And why couldn't Zach and I be friends? Casual friends. Zach was someone you could trust. Geoff and I did trust him. I could see why Payton liked him. . . . More and more, I hoped Payton and Zach would move past friendship to romance.

"What's that smile for?" Zach tilted his head to one side.

I hadn't even realized I'd been smiling. "Nothing. Just thinking."

I'd let my thoughts get away from me, and evidently they'd shown up on my face. Payton could figure out her own relationship. I wasn't a matchmaker.

"Driving down here, managing our renovation, it's not too much of a hassle for you, is it?"

"No. I'm good. Glad to help."

"We appreciate it. Even though I'm home now, I don't want to take this on."

"I don't expect you to. Well, I'll let you get back to your day." Zach pulled his keys from his pocket. "Are you coming to Payton's volleyball game tonight?"

"I hadn't even thought about it."

"You should. JV plays at five."

"Thanks for mentioning it. You just might see me there."

After Zach left, I called Winston back inside, waving at Gianna and Avery in their backyard. I could step outside, do the neighborly thing and chat for a few minutes, but closed the door instead. Maybe later.

Winston followed me back upstairs, where I made the bed and then settled in the middle with my laptop, away from the mess of the barely begun renovation. I'd take Winston for a walk later, once the workers showed up. *If* they showed up. For now, I'd check Facebook and Instagram.

But instead, I found myself typing the word *adoption* into the search engine and waiting for the page to load, holding my breath as if anticipating something mystical and magical would be revealed.

"I don't want to adopt. So there's no sense in talking about it."

Geoff's words whispered in my head. My hands hovered over the keyboard. I almost closed the tab. Almost.

But I didn't.

It was as if I was mentally squaring off with my husband.

I'm not talking about adoption.

I'm just doing research.

No harm in that.

All of that was true. Maybe if I gathered information, I could soften Geoff's adamant attitude and he'd be willing to look at what I'd found. His *no* didn't mean we couldn't talk about adopting a child ever, ever again.

I scanned the page. There were so many things to consider. American adoption. International adoption. Foster adoption.

No . . . I wasn't interested in adopting a puppy from a puppy mill. A laugh slipped past my lips, and I scratched behind Winston's ears.

Comic relief and a chance for my heart rate to calm down.

I'd take it slow. This wasn't a job. There wasn't a deadline. No one was waiting on me to organize and finalize this information and get it to them by a certain time. I could stop when I got confused. Reread things when the paragraphs got garbled. Walk away from my laptop if I needed to.

And I'd take notes. Lots and lots of notes.

I had the skills to do this. Researching adoption was not unlike gathering the different parts of a mortgage package. I just needed to take my time—and I had plenty of that.

But I'd also make sure I took care of myself and things around the house, too. I'd rest so that I'd be awake when Geoff got home at night. Maybe figure out some meals that worked well in a Crock-Pot. Keep up on things like the laundry and paying the bills. All the things Geoff and I struggled to stay on top of when we both worked full-time and that were compounded by my fatigue. It was time to make my first list. Title it *Things to Do Now That I'm Home Full-Time.*

Winston snuggled close. Even he was happy to have me home. Maybe . . . maybe unemployment was going to end up being a very good thing after all.

I'd keep telling myself that.

10

There was no running in the hospital hallways when she was wearing three-inch heels.

Besides being dangerous and decidedly unprofessional, it would spread through Mount Columbia like a rampant case of influenza if people saw Dr. Johanna Thatcher running, her white lab coat unbuttoned and flapping open behind her.

She'd walk, the model of decorum, nod and even smile at people she knew, and act as if being summoned to the CEO's office hadn't wrecked her schedule for the day.

She couldn't even remember what her schedule was anymore.

This call could mean only one thing . . . *the* long-awaited one thing. That after over six months of interviewing applicants, the administration had made a decision about the pharmacy director position. After proving herself more than qualified for the job, she was the best candidate and could drop the invisible-to-her word *interim* from her title. Own the position.

And yes, she'd handle the addition of the chemo site, too. She didn't have the experience like Dr. Axton Miller, but that didn't mean she couldn't do it. She'd already started reading up on the process. And once she'd negotiated her salary and signed on the dotted line, she'd focus on hiring an assistant so she could devote more time to the project.

The past months had been like waiting for the orchestra to tune up on the rare occasions she attended the symphony. And today, this moment, was almost like the first few magical notes that allowed her to relax deep within.

With this promotion, she could stop thinking *when* and focus fully on the *now* when she came to work every day— and she could also begin to discuss her plans for the medical center's future.

And plan her wedding.

Johanna stopped. She knew the hospital so well she'd arrived at the CEO's office without realizing it. She smoothed down the front of her lab coat, waiting for a ripple of excitement to overtake her. But today was almost anticlimactic. Her boss had groomed her for this position, all but promising her the job when he retired.

The last person she expected to see in Dr. Lerner's office was Axton Miller. He rose to meet her, hand outstretched, his smile creating crow's-feet around his eyes, as the CEO came around from behind her desk.

"Hello, Dr. Thatcher."

"Dr. Miller? I wasn't expecting to see you here." Her words hung in the air like an exposed electrical wire as she took his hand.

"I can understand why you're surprised to see Dr. Miller, so I'll get right to the point." Dr. Lerner positioned herself between them. "Based on his expertise, we've offered Dr. Miller the pharmacy director's position, and he's accepted."

No one spoke as Johanna struggled to process Dr. Lerner's words. This man, who stood smiling at her as if they were friends, had stolen her job. She licked her lips. Pressed her hand to her throat, letting it slide down to grip the lapel of her coat. "I see."

The CEO's smile was gracious. "Johanna, I know you expected the promotion—and rightly so, given your qualifications. Dr. Miller is hoping—we're all hoping—that you'll stay on as assistant director."

"I'd value you as a member of my team, Dr. Thatcher." The man nodded.

"A member of . . . your team."

"Yes. I'll be busy with quite a few things, so your corporate knowledge will greatly help my transition."

But apparently her corporate knowledge wasn't enough to secure her the promotion.

Instead of hearing the welcome strains of a familiar symphony, the words were off-key. Discordant.

She should have known better than to dream.

Johanna fisted her hands inside the pockets of her lab coat. "Congratulations, Dr. Miller. Of course I'll do what's best for the hospital to make the transition as smooth as possible."

"Thank you, Johanna."

"When will Dr. Miller be starting?" Johanna turned to the hospital CEO.

Dr. Miller—her new boss—answered her question. "Next week. My family will be joining me as soon as the house in Tucson sells."

"Of course."

"I'm planning to meet with the team next week—seven o'clock, before things get too busy. I'll let you know what morning. And you'll hold down the fort—"

Meet with the team. Hold down the fort. Did this guy always talk in buzzwords?

Dr. Miller had stopped talking. Johanna could only hope he'd spouted off more "team" type rhetoric.

Dr. Lerner spoke up. "I'll send out an e-mail with the announcement later today—ward off rumors."

"Of course." Time for another smile and an exit. She was overlooking something . . . what was it? Johanna swallowed hard. "Now if you'll excuse me, I need to get back to work."

Dr. Miller's handshake was firm, his smile open and genuine. Didn't he have the least bit of guilt that he'd taken her job? Or was he one of those "all's fair in love and war and promotions" kind of people? Did he believe that the best applicant had gotten the job?

BETH K. VOGT

Her eyes and the back of her throat burned. She blinked. Sniffled.

She was not a crier.

Johanna veered left into the nearest women's restroom, not stopping until she'd entered a handicap-accessible stall all the way in the farthest corner. Locked the door. Turned, leaning her back against it.

Her phone buzzed in her pocket, and out of habit, she looked at it.

Beckett.

How's your day going?

Ha. The man's timing was a bit off. How was her day? Maybe he would like to withdraw the question.

The time in Dr. Lerner's office had been like attending the symphony and watching the conductor walk up to the podium, take the sheets of music, tear them up, and toss them into the air before exiting the stage.

Nothing. No music.

A sob rose in her throat and she choked it down just as the door to the restroom swished open, someone invading what little privacy she'd found. Her desire to cry turned into a crazy urge to laugh, and she pressed both hands over her mouth.

She was going to lose it in the ladies' room—either that, or she was going to march back into the CEO's office, interrupt Dr. Lerner and Dr. Miller, and demand that promotion.

Her resolve disappeared with the flush of the toilet. The unseen woman had no idea Johanna was having a career crisis, standing in an oversize stall.

She could just as well face facts here as anywhere else.

Alone once again, she typed the truth in a text to Beckett.

I didn't get the promotion. Dr. Axton Miller got the job. He has expertise I don't have. He assures me that I'm an asset to his team. He and the CEO hope I stay on. And that's my Monday.

She sent the text. Put her phone in her lab coat pocket without waiting for Beckett to answer. Smoothed her lapels, her fingers brushing the place where her name and the words *Mount Columbia Medical Center* were embroidered in green thread.

This wasn't the first time she'd had to let go of a dream. She'd just forgotten how the pain sheared off a piece of her heart . . . and yet, somehow, her heart kept beating.

She kept breathing.

She didn't go backward. Didn't cry over spilled milk or broken melodies. And she didn't waste a workday hiding in the bathroom brooding over a lost promotion.

Johanna needed to stand up on her high heels and act like the professional woman she was.

She was an adult, not a ten-year-old.

If she played this right, she'd score a spot in the fifteen-item checkout line.

Hurrah.

Johanna tossed a prewashed bag of brussels sprouts into her green metal cart, planning to sauté them in balsamic vinegar, brown sugar, and honey. The dish would be a nice accompaniment to the sweet potatoes. Beckett's rib eye. Her salmon.

Now to find a crusty loaf of bread. And then maybe browse the pastry section.

She refused to classify tonight's meal as a pity party. The closest she'd come to crying over her lost promotion had happened in the ladies' restroom. No tears and wadded-up tissues would appear at the table. But there also wouldn't be the anticipated lavish dinner celebration at one of her favorite restaurants—The Peppertree, perhaps?

So she wouldn't be indulging in the pepper steak prepared tableside by a tuxedoed waiter, discussing all she could do now that she was the pharmacy director—no *interim* to impede her plans.

She'd eat comfort food instead—her kind of comfort food.

Johanna wandered past a display of high-end chocolates. Paused. There had been years when she'd been in the habit of buying several packages of these. Stashed them high on a shelf, indulging in them as needed as if stuffing her face might fill any ache in her heart.

She knew better now.

Besides, admiring glances were better than the short-lasting taste of chocolate, no matter how pricey.

As her cell phone rang, she sighed. Beckett, at last.

"Hey there." His voice was low. Distant.

She pressed the phone to her ear, straining to hear him. "Are you heading to my house?"

"No. Sorry. It turns out it's going to be a late work night. Again."

"What?" Her cart skidded right as she eased around the corner into an aisle, bumping the shelves of assorted teas. "You said you'd make it for dinner."

"I know what I said, but the superintendent needs me to handle something—"

"It's always something!"

"I'm scrambling to put a press release together." Beckett's words overrode her protest.

"Beckett, I've already bought everything to make a nice dinner for us."

That was stretching the truth, but he didn't need to know that.

"Just . . . just save it. You can cook it tomorrow. Or the day after."

Right.

She should be used to this. She'd been warned this was Beckett's life for the next year. Her life, too. She had nothing to complain about. But she didn't like dancing with two partners—Beckett and his still-hadn't-met-him boss leading her round and round in a never-ending waltz of inconvenience.

She relaxed her grip on the cart handle. Flexed her fingers. Even in a busy grocery store, she was alone.

"You still there?"

"Where else would I be?"

"I'm sorry, Johanna. I've got to go."

"I understand."

The silence on the other end told her the attempt to be a loving fiancée wasn't worth the effort.

The man probably didn't even remember she'd lost her promotion.

She closed her eyes. Organized her thoughts, her emotions, like the rows and rows of exotic teas in front of her. Box upon box. By flavor. By brand. By touted remedies.

For a moment, she seemed to catch the faintest hint of the aroma of lemon and mint tea. Heard the clink of delicate bone china teacups. A voice saying, *"Sometimes the best reward for a job well done is a nice cup of fresh-brewed hot tea . . ."*

Johanna opened her eyes, shaking her head. She didn't have time for this. She was in a grocery store aisle, not strolling down memory lane.

She retraced her steps, replacing each item she'd chosen. Brussels sprouts. Sweet potatoes. Salmon. Steak.

The overhead voice announcing some sort of sale price in the produce section might as well be the voice of some all-seeing god unveiling a truth. Other people might be running to grab half-priced organic fruit and vegetables. But Johanna was embracing the reality that Beckett loved his military career as much as she loved being a pharmacist. He reveled in being handpicked by the general. In the unrelenting fast pace, the endless demands.

Laughter floated over from the next aisle. At least someone was having a good day. Who was she kidding? Plenty of people were happy, including Dr. Axton Miller. Johanna couldn't move. Her thoughts jumbled together, a mixture of retorts to her boss and complaints to her fiancé.

Despite the rumbling in her stomach, Johanna wasn't hungry. She wanted to go home.

Jillian thought she was tired?

Her sister had no idea.

THE AROMA OF HOT PIZZA—three cheeses, onions, green peppers, and extra Canadian bacon—filled the air as Harper tipped and thanked the delivery guy, closing her front door with a smile and a firm kick of her bare foot, her nails painted a vivid orange.

"I thought he'd never get here." She balanced the boxes so the smaller container of cheesy bread wouldn't slide off.

I moved our glasses of soda so Harper could set the food in the center of the coffee table.

"You sure you don't want to sit at the dining room table?"

"Casual dining is fine." I handed her a paper plate, keeping one for myself. "Casual is all I do right now."

Besides, Harper's living room was comfortable. She'd

lost half her furniture during the separation proceedings but had found replacements at estate sales. A white couch with a coordinating floral-print chair. An oval wood coffee table. A slender wood floor lamp.

"I knew I should have cooked something."

"That's not what I meant." I added a piece of cheesy bread to my plate. "This is fantastic. It's not out of a Crock-Pot. It's not out of a can. And it's not a peanut butter sandwich."

"Well, when you put it that way." She slid two pieces of pizza onto her plate. "Life's just been a bit unsettled lately."

"You, too, huh? What's going on?"

"My divorce is final." She took a bite of pizza. Chewed. Swallowed. "I'm no longer legally married to Trent Adams."

The bravado in her voice was undermined by the sheen of tears in her eyes.

How had I lost track of this dreaded event in my best friend's life? Harper had been counting down the days like some sort of macabre ringing in a New Year . . . a new life she'd never wanted.

After I was diagnosed with cancer, people at work struggled to know what to say or what not to say. Should they ask how I was? Avert their eyes and walk past, saying nothing? So often they chose to say nothing. Was Harper getting the same kind of treatment from friends, family, coworkers at the bank? Did people even remember she was separated?

This was Harper. The friend who'd deluged me with positive thoughts, refusing to let me give up or give in to cancer. I'd be there for her like she'd been there for me.

I reached out and squeezed her hand. "I'm sorry. I should

have remembered. Trent's going to realize what a mistake he made—"

"Jillian." Harper shook her head, removing her hand from mine. She proceeded to shred a piece of cheesy bread. "He's getting married again. Soon."

"He's a jerk."

"So we've both said. Many times." Her laugh was weak. "Unfortunately, he never realized it."

Maybe changing the subject was best. I sipped my root beer. "How are things at the bank?"

"Funny you should ask."

"What does that mean?"

"It turns out they're downsizing. . . ."

"Hampton didn't say he was firing you!"

My outburst caused Harper to pull back. "What does that mean? Did you know something?"

"H-he mentioned something about the downsizing the day I was fired, but I—I couldn't say anything. And I didn't know who would be affected—never imagined it might be you."

Harper sighed, accepting my answer. "Well, this gives me a chance to update my résumé."

"Harper."

"It's just my life right now. Seems like it's all about starting over." She took another bite of pizza.

Wait.

"What aren't you telling me?" My gaze fell on a small stack of moving boxes in the corner of her living room by the front door. "What are the boxes for? Are you going to declutter and get into the minimalist lifestyle? Maybe adopt a capsule wardrobe?"

Harper didn't laugh.

Those boxes weren't a joke. There was more change coming—and I wasn't going to like it.

Harper refused to meet my gaze, concentrating instead on ripping up more cheesy bread. She was tearing up more food than eating it. "I don't know how to tell you, Jilly. This is the hardest part—telling you."

"Just say it." I gripped the side of the coffee table.

"I'm moving."

Now I was confused—but not chemo-brain confused, because I understood what my best friend had said to me.

"That's even less funny than you trying to shrink all the clothes in your closet to thirty-seven pieces."

"It's not a joke."

I pressed my fingertips against my temples, staring at her. "Harper . . . why . . . why would you even think of moving? Because the bank is downsizing? There are plenty of jobs here—"

"I'm not *thinking* of moving. I *am* moving." Harper slumped back against the couch, her lips twisted. "Trent is getting married again. I kept wondering how I was going to survive in the same town, watching his brand-new happily ever after. I kept wishing he'd move—get transferred or something. And then I found out I don't have a job anymore. That gives me the perfect reason to leave, to look for a job somewhere else. I want a change. I *need* a change, Jill."

Zach Gaines might as well have walked in and interrupted

Girls' Night. Told me that he'd found a massive crack in the foundation of my house. Bad wiring and faulty plumbing were fixable. Losing Harper? How was I supposed to fix that?

There were no questions or doubts in my friend's eyes. She'd already made up her mind—without talking to me about it. Probably because she knew I'd argue with her. Threaten to lock her in her room. Beg her not to go.

I took two huge bites of pizza, not because I was hungry, but to stop myself from saying all the negative things screaming in my head.

Harper's move wasn't some sort of attack against me or our friendship, but somehow her action pressed against the wounded part of my heart that reminded me I was never enough . . . where I was measured and found wanting.

I struggled to balance my lack with Harper's need for more . . . her need for a new beginning.

Moments ago, I'd decided to support my friend. I needed to follow through. I closed my eyes and chewed some more, trying to summon up encouraging words. Positive words. Something other than *"Don't do this. I need you. Please, please, don't leave."*

I swallowed and took a deep breath. "What's your plan?"

Not the most enthusiastic start, but I'd do better next time.

"I know this is going to sound like I'm running home to my mother, but hear me out." Harper half turned to face me. "I'm going to use my mom's condo on the Outer Banks."

"If you're going to run away, that's a great choice." I forced a laugh.

"Believe me, I have greater aspirations than becoming a beach bum. I'll be looking for a job, too. But this was the quickest exit route. And why not enjoy some walks along the shore while I reinvent myself, right?"

"It's a good idea, don't get me wrong. It would be an even better idea if I could go with you."

"I don't think Geoff would appreciate you running away from home."

And now our laughter united, the sounds of a regular Girls' Night. We were finding a reason to laugh, even if we were talking about Harper moving. Harper . . . the best of friends.

Oh, how I was going to miss her.

But not now . . . not while she was still here.

"You want help packing some boxes?" I wiped my fingers with a napkin.

"What?"

"I asked if you want to pack a couple of boxes tonight."

"You trying to speed up getting rid of me?"

"No. Never." It wasn't fair for Harper to ask me that when I wanted to hug her and cry at the thought of her leaving. "But I do want to help you like you've always helped me. So let's pack some boxes tonight. What do you want to start with?"

"Books?" Harper set aside her plate. "Books are easy."

"Okay, we start with books."

I had to laugh over Harper's *Books are easy* comment as I drove home later. I'd had no idea how many books my friend owned. Nonfiction. Fiction. Mysteries. Romances.

Biographies. As we tried to pack boxes, Harper would stop and reminisce about her favorite authors. Her favorite novels. Her favorite scenes. And then she'd hand me another book and my take-home pile would grow taller.

"I'm catching on to your plan. Give away more. Pack less. Pay less moving fees."

Harper had laughed then.

But I cried all the way home.

12

WHAT WAS THIS? A staff meeting or a breakfast party?

Dr. Miller—Johanna's new boss by way of stealing her promotion—had strolled into the conference room a few minutes after her, carrying a to-go carton of coffee and two large paper bags from a local bagel shop. Hadn't the man heard of reusable bags?

With a quick greeting, he busied himself arranging a variety of bagels, plastic tubs of cream cheese, plates and utensils, and a large bowl of mixed fruit on a side table.

"Did that myself." He nodded to the fruit. "My wife always says that it's time or money—and cutting the fruit took a little more time but was less costly."

"Nice."

So the man knew how to take his wife's advice, save money, and use a knife. What did he expect, applause?

If she was going to survive the next forty-five minutes, Johanna needed to tone down her snark, even if it was internal.

As the pharmacy staff began to arrive for the first of Axton Miller's "Let's get to know each other" meetings, he asked each person their name. No "Hello, my name is" adhesive tags. Just asked the name, looked the person in the eye, and repeated it. Soon laughter and easy conversation filled the room. Johanna watched the clock, seconds and minutes ticking away as Dr. Miller chitchatted.

She was wasting valuable time at this rah-rah fest disguised as a meeting. Her coffee cooled in her insulated travel cup, and she ignored the bagels and fruit salad.

One moment the room was a mix of people mingling, and the next, Dr. Miller had brought everyone together around the rectangular table positioned in the center. Johanna didn't even know how it happened.

"I'm excited to be here. I'm even more excited to finally meet each one of you. I know it's early, so thank you for coming." Dr. Miller's gaze touched each person as if he were walking around the perimeter of the table instead of standing at the head. "We are a team. I believe in the power of a team. As Henry Ford said, 'If everyone is moving forward together, then success takes care of itself.'"

Johanna choked on a sip of her tepid coffee.

Ten minutes and five quotes later, Dr. Miller dismissed

the team. As the group dispersed, he waved aside several offers to help clean up and came alongside Johanna where she stood in the back corner of the room.

"I get the feeling you didn't buy into everything I was saying."

Huh. Maybe she'd misjudged him. Behind all that motivational "be the team" talk, he was more astute than she gave him credit for.

"It's not that." And that wasn't the truth. "You just do things differently than I do, that's all."

"How often do you hold team meetings?"

"I don't . . . do team meetings." She went to sip her coffee again, only to find that the cup was empty. "We're a busy hospital. We know what we need to do and we do our work. I communicate through e-mails. Memos. It's efficient."

"Well, we'll be changing that."

And Dr. Miller also didn't beat around the bush.

"Team meetings are important. They build up a sense of camaraderie. That's one of the first things I want you to do— get team meetings on the calendar once a month. After these initial ones, of course." Dr. Miller offered a warm "come on over to my side" smile that revealed not-quite-straight teeth. "I like to know when people's birthdays are, too. And anniversaries. So we can celebrate them."

"Celebrate how?"

"Give them a card. Have a cake once a month for all the staff who have a birthday."

Now they were going to have birthday parties? Were they

back in grade school? Was he going to incorporate show-and-tell, too?

She swallowed her laughter, along with the desire to ask, *"Are you kidding me?"* Instead, she nodded. "I can get that information for you."

Because that's what a good assistant pharmacy director did, according to Axton Miller.

"What about you, Johanna?"

His question stopped her from saying good-bye. "What about me . . . what?"

"Are you married? Kids?"

"I'm not married. No kids. I'm engaged."

"Oh. If my wife were here, she'd ask if you'd set a date yet."

"No."

"So you're newly engaged."

"No. We've been together eight years. Engaged for three."

That earned her a laugh, although she'd said nothing humorous. "Not rushing anything, I see."

"Beckett, my fiancé, is in the military. His career has kept him busy—he's been deployed. And I'm dedicated to my career, too."

It was as if she were defending herself—her life choices—to him. She didn't even know the man. Didn't want to get to know him.

Didn't like him.

Just then Dr. Miller offered her another wide smile.

She was liking him less by the minute. He wouldn't be on the guest list for her wedding—maybe she should make that clear right now.

But instead, she asked him a question. It was only polite—and it turned the Q and A session back on him.

"You're married. Any kids?"

"Yes, my wife and I have two children—twins, actually."

Of course the man had twins. Having grown up with twin sisters, she knew no one ever ignored the fact that someone had twins or was a twin. For most people, twins were fascinating. And the man probably enjoyed all the attention.

"Twins?"

"Yes, fraternal twin boys. They're seventeen now. Seniors in high school. They've kept us on our toes and wrecked our grocery budget. My wife says she's ready for them to go to college, but I know she'll miss them. We both will."

"I imagine they keep you busy."

She was over Dr. Axton Miller. He'd stolen her job. Touted slogans and talked "team" like some positive-living guru. And now . . . now he was the father of twin boys. The man needed to go back to Tucson and live his perfect professional and personal life far, far away from her.

"Family?"

Had he asked her a question? "I'm sorry?"

"Do you have family in the area?"

"Yes. Family. We're all Colorado natives. Three sisters." She wasn't going to tell him that two sisters were identical twins. That one sister had died eleven years ago. She didn't want more questions. Didn't want sympathy. Didn't want to connect with this man in any way.

"If you'll excuse me, I need to go to the ladies' room."

With those words, she retreated to the bathroom again.

She couldn't spend the rest of her career hiding in the women's bathroom, avoiding the new pharmacy director. After months of anticipating nothing but advancement at Mount Columbia Medical Center, her future seemed as limited as the stall she sat in.

That thought was enough to make her want to call it a day before work even began. Maybe declare a sick day.

She was comparing her life to a bathroom.

Perfect. Just perfect.

This was the perfect time for me to be at Memorial Park. Moms of little kids were still watching the clock, hoping their babies and toddlers stretched their naps out a while longer. Meanwhile, moms of school-age kids counted down the last precious minutes to run errands or finish projects before their kids started heading home or they had to queue up in the carpool line.

I'd left my car on the far side of the park, clipped Winston to his leash, and made my way to the lake rimmed with trees. Not too cold yet, despite it being late October. No wind, so the surface of the water reflected the trees like a giant's looking glass.

But inside me? Harper's announcement that she was moving had churned up my emotions as if multiple Jet Skis had crisscrossed the lake, barely missing each other in their antics.

I'd only ridden Jet Skis a few times during family vacations, but I always remembered the time Payton challenged Pepper to a race and then got too close, ramming the front of Pepper's machine with hers, tossing Pepper into the water. She was unhurt, but that had been a costly accident, with Johanna yelling at them all the way back to shore like she was their mom—not that Mom was a yeller.

I kept my eyes open, as if by doing so, I could absorb the serenity of the scene in front of me. If I closed them, I was pulled into the tumult of my emotions.

Another text from Harper interrupted my thoughts— one of many she'd sent this week. Another one that I had to answer or ignore. Most had been ignored.

Some best friend I was.

How are you?

I stared at the text. It wasn't like I could ignore her forever.

Good.

Me too. Thanks for asking.

I was going to ask.

I wasn't sure if you remembered who I was. It's been so quiet on your end.

Ha. Very funny.

I'm being serious.

A second later, Harper switched to FaceTime.

"Why are you calling me?"

"I was hoping maybe I'd catch you at a weak moment and you'd answer the phone. Let me see your face."

"You're such a comedian today."

"Why are you avoiding me? And don't say you're not."

I couldn't argue with her. I had been acting like we were in middle school again, avoiding her instead of talking to her.

I leaned forward on the bench, cradling my phone

between my hands. "I'm trying to figure out how to be okay with all this. . . ."

"You don't have to be okay with it, Jill."

"I can't cry until the day you move. It could be months—"

"One month. Four weeks."

The lake in front of me was still calm, but the invisible Jet Skis had just collided.

"That soon?"

"I have one more week of work. My office is mostly packed up." She moved her phone around so I could see the walls bare of any photographs. Her diploma.

"And your house?"

"I'm getting ready to put it on the market. The good news is, it's a sellers' market right now. The bad news is, I met with the stager and they have all sorts of suggestions for making the house look good. Although I don't have that much. . . ."

That I knew. The separation and divorce had stripped her of a lot of things, material possessions included.

"I can come over and help you." And now . . . now I was offering to do the very thing I'd avoided since our Girls' Night. Was I trying to create some sort of shock therapy? "You know where I am?"

"Home?"

"No. I'm sitting at Memorial Park, by the lake." It was my turn to show her my surroundings, including Winston, who dozed at my feet. "Didn't we have fun at the balloon liftoff Labor Day weekend? Remember the Yoda and Darth Vader balloons?"

"That was so worth getting up early on a Saturday."

"Yeah. I loved watching the teams getting ready to launch the different hot-air balloons. So many designs and colors . . . seeing them sail over the lake." I settled back against the bench. "We just didn't know that you wouldn't be here for next year's launch."

"I could always come back."

"Can't make promises . . ." I blinked away the tears. I wasn't keeping *my* promise to not be sad while my friend was still here. "You're moving, Harper. Not dying. I'm sorry. You certainly didn't avoid me when we thought I might be dying."

Harper gasped, caught between laughter and tears. "I can't believe you just said that!"

"Am I right?"

"Well, yes."

"Well, then . . . I'm sorry I avoided you this week. I'm just . . . going to miss you, you know."

"I know. I'm going to miss you, too."

I swallowed hard, tasting salt. "Okay. Now that we've faced that, can I come over tomorrow and help you pack?"

"Sure. Absolutely."

"But I refuse to take any more books. Understood?"

"I can't promise. You want to look through my dishes?"

"Harper, I'm not taking stuff home with me."

"Oh, come on. There are some things I don't want to send to the thrift store."

Our banter settled into a normal rhythm again. I needed to figure out how to keep this up for the next four weeks. To laugh until it was okay for me to cry, even as fatigue settled heavier on my shoulders . . . slipped . . . and centered in my heart.

13

PAYTON WAS A NERVOUS WRECK—and all because she was hosting round three of our book club at her townhome.

"Will you calm down?" I debated stepping in front of her as she peered through the small glass window in her oven once again. "Why are you so worried?"

"I need to check these." She straightened, backing away from the oven, reaching for the door.

Now I did move in front of her. "Stop. You can't keep opening the door. Let the muffins bake."

"Why did I decide to make vegan jelly-filled muffins?" Payton's chin quivered. "It's not like Johanna is going to eat one. You might—"

"Don't worry about it. If they don't turn out or Johanna doesn't want one, we've got coffee and fruit salad—"

"Keurig coffee and cantaloupe and honeydew I sliced up. How's that supposed to compare to Johanna's French-press coffee and her homemade quiche? Served on china, no less." Payton opened a cupboard and started removing plates.

"Let me do that."

"Fine. Should I have bought juice?"

"Coffee is fine. And Johanna will probably bring her own coffee, anyway."

"You're right about that." She groaned. "I forgot to get cream."

"Like I said, she'll probably show up with her own coffee."

"Right. Right."

When she started toward the oven again, I shook my head. "Don't even think about it."

"Okay." Payton relaxed her shoulders and offered me a strained smile. "So why didn't you ride up with Johanna today?"

"She said she was leaving early to check in at the hospital, so I decided to drive myself. I thought she'd be here already."

"I'm glad she's not. No need for her to see me getting all crazy in the kitchen." Payton arranged three coffee mugs on the kitchen counter. "I don't know why I'm acting like this. I stopped trying to impress her years ago. It's not going to suddenly happen this morning."

"I didn't even know you wanted to impress Johanna."

"I don't. Not until something like this happens, and then some invisible switch gets flipped and I'm the little sister again, trying to make her like me." Payton grimaced. "Forget I said that, will you?"

"Said what?"

"Perfect response." Payton pulled the bowl of fruit from the fridge. Put it back. "No need to put this out now. I guess we need to clear the table in the breakfast nook before we set it, huh? Would you mind clearing my books off the table?"

"No problem. Up late studying again?"

"Yes. Zach came over and we studied for a while, then watched a movie."

"You two spend a lot of time together."

"As much as we can, what with him living in Winter Park." A true smile accompanied Payton's words. "He's become a good friend. Probably the best friend I have."

"Just friends?" I tried to keep the question casual.

Payton's smile disappeared and she hesitated before answering. "Just friends."

I waited to see if Payton would say anything else, but when she spoke, it was to change the topic. "Do you think Johanna is even going to show up today?"

"Of course she is." I began loading the dirty dishes piled up in her sink into the dishwasher. "Aren't you glad you started our sisters' book club?"

"Sometimes. I don't know. I was trying to do the right thing . . . trying to help us find some common ground, you know? I hear about women doing book clubs all the time, and I thought, *Why not?*"

"Based on the first two times we've gotten together, it doesn't look like books are our common ground."

"Then what is? The fact that we share the same genes?

The fact that we grew up in the same house? That certainly hasn't created a lot of closeness between us."

"You and Pepper were close . . ." I closed my mouth, the sentence unfinished. "I'm sorry. Maybe I shouldn't have said that."

"No. It's okay. You're right. It's like our family was some sort of genetic mathematical equation. Two plus two equals four Thatcher sisters. Johanna and you and then me and Pepper. No mixing and mismatching allowed."

Payton's eyes dimmed. She'd always seemed fine with how the boundary lines fell within our family and how they separated the two oldest Thatcher sisters from the two youngest. It made sense that way. But maybe she hadn't been . . . and then Pepper had died and she'd had to learn to live solo—a twinless twin.

And maybe that reality was the true reason behind the book club.

My cell phone pinged at the same time the oven timer went off.

"It's probably Johanna." I read my text. "Yep. She's here."

"Why don't you get the door, Jill? I'll see if these muffins are a success or a disaster."

I gathered the books from the table, stuffing them into Payton's backpack. "Where shall I put this?"

Payton slipped a pair of tattered oven mitts onto her hands. "Just set it at the bottom of the stairs for now."

"Got it. And relax." I slung the book bag over my shoulder with a groan. "How heavy is this thing?"

"Be thankful you don't have to lug it across campus."

When I opened the front door, Johanna stood there in a

stylish ice-blue peacoat paired with slim black jeans and short gray boots, a travel thermos in one hand and a cloth grocery bag in the other. Stepping inside, she placed the bag next to several pairs of Payton's volleyball shoes and discarded socks.

"What's in the bag? Payton's got breakfast covered."

"Books."

"Books?" Sure enough, a quick glance revealed a stack of hardback and paperback books. "Why did you bring a bunch of books? Are you cleaning your bookshelves?"

"No." Johanna shrugged out of her coat, tossing it on Payton's couch next to mine. "I thought we should consider reading a different book."

This was worse than if my sister had brought her French press and offered to make coffee for all of us.

I stepped in front of her. "Jo . . . don't do this."

"Do what? I'm offering a suggestion—well, several suggestions."

Payton appeared in the living room. "You two coming? The muffins turned out great."

I stepped to the side, pointing at the bag of books. "Ask her."

"Ask her what?"

"Ask Johanna what's in the bag."

Johanna tsked. "Jillian, you're being melodramatic."

Payton stepped forward. "What's in the bag?"

"I brought some books for us to look at—to consider instead of the biography that no one is reading."

Payton rested her hands on her hips. "And where did these books come from?"

"I bought them."

I knelt and began pulling books from the bag, forming a semicircle around myself. "You bought . . . as in purchased . . . a dozen books?"

"Yes. But first I did some research because I wanted a good variety. There's fiction and nonfiction. Another biography, if you want to consider that genre again. Historical. Mystery. An older one that was an Oprah book club pick. Romance, although that's not my favorite, but I'm open." Johanna took a few of the books from my hands as I removed them from the bag. "A thriller. Women's fiction. One that was made into a movie last year. All sorts for us to choose from."

I stared up at Johanna. "We already chose the book—"

"Fine." Payton's bare foot tapped the floor. "If we're reconsidering what we're reading, I want to read a comic book."

Johanna looked like she couldn't even be bothered to laugh at Payton's joke. "A comic book? Really?"

"We used to read them all the time on family vacations, remember?" Payton's reply was softened with a laugh. "Jo, you went out and spent I don't know how much money on a bunch of books . . ."

This was so familiar . . . what Johanna and Payton did best—facing off with one another. But it wasn't as hard-hitting as it could have been. For once, it was as if they were pulling their punches. Did Payton even realize she'd called Johanna "Jo"? Maybe, somehow, they had learned something this past year, something they'd forgotten during the first two book club mishaps—that there was no need to be brutal with one another.

Things had gone quiet as I mused on the difference in my sisters. Both Johanna and Payton watched me.

"Nothing to say, Jill?"

"You two are doing fine." I turned my back on both of them. "I'm hungry."

Once all three of us were in the kitchen, Payton concentrated on placing the muffins on a pretty glass plate, the slices of melon on another. Johanna had lugged her precious bag of books with her, setting it in one of the chairs at the breakfast nook table like an uninvited guest. We kept our conversation casual until we all sat down.

"It looks like you get to cast the deciding vote, Jill." Johanna sipped her brought-from-home coffee.

"No."

"What do you mean, no?"

"No, I'm not getting caught in the middle of this. Stop treating me like some sort of human tiebreaker." I couldn't have said that more plainly. "Payton, can I have some fruit, please?"

"How are we going to decide, then?"

"There's nothing to decide, Joey." I could only hope using her nickname would soften my betrayal. "We already agreed on what we were going to read—"

"But no one's reading it."

"Because life's been hectic. Things happen." I set my fork down. "I wasn't realistic about the house renovation. And I certainly didn't know I was going to lose my job. Payton's busy. We're all busy. But that doesn't mean we—that *you* change the plan. It just means it takes a little longer for us to read the book."

"I did read more this month." Payton smiled. "A whole chapter. Of course, I read it last night."

"I read a chapter, too." I placed a still-warm muffin on my plate. "See, improvement already."

"At this rate, it'll take us a year to finish." Johanna accepted the muffin Payton offered her.

"Then it takes a year."

Johanna obviously didn't believe in the "it's about the journey, not the destination" philosophy. She was counting pages, overlooking the value of spending time together. I wanted to shake her until she uncrossed her arms . . . and then hug her.

"If nothing else, we can choose our next book to read from the bag, right, Payton?"

"Absolutely."

"Next book?" Johanna looked as if I'd suggested that our next book be in a foreign language.

"You don't plan on disbanding the group after one book, do you?" I widened my eyes, then winked. "Since you made such an investment, you can select the next one we read."

"Now wait a minute . . ."

"Or maybe we should have her close her eyes and randomly pick one out of the bag."

"That is not how we're picking the next book."

Payton's snort almost covered up my giggle. Almost. Johanna's eyes narrowed . . . and then at last her face relaxed into a smile.

I tilted my head. "Are we okay here?"

"Yes."

"We're all agreed that we'll keep reading the same book?"

Both of my sisters nodded.

A small literary victory . . . but I'd take it.

I NEVER REALIZED what I was missing when I worked full-time. How pleasant late afternoon was when it was uninterrupted by phone calls and the pressure of things needing to be done and—when the workmen had gone home—their clamor replaced with calm. With my back resting against the arm of the couch, facing away from the now–open concept dining room and kitchen, I could ignore the uncompleted project.

I'd accepted the fact Geoff and I were still waiting for the countertops to be delivered and that they wouldn't be the trendy pressed-paper ones I'd originally selected. That was one easy way to cut costs, as Zach had pointed out. And he'd assured me I would be just as satisfied with the less expensive option. I had no choice but to believe him—and no budget, either.

And the wrong wood flooring had been delivered—another delay.

With Winston tired out from a walk, and the workmen gone, I'd moved downstairs instead of hiding in my bedroom. I chose to enjoy the warmth of Winston's furry body curled up against my bare feet. The softness of a blanket thrown across my legs. The chance to sip a cup of coffee while it was still warm, instead of finding it, hours later, neglected on the corner of my desk.

I shifted my shoulders, switching back to another tab on my laptop screen. I'd cut and pasted multiple paragraphs from the half-dozen open tabs into a never-ending Word document, trying to make sense of all the information about adoption I'd read for the past two hours.

International versus US. Foster adoption. Private adoption. Open adoption. And then the questions started. Should I contact a lawyer or an agency first? How much was this going to cost? How far into the process could I go without trying to talk to Geoff again? When would he need to get involved?

Juggling all this information was reminiscent of being at work, the information and questions and answers blurring together. Which website had I looked at last? Which requirements applied where?

Winston nuzzled my arm, his soft whimper drawing my attention. I ruffled his ears. "You want to go outside, don't you? Just give me a minute. . . ."

I had other things to do besides researching adoption, including figuring out some sort of decent dinner or deciding to order takeout or, since it was just me, skipping eating altogether. Continue the nonstop game of out-in-out-in with Winston. Maybe bundle up and take him for another short walk before it got too dark. Pick up the house some—at least make the bed from my midday nap.

But I wasn't ready to stop researching yet.

I stared at the "Contact Us" box at the top of one page. They asked for both an e-mail and a home address. I couldn't have an information packet showing up at the house. Maybe I could call instead. . . .

Wait.

I *could* call someone. Thea. Thea from work had talked on occasion about adopting her son, the ginger-haired, freckle-faced little boy growing up, picture by picture, in framed photos on her desk. It would be so much easier to ask questions of someone I knew—and it would be safer, too, until I was ready to talk to Geoff. Maybe he'd be more open to hearing someone's personal success story. I checked the time. How was it already five o'clock?

Please, please, please, let her still be there. . . .

"This is Thea Phelps. How can I help you?"

"Oh, Thea, this is Jillian. Jillian Hennessey. I'm so glad you're still at work."

"Jillian. Hi, how are you? We miss you around here."

"I'm fine." Winston yipped, jumping down from the couch. "Would you hold on one sec? I need to let my dog out."

I set my laptop aside, carrying Winston through the work area, my footsteps causing the heavy-duty plastic still covering the floor to crinkle, and opening the door so he could run into the backyard. When I worked full-time, Winston had spent his days in his kennel. Until I was home, I never realized how often he wanted to be let in and out. "Sorry. We're renovating the kitchen. It's a bit like walking through my personal construction zone."

"No problem."

"I realize it's the end of the day, but I was wondering if I could ask you a question or two."

"Sure. I was getting ready to leave, but I have a few minutes to spare."

I stayed by the back door, waiting for Winston to return and scratch to be let back in. "I remember you mentioning you'd adopted your son."

"Franklin? Yes."

"I'm considering adoption . . . started doing some research . . . and I didn't realize how complicated the whole process is."

Thea laughed. "I remember feeling exactly that way. It's like learning a new language."

"It is!" Her words cleared a bit of the muddle from my brain. I wasn't the only one who was confused by all of this.

"I assume you already know you can't pursue private adoption in Colorado—you have to go through an agency."

"Yes."

"Are you considering international or US adoption?"

"Probably US."

"That will make it easier for us to talk, since that's what my husband and I chose, too."

Winston was content to run in the backyard, so I remained standing where I was. "So what can you tell me about adopting?"

"Where to start? It's expensive—an average of twenty-five thousand dollars."

Thea wasn't telling me anything I hadn't already read, but hearing the number out loud shook me—especially when we were still dealing with the added costs of the renovation. "I gathered that from what I've read on some different websites."

"And it doesn't happen overnight. Just prepare yourself for that. My husband and I waited a couple of years before being selected. But it isn't always that long."

"Well, I'm already waiting five years before I can even try to get pregnant because of the medication I'm on after chemo and radiation." Might as well be honest with Thea if I was going to be asking her questions. "I'm hoping adoption might be quicker."

"What other questions do you have?"

"Adoption is just a bigger undertaking than I realized. There are different agencies. And do I contact an agency or a lawyer first? What was your experience like?"

"What if we met for lunch and talked then? It might be easier."

"That would be wonderful."

"Would sometime next week work for you?"

"Pick a day—my schedule is more flexible than yours."

After we chose a date, I stood there for a moment, my phone clasped in my hands, pressed against my heart. Talking, even for such a short time, with someone who'd already adopted a child made the process real. Attainable—well, if I didn't think about the cost. And meeting with Thea would be easier than scrolling through paragraphs of information that started blurring in front of my eyes. The undercurrent of excitement in Thea's voice fed my own eagerness.

"Who were you talking to?"

Geoff's question—his unexpected appearance—caused me to whirl around to face him.

"Thea . . . someone I know at the bank."

Geoff remained standing just outside the dismantled kitchen. "I don't have to ask what you were talking about. I heard."

"I . . . I didn't expect you home so early."

My words made it sound as if I was trying to hide something from him. I wasn't. Not really.

Geoff huffed a short laugh, removing his glasses and then rubbing the back of his hand against his jaw. "I imagined you wouldn't have had that little conversation if you thought I'd be coming home now."

"No. That's not what I meant." I turned my phone over and over in my hands. "I can—"

"Are you going to say you can explain? Because I really want to hear it, Jillian. Why were you talking to someone about adoption when I've told you that I don't want to adopt?"

With his words, Geoff built the invisible line between us

back into a brick wall, and anger simmered hot behind it. He could barely get the words out, his jaw was clenched so tight.

Why was my husband so angry?

"I wasn't trying to hide anything from you." I took a step, two, toward him. Stopped. "I was gathering some information so we could talk."

He slid his glasses back on. "We already talked about this."

"We did not." I pointed my phone at him. "You said no before we could discuss adopting."

"I said no because there is no reason to discuss it." Geoff paused. Looked away from me for a moment. His shoulders shifted as if he carried an invisible weight. "The truth is . . . the truth is, I don't want to have children, Jillian."

My husband might as well have said that he didn't love me. Or that he wanted a divorce. Or something even more absurd, like he was an alien. As his words echoed in my mind, I wanted to scream at him, *"Don't say that to me. You can't mean that. Of course you want children."*

I fought to remain calm. "What do you mean, you don't want children?"

"It's a self-explanatory statement." His words were rough. "I don't want to have children."

"Why didn't you bother to tell me this before now?"

"We never really tackled the kids-or-no-kids question when we were dating. It seemed like a nonissue. You didn't bring it up, so neither did I. Things moved so fast." Geoff adjusted his glasses as if he were having difficulty seeing me. "And then you were diagnosed with breast cancer right when we got engaged. It wasn't the time to say, 'Let's talk about kids.' I thought we'd have time to discuss all of this later."

"Discuss the fact that you'd already decided we wouldn't have children?" I couldn't keep a shrill note out of my voice. "You didn't think that was important? Why did we even go through the process of freezing my eggs?"

"Because it was important to you."

"Do you hear how you just contradicted yourself? First having children isn't important to me, then it is. What kind of explanation is that?"

"You had a lot on your mind and you obviously wanted the chance to have children—I didn't want to take that from you then, not when you were facing cancer."

"But you'll take that chance away from me now."

My knight in shining armor was slipping off his horse. Geoff, who had loved me in so many brave, amazing ways, was breaking my heart—and there were no tears in his eyes . . . no sign of emotion on his face at all.

With his declaration, I'd become married to someone I didn't know.

"Let's be honest, Jillian." Geoff shook his head. "Why all this sudden interest in adopting when you couldn't handle your job at the bank?"

"What . . . what kind of question is that?"

"It's a realistic one. How can you think about taking care of a baby when you can't handle something as simple as paperwork?"

His words reminded me, once again, of all my inabilities,

and lashed at what little self-control I had left. Geoff, who had always defended me, found me "less than," too.

I had no response. No defense.

I stumbled past him, up the stairs to our bedroom, slamming the door on the sound of him calling my name. I twisted the lock, securing my safety, before I crawled into bed, pulling the covers around my shaking body.

I couldn't have children.

In Geoff's eyes, I wasn't even capable of caring for a child.

But it didn't matter, because he'd already decided that the two of us would comprise our family. No sons. No daughters.

Just us.

15

PAYTON WAS AS COMFORTABLE in Zach's cabin as she was in her townhome. It was almost humorous to think back to the times she'd resisted coming here. But now the past events, with their misunderstanding and heartache, had been covered over with forgiveness and second chances. With friendship, an understanding of grace, and hope for a future for her and Zach.

A hope that neither of them voiced aloud.

Laz, Zach's dog, stretched out in front of the fireplace in the open great room with its large windows that provided a view of the mountains. Colin, Zach's coworker, and his girlfriend, Deanna, had just returned from a brief after-lunch walk and were watching the Seahawks game, something Payton could tolerate since it was a bye week for the Broncos.

Payton washed the lunch dishes, rinsing them and then handing them to Zach so he could dry them and put them away in the cabinets he'd custom-designed and installed.

"I'm impressed with your latest attempt at a vegan recipe." Payton offered Zach a bowl. "That black bean soup was delicious. I'm glad Colin and Deanna got to enjoy it with us."

"Me, too. I've come a long way from having nothing but a couple of dried-up pieces of fruit in my fridge, haven't I?"

"Yes, you have. You're quite a guy."

Zach slipped the damp dish towel over her head and down around her waist, pulling her close against his body. "And you, Payton, are quite a woman."

The air seemed to spark between them, all attempts at casual compliments disappearing.

"Zach, we're not alone!" That was probably a good thing—something planned by Zach. Payton's voice dropped to a whisper. "And my hands are wet . . ."

"Let me help you with that." Zach's husky whisper matched hers as he used the cotton cloth to dry first one hand, then the other, his touch warm and gentle. When he was done, he let the towel drop to the floor, wrapping his arms around her and pulling her even closer.

His gray eyes searched hers as he caressed the side of her face with his fingertips.

All she longed for was found in this man's arms. And this kiss—because, oh yes, he was going to kiss her for the first time—would be more than just a kiss. It would be a yes to him. An admission that she was in love with him. That she knew he was in love with her, too.

But he deserved better than that from her. Better than a yes now and both of them being sorry later.

Payton pressed her hand against his chest, half-turning away. "No, Zach."

He stilled. "What is going on with us, Payton?"

"Is this a 'define the relationship' talk?" She tried to lighten the mood with a laugh.

Zach stepped back, raking his fingers through his hair. "Of course it isn't. We can't have that kind of talk because we're still stuck at square one. At just friends."

"And that makes you angry?" Payton bent and picked up the dish towel.

"Yes." Zach groaned. "No."

Payton twisted the length of cotton material between her fingers. "I'm sorry."

"Payton, where are you with God?"

"I . . . I don't know."

"But you do know we can't do anything about this—what we feel for each other—until you figure that out, right?"

"I've told you that I don't know what I think, Zach. If anything, I'm more confused than I was a few months ago."

His mouth twisted with unspoken words, a V deepening between his eyes. "But you've been reading books. Coming to church. We've been talking. How can you not know?"

"And now you're pressuring me."

Zach's shoulders slumped. "I never meant to pressure you,

Payton. I'm sorry if I've made you feel that way. I just wanted to help . . . to answer your questions . . ."

"You want me to say I believe in God because you want more from me." She fought against the words building inside her but lost. "Sometimes I think you should just date Kelsey."

Zach stiffened. "Kelsey? What does she have to do with any of this?"

"She's the kind of girl you need in your life, Zach. Not me." One of them needed to speak the truth, no matter how bitter the words were. "She probably started going to church the day she was born. Knows all the right answers. Believes what you believe—there's no confusion with Kelsey."

Payton had seen Kelsey watching them during church services, probably wondering what Zach was doing hanging around with someone like her.

"Kelsey and I are friends. Nothing more."

"You and I are just friends, too, Zach."

"You're saying you don't love me?"

No matter what she did or didn't know about God, she knew how she felt about Zach. And she couldn't lie. Wouldn't lie. Zach deserved the truth. "Yes, I love you."

"Then I'm willing to wait . . . to hope . . ." He took a step toward her.

"But I can't . . . I can't fall in love with you." Payton raised her hands, fending off his advance.

"I don't understand."

She'd been walking an emotional tightrope for months. *Let's be friends. Just friends.* And today Zach was shaking the wire beneath her feet, threatening to send her tumbling. She wanted to ignore reason and leap into midair, to fall madly in love with this man, whose heart had pounded beneath her palm when he'd held her moments ago.

But she had to do the right thing so there were no regrets. No reason to say, "I'm sorry."

"I'm not a Christian, Zach." There. She'd said it—and he knew it. "I mean, I believe in God . . . I think. More than I used to. When I'm with you, it's easy to lean into your faith. Church is nice . . . it's not foreign to me. I like the worship music. I can even sing along now. And the sermons are encouraging. But sometimes I still feel like I'm on the outside looking in."

"Everyone starts with doubts, Payton. We can figure them out. Together." Zach clasped her hands, attempting to lead her to the couch in the living room. "Ask me. Better yet, we can talk about it, all four of us."

"Stop." She tugged her hands away, anchoring her feet to the kitchen floor. "You can't help anymore. I can't have a relationship with God so I can have a relationship with you . . . so I get some sort of approval stamp for falling in love with you. And I don't want to discuss this with Colin and Deanna."

Zach's eyes clouded over. "You know I've struggled with this, too. Tried to convince myself that we're okay . . . that we're friends . . . nothing more. I meant what I said, Payton. I'll wait—however long you need."

Sometimes, with all of her own battles, Payton forgot Zach faced his own.

"I'm sorry . . . I wish I could make a decision. It's not

just you." The complications rose up in her mind again. "I can't believe in God so I can wear Pepper's necklace—so I can make my dead sister happy. I have to do this—*if* I do this—for me."

How ironic. In her effort to find God, she was pushing away the man she never thought she could love.

Tightness closed her chest, seeming to make it difficult for her heart to take its next beat, and her hands trembled. She hadn't had an anxiety attack in months. But this was more like her heart icing over.

Maybe she could change her mind. Let Zach help her find her way.

No. She had to do the right thing—or forever doubt herself. Forever doubt her faith.

"So where does this leave us?"

"Maybe we break up?" Even as she asked the question, Payton realized how absurd it sounded. "I mean, I know it's not like we're dating . . ."

"Stop being friends? Stop loving you?" Zach reached for her hands again. "I can't change how I feel because you want me to, Payton."

She stepped away, her hands behind her back. "So we stop spending so much time together. We're fooling ourselves telling everyone we're just friends—telling ourselves we're just friends. We both want more. We both feel more for each other."

"But we can't have it." Zach's words shut the door on their future.

"I need time and space to figure this out . . . not just what

I believe about God, but why I believe it." The next words burned her throat. But she had to speak them. "Maybe we're not meant to be together at all."

"I don't believe that. And you don't either."

"I don't know what I believe. Or why. That's the problem."

The more they talked, the more their words snarled like a ball of yarn tossed back and forth between them. She told herself to leave, only to find herself in his arms, her face pressed against his chest.

"I love you, Zach. You're my best friend. . . . I haven't felt this close to anyone since Pepper died." The pain in his eyes when she looked up had to be a reflection of her own heartache. "You've taught me to believe there is a God. I'm going to do my best to find my way all the way to Him . . . and hope He leads me back to you. But if . . . if He doesn't, I'm going to believe it's for the best."

That was all the truth she could speak for now.

The warmth of Zach's arms was, once again, a safe haven for her. But she couldn't stay there any longer. She couldn't trust herself to be strong. To do the right thing and leave.

She stepped away, forbidding herself to say, "I love you" again. Hoping Zach would know not to say he loved her again because it would crumble her resolve.

"I'm going to slip out the back door. It's cowardly, I know." Payton brushed away the tears filling her eyes. "I don't care what you tell Colin and Deanna. They know something's going on—I saw him glance in here a few minutes ago."

Once in her car, Payton rested her forehead on the steering

wheel. Maybe . . . maybe she should go back inside. Sit. Talk with Zach and Colin and Deanna. Let them help her.

No.

She had to let her determination to do what was right, to figure out what she believed on her own, somehow be stronger than her fear of losing her way to God.

And be stronger than her fear of losing Zach.

THIS MORNING I didn't know who needed to get outside more—Winston or me. But then again, I knew I'd enjoy taking Winston for a walk more than I'd enjoyed my shower half an hour earlier.

I'd stood beneath the spray, hoping the warmth would seep into the chill that had encased my heart for the past week. But if it did, my heart would have to struggle to beat against the overwhelming losses I'd been dealt.

My best friend was leaving.

My husband had declared we'd be childless.

I had less than two weeks before Harper headed east. And when Geoff came home, we moved around one another like strangers who'd been chosen at random to be roommates.

The house was too quiet again this morning, despite Winston's insistent barks and the echoes of my last conversation with Geoff, where I found myself trapped between his revelation and his accusation.

"The truth is . . . the truth is, I don't want to have children, Jillian."

"How can you think about taking care of a baby when you can't handle something as simple as paperwork?"

Geoff's words pummeled my heart, making me doubt who I was in ways I never had before.

I had nowhere important to go, but I couldn't stay here. Maybe I'd be able to eat breakfast after taking Winston for a walk. One thing I could do well—I could walk our dog. I threw on the first coat my fingers touched in the little front hall closet—one of Geoff's zippered jackets lined with fleece that wrapped me in his scent. I stood there for a moment and savored the false sense of closeness. Then I fished a pair of gloves out of the basket on top of the table and managed to calm Winston long enough to clip his leash to his collar.

"Yes, yes, we're going for a walk if you'll be still for just a minute. . . ."

Wind bit at my face and neck as I stepped outside, pulling the door closed behind me. Maybe I should go back for a scarf and hat. But Winston tugged me forward, down the steps.

Onward.

As we rounded the corner, Gianna came toward us pushing a running stroller, Avery snugged inside a blanket decorated with hearts and stars, a fuchsia knit hat topped with a large pom-pom tugged low over her eyes. The two-year-old looked better than I did. Gianna and I did the typical make-eye-contact-smile-look-away routine until we were close enough to talk.

"Morning, neighbor."

"Out for a run?" I nodded toward the stroller, allowing Winston to sniff the wheels.

"Out—but not running. Avery and I were both a little stir-crazy this morning."

"I know the feeling."

"Where are you heading?"

I gestured at Winston. "Just a short walk."

Gianna pulled the stroller back and to the side, the rubberized wheels scraping on the sidewalk, maneuvering it so we faced the same way. "Mind if we join you? It'd be nice to talk to an adult."

There was no way I could tell Gianna, *"No, I'd rather you didn't join me."* Because then I might confess that I wanted her life. Wanted the chance to push a stroller with my own two-year-old in it who demanded my attention and interrupted my conversations and brought me dandelion bouquets.

"No, of course not. But I'm not a fast walker."

"This is more about mental health than exercising."

"For me, too, to be honest." I positioned myself on the outside, walking on the grass so Gianna could stay on the sidewalk.

"Last time we talked, the house renovation wasn't going as planned. What's the update?"

"The good news is we have new electrical and new pipes."

I infused as much excitement as I could into my voice. "The bad news is our budget is a mess."

"So you adjust, right?"

"Exactly. Which means our project is going like every other kitchen renovation."

"It'll look great when it's done, even if it's not exactly like you planned." Gianna responded to a small "Mommy!" from Avery by pausing long enough to hand her a plastic bag of Goldfish snacks. "When do you and Geoff celebrate your first anniversary?"

"In January."

"So no plan for kids anytime soon, right?"

"What?" Her question caused me to stumble. "No . . . no plans."

"I figured. A lot of couples wait nowadays—"

"It's not . . . not that." I pulled Winston back from where he'd slipped in front of the stroller, hoping Avery would share her morning treat. I scrambled between which answers to offer Gianna. "I—I had breast cancer and—"

"What?"

"It's okay—I'm okay. I'm finished with my treatment, but I'm on medication . . . for the next five years. And I'm not supposed to get pregnant while I'm taking it."

At least that was part of the truth.

"Oh." Gianna seemed to struggle with what to say. "I didn't realize."

I fluffed my short hair. "What? You thought I was just being trendy with this hairstyle?"

My neighbor gasped, and then she snorted, covering her mouth to muffle the laughter that followed. "That's awful!"

"Um, 'awful' is being diagnosed with breast cancer the night of your engagement party."

"Oh, Jillian . . . no!"

"It was rough." Where had this sudden burst of honesty come from? "I broke off my engagement with Geoff because I didn't think he should have to marry me . . . and then we ended up eloping."

"That's so romantic!"

Romantic. And awful, just like Gianna had said.

"But you're all better now?"

"Like I said, I'm fine." I found myself sharing more. "Geoff was amazing the entire time I went through my treatment. I had a partial mastectomy. Chemo. Radiation. Hence, the short hair and mostly nonexistent eyelashes."

"You sound really good."

Maybe I'd let Gianna believe that for a while.

We'd looped the block. As we neared my house, Zach's truck pulled up alongside the curb.

"Uh-oh."

"'Uh-oh' what?" Gianna scanned the area ahead of us.

"That guy getting out of the truck? That's Zach, the family friend who oversees the kitchen project for us—"

"That's nice of him."

"He drops by to check up on the guys while they're working—but I don't see any other trucks. I hope there's not another problem." Winston let out a bark, causing Zach to wave. "Gotta go. This was fun though."

At least that was the appropriate thing to say.

"It was. Let's do it again."

"Sure."

Zach leaned against his truck as I approached, but bent down to greet Winston, who continued to bark and jump until Zach picked him up.

"He likes you."

"The person he likes the most is your dad."

"True—because Dad feeds him all the time. Feed him and he'll defect to you."

"But I want to keep you and Geoff happy, too, remember? So no feeding this guy." Zach continued to hold Winston. "I wanted to do a walk-through. See where we are. Have a chance to talk with you before the guys got here."

"There's not a problem?"

"No. Why? Did you think there was a problem?"

"I guess I'm more nervous than I realized because I saw your truck and immediately thought you were going to tell me there was some sort of new issue we had to deal with."

"Nope. All good." Zach settled against his truck again. "You're happy with the changes we made?"

"The more and more I see the Corian countertops, the less and less I think about my first choice." I mimicked his posture, allowing space between us, staring ahead at the house. "Thanks for helping us make the right decision."

Zach laughed. "Glad to help."

"You did a beautiful job with the cabinets."

"I enjoyed designing them for you and Geoff." He shifted Winston in his arms. "So what else are you thinking?"

"Geoff told me how excited he was when he bought this house. I mean, he knew it was over a hundred years old. That it would need some updating. But overall, he thought it was a solid house. Then we started the renovation and discovered all these hidden problems."

"And now the kitchen is updated. Almost finished, once we get the floors down." Zach adjusted to my unusual answer to his question. "No one will know we had all those problems—or that you'd wanted French doors. I'm looking around for an extra special back door for you. Trust me on that, okay?"

Maybe that was Zach's attempt to comfort me while steering the conversation back to neutral territory, but I no longer cared about the renovation.

"Sometimes . . . sometimes I feel like I'm no better than this old house." I continued before Zach could try to formulate a response to my odd statement—the one I hadn't even realized I was going to make. Maybe all my honesty with Gianna had been a prelude to this. "I can put on clothes. Do my hair. Makeup. Not that I did that today. And I can hide all my problems. Unless someone gets close, no one knows I'm a year out from cancer just by looking at me."

That I wore a breast form.

That, despite my attempts to preserve my fertility, I was married to a man who didn't want children.

But even though I was being truthful with Zach, I wasn't willing to share those kinds of intimate realities.

Zach scratched behind Winston's ears. "Sounds like it's not the house that's bothering you, Jillian."

"Everything's a mess."

"Everything?"

"I'm unemployed. Harper, my best friend, is moving. And you know I can't get pregnant because of this medication I'm on." My laugh was brief. "You were there for that awkward family conversation. I tried to talk to Geoff about adopting, but he said no." I paused, realizing what I was on the verge of revealing.

Being this honest with Zach was like plowing a car into the house. I needed to stop, hit the brakes before I destroyed the kitchen, the custom cabinets, the new appliances . . . all of it.

I didn't even want to look at Zach. An apology slipped past my lips.

"Why are you saying you're sorry?" Zach tilted his head. "You meant everything you said, right?"

"Yes. But you came by to check on the kitchen, not have me dump on you."

"Look, Payton and I are . . . friends." Zach seemed to hesitate over the word. "In the past year, I've spent some time with your whole family. So why can't you and I be friends, too? Sometimes it helps to have someone outside the situation—whatever that situation is—to listen. I don't mind if you talk to me, but have you thought of talking to Payton about any of this?"

"Payton and I have never been close that way."

"Johanna, then."

"No." I'd just leave my reply at that.

"Okay. Well, I think Payton could help you—that she'd want to help you. But I'm here for now. I'm listening."

If Zach was still game to listen, then I'd take him up on his offer—this time.

"I was just so surprised that Geoff said no to adoption." I chose my words so I didn't reveal the whole truth—that Geoff didn't want children. Ever.

"You two didn't talk about kids while you were dating?"

That was a fair question.

"At first, I was surprised Geoff asked me out. That he kept coming back." For a moment, I allowed myself to savor the memory of those early days in our relationship. "And then we were just having fun. Falling in love. We only dated five months before we got engaged . . . and then . . ."

"And then you were diagnosed with cancer."

"Yes. For a while, I tried to talk myself out of marrying Geoff. After that came the months life was all about cancer."

"Maybe this is stating the obvious, but you and Geoff have had anything but the normal struggles of most newlyweds."

I couldn't argue with Zach. "And Geoff and I thought the kitchen reno would be fun. We couldn't have been more wrong."

"I never said the renovation would be fun, Jillian." A smile laced Zach's words. "I said it would be worth it."

"That's true."

"If you could, would you go back to the old kitchen? Undo all of this, knowing the extra cost, the problems we'd find? Have us not finish it?"

"Is this some sort of trick question?"

"No. No trick."

"I love the kitchen. The cabinets are beautiful to look

at—and they're spacious, so now there's a place for everything. I hated the dingy laminate floor and the old counters . . . it was all outdated. I can't wait to see the new wood flooring. And I know that the things I can't see are all sound, too. It's an investment that will pay off in the long run."

"I like what you're saying."

"It's obvious we couldn't have done this by ourselves. You're the craftsman when it comes to wood cabinets. And plumbing and electricity? We had to have experts do the work. It was a hassle—but you tried to shield us from that as much as possible." Some of the tightness in my shoulders eased. "I guess I'm more satisfied than I realized."

"Can you say the same thing about Geoff?"

"I'm not following."

"Okay, I admit that was a bit of a trick question." Zach's smile disappeared. "I've heard my pastor say that marriage isn't ever what we plan on . . . The person we marry isn't the person we find on the other side of 'I do.'"

"That's why I broke off my engagement . . . because Geoff hadn't proposed to someone with cancer."

"But Geoff didn't walk away, did he?"

"No."

"What about you?" Zach allowed Winston to squirm out of his arms, retaining a hold on the leash so he couldn't escape. "Are you going to walk away from Geoff because you two haven't figured out the kid issue?"

Zach's question was a direct hit. "That's not fair."

"You, of anyone, knows life isn't fair."

"But that's like asking me if I could be in two places

at one time. I want Geoff. I want children. I didn't know I had to choose. He didn't talk to me about this before he decided . . ." I stopped. Zach didn't know everything Geoff had decided. "I mean, he won't even talk about the possibility of adopting."

"That's not the point, Jillian."

"Then tell me what is the point."

"You spoke wedding vows with Geoff. I know you were in a judge's chambers, but that doesn't make those words any less binding. Did you mean what you said?"

Did I mean the "no matter what happens" intent of our wedding vows? When I stood in front of a judge, just me and Geoff and the specter of cancer and an uncertain future, did I mean it?

"Yes."

Zach was silent for a few seconds as if to let my answer settle into my heart. "Maybe what you need to do is stop thinking about how disappointed you are—although I can certainly understand why you're feeling that way. I'm just suggesting you consider a different perspective."

"What do you mean?"

"Has Geoff told you why he doesn't want to adopt?"

I replayed our conversations in my head. "Sort of."

"Sort of?"

"He gave me an answer, but really he just shut me down."

"Then go talk to him. Find out the real reason why Geoff doesn't want to adopt."

I stared straight ahead. "His answer also might not change anything."

"I know that. But at least you'll have asked him."

Zach, with his quiet voice and pointed questions, was turning me around, making me face my wedding vows. He wasn't being cruel or pushy.

He was also reminding me to think less about myself and more about my husband, who so often in the past had thought of me first.

"Can I ask you a question?"

I couldn't resist giving him a hard time. "You mean can you ask me *another* question?"

Zach half smiled. "Yeah."

"Go ahead."

"What got you through your cancer treatments—the chemo and the radiation? I mean, besides Geoff."

"Harper . . . she gave me a glass jar filled with positive thoughts. She wrote them out on all these colorful slips of paper and made sure I pulled one out each day."

"That's nice. And it helped, reading a positive thought a day?"

"Most days."

"Is there one of those thoughts that would help you right now?"

"I don't know . . . maybe." I closed my eyes, inhaling the scent of smoke. One of my neighbors had started a fire in their fireplace. "How about 'A single thread of hope is still a very powerful thing.'"

"I like it. Can you find even the smallest bit of hope inside you, Jillian? A single thread?"

"I can try."

It was the best I could do at the moment.

"That's a start. One thing I know . . . you love Geoff. And Geoff loves you. Remember that." He paused. "God loves you too, Jillian."

Huh.

Zach must have forgotten that the Thatcher sisters didn't believe in God—although maybe that was changing for Payton. But the idea of God loving someone as insignificant as me? I couldn't grasp it, but I also couldn't get angry at Zach for telling me that. Right now, if I could somehow find my way to a big, loving God who could fix the hurt and misunderstanding separating Geoff and me, I would run to Him without a backward glance at my doubts.

"I know you . . . your family . . . that we think differently about faith. But my relationship with God helps me through the hard times."

Zach was treading softly, not wanting to offend me. And he hadn't. He was saying, *"This helped me. Take it or leave it."*

Part of me wished that if I turned over all those slips of paper from the glass jar Harper had given me, if I pieced them together, I'd discover a map that led me closer to God . . . or offered me the ultimate words of comfort so I would be fine without Him.

Today, this morning, I would ask Geoff why.

But first he had to wake up.

I'd found my husband asleep next to me in our bed, dark circles under his eyes, his brown hair matted to his forehead.

Geoff hadn't even taken the time to hang up his clothes but tossed his khaki pants and button-down shirt on the wooden chair beside his dresser. The longing to be near me hadn't kept him in bed this Saturday morning—the sheer inability to wake up had.

Fine. I'd take it.

I'd stayed next to him for a while, appreciating the warmth of his body beside mine. The sound of his breathing. Resisting the urge to turn and curl closer to him. Rest my head on his chest. Touch his hair.

Even there, in the stillness of our bedroom, the questions snuck in, disrupting what little peace I'd gathered while lying next to my husband and pushing me from the bed. Geoff, my Geoff, with his jokes and his laughter and his kindness . . . what were his reasons for saying no to children? To expanding our family to include a son or a daughter?

Two hours later, I'd made breakfast—now brunch—in our almost-complete kitchen, the cement floor beneath the plastic covering cold on my feet. A quiche—using Johanna's favorite recipe. And the coffee would be hot and fresh, if not fancy. Winston had enjoyed a brief walk in the neighborhood, the cold hurrying us back into the warmth of the house. Now, at last, Geoff's footsteps sounded on the stairs.

"What time is it?"

"Ten thirty."

Geoff brushed his hair back, adjusting his glasses. "Sorry. I must have been really tired."

Was he apologizing for being home?

"You've been working hard, what with those extra projects.

And I know you're already prepping for the conference, too."
I pressed my lips together. I wanted my response to be pleasant, so shorter was better.

"Yeah. Just preliminary stuff, but I want to give it my best, you know? I'm researching the topic options, as well as presentation methods."

"Good idea. I took Winston for a walk. Wanted the house to be quiet so you could sleep."

"Thanks."

"Coffee?"

"Sure."

"Are you hungry? I made a quiche—Johanna's recipe. And fresh fruit."

"I thought something smelled good." Geoff nodded. "Sure."

He settled onto his heels, calling to Winston and scratching behind his ears, as I prepared the coffee and filled our plates. We pretended everything was fine. Easing our way around the kitchen. Around each other. Around the remnants of conflict that shadowed our days. We carried our breakfast into the dining room, Geoff sitting at the head of the table, me sitting next to him.

The room filled with silence. No easy banter. No laughter.

Maybe I should let go of my plans to talk to Geoff. Choose to relax. Have a pleasant day. See if I could get my husband to smile again. To look at me again.

No. This was a chance to talk—possibly our only opportunity, with Geoff so intent on avoiding me.

I waited until he was halfway through breakfast—and on

his second cup of coffee—before broaching what had happened a week ago. By then he'd at least made eye contact with me, even if he hadn't touched me.

"I was . . . I was hoping we could talk."

"Talk?" Geoff stiffened. "About adopting?"

I had to give the man credit for not dodging at least part of the issue.

"No." I shoved aside my plate. "I wanted to talk about why you don't want to have children."

Geoff gulped his coffee. He lowered his eyes. "Is this so you can argue with me? Tell me all the reasons we should have children?"

"No." I risked resting my fingertips on the back of his hand. How I'd missed being close to him. Physically. Emotionally. Even when he'd come home late at night and slipped into bed, he'd kept his distance, no longer drawing me close to him, curving his body around mine. He didn't pull his hand away now, but he didn't turn his palm up to curl his fingers around mine, either.

"Telling you why isn't going to change anything, Jillian."

"Yes, it will." I waited until he looked at me instead of staring at his plate. "If you explain, then I'll understand your decision. And your decision affects both of us."

Geoff closed his eyes. Opened them again. "Fair enough."

But even as he agreed to answer my question, it was as if Geoff moved further away from me. There was a fleeting glimpse of something bleak in his eyes. I almost said, *"Never mind. I don't want to know."*

But I had to understand why he was saying no to children. To our children.

"I have . . . a brother, Jillian." Geoff's voice had dropped to a whisper, but I didn't dare lean closer or ask him to speak up, for fear he'd stop talking. If he did, then I'd never make sense of the sentence that seemed to be a direct strike to my heart.

"His name is Brian. He's twenty months older than me. And you're probably wondering why you've never met him."

No. No, I was wondering why I'd never heard about Brian before now.

"Brian was always a handful for Mom and Dad—challenging them. Ignoring them. Ignoring teachers. Anyone in authority, really. When he hit the teen years, it was as if all the rebellion was turbo-charged. When he was seventeen, Brian ran away from home."

Geoff spoke with no emotion, his words as bland as if he were reading from a dishwasher installation manual.

"Where is he now?"

Geoff shook his head. "I have no idea."

"You've never heard from him again? Not once in all these years?"

"At first, he'd call every four months or so. But our parents told him to stop calling unless he was willing to come home and get his life straight."

"And?"

"That was the end of the phone calls."

"Don't you ever wonder where he is? Want to find him?"

"He left the family, not me." Never once had Geoff looked

at me as he spoke, but now his gaze connected with mine. "There was no reason to try and find him."

It was as if Geoff's words formed extra puzzle pieces that were supposed to somehow fit into our life story.

"Why didn't you ever tell me about Brian?"

"I don't . . . we don't talk about him."

"None of you—not your parents or you—talk about your brother? Ever?"

"I tried to ask my parents about Brian a few times, even though my mother kept telling me to stop. Then a couple of years later, I mentioned him again. My mother looked at me and said, 'Who?'" Geoff swallowed hard. "I never asked again. Over the years, it's become easier not to talk about him."

"Until now."

"What?"

"It was easier until now." I withdrew my hand from his, rubbing my palms together. My diamond engagement ring had twisted around and scraped against my skin. "Were you ever going to tell me about Brian?"

"No." Geoff's Adam's apple bobbed up and down. "Maybe. I don't know. What good would it do?"

"What good would it do to tell your wife that you have a brother?"

"It's bringing up the past, Jillian."

"Your past is affecting our future."

"Not really. I'd already made my decision not to have children before I met you."

"Because of your brother."

"He abandoned our family!" Geoff's voice rose before he stopped himself. "Why can't you understand that?"

"Didn't it ever occur to you that I might understand difficult family situations, Geoff? You just never gave me the chance."

"This is my family's issue, not yours."

"Not anymore. Not once we got married."

Silence.

None of this made any sense.

I slipped from my chair onto my knees beside him, wrapping my arms around his waist, hoping for some connection with my husband. Geoff stiffened, his arms resting on the table, his hands fisted together.

I couldn't fix this with a hug. This wasn't like trying to talk Geoff out of a bad mood.

Questions filled my mind.

How could your parents never talk about their firstborn son? Don't you miss your brother?

And then arguments filtered their way in between the questions.

How can you let something that happened when you were in high school determine what we do now?

Why are you letting fear stop you from becoming a father?

But I said none of these things. Instead I held my husband even as I tried to hold the invisible puzzle pieces he'd handed me as he told me about Brian. Winston came and nudged around us, settling with his head resting on Geoff's feet. I found my husband's hand, intertwining our fingers so that our wedding bands touched.

I needed to remember this . . . Our marriage was until death do us part. Not until I couldn't understand my husband.

Geoff shifted, burying his face in the crook of my neck, his ragged breathing warm on my skin. I waited for him to cry.

But no tears came.

Just more silence.

It was as if I stood at the edge of an open cavern, peering down into the opaque darkness. How deep was it? And if I slipped, would I ever stop falling?

17

JUST OUTSIDE the expansive glass windows surrounding the staff café, gray clouds hid the mountains from view. The overhead lighting created a cozy feeling, warming the tops of the rustic wood tables and cloth chairs scattered throughout the room. Several seating areas were arranged around a central stone waterfall, accented by lush greenery maintained year-round by a small, dedicated staff of horticulturists who also took care of the other plants in the hospital.

The café was one of the staff perks at Mount Columbia Medical Center—and Johanna usually appreciated it. But not today . . . not when she was having coffee with Axton Miller. Did the man think this was necessary now that he was her boss? She could only hope he didn't plan on making morning coffee sessions a regular occurrence, along with monthly birthday celebrations.

Despite Johanna's protests, he'd paid for both their coffees, along with his bran muffin. But only because his request for this meeting had caught her unawares—and she'd left the coffee she'd brought from home back in her office. They'd maintained idle chitchat while they'd waited for the barista to prepare their drinks, until she suggested she'd go claim a table for them. And now she waited for him to make his way through the room to where she sat at a small table for two. But the way the man stopped and chatted to first one group of people and then another—after saying good morning to the servers and cashier—she might be ready for lunch by the time he arrived.

The man was a schmoozer.

"I'm glad this worked out." Dr. Miller set his tray down across from her, unloading their coffees and his muffin and setting his briefcase on the floor before turning to hand the tray to a passing busboy. "Thank you, Billy."

Of course he knew that guy's name, too.

"I apologize for keeping you waiting, Johanna."

She mentally stumbled over his use of her first name. Fine. That was his decision—his freedom—as her boss. "No problem at all."

He peeled the paper wrapper from his bran muffin. "I'm glad we finally have a chance to talk. To get to know each other better."

Johanna knew everything she needed to know—or

wanted to know—about this man. She'd read his résumé. Twice. He'd taken the job she deserved away from her. They were not becoming work buddies.

"You did a good job as interim director, Johanna."

Had he put a slight emphasis on the word *interim*?

"Overall, things are in good shape."

"Overall?" Johanna set her coffee to the side. Okay. They'd talk.

"I've been talking to the staff, and from what I gather—"

"You've been talking to people?"

"Informally. Trying to connect, to get their view of things. And from what I've heard, I believe morale is down."

"You may think morale is down, but I know efficiency is up."

"Efficiency could be up because of fear—and fear is a poor long-term motivator." Any hint of a smile had disappeared from Dr. Miller's pale-blue eyes. "You can run fast when you're being chased by a bear, but it doesn't work well for real, long-term success."

Had the man just compared her to a bear?

She'd been a good pharmacy director during the job search. There'd been no complaints. None. And there'd been some customer compliments, too. She'd saved them all to a file on her computer.

Johanna refused to respond to his not-so-veiled suggestion that she was the reason employee morale was down. Let the man talk.

"What do you think we should do about this?"

Now he wanted her help dealing with a fabricated

problem? Not going to happen. She had actual projects that needed her attention.

"I think things are going fine."

"And I just informed you there are some issues we need to address." He buttered his muffin. "You've been here longer than I have. You know people better than I do. Why don't you come up with some ideas to encourage unity among our pharmacy team?"

Again with the unneeded request.

"This is a hospital, Dr. Miller, not a sports arena. We are taking care of patients, not . . . not playing volleyball."

He laughed. *Laughed.* "That's true. However, it turns out that team dynamics work on the court, in the boardroom, in the operating room . . . and in a pharmacy. Humans care about being valued and believing they are doing something important." He pulled a small navy-blue notebook from the pocket of his lab coat. Opened it and made a notation. "How about we meet Monday morning, after the Thanksgiving holiday, say eight o'clock, and you let me know what you come up with?"

Did Dr. Miller think one of his responsibilities as a pharmacy director included being a corporate leadership trainer?

Out of the corner of her eye, Johanna noticed the hospital CEO walk into the café. She had to at least pretend she and Dr. Miller were getting along when Dr. Lerner was around. That this was a pleasant chat over coffee, instead of the reality that he had tossed veiled threats at her from across the table.

Or she could leave. End the conversation now.

"That's fine. I'll talk to you on Monday."

Dr. Miller stood, stopping her with a hand on her forearm. "One more thing."

"Yes?"

He pulled a book from his briefcase. "I've read this book several times. I bought you a copy."

Not. Another. Book.

"It's *The Power of Positive Leadership*." He offered her the book, which meant she had to take it. "Go ahead and read the first couple of chapters. When we meet on Monday, you can tell me what you think."

"Thanks. I'll do that."

As if she had nothing else to do during the long Thanksgiving weekend but read a book and come up with ways to improve morale.

"This has been a good talk."

This wasn't a talk. It was covert accusations and a homework assignment.

And now . . . now the CEO was coming their way. Johanna was caught between a traitor and a saboteur.

Dr. Lerner nodded at Johanna. "Good to see you both. I knew you'd work well together."

"Johanna and I just had a good conversation about what we discussed yesterday."

Wait. He'd talked to Dr. Lerner about all of this? About her?

"Good. Good." Dr. Lerner pointed to the book Dr. Miller had just handed to her. "Johanna, you're reading Jon Gordon's book? It's excellent."

"Oh, I, um, I'm just starting it."

"My copy is highlighted and dog-eared."

"Well, that's quite a recommendation." Johanna eased away from the other two. "If you will excuse me, I need to get back upstairs. Thank you for the coffee."

Not that she'd tasted any of it.

"I look forward to talking again on Monday."

"I do too."

That was a lie.

The man had never outright threatened her. He was too slick for that. But she was smart enough to read between all the lines. He was gunning for her. Couldn't wait to take her down. Probably already had someone in mind for her job.

And now the CEO was sitting in the chair she'd vacated.

Fine. Let the two of them talk. She had work—real work—to do.

Johanna fast-walked to the elevator, slipping in among the group of people already on board, all the way to the back, and closing her eyes.

If only she could leave. Go home. Be by herself.

Why did she ever decide to become a pharmacist?

Because she was good at math.

And to help people . . . that, too.

She could always start looking for another job.

But she wasn't a quitter. Well, she wasn't anymore. She was an adult, not some young kid. She'd grown up and learned not to give in just because someone else didn't come through for her like they'd promised. Just because someone let her down.

Dr. Miller might have gotten the promotion she deserved,

but he wasn't kicking her out of her hospital by drumming up imaginary problems. She had a long-standing reputation at this hospital. And she had statistics—hard, cold facts— proving patient satisfaction and employee efficiency.

Johanna opened her eyes. The elevator was empty. Somehow she'd missed her floor. She pressed the correct number on the panel.

Whatever her boss was up to, he wasn't going to mess with her any more than he already had.

EVERY FAMILY had their holiday traditions. My family did, too—and Johanna, even more than Mom, ensured we maintained them, going so far as to come over the weekend before to get things ready.

Setting the table for Thanksgiving? We used Mom's china dinnerware she'd received as wedding gifts, decorated with black rims and delicate silver-and-black floral scrollwork, which Johanna had hand washed and dried. Of course, various accidents meant her collection had been supplemented with replacement pieces through the years. Grandmother's silver was polished—which grandmother, I couldn't remember—and the crystal goblets were unpacked and also washed and dried by Johanna.

Even today's activities had a certain order, with Johanna setting out the plates while I arranged the forks, knives, and spoons and Payton filled the glasses with ice water. Some things didn't change, even if we were adults, not little girls waiting for Mom to tell us what to do.

"I feel sorry for Thanksgiving." My admission was spoken aloud before I even realized it.

"You . . . feel sorry for Thanksgiving?" Johanna stared at me across the dining room table. "The holiday?"

Now I needed to try to explain myself. "Yes. It's confused."

"You're confused." Johanna smoothed the white table-cloth before centering the last dinner plate in front of Mom's chair. "Thanksgiving is a holiday—a day of the month that comes around once a year. It can't be confused."

"Fine. If you want to be literal about it. People have confused what Thanksgiving is about. The day has a split personality."

Johanna moved to the head of the table and began setting salad plates on top of dinner plates.

"It used to be a religious holiday, right?" Despite Johanna's disinterest, I continued. "I know, I know—everything we were taught in school got watered down. The Pilgrims thanking God for helping them survive the first winter in America? Remember that?"

"Not everyone believes—"

"I get it. But I'm talking about what's happened to Thanksgiving." I finished another set of silverware. Two forks. A knife. A spoon. All slipped into the cloth napkin Johanna had starched, ironed, and folded so that it formed a little pocket. "A lot of people spend the day watching football."

"Where do you think Dad and Geoff and Beckett are right now?" Johanna pointed toward the family room. "Even Winston is out there."

"Of course he is. If Dad's around, that's where Winston is." We shared a brief laugh. "Not that we mind. The men will do the cleanup. Wait . . . Does Beckett know about that Thatcher family tradition?"

"Not yet. Let the guy relax for now."

She was right. He'd be indoctrinated into that family tradition soon enough. "And then there are the people who planned what time they'll eat so it doesn't interfere with Black Friday shopping—which now starts later today."

"So what's your point, Jillian?"

"That I feel sorry for Thanksgiving."

"Right."

I needed to give up. Admit I was having a one-sided conversation between two people. Johanna was fine with Thanksgiving the way it was. She wasn't considering my point of view in a way that might change her mind. She was more concerned with setting one plate on top of the other and aligning the patterns just so.

Some things never changed, and that was never more true than in my family.

Payton entered, carrying the tray of glasses needing to be filled with water and setting it on the sideboard before adding them to the table.

"Did Jillian tell you that she feels sorry for Thanksgiving?" Johanna stepped back to give Payton room.

"What?"

"Jillian feels sorry—"

I could explain myself. "I was saying it's sad Thanksgiving doesn't even get a whole day anymore . . . It's this odd mishmash of be-thankful-watch-football-go-shopping-for-Christmas."

"I can't disagree with that." Payton circled the table, adding the goblets to each place setting. "The Christmas decorations show up in the store earlier every year, mixed right in with Halloween."

"Exactly! If anyone knows how to celebrate Thanksgiving, it would be Zach. At least he's saying thank you to someone." I finished another setting of silverware. "Where is he, anyway? Is he coming soon?"

Payton's hand slipped as she placed a glass on the table. "Um, he couldn't make it."

"Couldn't make it? Is he visiting family or something?"

"No."

I paused in my task. "You invited him, right?"

"We talked about Thanksgiving earlier this month, yes . . ." Payton never looked away from the table. "And he decided not to come."

"That doesn't sound like Zach at all."

"Well, it is Zach, okay? He's not coming."

The way Payton was acting made it sound like she and Zach had broken up, but they'd never been a couple. Had they?

Payton blinked back tears. Something was wrong, but she'd talk about it when she was ready.

Mom appeared in the door between the kitchen and the dining room, carrying a pitcher of water. "Is the table set?"

"Yes." Our voices blended together in one response.

"Good. Because, believe it or not, we've managed to coordinate all the food to be ready at the same time."

An hour and a half later, all of us sat around the table, some finishing their second helpings of Thanksgiving dinner. Meal preparation always took so long, with Mom ordering a fresh-not-frozen turkey weeks ahead. Making homemade rolls. Finding several new dishes to supplement our traditional ones when Payton decided to go vegan. And then we muted whatever football game was playing on TV and gathered around the table, Dad pulling out Mom's chair and placing a kiss on her cheek. Then he carved the turkey with a little bit of flourish, asking, "Who wants the leg?" which he promptly claimed. We started passing dishes of stuffing, mashed potatoes, rolls, butternut squash, shaved brussels sprout salad . . .

And then the feasting was over.

Some of us would go back to football. Dad would doze off—probably with Winston in his lap. Some would opt to take a walk later if it wasn't too cold outside.

"How is everyone?" I lobbed the question into the air, wondering if it sounded odd to anyone else. But then, we hadn't really talked that much beyond "This is delicious" and "Please pass me the rolls again" and "How's work?" while we were eating.

Beckett groaned. "I, for one, am glad to be off work today. The food was fantastic."

"My fantasy football team is winning, so I'm happy."

"Don!" Mom's reprimand was softened with a smile.

"The food was wonderful, Heather. It always is."

"Thank you." She reached for his hand. "And now you men do the cleanup and I can sit and hold Winston."

"What?" Beckett almost choked on a final bite of turkey.

Geoff laughed. "You didn't know, man? Welcome to the Thatcher family Thanksgiving tradition the women like best."

"I must have never made it here for Thanksgiving before now."

Johanna patted Beckett on the shoulder. "Dad is so happy to have you and Geoff here. He did this by himself for years."

"Where's Zach? We're down a guy."

Payton moved her food around her plate, the fork against china creating a sharp squeal. "He couldn't make it."

"Well, boys, I guess we're cleaning up before we watch any more football." Dad reached for Mom's plate, scraping the remnants of food onto his.

Thanksgiving—the national leftover holiday. Wasn't there some way to make it more?

I settled my fork and knife onto my plate with a soft clink. "Before the men start cleaning up, I wanted to try something new."

"Something new? What?" Johanna answered as if I were addressing her, the guardian of our family traditions.

"I thought we could go around the table and say what

we're thankful for this year . . . you know, just one thing we're thankful for?"

"I've heard of families doing that." Mom took Dad's hand. "Why don't you start, Jill?"

I couldn't argue with that. I'd suggested this little gratitude game. And with Mom's approval, no one else was putting up a fuss.

"I'm thankful for where I've come in a year—especially when I think about where I was twelve months ago. I'm thankful I'm done with my treatment." I fingered my hair. "And I'm enjoying this new short hairstyle. Who knew, right?"

That got a laugh from everyone, lightening the mood a bit.

"I'll go next." Mom sat up straighter. "I'm thankful we're all here together . . . well, not all of us. But you know what I mean."

"I second that." Dad squeezed Mom's hand, leaning over to kiss her cheek.

"Dad, that's not how it works."

"What? Jilly, are you telling me I can't be thankful for the same thing as your mother? I am."

I probably shouldn't critique people's responses, not if I wanted this to succeed. "No. No, you're right."

"My turn." Johanna spoke up. "I'm thankful for my job." Beckett cleared his throat.

"And for Beckett being here, of course."

"Thank you." Beckett smiled. "I'm thankful to be living here in the Springs this year—and looking forward to planning a wedding soon."

Johanna waved away Mom's unspoken question of *"When?"* "Payton, what are you thankful for?"

"I'm thankful for a lot of things . . . but I'll just say I'm thankful Jill is doing so well."

"Wow." I reached across the table for my sister's hand, our fingers not quite touching. "You picked me over volleyball."

Another round of laughter made its way around the table.

Geoff cleared his throat. "I'll be thankful when this kitchen reno is done. I never knew how much I'd appreciate things I can't see, like good pipes and up-to-date wiring."

My experiment ended with laughter, no surprise with Geoff going last. But now I realized how his humor deflected people's attention from what he didn't say . . . from realizing he'd stayed surface, being thankful for things, not a person.

Not me. Not even us.

Everyone stood and began clearing away the remains of the day, Beckett already talking about making a turkey sandwich.

My attempt to make something more of Thanksgiving wasn't a complete failure, but I doubted it would become a new Thatcher family tradition. Maybe if Johanna had suggested it . . .

Or maybe we weren't *that* family—the kind who wove a deeper significance into Thanksgiving Day.

Then again, maybe being thankful only worked if you were saying thank you to someone. A family member or friend who had helped you in some way. Encouraged you. Offered you something without being asked.

Or maybe Thanksgiving Day was about thanking God . . . if you believed in that sort of thing. Maybe thanking some invisible creator for blessing you with protection and care and family and friends would replace some of the emptiness I carried with me today.

Geoff slipped behind me, wrapping his arms around my waist. "I was thinking . . ."

"Yes?"

"We should take Winston for a walk."

I twisted to face him, giving him a quick kiss. "And you, Geoff Hennessey, are trying to get out of kitchen duty."

"What?" His eyes widened in feigned innocence.

"You can't fool me." I pushed him toward the kitchen. "We'll walk Winston after you do the dishes."

"If you say so."

"I do." I hesitated for a moment. "Geoff?"

"Yeah?"

"I'm very thankful for you—you know that, right? I wouldn't have made it through . . . everything . . . without you."

"Thanks, Jilly." He took a step toward me.

Hollers for "Hey, Hennessey, get in here!" and "Come on, you slacker!" interrupted the moment.

"Duty calls." He motioned toward the kitchen.

"Yeah."

"Keep me posted on the football game?"

"Sure. I'll be looking forward to our walk."

"Me, too."

⌒

How many chapters of this book did Axton Miller expect her to read? Two? Three?

She'd read only one chapter, one laborious page at a time, underlining a few sentences for good measure. But with every turn of the page she heard Dr. Miller's request. *"Why don't you come up with some ideas to encourage unity among our pharmacy team?"*

Her new boss was wrecking her attention span.

It didn't help that Beckett sat beside her on the couch, channel surfing his way through sports, infomercials, classic sitcoms, movies, and back through the cycle again.

He tossed aside the remote. "Come on, let's do something."

"I am doing something. I'm reading."

"I've been working nonstop since I got to Colorado. I finally have a day off. Let's go for a hike."

"A hike?" Johanna glanced around her living room. "Who are you talking to? The closest thing I have to hiking boots are brown leather and have two-inch heels."

"All right then, let's go to the Broadmoor. We can have lunch at the Golden Bee. Walk around the lake . . ."

Johanna held up the book. "Book. New boss. Meeting on Monday. Remember?"

"I'm bored." He sounded like a whiny five-year-old. A very handsome five-year-old, but still.

Did she have a fiancé or was she babysitting? Part of what attracted her to Beckett was his independence. If this was a hint of what it would be like when they were married, he wasn't the only one who was bored.

"What if you let me read another chapter—?"

"You do realize the general could call me at any time? Ask me to do something?" Beckett stood, holding out his hand to her. "Come on, Johanna. The Broadmoor? Lunch?"

"Fine." She closed the book. "The Broadmoor—but just for a couple of hours."

"Great! Can I bring your camera?"

"My camera?"

"Mine's at my apartment, so yours will have to do." He rubbed his palms together. "I can still get some decent photographs, even without my lenses and tripod."

"I thought we were having lunch."

"We are, but I'm not going to miss the opportunity to take a few photos. I'll even take some of you—my favorite model."

Now she had to put on some basic makeup and change her clothes. "Don't think flattery is buying you extra time. I've got to be prepared for my meeting on Monday. I know Dr. Miller wants to fire me."

"You are being paranoid." He took her hands, pulling her to her feet.

"I'm watching my back. The guy doesn't like me or the way I do things at the hospital."

"Don't worry so much. You've been at that hospital longer than he has—you've got clout. Just keep doing what you've been doing—"

"What I've been doing was good enough until Dr. Miller

came along with his padded résumé and talk of *team*. Now he's the golden boy and I'm back to being the assistant." The words tasted bitter on her tongue. But why not? She was bitter. What was the sense of networking and developing a strong relationship with her former boss if all of that failed her when she needed it the most?

Beckett trailed behind her as she changed her casual top for a sweater and opened the makeup drawer in her bathroom. "How do I know he doesn't have some other person waiting in the wings to take my place? Somebody he's already talked to Dr. Lerner about?"

"He can't shove you out of your job."

"He can if he convinces Dr. Lerner that I've ruined staff morale. As if we work at Disneyland and I'm supposed to make the pharmacies the happiest places on earth."

Johanna paused applying eye shadow to one eye. Thanks to all his talk about team, she couldn't think straight, much less read a book or formulate a plan to make everybody happy. What did he want her to do? Plan outings? Barbecues? Celebrate birthdays?

Yes. He did expect birthday cards and cakes.

Beckett wasn't even listening—he'd gone off looking for her camera. Not that it mattered. She'd handle the work issue herself.

She was tempted to bring the book with her and read in the car but left it at home. Maybe the drive and a walk around the Broadmoor—a *brief* walk around the Broadmoor— would clear her mind, even provide some inspiration for impressing Dr. Miller on Monday.

The five-star resort had gone through several renovations since the last time she'd been there, not that she could remember when that was. As they wandered after lunch, she couldn't help but be captivated by the beauty of the well-kept grounds and elegant decor, from the marble floors and the rich Persian carpets to the fountains and artistic floral displays, including a two-foot-diameter round brass bowl filled entirely with an orb of red roses. Beckett lagged by a roped-off area on the second floor of the main building where chefs worked on a stunning gingerbread house display in preparation for the annual Christmas lights festivities tomorrow.

"I don't know why I came along. All I'm doing is following you and watching you take pictures."

"And posing for me."

"Yes." She fluttered her eyelashes at him. "I'm really enjoying that."

"A beautiful woman and the Broadmoor as the backdrop. I wish I had my camera and lenses."

"Sorry, but we weren't driving all the way to your apartment before coming here." Johanna allowed Beckett to lead them back outside, across the stone bridge spanning the lake, where a flock of ducks and geese, as well as a duo of white swans, floated on the surface. He guided her into the west building. "We had lunch at the Golden Bee, just like you wanted. We already walked around the lake once, and we've been all over both sides of the hotel. Surely you have enough photos—"

"Oh, come on. Are you telling me you haven't had any fun?"

"I admit this has given me an idea." Johanna stopped inside the doors, surveying the marble floors and the shimmering chandelier hanging from an ornate ceiling mosaic in black, white, gold, and umber.

"Really? What?"

"What if we did our wedding here?"

Beckett lowered his camera. "Here?"

"Yes, here. At the Broadmoor. It's classy—the ultimate Colorado location for a wedding."

"If by 'classy' and 'ultimate,' you mean expensive, I agree."

"It's not like we can't afford it. And I'm not planning on a big affair—but I do want something memorable. The Broadmoor is definitely that."

"Are you saying you're finally ready to set a date?" Beckett took her hand, crossing the foyer toward the south lobby they'd visited earlier.

"I'm not the one who has been traveling all over the world with their job."

"I've invited you to join me a dozen times . . ."

"We are not having this argument, Beckett. You knew when you met me that I liked my job."

"And you knew when you met me that I was in the military."

She stopped in a long hallway lined with dozens of framed photographs of celebrities and dignitaries who'd visited the Broadmoor through the years. "Well, the military has you in the same town as me for once. Do you want to squabble about details of our relationship, or do you want to plan the details of our wedding?"

Whenever the topic of the wedding came up, this was what they did—they got sidetracked by quarreling, instead of getting serious and setting a date and then going through with it.

She wore an engagement ring, but there were some days when people asked her about Beckett and she almost asked, *"Beckett who?"*

"All right, let's plan our wedding. Here." He ushered her into the hushed room—no one there but the two of them. This could easily be her favorite area in the Broadmoor. Secluded. Providing varied glimpses of the resort, depending on whether she decided to relax in a leather chair or on a couch or at one of the small wooden tables positioned around the room, inviting people to sit and stay. Read. Unwind. Savor the refreshing sound of water spilling from the fountain topped by the figure of a lion. Maybe she'd toss a few pennies in it before she left.

"But first, I want a photo of you at that piano."

Johanna didn't move. Couldn't move. "At . . . the piano? I don't play the piano."

"I didn't say you had to play it—or drape yourself across the top. I just want you to sit there." Beckett took her hand again, pulling her, step by resistant step, toward the piano. "Let me have your coat and purse and sit down for a minute. The lighting is nice here."

Johanna settled on the bench in front of the grand piano, unsure what to do with her hands. She rubbed her palms together and then finally balled them into fists in her lap.

"You look like you're afraid of the thing. Relax. It's not going to turn into some sort of monster and eat you."

"I'm not afraid . . . Don't be silly."

She just couldn't breathe.

"Open the lid. Put your hands on the keys."

"Did you see the sign right there?" She turned the framed words—her salvation—so Beckett could read them. "It says guests aren't supposed to play the piano."

"We're not guests." Beckett removed the sign, setting it on the floor, out of sight.

"Very funny."

"No one's here but us." He eased open the lid. "Just sit there for a couple of seconds and act like you're playing the piano. You can do that, can't you?"

Yes. She could do that.

Beckett was right—no one else was in the room, although she didn't know why. It was beautiful, all golds and brocades, with a fireplace right next to the piano and windows framed by heavy curtains pulled back by golden cords to showcase views of the outside.

The sooner she did what Beckett asked, the sooner they could leave.

She shook out her hands, resting her fingers on the ivory keys, finding the natural placement with ease.

Still so familiar after all these years.

"Oh, that's good. You look like you're playing a song. . . ." Beckett's voice seemed to fade into the background.

People like to say, 'Practice makes perfect,' Johanna." Her piano teacher's eyes were half-closed as she spoke, her hands clasped together. "But you play so well already. Now I want you to discover how the music can come from your heart."

"But I played the song without any mistakes—"

"Tut, tut, tut. With enough practice, anyone can perform without mistakes." Mrs. Hill's reprimand was spoken with gentleness. "But that is not the same as knowing what a song means . . . letting the song own you . . . when you move past playing and performing to something more."

"I don't understand." Johanna's fingers were restless on the keys. For so long, what she'd done had been more than enough to please her teacher. Impress her.

"You will." Mrs. Hill rested her hand on Johanna's shoulder. "You will. Now try again—but this time, don't try so hard. Relax into the music."

Johanna closed her eyes, listening as Mrs. Hill began to hum the melody of the song she'd learned for the competition. Her fingers found the notes, even as her mind tried to find what her teacher wanted her to . . . some sort of connection with her heart . . .

"I thought you said you don't play piano." Beckett's words were intertwined with the melody Johanna hadn't known she'd been playing.

As her fingers stumbled on the keyboard, Johanna came back to the present with a discordant clash of notes. "I don't."

"Then what was that?"

"I mean . . . I used to play. When I was younger." She snatched her trembling hands away from the piano as if the keys burned her. "That? That was muscle memory."

Johanna pulled the cover over the keyboard again. Stood,

brushing past Beckett, ignoring the older couple who said, "That was lovely, dear." They must have stopped just inside the room to listen to her play.

Beckett grabbed her wrist. "Where are you going?"

"I'm going . . . going to find the concierge and ask him about wedding information. I'll meet you at the car."

"I'll come with you."

"No." She twisted loose from Beckett's grasp. Stepped back, holding up her hand like a shield, and then eased the action by leaning in to give him a kiss. She gathered up her coat and purse, words tumbling from her mouth. "No. Get a few more photos. Didn't you want to go by the alcove library again because there were some people in it the first time we looked? Do that."

A few moments later, she paused in the middle of the bridge, inhaling the fresh air. Her hands gripped the railing, the metal cold against her skin. She hadn't touched a piano in years—the closest she'd been was sitting in the orchestra section the few times she'd given in to temptation and attended the symphony.

She was not that girl anymore.

The memory was an unwelcome glimpse from her past. She escaped through the main hotel. Time to think about her life now. She had a book to read. Needed to figure out how to make the pharmacy staff feel important. Valued.

Yet another Broadmoor employee smiled and greeted her as he passed by. Every single one who had walked past them today had smiled. Said hello. Some had even stopped to ask how they were enjoying their day, if they were staying at the hotel, if they were from out of town.

Maybe it was as simple as that.

The Broadmoor was known for its exceptional customer service training—and she would bet morale was outstanding, too. She stopped just before exiting the lobby of the main hotel, retrieving her phone. Maybe there was even information online. A quick google of *Broadmoor employee training* pulled up thousands of hits. She clicked on the one about customer service and leadership tips.

"Come on, come on," she whispered. "Tell me something that will impress Miller."

She scanned the article, and her eyes locked on a quote in point five: *"You can teach a turkey to climb a tree, but why not hire a squirrel?"*—considered an unofficial Broadmoor hiring slogan. It went on to say that the Broadmoor didn't limit its selection pool of employees but looked for the best of the best from around the world.

Axton Miller's triumph in getting her promotion was still fresh in her mind.

She was the turkey and he was the squirrel.

Johanna closed the browser. It was like she'd been trying to one-up the man and he'd already anticipated her move and double one-upped her. He'd probably read this blasted article.

Fine. She was a fast learner. She might not like how the man played the game, but she wasn't going to make it easy for him to ruin her career and fire her. She'd spend the rest of the weekend learning enough of the lingo to make him think she wanted to play along. That she supported his feel-good team approach. In the meantime, she'd also gather the statistics proving what she'd said about overall efficiency. A nice one-two punch to counter his attempt to take her down.

It was the morning after my last Girls' Night with Harper.

Try as I might, I still couldn't quite comprehend the reality that there would be no more evenings with my best friend where we ate too much of all the wrong foods and talked and laughed, maybe watched a favorite rom-com like *Bringing Up Baby* or *How to Steal a Million* or tried a new restaurant and came away sane and satiated.

Harper exited the spare bedroom across the hallway, pulling her small rolling suitcase behind her. "I took the sheets off the bed."

"You didn't have to do that."

"It wasn't a problem. My mom always told me a good guest does that. Isn't it funny how our mothers' directions still follow us when we're adults?"

"Like writing thank-you notes?"

"Now that I don't do. I might send you an e-mail."

"I wasn't suggesting you do that—I mean, not to thank me. You do have to e-mail me to tell me all sorts of other things." We single-filed down the stairs, the suitcase thumping behind Harper. "Do you need any help?"

"No. Everything else is in the car—or on its way to North Carolina in the moving van."

The remains of our bagel-and-coffee breakfast sat on the kitchen island. "I made sure you've got fresh coffee in your travel mug."

"What travel mug?"

"The one I bought you for the trip." I nodded to the purple stainless steel container. "Surprise! I figured you needed something new."

Harper hugged me, her arms gripping me tight. How many hugs had we shared since she'd arrived last night?

"I do love this kitchen—it'll be perfect once the new floors are in." Was her comment an honest compliment or an attempt to forestall any tears? Probably both. "Zach made sure everyone did a beautiful job. So, you still think it was worth all the extra time?"

"Yes, and all the extra money, too. I mean, you hear other people's renovation horror stories, but somehow you hope you're going to skip that part. But I guess I wasn't being realistic. I keep reminding myself that ours wasn't as bad—or as costly—as some people's."

"Perspective, right?" Harper winked.

"I guess so."

Perspective—the great equalizer. Life could always be worse when I forgot to look at it through the lens of perspective. But doing that didn't mean there weren't problems to deal with. Putting something in perspective didn't erase the issues you faced. Didn't mean you could ignore them.

Harper's smile was the same one she'd pasted on the day Trent had walked out on her, when she'd believed he would come back to his senses—come back to her. The same one she'd worn when she'd cheered me through chemo and radiation.

Perspective helped you get through the hard times, but it didn't mean you could fix anything. Not that I was going to throw that cold dash of reality in my friend's face right before she hit the road to her chance for a new beginning.

"I have a gift for you."

"Another one? I really wish you hadn't. This—" she held up the insulated coffee mug—"I can fit in the car. But anything else . . ."

"It's not that big—and it's nothing ridiculous like a puppy to keep you company."

"You're too good a friend to do something like that."

I retrieved the glass jar filled with positive sayings Harper had given me. Placed it on the kitchen island. "I figured you might need this."

Harper shook her head, pushing the jar toward me. "What? No. This is yours."

"I took a photo before I removed the sayings from the mirror and put them back in the jar. So in a sense, I still have every single quote."

Harper removed the lid, sifting the slips of paper through her fingers. "I don't remember the jar being this full."

"I added a few of my own." I ran my fingers through my hair. "And I plan to text you every day with a quote—just like you texted me."

"Thank you."

I was only giving back to Harper what my friend had given me—a jar full of encouragement. A tangible reminder of our friendship.

Now Harper's fingertips traced the outline of the jar. Our friendship was changing . . . from Harper giving me so much to a season when I could give back, even as Harper moved away.

Trying to hold my friend close even as I let her go.

"Are you excited?"

"About a solo road trip to the Outer Banks? No. Not really. But I'll stop and see some friends and family along the way. That will make it easier."

"Does Trent know you're moving?"

"No. I thought about telling him. But then I realized he doesn't care. I mean, that's the point, right?" Harper's laugh was forced. "Talk about perspective."

In that moment, it was as if Harper used the all-powerful perspective button to mute her emotions. Like putting a silencer on a loaded gun so you wouldn't hear it go off—but the bullet was shot all the same.

I wanted to tell her not to pretend—with me or with herself. But she needed to do whatever was necessary so she could leave the life she'd hoped for behind.

"Are you and Geoff okay? I haven't seen much of him—"

"He knew we'd want time together last night—and he's not much for good-byes."

Harper touched my shoulder, her smile gentle. "Jill. This is me, remember?"

Of course Harper wouldn't let me keep things surface, even if she was leaving in less than an hour.

"No. No, we're not okay."

"What do you mean?"

"He's told me why he doesn't want children."

Harper hesitated for a moment, searching my face as if trying to guess what I was going to say. "Why?"

"He had . . . *has* an older brother."

Harper's eyes widened.

"Brian was rebellious and he ran away from home when he was seventeen. Geoff and his parents have no idea where he is now."

"But that doesn't make sense."

"I know it doesn't make sense." I pressed my lips together. Tamped down my emotions. I knew how to use a silencer, too. "But there's no talking to him about it. He's gone back to working late and leaving early. And I can't tell him to stop feeling a certain way."

"So what now?"

"What now? We're married—until death do us part, right?" Oh, I hoped my words hadn't gone astray and wounded Harper. "So . . . nothing. We don't talk about it. I imagine we'll figure out some way to get over this. Or through it. One of us will give in. I suppose it'll be me."

"But you want children."

"Yes. And for some reason, trying to take steps against infertility before my cancer treatment didn't indicate that to him."

"Why didn't he say something back then?"

"That's a very good question—but then Geoff had an answer for that, too." My husband seemed to have an answer for everything. "He said something about bad timing. I'd already said yes to Geoff when he asked me to marry him. And that was my first yes, wasn't it?"

I'd finally said out loud the thought that had been whispered over and over in my mind.

"Your first yes?"

"I said I'd marry him—what do I do now? Start saying no when things get hard? It seems like marriage comes down to whether we say yes or no to one another . . ."

I'd been debating all of this by myself, my answer shifting back and forth as if I were running from one side of a teeter-totter to the other, trying to keep it going up and down all by myself. Exhausting myself. Up. Down.

How was I supposed to choose?

The question followed me as I walked Harper to her car, carrying the glass jar and setting it on the passenger seat.

"I'm not very good at good-byes." Harper played with her car keys.

"Can we just not say good-bye?"

"What do we say then?" A smile twisted my best friend's lips even as tears filled her eyes.

I shrugged. "How about something like 'Talk to you soon'?"

"Or 'Text you soon'?" Harper giggled. "Or 'FaceTime you soon'?"

"Or 'I'll come visit you soon.'"

"I like that idea best of all." Harper locked eyes with mine. "I love you, Jillian. You're the best friend I've ever had."

"I love you, too, Harper. Just because you're moving cross-country, don't think you're getting out of best friend duty."

"We can still do Girls' Night long-distance, right? Skype?"

"Sure. We can eat snacks and watch the same movies together."

Harper pulled me into one of her bone-crushing hugs. "What am I going to do without you?"

"You've still got me. We've still got each other. We're a text or a phone call away, right?"

"When you say it that way, it doesn't sound so bad."

"New adventure—it's a good thing."

"Of course it is."

"I want to hear all about the beach life. Photos and . . . and everything. It's time you got on Instagram."

"You're texting me daily positive thoughts, right?"

"I promise."

I hung on, not wanting to accept another loss. Not because of cancer, but because of Harper's choice. I had to believe this was the best for my friend, or I couldn't let her leave. Neither of us moved. Neither of us breathed.

And then I stepped back, pushing Harper away. "Go on now. Be safe."

I had to hope for the best for Harper. And for myself.

Johanna set her travel mug next to the copy of *The Power of Positive Leadership*. It might not be dog-eared, but she'd read it. Every last page. Her second cup of coffee, brought from home, would do her more good than what the café served—even if they went out of their way to hire baristas who made it to order. And there would be no need to thank her new boss for anything. They would meet. Discuss the book. She'd tell him her suggestion—and then they'd part ways and be done with these coffee sessions.

Dr. Miller would not have the advantage this morning.

Until he arrived, she'd clean out her in-box. There was a reason efficiency had been up while she'd been interim pharmacy director.

She'd just finished skimming an article about patient engagement when a pair of dark-brown dress shoes appeared on the tiled floor beside the table. Johanna set her phone aside, facedown. Glanced up.

"Good morning, Johanna." Dr. Miller's smile creased the tan on his face, deepening the lines around his eyes and mouth.

"Good morning." She silenced her phone, tucking it in her purse to prove he had her complete attention.

"I saw you had coffee already." He motioned with the hand not holding a white to-go cup.

"I brought it from home."

He pulled out the chair across from her. "Did you have a nice Thanksgiving?"

Fine. She supposed they had to start with small talk.

"Yes. I spent it with my family and my fiancé."

"That's nice. My family and I decided to take a break from unpacking boxes and go skiing in Breckenridge. Everyone came back in one piece."

Weekend ski trips—they were one way to keep up on his tan. "A good weekend, then."

"I managed to keep the twins off the black diamond runs. They're both daredevils, but they're not quite ready for those yet." Dr. Miller twisted his wedding band. "Do you ski?"

"Some. It's been a while."

"What do you like to do for fun?"

Couldn't they just skip the get-to-know-you questions and talk about the book?

"I work out several times a week. Pilates. And I like to cook." Was that enough? "And . . . I'm in a book club with my sisters."

There. The book club was finally good for something.

"Oh, really? My wife was in a book club for several years back in Tucson. She misses it. She's hoping to find another one now that we're living here."

"This is just my two sisters and me . . ." She sounded rude. "We're all so busy, it's a way to make sure we see each other on a regular basis."

Now she'd exaggerated things to her boss—making it sound like she and Payton and Jillian cared about each other so much that they'd formed a book club to foster closeness. He probably imagined them sitting around a fireplace, drinking frothy cappuccinos, and reading a trendy bestseller.

Time to stop all this small talk and get down to business. She tapped the leadership book, retrieving her notes from inside the front cover. "I started reading the book, as you requested. Finished it, actually. And then I was at the Broadmoor last Friday with my fiancé—"

"Skipped the Black Friday sales, did you?"

"Yes." Johanna added a brief laugh. She had to at least pretend to appreciate the man's sense of humor. "The Broadmoor is known worldwide for its customer service. I noticed how every time we passed any employee, they greeted us. Said hello or good afternoon—at the very least, they smiled and nodded."

"Okay."

"It got me thinking about our employees. How we should encourage them to be pleasant to people they interact with in the hospital." Johanna backtracked. "Of course, I'm not saying they aren't already doing this, but it's always a good thing to remind them to smile. Say hello. To each other, other employees, patients. It will create a better mood overall."

"That's a good idea." He seemed to consider her suggestion. "I think the two of us should model that behavior for a few weeks before we ask outright for any changes, don't you?"

"Ye-es." He wanted her to smile? Fine. She'd smile.

"Instead of just saying, 'I saw this at the Broadmoor, so let's do it, too,' our employees will have experienced it firsthand—seen what we want them to do."

"Right."

"Back to the book. You said you read all of it?"

"Yes."

"You did what I asked you to do—and then some." He

leaned forward, his hands encircling his cup of coffee. "But you're not buying it, are you?"

Johanna shifted in her seat. "I don't know why you'd say that."

"First, you came here offering me an idea, not wanting to talk about something from the book."

"You asked me to read it. I did."

"Tell me one thing you underlined in the book—you know, something that stood out to you."

Ha! She'd gone through the motions of underlining sentences here and there—ones she suspected he would like—but she would never have read the book if Dr. Miller hadn't turned it into an assignment.

They were playing a game of professional dodgeball. She was trying to make the man happy, but he didn't want to know what she really thought.

His gaze hadn't wavered from her. Had he even blinked since they'd started talking?

"You wanted an idea about raising morale. I gave you an idea. And you agreed it was a good one."

"If all I wanted were suggestions, I could put up a suggestion box in one of the break rooms." Now he blinked. "I'm trying to figure out if we can work together as a leadership team."

He hadn't exactly put all his cards on the table, but he'd given her a glimpse of them. Fine. She'd call it.

"If you're just looking for some reason to fire me, why did I waste a long weekend reading some rah-rah motivational book?"

"You're an excellent pharmacist, Johanna." His words

should have encouraged her, but they seemed to hit a brick wall. "You have great credentials. I also know you wanted the pharmacy director position. I wasn't the one who hired me instead of you—but I did accept the position."

"I know—you have the expertise with the off-site cancer center."

"True. But Dr. Lerner also told me from the start that they liked the fact that I've turned around two other pharmacy systems struggling with morale and turnover problems—because that's a problem here at Mount Columbia."

He might as well have stood up and shouted, "You're fired" right then.

Johanna's skin chilled. She wanted to find the words to defend herself, but all that came out were repetitions of what she'd said before.

"I told you, Dr. Miller—we're performing well."

"At what cost?" Miller's voice lowered. "In terms of both money and our reputation, we'll run out of good people who want to work here. And then all those statistics you keep talking about? They'll fail."

She had no response.

"That's why I was hired, Johanna. And that's why I need to know if you're willing to be on my team. We want the same thing—success. We do things differently. I need to know if you can change."

"Of course I can change."

Dr. Miller rose to his feet. "Then prove it."

And with those words, he turned his back on her and walked away.

20

I SHOULD DO SOMETHING more to make today feel festive—more Christmassy. But tuning Spotify to holiday music would have to do. And there was the evergreen wreath, complete with a simple red bow, on the front door—thanks to some industrious high school kid showing up to sell greenery last week. With the kitchen floor still not finished, it was impossible to think about asking Geoff to pull out decorations and a tree, adding more disorder to the chaos.

I'd insisted on hosting round four of our book club, but it would be a bagels-and-cream-cheese kind of affair, with orange juice sufficing for fruit.

"No sign of snow." Payton hung her coat on the rack by the front door. "I wonder if we'll have a white Christmas."

"It's only the first day of December." Johanna shook her head, settling on the couch and balancing her travel thermos of coffee. I was tempted to ask if she had one for every day of the week, but refrained.

"Never too early to wish for snow on Christmas."

"Payton, do you want coffee?"

"Juice is fine. I drove through Starbucks on my drive down."

I joined Johanna on the couch, my book sitting on the coffee table—right where I'd abandoned it weeks ago. When was the right time to confess I hadn't read a single page since the last time we met? That it was easier to scroll through Facebook laughing at inane cat and dog videos or memes, skipping everyone else's posts about how their life couldn't be better, their children more perfect—or worse, political wrangling that never swayed anyone's already-settled opinion.

Might as well go first—live the "confession is good for the soul" principle. One day I needed to figure out who said that.

I twisted my engagement ring and wedding band around my finger. "I'm going to be honest with both of you and admit I haven't read any more of this book."

"What?" Johanna looked as if I had just said I had a new book for us to read—but I wasn't that Thatcher sister.

"I wanted to. I liked the first chapter. But I—I just haven't been able to."

"What do you mean?"

Why was Johanna so surprised? Did she really expect me to get my life in order in four weeks?

"If you'd stop interrupting her, maybe she could explain." Payton stepped up, ready once again to take Johanna on.

"You know what? I'm not up to you two arguing today."

My words silenced my sisters. They both looked like I had yelled at the top of my lungs.

"I'm not climbing back in the ring with you two. I'm done being the referee every time you decide to duke it out. We formed a book club, not a fight club."

Now that I'd said all of that, part of me wanted to return to my assigned position in between Johanna and Payton. Or even better, go upstairs, crawl back into bed, and go to sleep. But I was going to stay. Talk this out.

I pressed the heel of my palm against my forehead. "I lost my job at the bank because of this stupid chemo brain. And I can't get a job for the same reason. I should have all the time in the world, right? But no matter how much time I have, I just can't function. I wake up . . . and I'm tired. All the time. I struggle to get things done. Going to the grocery store to get the stuff for today, I forgot to get the fruit for the fruit salad . . . and Winston's dog food. And the toilet paper."

"We all do that, Jill."

"Sure. Sometimes. But this is my life, Payton. Every single day. All day."

"You'll get better, right?" A faint echo of Mom's voice laced Payton's words. "It'll just take time."

"I don't know. Maybe. Some people—breast cancer survivors, researchers—say yes, you get over this in three months." I sipped some orange juice, welcoming the tangy relief on my dry throat. "Well, I'm past that expiration date, obviously.

Others say they're still struggling with symptoms years after their treatment."

I'd been honest with my sisters this far . . . why not be completely candid?

"And because I can't get pregnant—now or maybe at all—I thought Geoff and I should look into adoption . . . but Geoff said no. Not just no to adopting, but no to any children at all. Ever."

"What?"

"Why?"

Johanna's and Payton's questions hit me at the same time. A duo of quick, sharp verbal stabs.

I choked back the tears threatening to stop me from telling them everything. "Oh, now this . . . this is when it gets interesting. It turns out that Geoff has an older brother, Brian, who ran away when he was seventeen. And because of how his brother abandoned the family, now Geoff doesn't want to have children."

"That doesn't make sense." Johanna spoke the words with authority as if I'd never thought of that.

"I know it doesn't! But Geoff's decision is all tangled up in his head and it makes sense to him. He'll marry me with all my mess and the possibility my cancer might come back, but the thought of having a child, of being a father . . . because of what happened when he was a teenager . . . he can't go there."

Trying to explain my life to Johanna and Payton, my husband's decision, was like trying to explain math to someone when I didn't understand it myself. All the numbers and symbols jumbled together, creating white noise in my head.

"I'm so sorry, Jill. I just never imagined . . ." Payton's voice trailed off.

"It's crazy, right?" I rubbed my hand over my eyes. "Sounds like a soap opera, but it's my life. The reality is staring me in the face every morning when I wake up. I mean, I have trouble remembering a lot of things, but there's no forgetting this."

We sat in silence for a few seconds, and then Johanna's whisper positioned her front and center.

"If the theme for this morning is honesty . . . I might as well confess work is a bit of a mess right now." Johanna set her thermos on the coffee table, moving a coaster in place before she did so. "And this isn't some sort of sisterly one-upmanship, Jilly."

"What are you talking about? Aren't you enjoying your promotion?"

"I never got the promotion. Months ago when I announced to the family that I was the pharmacy director? That wasn't the truth. I was made the *interim* director while they were doing the hiring search." She rubbed her palms against the material of her pants. "I'd been all but promised the job by my boss when he retired. And then a late applicant showed up and trumped my résumé with his."

"Johanna!"

"Why so shocked, Jill? Because I lied?"

"No . . . no. I'm so sorry." I could only imagine how disappointed Johanna was. "I know how much you wanted that promotion."

This was like finding out your crisp, new hundred-dollar

bill was counterfeit. Johanna's life was always so perfect. She didn't make mistakes. She always had a plan—and then she executed it, the way she wanted it done, when she wanted it done.

What else had she told us during the past six months that was false?

"I know you've got to be upset, Johanna."

"Thanks." Johanna's curt reply brushed aside Payton's attempt to understand.

"How's it going with the new director?" I rushed in with a question, hoping to cover up Johanna's brusqueness.

"Oh, well, there's the other lovely part of all of this. We do not get along. At. All. He's like some life coach on steroids and a steady diet of coffee chased with Mountain Dew."

I wanted to laugh at Johanna's over-the-top description but didn't dare. "Are you going to quit?"

"I guess that's the question. Am I going to quit . . . or is he going to fire me?"

Payton surprised both Johanna and me with a laugh.

"What's so funny?" Johanna sounded more irritated than curious.

"It looks like the Thatcher sisters have found their common ground at last."

"What do you mean?"

"We're all a mess. Ironic, isn't it?"

Not Payton, too. "I thought you loved being back in college and coaching the high school team."

"No real complaints about my college life . . . except I'll never enjoy taking tests and writing papers."

"Then what's going on?"

"Zach's in love with me—"

"Everyone knows that," Johanna scoffed.

"And we agreed we can't have a relationship."

"You can't have a relationship? What does that even mean?" Johanna's focus was now lasered on Payton. "You love the guy, right?"

"Johanna, you may not understand this, but Zach's a Christian and I'm not."

"This is about religion? So tell him he can believe what he wants—kind of like you rooting for the Broncos and him rooting for the Chiefs, or if he was a Democrat and you were a Republican."

"That's not how it works."

"People make that work all the time. They just don't talk about it during the play-offs or election season."

Payton was sinking farther back into Geoff's chair. "Johanna, can we please not argue about this today?"

Johanna crossed her arms, her expression softening. "Fine. No arguing."

And this . . . this was a modern-day miracle for our family.

Payton teared up again. But was it because of Zach or because Johanna backed off?

If no one else would, I was going to celebrate this occurrence. "Well, we may feel like we're sitting at the bottom of the barrel, so to speak, but we're together, right?"

Payton sniffed, offering a smile. "That's true."

"Isn't this when we brainstorm how to get out of here?" Johanna, ever the leader, was already planning our exodus.

"No." I raised my coffee mug. "We enjoy the moment."

"Are you kidding me?"

I raised my coffee higher, motioning to my sisters. "Here's to the Thatcher sisters, together at last."

Payton raised her coffee cup. "Together at last."

Johanna shook her head. "You two are crazy."

"Come on, big sister."

"Fine." Johanna raised her thermos. "Together at last."

The music of our combined laughter, such a rare sound, lasted for a moment.

Johanna lowered her cup, staring us both down with her "Listen up, because I'm the big sister" glare. "But we're not staying down here for long."

"Agreed." Our voices melded together again in a promise, a family likeness in our smiles.

21

I RAN MY HAND along the pewter-colored countertop, trying to overlook how it didn't flow into a waterfall edge as I'd hoped. I focused on the beautiful backsplash with pewter-and-stone accents that one of Zach's friends, who was learning how to install tile, had designed at half what the labor would have normally cost us.

"So, even though you've had to make adjustments, are you happy with the kitchen?" Payton's question pulled me from my assessment of the room.

"Yes. In some ways, I like it better."

Just then, Winston skittered through one of the unexpected adjustments to the kitchen, which was fast becoming one of my favorites—the single back door with a large, multipaned glass window to let in the sunlight for me . . . and a doggy door for Winston.

"Zach calls that door 'a moment of accidental brilliance.' Whatever it is, I'm glad we ended up with it rather than the French doors I'd wanted."

"I think Winston likes it better, too." Payton ignored the mention of Zach's name.

"We all do." I sidestepped past Winston. "You want some coffee?"

"No, thanks. I'm meeting with Sydney to finalize plans for the beginning of club season after this." Payton bent and picked up Winston, who had been dancing around her feet, demanding attention.

"Right. Can I get you some water, then?" When she agreed, I retrieved two bottles of water out of the fridge. "I've never been so thankful to have a mostly functioning kitchen again in my life."

"So the floor is the last thing left to do?"

"Yes—and that'll be installed next week, now that the right flooring has arrived. Zach said between that and a few final touches here and there, we should have everything complete by Christmas."

"And then you and Geoff and Winston—" she ruffled his ears—"will have the house all to yourselves again."

"We're all looking forward to that. But Zach has been great through all this—and I know he helped us out, gave us a price cut. Because of you."

"Well . . . that's just who he is." Payton's face remained neutral at every mention of Zach, as if she didn't know him.

"Come on, Payton, I know you miss the guy."

"I'm fine."

I wasn't buying it, but I hadn't asked her to come by to argue about that.

"How about we go sit in there? I'll bring the water." I motioned toward the living room. "I appreciate you coming by . . . because I wanted to talk to you about something."

"You did? What?"

"Well, Zach actually suggested I talk to you . . . after I talked to him about some of it."

Payton settled Winston in her lap. "I don't follow."

"During our book club the other day you said that you and Zach can't be together because he's a Christian and you're not."

Payton's mouth twisted. "Right."

"I don't understand. If you love him and he loves you, why can't you guys just agree to disagree?"

"You mean like Johanna suggested? It doesn't work that way, Jill." Payton's attention never strayed from Winston. "Zach's faith is too important for him to want to be with someone who doesn't believe the same thing he does. And besides, the Bible says a believer shouldn't marry an unbeliever."

"But I thought you believed in God."

"I do believe in God. But there's more to it . . . to faith . . . than that." Payton closed her eyes. Hesitated, as if gathering her thoughts. "I thought you wanted to talk about something else—not about me."

"I'm not trying to fix you and Zach. We're not in high school anymore, so I know that's not my job. I'm trying to understand you a little better before I talk about me."

"I'm sorry, but I don't want to talk about me . . . about Zach right now. It's just too hard." Payton twisted off the cap of the water bottle but didn't take a drink. "What's going on with you?"

"I thought when I married Geoff that I'd be happy, but I'm not." I didn't know if my admission surprised me or Payton more. "Isn't that a horrible thing for me to say?"

"Surprising, yes. And honest. I think we've both seen enough marriages end in divorce that we know it doesn't guarantee happiness."

"I guess I somehow thought Geoff and I would be different." I shook my head. "It seems like I got engaged and then the past year of my life has been one long undoing. No more good health. No dream wedding. No perfect husband. No . . . no . . . no . . ."

"And no children."

"No children." Saying the two words seemed to scrape my throat raw. "How can Geoff do this to me?"

I'd forgotten I was even talking to Payton until she'd stated the blatant truth I lived with every second of the day. Only sleeping allowed me to forget. It was as if I was laying all my losses on the table, trying to sort them out, going through the emotional debris of the last year. Which reaction was real? Which one was fueled by fatigue?

"My life feels like . . . well, more like a house renovation."
Great. I was back to that word picture, the same one I'd used
when I talked to Zach. I could only hope Payton understood. "Every time I turn around, something else is wrong.
My emotions are as exposed as the walls of my kitchen during the beginning of the work, when they'd stripped out the
drywall to rewire the house."

I stopped, unsure if I was saying too much.

"Go on."

"I love Geoff. And I believe with all my heart that he loves
me. But I don't know him anymore." I pressed my hands to
my face. "That sounds like a line in a movie!"

"It's understandable."

"You know how I got through cancer, Payton?"

"I know Geoff helped you . . ."

"A glass jar full of quotes like 'One positive thought in the
morning can change your whole day' and 'Every day may not
be good, but there's something good in every day' and 'This
too shall pass.'"

"Okay."

"Now I'm facing this huge reality that I won't ever have
kids and I can't think of one positive thought to help me
live with that reality. Not that it matters because I gave the
jar back to Harper so she could take it with her to North
Carolina. I thought she might need all those 'You can do it'
statements more than I do."

Payton took a sip of her water. "I can understand why
this is so upsetting to you, Jill, but I'm not sure why Zach
suggested you talk to me—"

"Payton, you're not who you were a year ago. You . . . you dealt with Pepper's death after avoiding it for ten years. Told the truth to the family. You handle Johanna better—"

"Sometimes, Jill. Sometimes."

"What helped you?"

"Zach helped me. His faith . . ."

"But don't you have faith, too?"

"I don't know. I'm still trying to figure it out, still asking questions . . ." Payton paused, pressing her lips together. "Yes, I believe in God, but there are still things I'm confused about. . . . I—I think you should talk to Zach again."

"But he told me to talk to you."

Payton stared at me for a moment, seeming to struggle for words. Then she stood, shaking her head. "I can't help you . . . except to say talk to Zach. Or someone whose faith is stronger than mine. I can't offer you anything when I'm trying to find my own answers."

I stopped Payton before she rushed out of the house. "I'm sorry for upsetting you."

"No, I'm sorry that I couldn't help you." Her smile wavered. "I . . . I just don't have any answers for you. Or for me."

22

THE FIRST OFFICIAL PRACTICE of Club Brio's "evens" teams was over. This was the first chance for the girls who'd been selected for two teams of fourteen-year-olds, two teams of sixteen-year-olds, and one team of eighteen-year-olds to run through a few drills and line up on opposite sides of the net for a low-key scrimmage.

Payton liked the looks of her sixteens team. Her setter had good hands and was just as excited to work with a left-handed middle as Payton was to coach her. Her libero was going to rock the back row. Now all she had to do was make certain her pin hitter positions were anchored down—and that she was prepared to back up Sydney's "no drama on or off the court" speech given earlier this evening. She could only hope the girls' parents went along with the no-drama edict, too.

Sydney hugged one of the younger girls from a fourteens team—a new setter who had come over from another club—and waved good-bye to the girl's parents as Payton did a final check of the gym for random volleyballs that had been overlooked during cleanup.

"Where's Zach? I expected him to be hanging out at the gym, watching his favorite coach, waiting for the chance to take you to coffee." Sydney grabbed one side of the canvas ball cart, rolling it across the gym as she walked backward toward the equipment room. "Or are you meeting him somewhere?"

"Um, no." Payton tossed two volleyballs into the cart.

"No? Just no?"

"Pretty much."

Sydney locked the equipment room, pocketing the keys. "Payton, what kind of answer is that?"

Payton called a final good-bye to Cassie, her new middle, before answering. "You know Zach and I aren't dating, right?"

"No . . . Is this a 'we were dating but now we're not' kind of thing?"

"We were never dating."

"I'm confused—because you guys certainly looked like a thing."

As she shrugged into her hoodie, Payton wanted to admit she was confused, too—but she wasn't. She knew exactly what was going on—or rather, why nothing was going on between Zach and her.

Why the necklace Pepper had left her had become some sort of symbol of the religious and romantic mess of her life. Give the right answer, believe the right way, and she got to wear the necklace. She got God and Zach, too.

Some nights she fell asleep and dreamed she and Zach were back in the cabin, back in the kitchen . . . and that she ignored her hesitation and held on to him, told him she loved him, promised she'd never let go . . .

And then she woke up. Stark, unsatisfying reality replaced her wishing.

But she'd survived sleepless nights and troubling dreams before. She would again.

She doubted she'd ever figure out what she believed about God. If she believed in Him for herself alone. And then Jillian asked her questions. What a waste of time.

"What's holding you back from being with Zach?"

"I am."

"What does that mean?"

"It means Zach's a Christian and I'm . . . I'm still trying to figure out what I believe. Why I believe."

"But aren't you going to church with him?"

"Yes, I was. But I know enough to know attending church isn't the same as believing in what . . . in who Zach believes in."

"So you don't even believe in God?"

"I do. More than I used to."

"That's an unusual answer."

"Sydney, I grew up in a family that didn't talk about God. We didn't go to church. I mean, we weren't even one of those families that went to church on Christmas and Easter." Payton sank onto a bottom bleacher, the metal cold through her sweatpants. "When Pepper started hanging with Christians before she died, I was so hurt and angry that I didn't want to hear anything she had to say. And at first, I was hostile toward Zach, too—for a lot of reasons, but I definitely didn't want to hear anything he had to say about God."

"So what changed?"

"I did, I guess."

"What do you mean?"

"This past year, with everything that went on with Jillian, and me telling my family the truth about the snowmobile accident that killed Pepper . . . I changed. And Zach became a friend. Someone I trusted. He never pushed what he believed. I got curious."

Retelling the story, even in shortened form, was like . . . not a walk down memory lane . . . more like cruising through a familiar neighborhood, maybe one you grew up in. Passing by houses you remembered. You didn't want to move back there because not all the memories were pleasant, but you wanted the chance to recall some things. Some of the neighbors. Some of the days gone by.

The gym had gone dark, just the emergency lights on, and Payton hadn't even noticed. They needed to leave. But she wanted to stay. Wanted to hide.

She at least needed to offer Sydney the chance to go home to her husband and kids. She wasn't one of the teens Sydney was coaching—mentoring—anymore. But just like years ago when Sydney had been her coach, Payton still valued her insight.

"We should leave."

"Keep talking." Sydney leaned over so that their shoulders touched. "So the lights are out. It's not like anyone is going to lock us in. I've got the keys."

Payton bumped their shoulders before continuing, a silent thank-you for Sydney's understanding.

"Curiosity—even a strong curiosity—isn't the same thing as believing like Zach does. Like Pepper did. Zach and I both know we can't be more than friends if all I am is curious—no matter what we feel for each other. Lately it's like he's pushing me to decide what I believe so we can finally move forward, admit that we love each other."

"Why do you say that?"

"Oh, little things like saying, 'You want to talk about the pastor's sermon?' or 'What did you think of the book I gave you?' Or he just happens to find another book he thinks I might like." Payton groaned. "I'm in college! I barely get through my required reading for my classes."

"Payton . . ."

"And then he told Jillian to come talk to me about her problems . . . as if I could help her. How could I do that when I don't even know what I believe for myself?"

"Payton, this is Zach—the guy you said you trust. Do you really think he was setting you up somehow? That he was pressuring you in some covert way by sending Jillian to talk to you? Maybe he really thought you could help your sister by being there for her."

"I'm just confused, Syd."

"But you do love him."

"Admitting that doesn't change anything."

"You're telling me that you're nothing more than an interested bystander to Zach's faith?"

"Say I decide to go all-in with God. How can I be sure it wasn't somehow connected to Pepper? Or worse, how do I know that I don't believe in God just because I love Zach?"

"So Zach becomes your bonus prize, huh? Not bad."

Payton shook her head. "How can you joke about this?"

"Because you, Payton, need to lighten up."

"This is an important decision, Sydney."

This was like all the times Sydney had coached her through a match. The pressure would be on—the score 23–22—yet Sydney stayed calm. She'd call a time-out, gather the team in a huddle, refocus them off the score or a couple of bad plays or a bad call, and remind them to be a team and play their best. She was never one of those coaches who yelled at their players. She never got yellow carded for arguing with a ref.

Here she was, calm again when Payton was off her game. Sydney's family was waiting for her. And based on the way her stomach had just growled, Sydney was as hungry as Payton was. Still, she didn't rush the conversation.

Couldn't Payton just pretend she was in high school, let the coach call the plays?

No. Too much had happened for Payton to play make-believe.

"You're getting mental, Payton."

"What?"

"Remember when we'd be playing an important set—"

"You always told us every set was important."

"Nice to know you remember. Now don't interrupt when I'm coaching you." That quick moment of laughter eased a bit of the tension. "You always played your best—the team always played their best—so long as you didn't get stuck in your head. Stop overthinking this."

"How can I not think about this?"

"I said stop *over*thinking it. You've been trying to decide what you believe about God for months now. I know you've been talking with Zach about what he believes. Asking questions. I know you've been listening to those sermons when you're sitting in church—hearing the truth about God. That it's not about religion, but reconciliation and relationship. Am I right?"

"Yes."

"Then don't complicate what you know, what you believe, with Pepper and Zach."

Without her realizing it, Sydney had slipped her arm across Payton's shoulders, pulling her close.

The simple embrace reminded Payton that she wasn't alone.

"What do you believe, Sydney?"

Sydney shook her head. "Oh no. We're not going there. Not tonight."

"What? We can talk about what I believe or don't believe, but I can't ask you what you believe about God?"

"No, you can't. Not now. You're already weighed down by Pepper's faith. By Zach's faith. I'm not about to toss my faith into the mix. But I do want you to know that whatever you decide, I'm here for you, Payton. Nothing changes that."

"I didn't ask you a fair question, did I?"

"Timing is everything."

"Yes."

Through the years, Sydney had offered to pray for her and other girls on the teams, so Payton knew she believed in God. She knew Sydney's faith was important to her, even though she didn't talk about it unless she was asked. Yet, here Payton had asked, and Sydney refused.

And for good reason.

Maybe part of Payton hoped Sydney would persuade her so she wouldn't have to wrestle this out alone . . . well, wrestle this out with God.

The sound of their breathing filled the darkness.

"Payton?"

"Yeah?"

"I love you."

"I love you, too, Syd."

"And Zach loves you—no matter what you decide."

"I know."

But that didn't mean they'd end up together.

"And God loves you, too. He always has. It's always been about more than Pepper and Zach, you know—and less than them, too."

"What do you mean?"

"Even if there'd never been Pepper and there'd never been

Zach, it would still come down to you and God—and this question." Sydney stood with her, and they walked through the gym, stopping at the front doors leading outside to the parking lot. "Saying yes to Him isn't so frightening if you can remember He loves you."

Sydney's words stayed with Payton as she drove toward Denver.

"Saying yes to Him isn't so frightening if you can remember He loves you."

She was frightened.

Not of God . . . but of getting all of this wrong. Frightened that one day, when she got to heaven—because if she believed all this, then she was saying she believed in heaven, too— she'd be face-to-face with God and He'd say, "You almost got it right, Payton. But be honest. Wasn't your so-called faith really more about what your sister wanted? And about Zach Gaines? It wasn't about Me."

Even a loving God wasn't going to overlook that kind of a self-centered miss.

But maybe . . . maybe faith wasn't so much about believing enough. Being enough. Maybe faith was realizing that the truth of who God was, and what He promised, was enough for all her doubts.

23

JOHANNA SMOOTHED the gray-and-pink paisley duvet over her bed, the material soft against her skin. She gathered the two king-size pillows, Beckett's aftershave lingering on one, and arranged them against the tall gray padded headboard, covering them with shams that coordinated with the duvet. Then she folded a pale-pink blanket across the foot of the bed. This room stood in direct contrast to every other room in her house, but this was where she came to rest.

Maybe today was the day she and Beckett would start planning their wedding.

She'd gone online several times and looked through the Broadmoor's Celebrations photo gallery and scanned the details in the virtual brochure. They'd celebrated their eighth anniversary this past summer. What were they waiting for—to reach a decade? She'd browsed several wedding dress designers to begin narrowing down her dream dress and even gone onto Pinterest and looked at wedding bouquets. She wasn't quite ready to create boards, but she'd lost herself for almost two hours in all things bridal. She knew what she liked, but there was something fun about browsing others' creative ideas. There was so much more to getting married than changing her status from "engaged" to "married" on Facebook.

Things would be quiet today, or so Beckett had promised as they'd fallen asleep last night. When he came back from his run, she'd suggest they go have a late breakfast at Garden of the Gods Café and consider possible dates. Take her iPad and look at the Broadmoor's information together.

Beckett's phone buzzed on the bedside table.

Johanna groaned.

So much for a relaxed day together, making wedding plans. This was probably the superintendent, needing him to do something urgent right away. It was always urgent, whatever it was.

A photograph of Beckett standing with his arm around a woman filled the phone screen. An unfamiliar woman, with a killer body accentuated by tight jeans and a skimpy top, identified as "Iris."

The repeated buzz of his phone was as good as an electric shock up her arm, traveling straight to her heart.

"Hello?"

A moment's silence and then, "Is Beckett there?"

Again there was silence as if the two of them were circling the phone, sizing each other up across the line. Fine. She'd go right ahead and confirm Iris's suspicions.

"I'm sorry. Beckett's in the shower right now." A white lie—but he'd need a shower when he came back from his run. "Can I give him a message?"

"No . . . that's all right. Just tell him that Iris will call later."

Touché. Pretty little Iris didn't scare easily.

"I'll do that." Johanna disconnected the call, tossing Beckett's phone onto the end of the bed as if her hand had been scorched from a lightning strike.

The woman might as well have shown up in her bedroom, asking Johanna if she could talk to Beckett.

Johanna retreated to her closet, dropping her robe to the floor, changing into black leggings and a long-sleeved purple top. She twisted her hands together, willing them to stop trembling—her entire body to stop shaking. She paced the length of her bedroom, pausing long enough to yank open the floor-length curtains, flooding the room with light. She stared out at the winter sky, not moving even when Beckett's "I'm back!" sounded through the house. His footsteps announced his approach. She only turned as he entered the room, unzipping his jacket, pulling off his cotton hat, his hair damp from his run.

"You got a phone call."

Beckett muttered something unintelligible, leaning over, his hands on his knees. "What did the superintendent want?"

"It wasn't your boss."

"It wasn't?"

"No." Johanna swallowed, tasting acid in the back of her throat. "It was Iris."

Beckett failed at a poker face. "Iris?"

"Yes. *Iris.*" She would never have those flowers in her house again. "She looks pretty based on the photo on your phone—if you like your women buxom and overly made-up. Apparently you do."

"Johanna, I can—"

"Explain? Go right ahead, Beckett. I'm waiting to hear this."

"Iris is a friend."

Of course she was.

"A friend with benefits?"

Beckett pressed his hand to his forehead. "I met her in Wyoming."

Location, location, location. As if where they met made any difference. "I see. And you became . . . friends."

"Yes."

Beckett was answering all her questions . . . and telling her nothing. How much did she really want to know?

Everything. But it appeared Beckett was going to make her drag the information out of him.

"You dated her."

"Yes."

"Did you sleep with her?"

Beckett glanced down, then back up, meeting her eyes. "Yes."

"You slept with this woman when we were engaged?"

"Oh, come on, Johanna!" He squared off with her, hands on his hips. "Do you really call this an engagement?"

His sudden attack almost caused her to stumble backward, but she dug her heels into the carpet.

"You proposed to me three years ago at our favorite restaurant. I said yes. I'm wearing a ring that you bought me, after taking me shopping, telling me to pick out whatever I liked. You keep saying, 'Let's plan the wedding.'" Johanna sucked in a breath. "Yes, I call this an engagement."

"But every time I push for us to get married, you come up with a reason to hold off—"

She took a step forward, her heart pounding in her chest, causing a rushing in her ears. "And that gives you a reason to cheat on me?"

"Johanna, I'm sorry . . ."

"Don't. Don't say it." Johanna picked up his phone from the bottom of the bed and threw it. Beckett ducked, so it hit the wall next to the door, falling to the floor.

Beckett scrambled to retrieve the phone, cursing when he saw the shattered screen. "What are you doing? What if the superintendent needs to call me?"

"Do you think I care?" She advanced another step. "You're standing here, telling me you cheated on me while you were stationed in Wyoming. . . . You're probably still cheating on me."

"No." Beckett held his hands up. "No, I'm not."

"I'm supposed to believe that when Iris just called you?"

"I don't know why she called—"

"Get out!" Johanna shoved his shoulders. "I mean it, Beckett! Get out!"

It was as if she'd spun out of control, like a top let loose of its string, spinning, spinning, spinning . . . waiting to topple over.

Beckett tried to grab her hands, but Johanna dodged his grasp and ran out of the room. He followed her down the hallway, through the dining room and living area. She pulled the front door open, turning to face him. "Leave."

"Johanna, we need to talk."

"No. No talking." She shook her head. "Get. Out."

"Come on . . . At least let me get dressed."

"I'm sorry if this is inconvenient for you." She grabbed his boots that sat by the door. His car keys from the front table. Shoved them into his arms. "Good-bye, Beckett."

This was like some scene in an awful movie. If she'd been watching it, she would have laughed at the overly dramatic female lead. Wondered why the woman was crying over this guy, even as she slammed the door on yet another apology.

Johanna pressed her hands against her eyes. She was not going to cry over a man who dated her for eight years . . . proposed to her . . . and had probably cheated on her the entire time.

But it didn't seem she had a say in the matter, because no matter how hard she tried to stop them, the tears kept coming.

And then she realized she wasn't crying for Beckett. . . . She was crying for herself.

I tugged on a bright-red sweater, smoothing the hem along my waist. Too bad I didn't have a silly pair of holiday socks or even a dangly pair of jingle bell earrings for an extra touch of cheer. Christmas was less than two weeks away and I was still struggling to find my way through this season.

The lights seemed too bright, the music too loud, the joy too forced. I found myself stuck in some sort of in-between place. I had so many reasons to be happier than I was a year ago . . . and yet, I wanted even more.

My body had fended off cancer's attack . . . and I resisted the consequences of the battle.

My relationships with Johanna and Payton? There'd been

some improvement, but we maintained our customary roles and distance, despite monthly get-togethers and the echo of Pepper's exhortation to be sisters.

I was married to a man who'd refused to abandon me when life stripped me of what little beauty I had—and now he denied me one of my heart's deepest longings.

Today . . . today I would settle for wearing a red sweater while decorating our first Christmas tree together. We might not find the elusive peace that was supposedly a part of the season, but we'd be together, navigating our way around the areas in our relationship now marked "No trespassing." Ignoring how we'd hurt each other and choosing to be a happily married couple.

"Are you coming, Jill?" Geoff's question, called from the bottom of the stairs, pulled me from my thoughts.

"Yes. I'll be right down."

Time to face the day. No, time to have a good day with my husband.

"I'm still adjusting to the house with the kitchen all finished." Geoff straightened the fresh fir tree in its stand where we'd positioned it by our front window after bringing it home last night, the outdoorsy scent filling the room.

"Christmas music playing, we're decorating our first Christmas tree, and the floor's done before the holidays, just like Zach promised. Something happened according to the original plan."

Geoff offered me a grin. "Merry Christmas to us, Mrs. Hennessey. We survived the kitchen renovation."

"Yes. Merry Christmas to us." I knelt on the living room

floor next to our single box of ornaments. "How do you think Winston will do with the tree?"

"Winston? Why would you even worry about him?" Geoff tossed his answer back over his shoulder.

"You're not worried?"

"To be honest, I had nightmares about it last night—but in the dream he was a Saint Bernard—a supersize Winston. Remember the *Beethoven* movie that came out when we were kids?"

I held up my hands as if fending off an attack of an oversize dog. "Now that would be awful."

He set down the white lights he'd been stringing to go drag a couple of boxes from behind the couch. "Not going to happen, because I got up early this morning and purchased a few childproof gates to keep Winston from messing with the tree."

"You did?"

"Yes. I decided not to wake you up to join me."

"I'm not really sure I want plastic gates all around our Christmas tree. I mean, think of how it'll look—"

"Well, think of how it'll look in here if Winston knocks over the tree." Geoff motioned around the room, frowning as if the disaster had already occurred.

"But the living room isn't that big."

"It'll be fine."

"Right. What do I know? I'm just Jillian." I muttered the words under my breath.

Geoff paused with a string of lights in his hands. "What did you say?"

"Nothing. Let's just hope Winston doesn't jump over the barrier."

"We'll keep a close watch on him the first couple of days. He's a smart boy." Returning to the lights, Geoff plugged in the strand he'd woven through the branches and stepped away. "There. That's all done."

I started sorting through the box, placing ornaments on the coffee table. "We don't have that many decorations to put on the tree."

"That will change the longer we're married. Which reminds me—" he retrieved a small package from the mantel—"here's one to add to the collection."

"What's this?"

"A gift. Something I picked up for you earlier this week."

I sat on the couch, Geoff kneeling in front of me, a smile on his lips. Inside the plain brown paper bag was a circular white clay Christmas ornament. The words *Our First Christmas Married* were encircled in hand-painted twinkly Christmas lights.

"This is perfect." I leaned forward and kissed him.

"Tradition, you know." He stole another kiss, the taste of coffee on his lips. "I figured we needed one."

"We do." I traced the words. "I'll put it up high so that if Winston does manage to get over the gates, he won't get to this."

I turned the ornament over in my hands. Here I was, worrying about our dog and using childproof gates. Protecting an ornament celebrating our first Christmas as a married couple.

Would we ever put up a *Baby's First Christmas* ornament?

The question slipped into my heart like a thorn. Quick. Sharp. For now, and possibly forever, the answer was Geoff's adamant *no*.

Better to savor his kiss. Our closeness. Today was the best time Geoff and I had spent together in weeks. The only way I could protect this was by not thinking too far ahead into the future.

By not wanting more.

Just adding the lights among the branches already made our tree look festive and would cause our small assortment of decorations to sparkle. Time to finish unpacking the ornaments—ones I'd purchased through the years while I'd been on vacation or had received as gifts. Others Mom and Dad had chosen from the family's collection and given to us after Geoff and I had eloped.

A tiny slice of cake decorated with a red rose from when I'd taken cake-decorating classes one summer.

A small frame with my high school graduation photo in it.

A blue Colorado columbine.

"Do you think your parents might let you have a few family ornaments to add to these?"

Geoff stood, hanging the ornament he'd just been given on one of the high, center branches. "My mom isn't really into sentimentality. She prefers doing themed Christmas trees every few years. Once she's done with a particular design, she gets rid of all the decorations."

"Oh."

"She mentioned she did something new this year—angels, maybe? We'll see it when we're over there on Christmas Eve."

"That'll be fun." But now I'd need to find a substitute gift for the Santa Claus ornament I'd bought them.

Between the two of us, the tree was decorated in less than fifteen minutes.

"Shall we let poor Winston out of his kennel?" Geoff stood back and surveyed our efforts. "See what he thinks?"

"Yes. He caught on pretty quickly about staying away from the kitchen."

"He does like having you home."

"That's true. More walks for him." And Winston never minded that I napped during the day—not once he learned that I'd let him up in the bed with me.

"Well, now he has a new distraction."

For the next few minutes, we sat with Winston on the floor in the living room, our backs against the couch, our shoulders and legs touching, Geoff correcting the dog when he got too close to the plastic barriers.

If Geoff was this good with Winston, surely he'd be good with children. Our children.

I shifted against the couch, unable to stop a soft sigh from escaping.

"Is something wrong, Jill?"

"You know the kind of year we've had." I remained facing forward, my eyes on the tree.

"You've done beautifully."

"Some days . . . but there were so many days I didn't feel brave. Or when I wondered why I had to get cancer."

"But we got through it."

"I know . . . but at what cost?"

"I don't understand."

I pulled the list out again. The one I never forgot. "There are some consequences you can't fix, Geoff. Effects of medication, infertility . . . finding out you don't want children." I'd said it all. "There's no changing any of it."

Next to me, Geoff stiffened. "You're acting like surviving cancer doesn't matter."

"No . . . no, that's not what I'm saying. Of course I'm thankful every day that I beat breast cancer. But being grateful for that doesn't mean these other things don't hurt. Surviving cancer isn't some massive dose of Novocain that numbs any other kind of pain in my life." I gathered a breath. "You can't have children? Take a dose of your post-cancer medication. Your best friend moved? Don't be sad because, you know, you got through a mastectomy and chemo and radiation. Cancer's gone."

"Are you ever going to be happy, Jillian?"

His words jarred me. "What?"

"Are you ever going to be happy?" Geoff twisted away from me, leaning forward on his knees. "Because I've tried, really tried, to make you happy . . . and even if I said okay to adopting—which I'm not going to do—I still don't think you'd be happy."

Geoff's question stunned me. "Is that what you think this is all about—my being happy or not being happy?"

"What else am I supposed to think?" He spread his hands wide, shaking his head. "You're always wanting more . . . more than I can give you."

His words were an echo of what I'd shared with Payton.

"I didn't realize until the last few days that I was expecting you to make me happy, Geoff. I didn't realize until right now that you feel like you have to make me happy." I wanted to touch him, to reconnect with him, but I also wanted to give him space if that's what he needed. "I'm sorry."

Winston had edged in between us, resting his chin on my knee. He always sensed when I was upset, sometimes sooner than Geoff did. "I've talked to Zach and Payton some about how I've been feeling . . ."

"You've talked to Zach Gaines?"

"And Payton, yes. I told Zach that I was struggling—"

"In our marriage?"

"Some . . . yes. And how I was struggling with the after-effects of the chemo and losing my job. I told him I felt a little like this old house—like I was undergoing some kind of life renovation." I laughed, but Geoff didn't join in. "Zach suggested I talk to Payton—and she suggested I talk to Zach. So I'm back to square one, trying to figure this out on my own."

"Why didn't you talk to me?"

I hesitated. "We haven't been communicating very well lately."

"I know you're unhappy, Jill, but you can still talk to me."

"No, Geoff, I can't." My voice cracked. "Don't you understand how you made me feel when you said I wouldn't be a good mother?"

"I'm sorry. I never should have said that. And I should have apologized sooner—"

"You might as well have been my grandfather when you said that." My body started shaking as I flung the words at him.

"What?" Geoff's eyes clouded. "That doesn't even make sense—"

"I've been . . . second-best my whole life, Geoff." I fought to speak, trying not to cry, my throat getting tighter. "The lost-in-the-middle Thatcher sister . . ."

"Why are you saying something like that?"

"Because it's true. . . . It's been true forever." Tears blurred my vision. "Just Jillian—that's me."

With those words, I buried my face in my hands and sobbed.

As Geoff tried to pull me into his arms, I resisted—a feeble attempt that lasted only a moment. Even when everything was so wrong between us, he was still my safe place. My sobs were muffled against his chest, and my tears stained his shirt, but he held me until there were no more tears left.

Geoff shifted me so that I rested against him. "Can you explain what that was about? I really want to know."

I swiped at my face with the back of my hand. Sniffled. "It won't make any sense. . . . It was so long ago."

"Just tell me. Please."

"One summer when I was twelve, I took cake-decorating classes. I had so much fun learning how to make frosting. How to make roses." I closed my eyes, gathering my breath. "Then I asked my mom if I could make my grandfather a birthday cake."

"That's a nice thing to do." Geoff kept his voice pitched low, the words rumbling in his chest.

"I worked on it Saturday afternoon. Made the icing twice. Wrote *Happy Birthday* in bright-red icing on top. It wasn't perfect—a little lopsided two-layer cake, but . . ."

"I'm sure you did a great job."

"Pops didn't think so. Mom drove me over early on Sunday so I could show him. I remember he asked where Johanna and the twins were. Nonie told him it was just me. I was always just Jillian, especially to Pops."

"She didn't mean it like that—"

"It's the truth." A reality I could never escape. "I don't know why it mattered so much that Pops like me . . . notice me. When I was younger, I would draw him pictures and he would always say, 'What is this?' I would make him cookies and he'd say something like 'Why are these cookies so flat, girl?' I thought the birthday cake would finally do it."

"What happened?"

"When we came back that night, we ate the German chocolate cake Nonie had made him—it was his favorite." Retelling Geoff the memory burned my throat. "I kept thinking they'd bring out my cake. Kept waiting. Nothing. When we were getting ready to leave, I snuck back into the kitchen . . ."

"Did you find your cake?"

"Yes. It was in the trash."

"Oh, Jill—"

"I mean, why did I ever think he'd eat my cake? It shouldn't matter after all these years . . . I'm an adult . . . but it seems like I can never get away from being 'just Jillian.' I'm stuck in the middle . . . and whatever I do just isn't good enough."

Geoff pulled me closer. "You're not 'just Jillian' to me— you never have been. I love you because of who you are. And I'm sorry I hurt you the other day. That I didn't value you."

"It's okay."

"No, it's not okay. Forgive me?"

"I do."

Memories and tears now stained the day, even as I sat in my husband's embrace. It seemed, more and more, life was a precarious balance of yesterday and today—and I had no idea what tomorrow would bring. Or how to prepare for it. How to be enough.

25

THE RUMBLE OF ZACH'S TRUCK, the crunch of the tires on the gravel driveway, preceded his arrival.

Payton leaned against the back of her car, hoping to achieve a relaxed look. Casual. Boots. Jeans. Winter coat. Beanie hat pulled over her hair. But trying to appear calm was absurd, since she hadn't seen him since before Thanksgiving—and now she'd shown up, after nothing but a text, at his cabin.

Five weeks of separation—no phone calls, no coffee get-togethers, no meeting for church, no *anything*—and she'd missed him every single day. Went to sleep longing for him—the sound of his voice, his laughter, his questions about her classes and her volleyball team—and woke up some mornings with the dream of their last conversation creating an ache inside her that lasted all day long. She wouldn't have blamed him if he'd ignored her when she contacted him yesterday morning. Deleted her "Can we talk?" text without responding. But this was Zach, and he understood her better than anyone else ever had.

He pulled the truck up alongside her Subaru, the glimpse of his profile causing a fresh ache to rise up inside her. By the time his boots hit the ground, she was on the other side of the truck.

"How long have you been here?" His question appeared in small white puffs.

"Not long. I know your Sunday morning routine."

"You were welcome to join me . . ." Zach tucked his hands into his jeans pockets. "You know that. Sorry."

"I do." She offered him a smile, trying to bridge the distance between them. "It was just that I had a long Saturday—some private lessons—and then I was up late last night, trying to finish up some things . . ."

"No problem."

He probably thought she was offering him excuses.

"Go for a walk with me?" She nodded toward the field and wooded area behind her.

If her request surprised him, Zach didn't let on. "Sure. Can we take Laz?"

"I already let him out. He's off running around." She shrugged. "Hope that's okay. He was barking like crazy."

"One of his favorite people was here—what did you expect him to do?"

Payton motioned toward the house. "You need to put anything in the cabin first?"

"I'm good." He shut the truck door, pocketing his keys.

Neither of them spoke as they left the cabin behind. The midmorning air was crisp and clean, and areas of leftover snow sparkled in the sunshine. They both headed toward Pepper's bench without either of them acknowledging their destination. In some ways, today was like returning to the beginning of their relationship—back when Payton had resisted Zach's first invitation to see the bench he'd made in honor of her twin sister's memory. Now, it was one of her favorite places to be . . . with him.

They'd both tucked their hands in their coat pockets, a light breeze tugging Payton's hair beneath the cap. Zach's arms were pulled up close against his body as if he were protecting himself.

"How've you been, Payton?"

"I wanted to tell you—"

Their words ended up in a tangle of awkward bursts of laughter.

"Before we do the 'You go first. No, you go first' thing, can I just say that I'd like to go first?" Payton rushed ahead.

"Okay."

"I've done a lot of thinking since we saw each other in November. I even had a bit of an interesting conversation with Jillian—"

"She did talk with you, then?"

"Yes, although I didn't know you'd told her to until I suggested she talk with you." This time they laughed, easing some of the tension between them. "Did she talk to you again?"

"No."

"Oh, well, maybe she's planning on it." The conversation was drifting off course. "I even talked with Sydney . . . but mostly I've been thinking since the last time I saw you. A lot."

"Has the talking and thinking helped?"

"Well, I don't think my conversation with Jillian helped her very much."

"You don't know that."

"I'm certain about that, Zach. You can't answer someone else's questions when you're still struggling with your own."

Zach nodded but remained silent.

"That's what it's been like for most of the time we've been apart. Trying to figure out who I am and what I believe. Why I believe."

"I've been . . ." Zach caught himself. "Go ahead. I promise to not interrupt again."

He was probably going to say he'd been praying for her. He had been for months—nothing would have stopped him.

"I'll start with Pepper." The threat of tears surprised her. "The truth is, I can imagine my life without Pepper. I mean, I've done that for years now. I don't think I'll ever stop missing her, but I've learned to be me without Pepper. More successfully, now that I've told my family the truth."

She paused, waiting to see if Zach wanted to comment. Nothing.

"And . . . I can even imagine life without you—although it would break my heart in a way I can't even begin to express."

Zach stumbled. Regained his footing. "I get it, Payton. I understand."

She'd known telling him this way would confuse him, but she didn't know any other way to help him understand what she'd discovered.

He kept walking, his boots crunching on the sticks and dried ground, refusing to look at her.

And she had to tell him the whole truth.

"Zach, let me finish, please. It's important for me to tell you everything."

"Fine." His voice was rough as if he was fighting a cold. His eyes red-rimmed. "I owe you that."

"So Pepper . . . you . . . but after living most of my life without God, now I can't imagine continuing that way. I'm not even sure how it happened. It's as if God's been walking alongside me for months now. As if He's been saying, 'Take your time, Payton. No rush. You've got questions? Ask them. This isn't a test. I'm only asking you one question—if you believe in Me for Me. We can figure out the particulars along the way.'"

Zach stopped walking. Turned to face her. "What are you saying?"

"I'm saying I know what I believe about God. I know that I *do* believe in God. And I believe—just for me. Not because I have to make Pepper happy. Not because I love you." Payton held her hands out, palms up. "For me, faith has been more like a slow walk toward the sunrise. Me moving toward God . . . and God moving toward me. Asking questions. Reading books. Talking with you. Watching you.

Going to church. Even my friendship with Sydney that started back in high school was part of it."

"So you and God . . . you're good?"

"Completely good. The best we've ever been."

She knew she didn't have to explain herself to Zach—make sure he approved of where she was or how this all came about. This wasn't about satisfying Zach. It was about sharing the truth with him . . . the truth that changed everything for her.

And for them.

Zach's eyes filled with tears as he pulled her close. Payton wrapped her arms around his waist, resting her head against his chest and treasuring his nearness, something she was afraid she'd lost. But too soon, he held her away from him, resting his forehead against hers.

"Not to be pushy or anything, but where does all of this leave us?"

"I love you, Zach Gaines." She framed his face with her hands, his jaw rough beneath her fingertips. "I fell in love with you as I was falling in love with God. The two are intertwined. I thought that was wrong . . . that I couldn't be falling in love with you and finding my way to God at the same time. But now I realize I wouldn't have it any other way."

His kiss took her breath away, his lips cool against hers, his hands stealing up so that his fingers tangled in the ends of her hair. "I love you, Payton. I've wanted to tell you that for so long."

"Kiss me again, please." She whispered the words, their lips close. "That was even better than I dreamed."

26

AN APOLOGY WAS NOT the best way to start her third meeting with Dr. Miller. But since she was showing up a good ten minutes late, based on the last time she'd checked her phone, there was nothing else she could do.

Johanna could have postponed the meeting. Called in sick. Struggling to sleep the last ten days had left her pale, with dark circles under her eyes. Any cover-up attempts only seemed to highlight her exhaustion.

"I'm sorry for not being here on time." Johanna pulled out the chair across from Dr. Miller, motioning for him to remain seated.

"It happens, Johanna." His eyes narrowed. "Do you want to get some coffee?"

"No. Thank you. I forgot mine at home."

"Not a fan of the café coffee?"

"No. Not really." He was probably trying to make a joke. She hadn't laughed and couldn't force even a small smile to form with her tight lips. "I like French press with fresh-ground beans and real cream. My sisters say I'm a coffee snob."

"And my wife says I'd drink mud if she set it in front of me."

Another joke. At least she'd caught on this time. Had the chance to laugh. And without meaning to, she'd provided her boss with more personal information. That should make him happy.

Of course he had the book. Again. Her copy was somewhere at home. She could tell him that she'd reread it. Even underlined more parts of it because she knew he'd wanted her to.

Or she could tell him the truth.

If she was going down, she'd go down telling the truth.

"Dr. Miller . . . Axton." Should she be formal or informal with him when she was being blunt? "The leadership book you asked me to read? I suppose if I owned the Broncos or ran Anheuser-Busch, I'd buy into the positive-leadership philosophy more. But when it comes to running hospital pharmacies, I'm more a 'know the rules, follow the rules, pay attention to the details' kind of person."

"Casual conversation over, I see." He slid his cup to the side of the table. "So you're saying that you don't see the benefit of developing strong relationships, of ensuring good communication?"

"You may think you've built a strong relationship and discover you haven't. That's why I value structure and rules."

She and the man across from her could be talking about two very different things and not even be aware of it. Sitting so close and be miles apart. And they were—he just didn't know it.

Johanna tucked her hands in her lap, shielding the now-bare ring finger on her left hand. No need to give her boss a clue that something was wrong. This was business. Not personal. Business.

"And love?"

She couldn't have heard him correctly. "What was that?"

"I assume you don't agree with the author's principle on loving tough. The need to love someone enough to work with them—to fight for them."

"The author sounds like a self-help guru."

"You do acknowledge that employees are people, right?"

"Yes."

"Well, there's something we agree on." He grinned. "Common ground at last."

Her cell phone buzzed right as Dr. Miller declared that minor victory. A quick glance proved it was Beckett. Again.

Johanna, call me. Please.

"Do you need to answer that?"

"No. It's not important." She slid her phone back into the pocket of her white lab coat. "You were saying?"

"Johanna, I was hoping for something different this morning."

Welcome to the club, Dr. Miller. You're not the only one deal-ing with disappointment.

He wanted something different? Fine.

"I can save us both a lot of time and energy." The back of her throat burned. "I . . . I quit."

She might as well be back at home, in her bedroom, staring at Beckett's phone screen just before she shattered it. Only this time, her actions—not someone else's—were destroying her future. It didn't matter. Dr. Miller was prob-ably counting down the days until he fired her. At least she'd beat him to it. Quitting like this left her in charge.

But instead of accepting her resignation, he stared at her, brows furrowed. And then, "What's going on, Johanna?"

"What's going on? The last time we met, you wanted to know if we could work together. You asked me to prove I could change. You're all about team and positive leadership and . . . and love." She forced the word past her lips. "I want things to be efficient. Black and white. I'm not interested in changing."

"What else is going on?"

"Besides the fact that I just told you I quit? Nothing."

He sat back, staring at her and doing the not-blinking thing again. "You look upset about something. Is everything okay with your family? Your fiancé?"

Oh no. They were not going there.

"Dr. Miller, you are my boss, not my friend or my mental health counselor. We are talking about work-related issues, not about things that are wrong with my personal life—not that I'm saying there are problems with my personal life."

"Fine. I'm your boss." He rapped his knuckles on the top of the wood table. "And I'm ending this conversation because I *do* think there's something personal going on that you don't want to talk about. You are too valuable an employee to lose because you are not thinking clearly."

Johanna tried to keep up. Tried to process everything he was saying. Now she understood how Jillian must feel every day. "You're not accepting my resignation?"

"No, I'm not. We haven't worked together that long, but I know enough about you to know you are not a quitter." He pushed his chair back. Stood. "I'm taking some time off between Christmas and the beginning of January. We'll talk after then. I'll contact you."

"But—"

"That's all for today, Johanna. I would tell you to take the day off, but I also know you'd probably argue with me. If you want to, take a half day."

And with those words, he left her sitting at the table.

Was everyone in the room watching them? Watching her? All she wanted to do was lay her head down on the table and, for once, let the tears fall—in public. But instead, she stiffened her shoulders. Stared straight ahead. Waited for her heart to settle back into a regular rhythm. Then she stood and exited the café, ignoring everyone else in the room.

As she passed an atrium located near the staff café, the soft notes of piano music caught her attention. For a moment, she stopped. Who would be playing a piano? The slight form of an older woman wearing a pale-blue pantsuit sat at the grand piano positioned in the atrium—where hospital volunteers sometimes performed during the day to entertain, to lift the spirits of patients and visitors . . . of employees, too.

Soft winter sunshine streamed down through the windows, surrounding the piano and the player in a golden glow. Johanna escaped into a shadowed corner and closed her eyes, exhaling as the music found its mark.

It was as if the woman offered her a cup of water, lifting the glass to her parched lips and whispering, *"Drink . . . drink."* How she longed to lean in, to accept what the woman offered. What she'd missed. To let each chord touch the dry fragments of her soul.

There'd been no music in her life for so long.

For a moment longer, Johanna stood with her eyes closed. And then she shook her head as if to dispel the pull of the music and walked away.

27

"THANKS FOR LETTING ME drop by on short notice." Payton slipped off her coat, a light dusting of snowflakes spread across the dark material and the layers of her hair.

"It's snowing?" I kept Winston snugged up in my arms, shushing his barks.

"It just started. Hey there, good boy." Payton ruffled Winston's ears before hanging her coat in the closet. She bent over to pull off her boots. "That feels so good to have those off my feet. I much prefer my volleyball shoes."

"Are you driving back up to Denver tonight?"

"Yes. It's not supposed to snow that much, and I don't worry about driving unless the roads get icy."

"Come on in." I tightened my grip on Winston, who was now determined to jump into Payton's arms. "You look nice."

"We had a Christmas party for the volleyball club tonight." She tugged at the sleeves of her soft white sweater.

"Sounds fun."

"It was. It's a chance for the girls to hang out together, get to know each other a little bit before the season starts in January." Payton followed me through the living room, sidestepping past the childproof barriers surrounding the Christmas tree, and into the kitchen. "I remember doing the same thing when Pepper and I were in club together. We always knew a couple of the girls, but some were from competing high schools."

"Competitors one month, teammates the next."

"Yep. Strange, right?" She leaned against the island. "The crazy world of volleyball. Another tradition I liked was the end-of-the-season parties. Sydney always took a moment to encourage each girl individually—saying how we contributed to the team. It was so important to me—and to Pepper, too. Sydney always saw us as individuals. Never once mixed us up."

"That's impressive. I remember how you hated it when teachers thought you were Pepper."

"Or when they thought Pepper was me. We dealt with that all through our school years. Sure, we were identical twins, but we weren't the same people. Of course, there were times we did trade places as a joke. . . ."

This conversation with Payton was some sort of optical illusion. I was talking to my sister but seeing a side of her I'd never glimpsed before—relaxed, casual, smiling . . . reminiscing about Pepper. No hesitation. No hiding. No secret marring the past, present, or future.

"Do you want coffee or anything?"

"That'd be nice. If I have some now, I won't need to drive through and get any on the way home." Payton glanced around. "Where's Geoff?"

"At work."

"I guess I shouldn't have asked. . . ."

"He's trying to wrap up a couple of projects so he can take time off between Christmas and New Year's."

"Nice."

"Well, his boss encouraged it because he has so much unused vacation time." I handed Winston to her. "Why don't you take Winnie and go sit in the living room while I fix our coffees."

"Sounds good."

By the time I carried in two mugs of coffee—Payton's sweetened with the right number of sugars, mine simpler with a single sugar and a splash of cream—she was on the couch, feet tucked up underneath her and Winston snoozing in her lap.

"That is a happy puppy."

"We're both happy." She inhaled the aroma of coffee and grinned. "This is perfect."

"It's not French press."

"I'm not Johanna."

"Point taken." I raised my mug in a salute. "So how are you?"

"That's what I wanted to talk about."

Oh.

Payton sipped her coffee, staring into the mug as if she were reading something—a script, maybe?—before saying anything. "So, the last time we talked, you were having a hard time. . . ."

"Wait . . . I thought we were talking about you."

"We were. We are. I promise this will all make sense. Okay?" Payton waited for me to nod before continuing. "And you said Zach suggested you talk to me."

I nodded again.

"I wasn't a whole lot of help to you—"

"That's why you stopped by? To offer some kind of belated apology because you couldn't help me deal with my problems while you're still dealing with your own?"

"Well, yes and no."

I set my untasted coffee aside. "I'm still confused."

"I'm sorry—for confusing you now and for not helping you back in November when you were having such a hard time."

"It's okay, Payton. You aren't required to be some sort of answer lady for me." I shrugged. "You have your own things going on in your life."

"That was the problem—I was so worried about all the right answers back then. About getting everything perfect with God. That's what I wanted to say I was sorry about. I should have just listened to you. Listened to your story. What you were thinking about. Struggling with. Maybe told you my story, if you wanted to hear it."

Payton was trying to restart a conversation that I'd walked away from weeks ago. It was like coming back to a fire that had been doused and stirring the ashes—but no spark remained. I didn't want to have this conversation, didn't want to revisit this missed opportunity.

"My story's not that important."

"Why would you say that?"

"Because it's the truth. If there's one thing I've learned since I was diagnosed with cancer—no, even before that—it's that my story . . . me . . . I'm not important."

"Jill! Who told you that?"

"Everybody. Everything. I'm stuck in the middle of all that's perfect—and reminded again and again that I'm not."

Payton's eyes widened. "That's not true!"

"You've never fought to be seen when you're surrounded by the professional perfection of Johanna and the athletic success of not one but two younger sisters. You've never had the tag of 'just' stuck on you. It's *just* Jillian. Such a small word, but it points out all I'm lacking every time it echoes in my head."

"Who said that?"

"Pops did, for one. But he got it right. Jillian Thatcher Hennessey—it's just me. Nobody important. If you're looking for me, you'll find me stuck in the middle."

Payton wanted a story? This was mine. Nothing impressive. Nothing anyone would want to read. A throwaway.

The word *just* scorched my throat even as it branded my heart.

"Jillian, that is not the truth!"

"It's the truth I've lived with all my life."

"That is going to stop today."

My weak laugh didn't even begin to push away Payton's words—to hide the fact that I'd ever wished I were more than just me.

"There were a lot of good things about our family. Football Sundays. Cookouts. We knew Mom and Dad loved us." Payton stared down at her coffee again. Shook her head. Continued. "But we didn't grow up knowing about God. That He's real. That He loves us. That having a relationship with Him changes everything we believe about ourselves . . ."

"We weren't a churchgoing family. Although I guess that changed for Pepper . . ."

"And I wouldn't listen to her. I couldn't handle how it changed her. It scared me—but not anymore."

"I know you believe in God—"

"It's more than that. I was all confused, thinking I had to believe in God for Pepper. For Zach. I realize now my relationship with God is mine—not because I have to make anyone else happy."

"That's great."

"And now I'm going to tell you what Pepper told me when I was sixteen. God is real. He loves you—like crazy, crazy loves you." Payton's laugh was strong. Vibrant. "That's what she used to say."

"Sounds like Pepper."

"Believing in God didn't change her personality, that's for sure."

I caught a glimpse of Pepper's irrepressible joy in Payton's smile. My sister looked different. Younger. Like the Payton she was before Pepper died.

Miraculous. Could believing in God do something like that for me, too?

"If I believe that—that God loves me—then what?"

"Then your story changes."

"What do you mean?"

"God started our stories the day we were born—we just never knew that growing up. The minute we realize that, things change. Our thinking changes because we're more aware of the Author of our story."

"That's an interesting way to put it."

"There's a verse—Zach would know where it is in the Bible—that says God started something good in us and He will finish it."

I shook my head. "I'm not sure I believe that."

"It's the truth." Payton leaned toward me. "That's one of the ways your story is going to change."

"When?"

"When . . . what?"

"When does it change?"

"Now. Right now."

"How?"

"Um . . . if Zach were here, he'd pray."

"Will you pray with me?"

Payton hesitated, her blue eyes wide. "I—I've never prayed with anyone except Zach—and he always prayed. I listened. I'm still new at this."

"Does being new at this mean you can't pray with me?"

"No-o."

"Okay . . ." I hesitated—but was it because Payton was nervous or because I was? "Then will you?"

Payton was quiet for so long, I almost expected her to say no. Her yes escaped on a long exhale. She stood, coming to kneel beside my chair, and held my hands. Her whispered words shook, causing me to lean in.

"God, I'm still getting used to talking to You . . . but now I'm talking to You for my sister Jillian. You're the Author of her story. I know You say that in the Bible somewhere. And I know You love Jillian just like You love me and like You love Pepper . . . and Johanna, too, but I don't think she's ready to hear that yet." Payton cleared her throat. "Anyway, I know You have lots of good things for Jill . . . and that You think she's beautiful . . . and You want to have a relationship with her so she knows You and talks to You and finds peace and hope and everything she needs right now."

As Payton prayed, I relaxed into her words . . . words that replaced the brand on my life with a blessing. It was as if someone was turning the pages in my story to a new chapter . . . something so unexpected, woven through with hope.

There was no going to sleep once Payton left. I wanted to stay awake, to hold on to the sense of newness wrapped around me. The belief that there was more to my life than I'd ever imagined . . . and I had to tell someone.

So I'd hugged my sister good-bye, gathered Winston in my arms, and waited. An hour or so later, Geoff's car pulled into the driveway, the headlights sweeping across the house. Winston went on alert, but I shushed him back asleep.

Geoff stopped just inside the front door. "I wasn't expecting you to still be up."

"It's only ten thirty. How are the roads?"

"Not bad. The snow's sticking some, but the plows are out already on the main roads and the highway. We could get a few inches."

"Payton should be fine, then."

"Payton?"

"She stopped by after a volleyball thing. Left about an hour ago. I was worried about her driving to Denver, but she said she'd be fine."

"Monument Hill might have been icy." Geoff came and sat beside me on the couch, resting his arm across my shoulders. "What are you doing?"

"I was thinking we needed to put something else on the mantel."

"On the mantel? You mean for Christmas? There's not much room."

"But something . . ."

"We've already got the candles there. And Christmas is less than a week away."

"True." I paused. "What would you think if I found a little Nativity scene?"

"Like a manger scene?" Geoff tilted his head as if trying to imagine what I was talking about. "Shepherds and wise men and stuff?"

"Yes. One of those would be nice, don't you think?"

"I guess. If you like that kind of thing."

Maybe I should have suggested we put up a gaudy light show in our front yard, with a gigantic blinking-nose Rudolph beside a waving Frosty the Snowman and thousands of multi-colored lights orchestrated to Christmas music—then at least I would have gotten some sort of reaction out of Geoff.

A subtle segue into what I wanted to talk about wasn't working. "God is a part of Christmas, right?"

"God."

"Yes. *God*. Payton talked with me about what she believes, about how she's not questioning her faith anymore. What she said made a lot of sense. In the end, she prayed for me. . . ." I wanted to beg Geoff to understand, to not pull away from me. "And I'm going to do things differently now."

"What does that mean exactly, besides wanting to put a Nativity up on our mantel?"

Geoff's question was a fair one—one that I'd been asking myself since Payton left. "I'm not sure. Except that I have more hope than I've had for a long time. And I want to try and find out more about God. Who He is and how He can help me live with the reality of what my life is like."

"What your life is like . . . because you're so unhappy with things?"

"No . . . Geoff, I love you, but like you said, you can't make me happy. You can't fix all the things I'm dealing with."

"So you're religious now?"

"I don't think so." Was that all I was? It had seemed like more when Payton prayed for me. "I don't think Payton or Zach is religious. Do you? I mean, both of them believe in

God. Love God. And they say their faith helps them. Payton almost radiated peace tonight. She could talk about Pepper without tensing up, without looking so sad. That's what I want."

Trying to explain it all to Geoff when I still had unanswered questions and when I faced his doubt, his resistance, was like trying to follow directions on a GPS when it kept recalibrating.

Geoff removed his glasses, rubbing his eyes. Placed his glasses back on. Smiled his familiar smile that so often warmed my heart. But now it looked forced. "If you're happy, then good. That's great. I'm okay with all of this."

There was that word again. *Happy.*

"I . . . I'm not asking for your approval, Geoff."

"Then what do you want me to say, Jillian?"

"Nothing. I just wanted to tell you. This is important to me. You're important to me." I hesitated for a moment. "I don't know that this guarantees me instant happiness, but I think it will change me in ways I don't even know yet."

Geoff huffed a short laugh. "I have no idea what you're talking about . . . but again, if it makes you . . . makes things better for you, that's great."

I settled back against the couch. "Thank you for that."

"How does this change us?"

I hadn't even considered the question. "I just didn't want you to be surprised if . . . if I decide to go to church. I thought I might try that. You wouldn't want to go with me, would you?"

"Church? I've only gone to church for weddings . . ."

"I know. Me, too." The words *and funerals* echoed in my head. "I'm not even sure where I'll be going. Payton said she'd talk to Zach and let me know about some possibilities in the area."

"So . . . church."

"Like I said, I thought I might start there."

"Fine." Geoff held up his hand. "I'm not approving . . . just processing."

"I know. I still am, too."

"Is it okay with you if we head upstairs? It's been a long day."

"Sure."

"If you want to turn off the tree, I'll get Winston. Come on, buddy." He scooped Winston up in his arms, leaving me to follow behind.

I was tempted to remain downstairs, sitting in the festive glow of the Christmas tree. Geoff's reaction had dulled the warmth that had wrapped around my heart while Payton prayed.

"God, I'm really new at this. I don't need a Nativity scene . . . but it would be nice if Geoff could understand just a little bit." I pressed a hand to my heart, where the brand "just Jillian" ached. "I don't even know if I can talk to You like this. But could You help me find my way to You . . . and help me understand what You say about me?"

28

Too bad she didn't have any hobbies.

But Johanna didn't knit or crochet or *craft* in any way, which meant there was nothing for her to do at home except be here. Of course, she could read the book club biography . . . but what was the point of being the only Thatcher sister committed enough to do that? Her Christmas gifts for her family were all wrapped and ready to go. Online retailers, with their gift wrapping, were a wonderful way to be efficient.

Johanna curled up in a corner of her couch, wishing for once that she'd purchased a throw of some kind that she could wrap around her body for warmth. For comfort. She could always watch TV—a Christmas movie, maybe?—but couldn't bring herself to voluntarily participate in *merry* anything.

If she could, she'd skip Christmas this year. Go all Scrooge on her family and anyone else who came near her—Axton Miller included—and "Bah, humbug!" her way through to the New Year.

But if she did that, she'd get multiple "What is wrong with you?" phone calls from her mother. From Jillian. Maybe even from Payton.

There was nothing wrong with her—and everything wrong with Beckett Sager. But she would not be discussing him with anyone.

Christmas was the day after tomorrow. It had been over two weeks since she'd found out about Beckett's "friend" Iris. Since then, she'd ignored all of Beckett's texts. All of his phone calls. He'd even e-mailed her once, desperate, stupid, *unfaithful* man that he was, but she'd deleted the message without reading it. It was best that way. There was nothing he could say or do to fix how he'd destroyed their relationship. Their future. Their just-begun-to-be-planned wedding.

To change her mind.

But since he hadn't tried to contact her today, she could assume Beckett had come to his senses and given up. At last.

She would get over this. Get over being in a long-term, long-distance relationship that ended with infidelity and failure.

"No pressure . . ."

". . . and plenty of space."

Their humorous little motto mocked her now. No pressure. Plenty of space.

And no commitment. No trust.

She could be listening to all the sad Christmas songs . . . but she wasn't that kind of woman. She'd skip it all this season, except the unavoidable, piped-in music at the hospital and in the stores.

Johanna rubbed the palm of her right hand against the back of her left hand. She'd adjust to not wearing her engagement ring, too. The ring was just a thing—a very expensive, beautiful thing that she'd taken off and tossed into the top drawer of her dresser. She'd figure out what to do with it after the holidays.

A metallic rattle of the doorknob followed by a soft click caused Johanna to turn, crouching on her couch. The front door swung open, and Beckett walked in.

Johanna fought to catch a breath. "What are you doing?"

"Key." He raised his hand, her front door key held between his fingers.

"Give it to me—and leave."

"I will once we talk." He pocketed the key in his dark jeans.

She rose from the couch, meeting him before he could advance farther into the room. "There is nothing for us to talk about."

"After eight years together, Johanna? Nothing?"

She closed her eyes. She used to think he was so handsome. Now all she could think of was him kissing Iris . . . being with Iris . . . "It's funny how eight years can suddenly mean nothing, Beckett."

"Are you really so surprised that I slept with someone else?" He stood with his hands on his hips, his winter coat unbuttoned.

"What kind of question is that?" Johanna stood her ground, determined not to let him see how the question rattled her.

"I mean, I'm a guy. I traveled a lot. We had a long-distance relationship. I was deployed overseas."

"Are you saying all those things give you permission, *the right*, to cheat on me?"

"You never slept with anyone else while we were dating?"

"You and I obviously have a very different idea of what it means to be in a committed relationship—to be engaged."

"It would have been different if we were married."

"And I'm supposed to believe that." She mirrored his hands-on-hips posture.

Johanna's heartbeat seemed to be slowing, her chest aching more with every dull beat. The pain was laced with the humiliating reality that she'd been fooled by Beckett for years.

When he opened his mouth again—most likely to defend himself—Johanna raised her hands. "Beckett, stop talking. You're only making it worse."

"I'm trying to explain . . ."

"Fine. I accept your explanation. You're a guy. The kind of guy who sleeps around even though he's engaged because he's in a long-distance relationship. And because he travels. Now give me my house key." She held out her hand, pulling back once he dropped it into her palm.

But as he turned to leave, she stopped him. "Wait."

Giving him a wide berth, she went to the front hall closet. Pulled out the black garbage bag where she'd dumped all his stuff. A spare uniform. Casual clothes. Another coat. Shoes. Dirty workout clothes. His toiletries that she'd put in a ziplock bag. Several framed photographs of them. And every photograph he'd taken—removed from their frames and tossed into the bag, unprotected.

This was what it came down to. This was how their relationship ended after eight years—with her handing him bits and pieces of his belongings. The bag wasn't heavy. She could throw it at him if she wanted to. Or dump it out on the ground. But she was a better person than that. A better person than Beckett. Johanna dropped the bag at his feet.

Beckett crossed his arms, staring at her. "Is the ring in there, too?"

"The ring."

"Your engagement ring, Johanna. Did you put it in the bag?"

Her engagement ring.

"You broke up with me. It's customary for you to return the ring . . ."

She couldn't hold back a sharp laugh. "You're lecturing me on traditions or customs . . . That's like Benedict Arnold telling someone what loyalty means."

Johanna pivoted and escaped to her bedroom. Yanked open the top drawer of her dresser. Shoved aside a layer of lingerie. Oh, she needed to throw all of that out, too. Found the ring where she'd thrown it after removing it the day she'd kicked Beckett out.

It was an elegant ring—an oval-cut diamond set on a slender band of smaller diamonds.

And she hated it to the point that her stomach roiled. She clenched the broken symbol in her fist until she stood in front of Beckett again.

He held out his hand and she dropped it into his palm, snatching her hand back, careful once again that she didn't touch him.

"I'm not a leper."

"No. You're a cheater. And a liar. Those are worse."

He stuffed the ring in his coat pocket. Picked up the trash bag. Turned. Paused. "It's been fun, Johanna."

"Oh no, Beckett. It's been fake—all of it."

When she slammed the door, it seemed to reverberate through her entire body.

If only she'd found the ability to say, *"Good riddance"* or *"I won't miss you."* Or if she could tell herself that she was glad. That she was relieved.

But all she wanted to do was ask him why.

And then she remembered he'd told her why. He slept with Iris—and most likely other women—because of their long-distance relationship. And because they weren't married. And because he was a guy.

29

GEOFF AND I WERE HAVING our own "not a creature was stirring" Christmas Eve moment at his parents' house.

After one last reminder that they'd see us in the morning, his mother and father—or Lilith and Felix, as they requested I call them—had disappeared upstairs to their bedroom, dimming lights as they went. Once I'd changed into my pajamas and robe, Winston had followed me through the darkened house into the living room, curling up on the carpet in front of the gas fireplace.

Geoff appeared moments later, carrying tall glass Irish coffee mugs. "I thought tonight called for some hot chocolate."

I tucked my bare feet up underneath my body. "Is that whipped cream?"

"I found some left over from dessert." He shrugged,

managing to hold the mugs steady. "Of course, the house-keeper is going to wonder what happened to it."

"Geoff!"

"Don't worry—she's always liked me." He handed me a mug, placing his on the side table, and sat beside me, resting his arm around my shoulders. "A nice, traditional Christmas Eve. Hot chocolate with real whipped cream. A fake Christmas tree. And a fake fire . . . All we need is a selection of Christmas music to complete the mood."

I snuggled closer. "No. I'm good. I'm enjoying the quiet. Now, if you could arrange for snow . . ."

"You heard the weatherman. No snow for Christmas. Sorry."

"A girl can still hope to wake up tomorrow and find out the weatherman got it wrong. Even if the girl is in her thirties." I sipped my hot chocolate, wiping away the whipped cream left on my top lip with my tongue. "I think your parents liked their Christmas gift."

"They liked it even more when they found out we were going to the theater with them. You, Mrs. Hennessey, had a brilliant idea." Geoff shifted so my body fit closer to his.

"You helped me choose which show we're going to see." I clinked our mugs together. "Job well done. I'm so glad they're excited. I wish we could have done more, but with the renovation . . ."

"Don't worry, Jill. They're happy. They're glad we're here tonight, and they're looking forward to going to your parents' tomorrow for dinner."

"It'll be pretty casual, compared to tonight . . ."

"That's one of the things I like about being with your family."

A comfortable silence settled between us, one void of all our recent struggles.

How was it that Christmas had the ability to pause real life? To just for a few moments, a few days, hush some of the unresolved tensions? Sitting here, I could close my eyes . . . could pretend to believe in all the things I had when I was a little girl. Not in Santa Claus, but in the magical "more" that Christmas promised.

Magic wasn't all that hard to embrace while we were at Geoff's parents' home. The decor was a silver, gold, and blue theme, complete with a designer Christmas tree overloaded with fake snow and matching ornaments—not a single one with sentimental value. The mantel mirrored the color theme with a lit garland decorated with more coordinated ornaments and tall silver pillar candlestick holders. A silver cashmere throw was draped across one chair while a "Merry Christmas" pillow was tucked into its companion, and other silver, blue, and gold embellishments graced the room. A large abstract painting of an angel hung over the mantel.

Again and again, my eyes were drawn to this painting.

There was no Nativity in Geoff's parents' house, but that didn't mean I wasn't thinking about God this holiday season. For the first time, the concept of angels and shepherds and a young Jewish couple's plan for marriage interrupted by an unexpected, God-ordained pregnancy lingered on the outskirts of my thoughts as more than a story—as part of my fledgling faith journey.

"Why so quiet?"

"I'm thinking about the Christmas story."

"The Christmas story? Which one? Scrooge? Or Charlie Brown?"

"The Bible one."

Geoff covered any hesitation by taking a gulp of his hot chocolate. "Did you enjoy going to the Christmas Eve service earlier today?"

His question was nice—and unexpected. I'd managed to slip away to a church close by before any preparations for dinner had begun. My first time in church since Payton had prayed for me. I'd invited him to the candlelight service, thinking maybe he'd want to go with me.

He hadn't, but asking now was an acknowledgment of something important to me, if not an expression of real interest.

"It was odd to attend a candlelight service at ten o'clock in the morning. I was surprised by how many people were there—the sanctuary was packed. I should have arrived earlier."

I waited for him to ask for more details. Nothing.

"But I liked it. We sang some Christmas carols. Well, I tried to. At least they put the words up on screens in the front of the auditorium. And I liked the pastor's sermon—it was brief, but still meaningful."

Still no response from Geoff. Maybe he hadn't been all that interested. But for some reason, I kept talking, kept sharing, as if something I said would spark his curiosity.

"My favorite part was when they darkened the sanctuary

and we all sang 'Silent Night' and everyone lit each other's candle, one by one."

"Why was that your favorite part?"

Finally a question . . . and one that I struggled to answer.

"Because . . . I felt some of the peace I think Payton has—that I'm looking for."

It was like trying to translate something for Geoff when I barely knew the language myself. I mixed up the words. Definitions eluded me. Had I ever understood what peace was—peace that reached deep into my heart? Or had I settled for something temporary, like the warmth of the hot chocolate as I sipped on it?

Geoff didn't respond, shifting against me, clearing his throat . . . and then, "I have a Christmas present for you."

"What?" I startled, splashing a bit of hot chocolate on my robe. "Geoff, we agreed no presents this year, not after the extra expense of the kitchen."

"You know, when someone gets you a gift, you're supposed to say thank you."

I rubbed at the dark stain. "Not when we agreed no gifts this Christmas."

Geoff reached beside the couch and set a large red gift bag, white tissue paper sticking out of the top, on my lap.

I handed him my hot chocolate so he could set it on the side table. "Where did you hide this?"

"Ho, ho, ho." Geoff moved over a bit, giving me room. A smile accompanied his Santa laugh, but it seemed forced. "My elves helped me. But before you open it, I have to tell you something."

My hands stilled against the tissue paper. "What?"

"I—I haven't been completely honest with you." Geoff removed his glasses, rubbing his eyes as an exhale escaped.

"Is this about Brian? You want to talk about him now?"

"No." Geoff slipped his glasses back on. Straightened them. Rubbed his hand across his mouth. "No. I need to tell you about . . . about Kyler."

Kyler.

"Who is Kyler?"

"My younger brother."

My vision blurred, the room seeming to darken for a moment. I shook my head, trying to refocus on my husband. "Is this some kind of joke?"

"No. I would never do that to you."

"But you'd date me . . . marry me . . . without telling me you have not one, but *two brothers*?" My voice shrilled on the last words.

"I couldn't."

"You . . . couldn't."

"You have to understand my family. We don't talk about Brian. Or Kyler. Ever." Geoff's voice rasped on his brothers' names, as if a heavy wooden door, long closed, had been pulled open mere inches.

My hands clutched the sides of the gift bag. "And this? What is this?"

"Ever since I told you about Brian, I knew I had to tell you the whole truth." Tears filled my husband's eyes. "But Kyler . . . losing him . . . was harder than what happened with Brian. I mean, Brian left because he wanted to . . ."

The way Geoff's words faded into silence chilled me. "What happened?"

"They adopted Kyler when I was five." For just a moment, Geoff's eyes warmed again. "Mom and Dad were so excited . . . and I was going to be the best big brother ever."

"Was Kyler a baby when your parents adopted him?" I struggled to move past all the emotions warring inside me. To listen. To visualize the story Geoff was telling me.

"No. He was two. He'd been in foster care, so we didn't know his biological parents or much of his medical history." Geoff twisted to face me. "Kyler was so much smaller than Brian and me. Quieter than us. The doctors said something about 'failure to thrive'—not that I knew what that meant. Brian kind of ignored Kyler, said he didn't want to be bothered. But Kyler always tried to keep up with me—and I encouraged him. Let him tag along anytime he wanted. I probably shouldn't have."

Just that admission gave me a glimpse of an unseen adversary that preyed on my husband all these years later.

"Then when he was seven, all three of us got a virus—it was going around the school. Kyler couldn't shake it. He ended up in the hospital because his body was overwhelmed—he was going downhill rather than getting better. They ran some tests . . . and that's when they found out he had a congenital heart defect."

"Oh, Geoff . . ."

"Before my parents could even begin to process the news . . . or talk to the doctors about what was going to happen next . . . Kyler's heart went into an arrhythmia. They couldn't resuscitate him."

Geoff's voice trailed off into silence again and he stared straight ahead. I almost said something, prompted him to keep talking, to tell more of the story. This might be the only time he'd share about Kyler. But I remained still, the unopened gift separating us.

"I was going to visit him after school. That was the routine. Brian and I went to school while Mom stayed with Kyler and then we'd go up with Dad in the evening and see him. I never thought . . ."

When Geoff didn't continue, I forced myself to ask the question. "How did you find out?"

"Dad picked us up from school. We usually rode the bus home and stayed at a neighbor's until Dad got home from work. But that day . . . we were called into the office right before school got out. And Dad was there . . . He told us . . ."

Geoff's shoulders rose and fell with his rapid breathing. "I'm sorry, Jillian. I'm sorry I didn't tell you sooner. . . . It's just that, after all these years, it's become easier not to talk about him."

"What changed your mind?"

"I kept hearing myself telling you that I'm trying to make you happy—and yet my decision to not have children hurts you. I knew I had to be completely honest with you, no matter how hard it was going to be. I thought we could start the New Year off with no secrets between us." He repositioned the gift in my lap. "Would you open your gift?"

"Now?"

"Please."

I did as he asked, removing the tissue paper and pulling out a small blue photo album. "What's this?"

Geoff was silent as I placed the book in my lap, and then his fingers traced the words *Family Photos* embossed on the front cover in silver. "Something I wanted to share with you."

"I don't understand."

He shifted closer again, opening the front cover and settling the album across both our laps. "These are some of my favorite photos of Kyler."

And with those words, Geoff invited me into his past.

His hand shook for a moment, and I almost said he didn't have to do this. Didn't have to show me the photos.

But I knew he needed to.

And oh, how I wanted him to.

"I was so excited when I found out I was getting a little brother." Geoff's voice was hushed in the light of the Christmas tree and the fireplace. "I'd kept asking my parents for a baby brother or a sister. Brian didn't care—he always laughed when I said something. I told Mom and Dad I was hoping for a brother. The Hennessey brothers, you know? It took a long time. Brian and I were only twenty months apart, but I didn't know that my mom had several miscarriages after me and then ended up having a hysterectomy. I mean, you don't tell a little boy those kinds of things until later . . . and my parents, well, they just don't talk about anything like that. I don't know why they decided to adopt. Sometimes I think it was more for me than for them."

He turned the first few pages as he talked, revealing

photos of my then-five-year-old husband and his two-year-old brother. Smiles and silent laughter on their faces.

The two boys sitting on the couch together. Tucked into bed together, their mother sitting on the edge of the bed. Geoff reading books to Kyler. Building block towers. A hodgepodge, out-of-order sequence of photos of Geoff and Kyler. Each photo unlocking a memory for Geoff.

"We had chocolate cake and chocolate ice cream for his third birthday. He was a mess. And that's us on the first day of school—not kindergarten for Kyler, first grade. He said kindergarten didn't count because we weren't in the same school."

His memories were adding color to the mental portrait of my husband—each word a brushstroke filling in more details. My husband had more than a difficult relationship with an older brother who'd disappeared years ago. He was a big brother whose smile was altogether different when he talked about his little brother.

And then the words stopped as Geoff stared at one photo.

I hesitated to intrude on this memory.

"This—" Geoff traced the edges of the photo—"this was one of our last photos together. I can't say it was the last one taken. But it's one of my favorites. Mom took it while we were all walking to the park one day. Me and Kyler running ahead, and Mom and Dad behind us."

There they were, the photo a bit blurry with their legs caught in midmotion. Two boys running together, Kyler looking up at his big brother.

"You never thought you wouldn't see him again."

"No." Geoff seemed to choke on the word. "Kyler liked for me to sit with him at night in the hospital, to read him books. The day . . . the day he died, I had get-well cards from all his classmates . . ."

Geoff covered the photo with his hand as if he couldn't bear to look at it. Then he closed the photo album. Tapped the cover.

I waited.

"There's a couple of other things in the bag." Geoff pulled it up off the floor.

"There is?" Reaching inside, my fingers touched the worn edges of another book. "What's this?"

Geoff's eyes shone with tears. "That was Kyler's favorite book. He loved when I read it to him."

I couldn't help but smile at the yellow animal covered with multicolored spots lounging on the cover of the book beneath the title *Put Me in the Zoo*.

"I read this book so many times, I had it memorized." Geoff closed his eyes. "'I will go into the zoo. I want to see it. Yes, I do.'"

"It sounds like you still have it memorized."

"I guess so . . . maybe." Geoff cleared his throat. "He loved Grover from Sesame Street, too. I practiced until I could talk just like Grover for him."

"Are you going to let me hear that?"

"No . . . I don't think I can do the voice anymore."

"So is there a Grover book in the bag, too?"

"No . . ." Geoff waited as I reached for the bag again.

My hand found a bundle of softness. I gathered it together and revealed—"Is this a baby blanket?"

"It was Kyler's. Yes."

"Oh, Geoff . . ."

"He brought it with him when my parents adopted him. He slept with it. Dragged it everywhere. Mom could hardly get a chance to wash it."

I spread the soft white cotton blanket decorated with blue floppy bunnies and yellow chicks, the binding worn.

"When Kyler died, I came home . . . and took the blanket and this book from his room. And a few weeks later, I took some of my favorite photos and put them in this album—I bought it at the store. I put them away in my closet because Mom and Dad didn't want to talk about it . . . to talk about Kyler . . . and Brian was okay with that, too."

Geoff's voice had faded away, softer and softer, as if the strength to recount all the memories had stretched him too thin.

There were no tears.

Just a silence, a loss, I couldn't speak into.

⁓

The local weatherman's forecast of no snow for Christmas had been correct.

The classical holiday music piped through the Hennesseys' in-home stereo system set the appropriate, if somewhat muted, mood for the day. The coordinated and oh-so-expensive decorations along the winding banister and in various spots in the foyer and other rooms might last until the first of the year—or would Lilith have the normal decor restored before then?

Geoff and Winston were both still asleep upstairs, but I found my way to the kitchen, with its gourmet stainless steel appliances and black granite countertops, where Lilith had just closed the oven door on a breakfast casserole. Geoff's mom fit into her perfect surroundings, already dressed for the day in sleek black pants and a white blouse, her brown hair styled away from her face, her hazel eyes so like Geoff's.

"Can I do anything to help?"

"No, dear. The housekeeper did all the prep for me. All I had to do was put the casserole in the oven and then pull everything else out of the refrigerator once this is done." She motioned to a glass pitcher on the counter, next to four fluted glasses. "There are mimosas if you'd like one."

"No, thank you. I'll wait for everyone else. May I set the table for you?"

"That's already done. It's simple enough with the four of us."

Just the four of them.

"I wanted to ask you something."

"Yes?"

"Your Christmas decorations? They're lovely."

"Aren't they? The company I hired did a wonderful job. I tell them what theme I want, so it's personal. Did you say you wanted to ask me something?"

"It's that Geoff and I are just starting out with our decorations. We have a few ornaments from my family. I was wondering if we could take one or two from your tree—family tradition, you know?"

"Family tradition?"

"Yes."

"Certainly, Jillian. I'd rather you not spoil the larger tree in the living room. Just take something from the back of the tree—the one downstairs in the family room. The decorations are staying up until after the New Year."

"Of course."

This was like asking for something and getting a yes, but knowing the person wanted to say no. The entire time we talked, Lilith kept moving, pulling items from the refrigerator, gathering serving utensils. She never once made eye contact with me.

"I was wondering if I could talk to you about something else . . ."

"Yes?" Lilith glanced at the timer on the stove, a not-so-subtle hint that our conversation had a time limit.

"I wanted to say . . . to tell you . . . that Geoff told me about both Brian and Kyler."

Lilith opened a drawer next to the stove. Removed a knife. Eased the drawer shut without a sound. "Oh?"

"Yes, we were talking . . . and he told me about what happened with Brian . . . and how Kyler died."

"I see."

"I wanted to say I'm sorry—"

"Jillian." Lilith gripped the handle of the knife. "That conversation. It was between you and Geoff, correct?"

"Yes."

"I don't understand why Geoff felt compelled to talk about . . . any of this all these years later, but I think it's best what was said remains between the two of you."

"But—"

"This is not something we talk about." Lilith's voice firmed.

"Why not?"

"Felix and I always thought it was easier, best . . . for Geoff, for the family, if we handled it this way."

I assumed the word *family* only included her, Felix, Brian, and Geoff. Lilith had always been reserved, but now it was as if she'd vacated the room once I'd mentioned her other sons. Her voice had gone flatline, even as she placed the knife on the counter, next to a cutting board, and removed a shiny red apple from the white ceramic fruit bowl.

Perhaps if I took it one brother at a time.

"Surely you had to know Geoff was going to miss his little brother . . . that he needed to talk about Kyler after he—"

"Don't begin to think you can tell me how Geoff felt . . . or how it needed to be handled. I had plenty of people telling me their opinions years ago. 'Let him cry. Don't let him cry. Take him to counseling. Counseling will mess him up.'" Lilith focused on halving the apple. Quartering it. Removing the core. And then making precise slices. "Felix and I decided the best way to handle it was to get back to normal as quickly as possible. After all, it had only been five years . . . We could go back to the way things were . . ."

"You think he just forgot—?"

"Yes, I do. We went to the funeral. Came home and never spoke of it again."

"So Geoff . . . and Brian . . . went to Kyler's funeral."

At the mention of both Brian's and Kyler's names, Lilith's slicing paused and then resumed again. Swift. Precise. "Yes. We were going to leave them with friends, but Geoff insisted on going. Demanded to go. I gave in, but only once he agreed he wouldn't cry. We would do this right. No crying. And of course, I had to bring both of them."

It was as if I were standing in front of one of those crazy mirrors where everything was distorted. Lilith was a mother. Brian's mother. Geoff's mother. Kyler's mother. But she chose to forget her eldest son when he ran away from home and her youngest son when he died.

The only sound in the kitchen was the rapid hiss of the knife blade as it sliced through the apple, over and over again.

The timer dinged, causing me to jerk.

Lilith set the knife next to the pile of apple slices on the cutting board. Checked the casserole, closing the oven door silently.

"This needs about ten more minutes." She washed her hands at the sink. "My husband will be coming downstairs in a few minutes. He expects a nice Christmas breakfast. So does Geoff."

"Yes." I struggled with the change of conversation.

"Then I suggest we keep this between the two of us—as if this conversation never happened. Don't you agree?" Lilith began scraping the delicate apple slices off the cutting board, into the trash can. "Jillian?"

"Yes. Yes, I agree."

I had no choice.

"Good. Then why don't you go select an ornament or two off the family room tree. One of the angels and one of the stars might be nice."

"Thank you."

I'd been dismissed. Another one of the incidents to be forgotten in Lilith's life—a more easily forgotten one.

30

I could check one thing off today's to-do list. I'd gone grocery shopping. And thanks to writing the list in my phone—so I couldn't forget it at home or lose it somewhere in the house or on my way to the store—I'd been successful and gotten every single item. Of course, I'd had to check and recheck the list multiple times before I left the store—and even one last time while I sat in my car and waited for the defroster to clear the ice off my windshield.

It was a small victory, but I'd take it.

I'd overlook the fact that I'd taken a short nap before going grocery shopping.

And that I'd postpone cleaning the house until tomorrow.

There would be no more adoption research taking up my time. No meeting with Thea, who had accepted my brief text about not being able to meet without asking any questions.

Putting away the eggs, milk, oranges, and packaged salad gave me a chance to appreciate my new fridge—which worked beautifully, even with the hidden ding on the side. Stacking my canned goods in one of the cabinets made me thankful once again for Zach, even as I wondered if he and Payton had figured things out. I hadn't asked her about that when the family celebrated Christmas, although Payton mentioned he'd gone to see his parents in California. So they must still be talking a little bit. And not once was I distracted by having to stop and let Winston out or in. The doggy door, outfitted with a little *Wipe your paws* mat, was fast becoming a favorite add-on to our kitchen.

Once the groceries were put away, I took the time to peel an orange, piling the sections in a small bowl. After rinsing the juice from my hands, I rewarded myself with a phone call to Harper, who answered immediately as if expecting my call.

"Jillian! How was your Christmas?"

"Good. The usual Thatcher affair." I stretched out on the couch, my snack nearby. "Except Zach wasn't there this year because he and Payton . . . they're not seeing each other anymore."

"So they *were* seeing each other."

"No, I phrased that wrong." I took a quick bite of orange, savoring the refreshing tartness. "It's complicated . . . and they decided it was too complicated. Does that make sense?"

"I'll trust you that it does."

"Although Payton did mention him briefly, and she seemed less tense, so maybe they've decided to be friends again. I don't know." I paused for a moment, rethinking over the day. "Beckett wasn't there, either. Which is odd. I find it hard to believe he had to work on Christmas. But that was Johanna's story, and she stuck with it."

"I seriously doubt that anything's wrong with Johanna and Beckett. Those two have been together forever."

"You're right." I patted the couch, inviting Winston to jump up beside me, moving the bowl to the side table. "It's so good to hear your voice. I'm going to pretend you're still here in the Springs."

"And I'm going to enjoy the view outside my mother's condo while we catch up."

"That's not nice."

"It actually is a very nice view of the ocean."

"And that was nicely played." I closed my eyes, allowing myself to relax. "Did you have a good Christmas in North Carolina?"

"If by 'good' you mean 'quiet,' then yes, I had a good Christmas."

"What did you do?"

"I took a long walk on the beach in the morning. Then I took an even longer one in the evening."

"And in between?"

"In between I watched *Miracle on 34th Street*, *Christmas in Connecticut*, and *It's a Wonderful Life*."

"Not *White Christmas*?"

353

"No, I decided to go with all black-and-white Christmas movies this year. Might have started a new Christmas Day tradition."

"Maybe I'll try that next year. Sounds like a good idea." Time for another slice of orange, the fruit moist on my fingers.

"Except that *It's a Wonderful Life* always makes me cry."

"But in a good way, right?"

"I guess so . . . most years."

"Are you getting settled out there?"

"Sure. I mean, there's nothing to settle. Most everything I own is in storage. And I'm not working yet."

"You'll start the job search up again in January, right?"

"New Year, new job." Harper's tone brightened. "You want to know what I pulled out of the jar today?"

"Tell me."

"'The best time for new beginnings is now.' Perfect timing, wouldn't you say?"

"Absolutely."

"I only had to try seven times before I found it."

The sound of Harper's laughter was its own kind of gift. Harper never stopped looking for a silver lining to any cloud. Never stopped hoping, even when her husband stopped believing in their marriage.

"What about you, Jilly? How was Christmas for you?"

"It's been . . . different." I reached for another bite of orange, my movement unsettling Winston, who jumped down from the couch.

"Are you and Geoff better?"

"Some." That was the truth, wasn't it? "He hit me with something unexpected on Christmas Eve."

"Please don't tell me that he's got some horrible hidden vice like gambling or . . ."

"He has two brothers. Not one. Two."

"What? Jillian, that's ridiculous."

I buried my face in one hand, my phone clutched in the other, allowing Harper to sputter away. Her reactions were no different than mine had been.

"Are you still there?"

"Still here." My reply was muffled.

"Why aren't you saying anything?"

"I was waiting for you to be done with all your 'This can't be true' statements."

"I'm sorry. I just can't believe this—"

I settled back against the couch. "I know. But it's the truth. Geoff's older brother ran away from home. His younger, adopted brother, Kyler, died. And the Hennessey family doesn't talk about either of them."

"That's so wrong."

"It's how his parents coped. Not that I'm defending them."

"What are you doing?"

"I'm trying . . . trying to understand my husband. Why he didn't tell me all of this sooner. Trying to figure out how we move forward. I have to believe it helped Geoff to talk about his brothers." I sat up so that I could see our Christmas tree. "Of course, that doesn't mean anything changes for us."

"You don't know that."

"Hoping Geoff might change his mind about having

children? It's like holding my breath . . . I can't survive that way. The other night, he showed me photos of Kyler and him, and it was like inhaling a precious gasp of air. But now I'm back to holding my breath again. Waiting . . . waiting to see if anything changes."

I found myself taking a deep breath as if talking about all of this with Harper had reminded me that I needed to breathe, to fight past the pressure building in my chest and just keep inhaling and exhaling. Believing I could live this way.

"But I'm trying . . . trying to be more hopeful." My gaze was captured by the tiny Nativity I'd purchased on sale and put on the mantel—a simple manger scene with Mary, Joseph, the baby Jesus, a shepherd with a couple of sheep. No wise men. No angels. I could always add more pieces to the collection if I wanted to, but then I'd need a larger mantel.

"Positive thoughts, huh?"

"No. Although I'm glad my texts are helping you."

"What? They don't help you, too?"

How did I explain all of this to Harper?

"The positive thoughts you gave me last year? They were great. But I needed something more after I got fired. And because I don't know how long I'll be dealing with chemo brain." I needed to back up. "I kind of thought I'd get through the mastectomy and the chemo and radiation, and things would be all better. That I'd marry Geoff, and things would be good finally, but . . ."

"But things didn't work out that way."

"No. Is it awful to say that?"

"You can say anything you want to me, Jilly. You know that."

"I love Geoff—nothing changes that. Nothing." My mouth had gone dry, the fresh taste of orange souring. "But I can't just think myself out of the whole 'no children' decision he's made for us. Or out of night sweats and the constant fatigue."

"So what? You're going to counseling?"

"No." If only I were sitting across from Harper right now so I could see her face. "I'm going to church."

"To *church*?"

"Well, it's more than that. I talked with Zach and Payton . . . and I'm trying to figure out what I believe about God."

"God." Harper's voice echoed the same flat tone that I'd heard in Geoff's. "You believe in God?"

"Yes. I want to. I need to."

This was the first time I'd ever struggled to talk with Harper. It was as if we'd been riding the same up escalator together, and now I'd switched to the escalator going down. I was stepping, stepping, my feet out of sync, trying to stay alongside her.

Cancer had cost me so much. Was choosing to have faith—whatever that was going to look like—going to cost me my best friend, too?

"What are you looking for, Jill?" Harper's voice was serious.

"Hope, I guess. No, not I guess. *I know.*" I pulled my knees up onto the couch and hugged them close. "I'm tired all the time, but not just physically tired. I want to figure out how to not be torn apart by my circumstances. My cancer may come back or not. Geoff may change his mind and decide he wants kids—or he may not. I may wake up one morning and feel like myself again. Or not. But no matter what, I want hope. I want to figure out who God is and if He can give me that."

"And I thought I was being brave, moving across the country to start my life over."

"I don't feel very brave."

"You're facing some tough circumstances—and you're asking some tough questions."

"Are we okay?"

"Yes. Absolutely. Nothing's going to change our friendship."

I knew Harper meant what she said, just like she'd meant it when she said moving across the country wouldn't change our friendship. But our relationship had already changed. There'd been no Skype Girls' Nights since she left. Maybe that was because it was the holiday season—or maybe it was because the move had altered things. Our friendship wasn't going to be the same.

I could keep fumble-stepping up the escalator or I could stop and slide back down to the bottom.

But Harper and I needed each other.

"Jill, I was going to ask a favor of you." Harper's words brought the escalator to a sudden halt.

"Go ahead and ask."

"Do you remember Gail Ferguson at the bank?"

"I think so. She was a teller, right?"

"Yes. She texted me that she was diagnosed with breast cancer—"

"No!" Harper's statement created an instant connection between me and a woman I barely remembered.

"I know. It's awful. I don't know all the details, but I wondered if you'd be willing to talk with her. Maybe give her some advice?"

I rested my chin on my knees. "But I don't know her—why would she want to talk to me?"

"You may not know her, but you understand what she's going through. That's what she needs—someone who understands. Who can listen, maybe answer some questions."

It wasn't like my days were busy with commitments. What would meeting with Gail cost me—an hour or two at the most? She could talk, and I could smile, nod, say, *"I understand."*

Easy enough.

"I guess I can do that."

"So I can give her your number?"

"Sure. Tell her that she can text me. Maybe we can get together after New Year's."

"I will. I know this will mean a lot to her."

Harper and I chatted for a few minutes more, promising to connect next week. As we hung up, my thoughts turned to Gail. I didn't know her, but my heart hurt for her. The unknowns she faced. The decisions she'd have to make. How fighting cancer would change her life.

I'd wait and see if she texted. I could always change my mind about meeting with her.

But I wouldn't.

31

"Here we are again . . . The Thatcher Sisters' Saturday Morning Book Club made it into the New Year." I raised my fluted glass of orange juice in a toast to Johanna and Payton. "Happy New Year to us! That's an accomplishment, isn't it?"

"Happy New Year—and happy anniversary to you, Jill."

"Yes, happy anniversary." Payton joined in with Johanna's impromptu toast. "Do you and Geoff have plans to celebrate?"

"Nothing fancy—just a quiet dinner at home tonight." I held up my hand, stalling any protests. "That's what we want. The budget's a little tight, what with finishing the reno and the holidays. And we're both ready for something low-key."

"Then that's perfect." Payton offered a smile. "So is that our official name now—the Thatcher Sisters' Saturday Morning Book Club?"

"It doesn't have to be. I just kind of said it this morning."

"Some book club we are. The real question is how much of this book we've read." Johanna tapped the cover of the biography next to her plate.

"Again with the total chapters between us?" Payton shrugged. "Less than ten, unless someone has read more since the last time we got together."

Johanna took a sip of her ice water. "I think we should abandon any idea of naming our little group and admit that your book club idea is a bust, Payton."

"Don't judge a book club by just how many books, or chapters, we've read. We've gotten together the last five months. That's a good thing, right?"

"True, even if the last time we met we were all sitting at the bottom of the barrel, as I recall." Johanna took a small bite of the vegan overnight oats she'd made for today. "Any change in virtual location since the last time we got together?"

This was my cue.

"For me, yes."

Johanna set her spoon down, more intrigued by my announcement than her breakfast. "You and Geoff come to some sort of agreement about children, Jill?"

"No. It's a nontopic for us now."

"So you're just not talking about it? Or have you decided you don't want children?"

"I still want children. And Geoff hasn't changed his mind. But I'm trying to give him time to tell me more of his story."

"What does that even mean?"

I guessed I was going to be grilled by Johanna instead of saying what I wanted to say. "On Christmas Eve, Geoff told me that he also had a younger brother, Kyler."

Both Payton and Johanna gasped.

I hurried on before they could begin asking questions. "Kyler was adopted. He died from a congenital heart defect. It was even more difficult for Geoff to talk to me about Kyler than it was for him to tell me about his older brother." I swallowed back the sob that rose in my throat. "I know how crazy this all sounds . . . but Geoff and I have had a complicated relationship from the beginning, haven't we?"

"Why didn't he tell you all of this sooner?" Johanna spoke up.

"His parents don't talk about either Brian or Kyler— and Geoff just followed their lead. What else could he do?" I twisted my hands together. "I tried to talk to Lilith about Kyler on Christmas morning and she shut me down. Told me, 'This is not something we talk about.'"

"How could she say that?" Payton shook her head.

"She thinks it's the best for her family." Not that I could convince my sisters of something I didn't believe. "But Geoff is talking about Kyler now. He even showed me a photo album of the two of them."

"That must have been so special—and difficult at the same time."

"I know it was good for him. For us." The more I said it

out loud, the more I believed it. "He doesn't ever talk about his older brother, Brian. His family doesn't talk about anything beyond the surface. But I think Geoff needs to remember his little brother. Talk about him. I love Geoff enough to listen . . . and wait."

"Process the grief." Payton's words were soft.

"Yes." If anyone could understand how much Geoff was hurting, Payton could, after bottling up all her emotions about Pepper's death for ten years.

Johanna shifted in her chair. "Are you hoping if Geoff talks enough about Kyler that he'll change his mind about children?"

"No. Maybe. I guess . . . I guess I'm giving God time to change me."

And now . . . now I waited.

"God?" Johanna asked the question while Payton offered me a smile.

"Yes. God."

"What do you mean, Jill?" Johanna's voice sharpened.

"After talking to Zach and Payton and then talking with Payton again before Christmas—"

"You're not going to say you're becoming a Christian, are you?" Johanna asked the question as if I were about to announce I was going to perform on Broadway. Or become a fisherman off the coast of Alaska. Or maybe do something fantastical like join the circus as a clown.

"That's exactly what I'm going to say, Joey."

"Why?"

"Why what?"

"Why are you doing this?" Tight lines formed around Johanna's mouth, her eyes narrowing. "You're smarter than this."

"It's not about being smart or not being smart." I refolded my cloth napkin in half just to give myself a chance to gather my thoughts. "It's about wanting hope in my life again."

"And some sort of made-up god gives you that?"

"Yes. Believing in God, the real God—that He loves me, that He has a plan for my life—gives me hope."

"Even if that plan includes cancer? And no children? You're okay with that kind of god?"

"I'm new at this, Johanna. I don't understand how all of this works. Why my life includes cancer . . . and, very possibly, no children." I forced myself to meet Johanna's eyes. "But yes, my faith, as new as it is, helps me. Life's not perfect. And I'm not perfect. But for the first time, I'm beginning to be okay with that because I don't have to have all the answers. I don't have to fix everything. I don't have to pretend like nice thoughts are enough . . ."

"Nice thoughts?"

Trying to explain all of this to Johanna, who was battering me with questions, was like being the new kid in school and having to stand up in class, introduce myself, all the while wondering what everyone else was thinking. If they would like me. Accept me.

"Here's one for you: 'Positive thoughts generate positive thoughts and attract positive life experiences.' Do you like that one? I said it over and over again for months . . . and I still felt like 'just Jillian.'"

"What are you talking about?"

"Of course I'd get cancer . . . not you. Not Payton. It's just me, *just Jillian*. I didn't matter that much anyway, did I? Stuck in the middle between the superachieving older sister and the amazing twins . . . who saw me?"

Johanna gasped. "Jilly, that's not true—"

"It is. It's the truth I've lived with for years. *Just. Jillian.* Do you know how long I've worn those two words like a brand on my soul?" The tears wouldn't be held back now. "My life has been all about losing and can't have and won't have, and I want something more . . . I hope there's more. And guess what? God wants me just for me." I sucked in a deep breath. "I'm not settling, Jo, so don't even say that. I'm going to figure out how to love my husband for who he is right now . . . although I don't even know what that means."

Maybe I shouldn't have said anything. But I had to tell my sisters sometime. Johanna remained frozen in her chair, but Payton came and knelt beside me, tears in her eyes.

"I'm sorry, Jill." Payton's hand rested on mine. "I know I said it before, but I'm sorry we stuck you in the middle so often."

I inhaled a shuddering breath, unsure what to say.

Payton squeezed my hand. Hesitated for a moment before saying, "And I understand."

I dropped my voice to a whisper. "I know you do."

Payton positioned herself so that she could look at both me and Johanna. "Since we're on the topic of faith this morning, I'll say that I've done a lot of thinking about God and why I do or don't believe in Him. It was all mixed up with

Pepper and Zach. I finally realized that of course it would be. Pepper was the one who first talked to me about God. And then Zach continued the conversation. I realized I could love God, believe in God, just for myself—and still love Pepper and Zach, too."

"Everyone knew you and Zach were in love with one another, Payton." Johanna seemed willing to ignore the topic of God and address their relationship.

"Well, we couldn't do anything about our feelings for one another until I knew where I stood with God."

"That's one of the reasons I don't like religion—too many can'ts and don'ts." Johanna leaned back in her chair, crossing her arms.

"I don't want to discuss 'religion' with you, Jo." Payton's eyes brimmed with joy. "But what would you both say if I told you Zach and I are getting married?"

If I hadn't been holding on to my sister's hand, I might have toppled over. "You're marrying Zach?"

"Yes."

I held her hand up. "You're not wearing a ring."

"I left it at home today."

"You have an engagement ring and you left it at home?"

"I figured you and Johanna would notice it pretty quickly."

"Payton, this is crazy."

"What? Getting married or not wearing my engagement ring?"

"Both, I think."

Payton shook her head, overtaken by another laugh. "Wait until I tell you when we're getting married."

"When?"

"Zach and I were thinking of February."

"Next month?"

"Yes. We want something simple. Just family." Payton paused. "We want to have the ceremony up at Zach's cabin, by Pepper's bench."

"An outdoor ceremony? In February?" Johanna spoke up at last.

"I realize we'll all probably be wearing snow boots and coats and mittens. We'll look a little wintry in the wedding photos. Who knows? It might even be snowing. But we'll make it work. And the ceremony will be brief. It's not like we can even have any music outside. I admit I'm a little disappointed about that, but like I said, it's just family, so that's okay."

"After the ceremony, what are we going to do? Go to Zach's cabin for hot chocolate?"

"That would be fun." Even Johanna's bit of sarcasm couldn't dim Payton's happiness. "But no, we'll drive into Breck to a nice restaurant for dinner, and then Zach and I'll leave you all to figure out what else you want to do for the rest of the evening."

All that time I'd never been certain what was going on with Payton and Zach. And then she'd said nothing could go on between them. Now here she was, telling me they were getting married in a month.

"Congratulations, Payton." Johanna's response was oddly brief.

"That's all you're going to say, Jo?" I never thought I'd have to correct my oldest sister on her manners.

"Of course I'm happy for you and Zach, even if an out-door wedding in February in Winter Park is a bit . . . unique." Johanna's glance wavered. "But I won't be joining the two of you on the 'got God' side of the line this morning. I didn't quite anticipate this two-against-one religious turn of events."

"We're not against you, Johanna." Payton rose and returned to her chair.

"It certainly seems like you two are on one side and I'm on the other—the more reasonable, logical side, I might add. Our family has done just fine without religion. I don't understand why you both seem to feel some need for it now."

"There's more to life than 'doing fine.'"

"That's not what I meant, and you know it. We're all successful—"

"If you call all of us being at the bottom of the barrel successful."

"Can we just drop this conversation? I'll even congratulate the two of you on this God thing, if you want."

"It's fine, Johanna." Even Johanna's reaction couldn't erase the smile from Payton's face. "You don't have to say anything else."

"Like I said, I am happy for you and Zach."

"I want you and Jillian with me when I get married, so we'll need to talk dresses."

"That'll be fun. Have you told Mom and Dad yet?"

"Zach and I were planning on telling them tomorrow."

"Will Dad be walking you down the aisle, then?"

"No. It'll be very casual. No aisle. We'll all meet at Zach's—the pastor and his wife, too—and then walk together to Pepper's bench. We can talk about this more tomorrow. Do you think Beckett will be able to be there?"

"No." Johanna's voice seemed to chill. "No. He won't be there."

"His schedule isn't going to slow down anytime soon, is it?" Payton shook her head. "Do you think he can ask his boss to have the day off for the wedding?"

"That won't be necessary."

"It won't be *necessary*?"

"It seems as if all of the Thatcher sisters are starting the New Year off with some big life changes. Now's as good a time as any to tell you that I broke things off with Beckett." Johanna raised her hand to reveal the absence of her engagement ring.

"Johanna!" Payton stood again, rocking her chair back.

"What happened?" Even as I asked the question, Johanna's jaw clenched.

"The guy cheated on me." She pressed her lips together. "And that's all I want to say about it, okay?"

"Johanna—"

"Since I seem to be the only Thatcher sister still sitting at the bottom of the barrel, I might as well tell you that I also quit my job."

I couldn't have heard her right. Johanna quitting her job was even crazier than her breaking up with Beckett. "Why would you quit?"

"Because my new boss and I have fundamentally different philosophies when it comes to managing employees." She forced a laugh. "But do you want to hear the funny thing?"

"There's something humorous about you quitting your job?"

"Axton Miller wouldn't accept my resignation. He said I wasn't a quitter—"

"He's right. You're not."

"And then he said he would talk to me in a few days."

"And?" Payton sat back in her chair.

"That all happened the week before Christmas. We haven't talked since then."

It was as if Payton and I had climbed out of the barrel and were staring down at Johanna—not that Johanna would want to think of it that way. I had to be careful what I said or did next. My older sister didn't like to be taken care of. But I could do a little something for her.

"You haven't drunk any of your coffee, Jo. It's probably cold. Let me reheat it for you."

"No. It's okay. I'm just going to have water." Johanna placed her porcelain cup to the side. "It hasn't set right with me this morning. I knew I needed to buy new coffee. Old beans and stress don't mix."

Johanna had just admitted out loud that she was stressed.

"What are you going to do now?" Payton stirred her oatmeal. "Just wait until your boss calls you?"

"At this point, yes. It'll probably be early next week—"

Payton sat forward. "You are not waiting for your boss to call you."

"I'm not?"

"No. You're going to call him."

"I am?" Johanna huffed a laugh.

"Yes. Call him. Either ask to meet with him or talk to him over the phone. You decide. Tell him you've had time to think about things and that you want to keep your job."

"Weren't you listening, Payton? I don't want to keep my job."

"Yes, you do."

"Why are you an expert on my life all of a sudden—able to tell me what to do? Why would I want to keep my job? I didn't get the promotion. I can't work with this guy . . ."

"Have you even tried to work with him?"

Johanna pressed her fingertips to her temples. "I don't want to try. He talks about teams and tough love and wants to celebrate people's birthdays . . ."

"Sounds to me like you have been listening to him. Now you're just being stubborn—and I do know what that looks like. I didn't ask if you wanted to work with him. I asked if you've *tried* to work with him."

Johanna glared at Payton, not saying a word.

"I didn't think so."

I figured it was my turn to be persuasive. "You've stayed in this job for years. Haven't moved for Beckett—and we're glad you didn't. And now you're going to quit?"

"They didn't give me the promotion."

"Fine. That's another reason to stay. Prove them wrong—show them that you deserved to be the pharmacy director. At the very least, stay while you look for another job."

"Fine."

"You'll call him?"

"I'll consider it."

I sat back in my chair, satisfied. Bit by bit, we were dragging her up out of the barrel. "That's something, Payton."

"I'm sorry about Beckett." With her words, Payton bound the three of us together. "You didn't deserve to be treated like that."

"He said we didn't have a real engagement . . . that I wouldn't ever settle on a date and start planning a wedding. As if that gave him the right to sleep with another woman."

"It's not your fault."

Johanna shrugged. "I'm just glad I found out before we got married."

"I know you're hurt."

"I'm not hurt. I'm angry. I'm not going to waste any time being hurt or sad . . . I shouldn't even be thinking about him." Johanna's voice cracked.

"Oh, Jo—"

"How could he do that to me?" Her shoulders shook even as she brushed away the tears. "He's not worth crying over."

The uncharacteristic display of emotion was like finding out a seismic fault line ran right through your property, right beneath the foundation of your home.

"He may not be worth crying over—" I offered Johanna a smile wet with tears—"but you are."

Johanna sat in her car outside the Pilates studio close to her house. The time in class had allowed her body to relax—her mind, too. The workout was strenuous but familiar. And now other classmates—women she said hello and good-bye to and maybe "That was an excellent workout"—returned to their cars. Started them. Left the parking lot, heading home to their families. Maybe to get ready for a date or a quiet night at home. But she sat there, the engine running, the defroster clearing the windshield as warm air filled the car.

She needed to make the call. Stop talking herself out of it.

Jillian's and Payton's admonitions to talk with Axton Miller had stayed with her all day. To call him first. To not quit. To at least try to work with him. To prove to the hospital administration that they should have given the promotion to her. If she was going to talk with him, she needed to do it sooner rather than later.

Now.

She tapped his number into her phone—one of the advantages to having access to the hospital computers—and waited.

"Hello?" a high-pitched, bubbly female voice answered. "This is the Millers'."

"Is Dr. Miller there, please?"

"May I ask who's calling?"

She couldn't blame the woman for asking—not after the Iris misadventure. Of course she'd asked for Dr. Miller. Not Axton. And her face hadn't shown up on his phone screen— if this was his cell phone. Maybe the man had a landline.

"This is Dr. Johanna Thatcher. I work—"

"Oh, Dr. Thatcher! Yes, Axton has told me quite a bit about you."

She was sure he had. "Well, I—"

"He's so excited to work with you. Says your skill set and

his are a perfect match. He's always evaluating things that way. Strengths. Weaknesses. What's best for the team. But I'm sure you've figured that out already."

Johanna leaned back in the seat, staring at the storefront of the Pilates studio. There was no getting around Dr. Miller's wife. "Yes. I have."

"You should have seen him when he coached our sons' soccer teams when they were younger. Same lingo. And they were only eight at the time."

"Really?"

"If nothing else, my husband is consistent."

"That's good to know."

"Now that the holidays are over, I'm looking forward to meeting you." Apparently Mrs. Miller had nothing better to do than talk with her today. "I've told Axton I'd love to have you over for dinner. And your fiancé, too. Axton mentioned you were engaged."

Of course he did.

"There's no need—"

"I love to cook. And the house we bought has a gourmet kitchen, so I need to take advantage of that, don't I? Any food allergies? Shellfish? A lot of people are allergic to shellfish."

"No." Although she did have an adverse reaction to people who talked too much.

"Good." Voices sounded in the background. "Hold on—Axton, this phone call is for you, not me. It's Dr. Thatcher."

During the lull in conversation, Johanna tried to get her bearings. She lifted her damp hair off her neck, shifting in the seat and lowering the heat. Maybe she should have waited to call until she got home. But if she had, she would have talked herself out of calling.

"Johanna? This is a bit of a surprise." Dr. Miller's voice jolted her second thoughts up against her determination to confront her boss. "Is anything wrong?"

There were so many ways she could answer his question, but she'd stay professional.

"No. Nothing's wrong. I wanted to follow up on our last conversation."

"I see. I planned on talking with you early next week."

If this was his subtle way of saying she shouldn't have called—of saying he didn't want to talk with her right now—too bad. She wasn't backing down now.

"I apologize if this is inconvenient, but it won't take long." She rushed ahead. "I wanted to tell you that I agree with you."

"You . . . agree with me?"

"Let me clarify. I'm not saying I buy into all that positive-leadership stuff. I'm still thinking about that."

"What do we agree on, then?"

"I'm not a quitter."

His laughter coaxed a small laugh from her. It was as if they took one small step toward each other.

Johanna released her tight grip on the steering wheel. Flexed the fingers of her right hand, encouraging blood flow.

A shared laugh didn't make her friends with this man.

"Do you think we could agree on one more thing?"

Here it came. He was already wanting more from her.

"Possibly."

"Possibly." Another chuckle. "We're making progress."

"Nice."

"Would you agree to be more open-minded to my approach to raising morale? To not counter with efficiency ratings every time we discuss my plans?"

Johanna grabbed the steering wheel again, choking back her instant rebuttal. "You're asking me not to quit . . . and in the same breath, you've asked me to change."

"Yes—and not for the first time. The truth is, to work together, we would both have to change. I also used the term *open-minded*—that implies being willing to consider my suggestions. Can we start there?"

"I can agree to that."

The tension inside her loosened, like a soldier transitioning from attention to at ease. Not that she wanted to use military analogies right now.

The first step would be to stop thinking of her new boss as the enemy.

"We're in agreement, then?" She could hear the smile in Dr. Miller's voice. "You're not quitting?"

"Agreed. And you're not planning on firing me."

"No, I'm not. I never was. And you're willing to consider the concept of positive leadership."

She inhaled. This was a little harder to do than she'd realized. "Yes."

"You're reading the book?"

". . . I've read the book." He'd ask several things of her, so it was only fair that she could ask something of him. Perhaps he would see it as her willingness to try to learn. "Would you be willing—when we meet the next time—to share with me two, maybe three principles that you think are key?"

"If you'll tell me one thing you liked about the book."

"A few weeks ago, I would have said, 'The end.'"

That honest comment earned her another laugh. "But you won't say that now, right?"

"I just did. But I'll come up with something else before we talk next. I'm being open-minded, remember?"

Someone talking in the background delayed his response.

"I'm sorry, Johanna, but my wife told me to try to arrange having you and your fiancé—Beckett, right?—over for dinner. Shall we put something on the calendar for later in the month?"

His words chilled her as if she'd rolled down her car windows, letting the January wind ransack the interior of her car.

"Oh . . . um . . . I'm not at home right now. And Beckett's schedule is awful." She pressed her fist against her lips.

Calm down.

"Let me talk with him and you talk with your wife and we'll compare calendars."

"Sounds good. I'll see you at the hospital on Monday."

"Yes."

"Happy New Year, Johanna."

"Happy New Year, Axton."

Johanna tossed her phone onto the passenger seat next to her workout bag. She'd agreed to be open-minded with Axton Miller. Fine. But one thing wasn't happening. There'd be no get-together dinner with his family.

32

HERE I WAS, once again, fortifying myself with a cup of coffee. Gail and I had agreed to meet at Third Space Coffee, so getting something to drink appeared normal, not like an attempt to strengthen myself to talk with someone I didn't know. What was that saying? *"First I drink the coffee, then I do the things."*

Well, today was a huge thing I'd never done before. Meeting with someone I barely knew to try to help her as she faced a battle like the one I'd just walked through—not unscathed, but I had come out the other side alive. And that was something . . . something I could share with Gail.

Even so, I should have ordered a larger drink.

I pulled out my phone and texted Harper.

You there?

Yes. Looking online at jobs. What's up?

I'm meeting with Gail during her lunch hour. Waiting for her to show up.

☺ **You'll do great, Jill. I know you can help her.**

Her experience is going to be different than mine.

Of course it will be. But you, better than most people, can listen to her and calm her fears.

"Jillian?"

The soft questioning of my name had me almost dropping my phone. The woman standing in front of me seemed somewhat familiar. Gail—and I had no reason to think this wasn't Gail—was ten, maybe fifteen years older than me, wearing a long hooded down coat and fur-lined waterproof winter boots.

Hesitant. Scared.

"Yes. Yes, I'm Jillian." I wanted to hug her. Tell her it would be okay. Maybe that's all I needed to do today. But I couldn't . . . couldn't hug someone I'd just met. "Do you want some coffee?"

"I got some black tea, actually. I ordered when I first came in. I'll listen for them to call my name."

"I'm not sure we ever talked when I worked at the bank."

"No. I don't think we did. I knew Harper—"

"Harper knew everyone."

Gail's laugh brought light to her eyes, easing the tightness around her mouth. "Yes. She's wonderful. I was so glad when she mentioned you. I hope you don't mind that she did."

"No, of course not." As I reassured Gail, I realized I meant it.

"I just don't know who to talk to. Being diagnosed with breast cancer is just so sudden—although I realize that's probably not that unusual." She paused as the young barista with a long blonde braid brought her tea over. "Thank you."

We both paused, sipping our drinks. Catching our breaths.

"I forgot that you were so much younger than me." Gail removed her coat. "You must have been so shocked when the doctor told you that you had breast cancer."

"Yes—I was. But I think every woman is, no matter what age. Did they find something on your mammogram?" I bit my bottom lip, remembering my determination not to let this morning be about me and my cancer journey.

"No. I found a lump in early December. I'm not one of those women who does monthly exams—I mean, I know I should. But I saw a public service ad on TV and when I took my shower that night, I—I found something in my left breast. I thought I was imagining it, so I checked a couple of times. And then I thought I should see my doctor, just to be sure. She found something, too, during her exam. And that was that."

"I'm sorry."

Gail sipped her tea, possibly in an attempt to hide the tears in her eyes. "Of course, with the holidays, everything has been slower. My doctor ordered a diagnostic mammogram. I've also had a biopsy . . ."

"I remember all of that. Do you have your diagnosis?"

"Stage 2b. One lymph node had cancer. No other spread." Gail spoke as if she'd practiced saying those words over and over again. "Now it's January and we're going to decide what to do next. Mastectomy or lumpectomy with radiation to the site. Maybe chemo."

Listening to Gail talk was like listening to someone retell my story. In some ways, we were so similar, starting with the cancer catching her unaware. Maybe women with a family history of breast cancer lived with the fear every day, but Gail and I, like so many other women, had been minding our own business, not expecting cancer to interrupt our plans, to take over our lives.

Gail wore no wedding ring on her left hand. But I couldn't assume she wasn't married. Or that she didn't have a significant other.

"How is your family handling all of this?"

"My family?" Gail almost looked confused, as if she didn't understand my question. "I'm divorced. No husband. No boyfriend. My parents live in Minnesota."

"Any kids?"

"A daughter and a son."

"Have you told them?"

"No. I didn't want to ruin the holidays."

I tried to not show my surprise. "No one suspected anything?"

"My daughter spent this Christmas with her husband's family. And my son is in college—and well, you know how kids are. He was home, but he was so busy with his friends that it was easy to not say anything. I didn't want to worry him."

"I can understand that. I didn't tell anyone in my family right away, either." Yet another thing in common with Gail Ferguson. "So when are you going to tell them?"

"I thought maybe you could help me figure out how to tell them."

Me?

A little more than twelve months' head start made me an expert when it came to breast cancer—at least to Gail. There was no need to let on how much I struggled with all the aftereffects—not now, anyway. This morning was about encouraging her. I was a little farther down the road than Gail, which meant that, if I chose, I could double back and walk alongside her. And I understood not wanting to tell family right away. Our reasons might be different, but I still understood.

All the other people in the room—the trio of women sitting together, laughing and talking, the college-age guy hunched in front of his laptop, blocking out any noise with a pair of blue earbuds, the man and woman sitting together on the couch—they were leading normal lives. Expecting things to go as they planned. But behind their brand-new calendars and just-begun-to-be-filled schedules, they didn't know what the day held. Not really. Disruption was a phone call, a text, a lab report away.

I didn't know any of them. Couldn't help them.

Until Harper had asked me to meet her, I hadn't known Gail, either. Now I did. And I knew what Gail was facing—the doctors' appointments, the decisions, the questions—even better than she did.

The first domino fell the night of my engagement party. Only now did I know all that was set in motion with Dr. Sartwell's phone call. Only now did I know how much I'd lose . . . and how much I'd gain in the process. I didn't want Gail to walk through all the losses alone.

But I wasn't the one to walk alongside her. Revisit all those places. Could I be of any help to her when I was still enmeshed in my own struggles? But then, hadn't Payton wrestled with the same doubts—wondering if she could help me when she didn't have all the answers? Until she'd realized it wasn't about having all the answers.

"You should tell your family—your children and your parents—right away. As soon as you can. They need to know." What was the best way to do this when her family wasn't all in the same town? This wasn't the time to struggle to think. "You can set up a group Skype session . . . something like that. Then you can tell them at the same time, and you don't have to do it more than once."

"I hadn't thought of that."

I hesitated to say anything more, but the offer couldn't be stopped, no matter how much I tried to resist it. "I could help you figure out what to say, if you want—anticipate some of their questions. You won't have all the answers, but we can try to figure out as many of the questions they might have as we can. Then you can always tell them you'll get the answers to any others."

"Good."

I took a sip of my coffee to give myself time to gather my thoughts. Wait. I'd made a list of possible talking points, but hearing that Gail's family didn't know had thrown me so much that I'd forgotten.

I opened my note in my phone. "You said you're figuring out your course of action, right?"

"Yes."

"When's your next appointment?"

"I see my doctor on Thursday."

"Don't be afraid to ask for a second opinion. It's important that you trust your doctors."

"I'll keep that in mind, although so far I'm happy." Gail had been tapping notes into her phone. "Anything else I should think of?"

"Right now, telling your family is the first step. And then figuring out what you're going to do. That will determine a lot—like how your job is affected."

"Thank you for everything, Jillian. You've been such a great help."

"Feel free to text me if you ever want to ask anything else." That was only the right thing to do. And a text was more impersonal than a phone call.

Gail tucked her hair behind her ear. Surely she'd thought about losing her hair. About the possibility of losing a breast. Now, when we'd just said good-bye, wasn't the time to say, *"Oh, wait, I forgot to mention . . ."*

Her doctors would address all those realities, just as mine had.

How odd that I was the one with the expertise. The one answering the questions, not asking them. It was as if, because of my past, I could so clearly see Gail's future . . . I was some macabre version of a fortune-teller.

All the way home, I warred with the desire to weep for Gail and the knowledge that tears did no good. There was enough sorrow wrapped around cancer . . . and not enough tears to quench it.

Both physical and emotional exhaustion pressed against me as I sat on the edge of my bed, ready to forget my time with Gail. To close my eyes and sleep. But my thoughts whirled with all the questions Gail needed to ask her doctors—and all the possible answers she'd receive.

I just got back from meeting Gail.

My text to Harper was sent almost without my realizing it.

I know you helped her.

I didn't do much. I listened. Offered some suggestions. Told her to tell her family.

They don't know?

No. She didn't want to mess up their holidays.

I couldn't have done that.

Everyone handles things differently. Anyway, I just wanted to let you know.

Thanks, Jill. Thanks.

I stared at my phone.

I could have done more.

I should have done more.

Meeting for coffee, that was one thing—one emotionally safe thing. If I did anything more, it would be like revisiting the scene of an accident. No, worse—it would be as if someone had filmed the accident in slow motion, and I'd be watching it again, knowing what was happening, unable to close my eyes, unable to mute the sounds.

I'd told Gail she could call or text if she had any more questions.

"God, help me . . . God, help me . . ."

Where had those words—that rough prayer—come from?

All during our time together, I hadn't mentioned God . . . still didn't know how to do that. *If* I should do that.

As much as I didn't want to get more involved with Gail, with all I knew her future held, I knew there was more I could do for her.

Gail, this is Jillian. I'd be happy to go with you to any of your doctors' appointments, if you think it would help. And I'm praying for you.

I waited. No response after twenty minutes. That was okay. Gail might be busy. Or she might not want a just-talked-to-you-once stranger to go with her to an appointment.

But I'd done what I thought I should do. And surely God listened to less than perfect prayers like mine.

Back when I was in middle school and high school, occasionally I'd been asked to let someone who was considering coming to the school shadow me for the day—attend classes with me, go to lunch with me. It was one day of my life—my school life, surrounded by teachers and classmates.

The offer I'd made to Gail? It was open-ended. And if she said yes, I'd be stepping into something personal to her. To me.

But I wasn't going to rescind my offer. I couldn't.

My text was still there, unanswered, but it was the right

thing to do. I hadn't stopped to think about all the reasons I wasn't qualified to help Gail. My fatigue. My inability to focus. I could sit beside her and listen, even if I was tired. Take notes. Be a presence . . . a very new friend who'd gone before her.

33

SNAGGING A BOOTH at Over Easy before the usual Saturday morning rush was worth leaving the house at seven o'clock. Winston had just raised his head from where he snoozed on the end of our bed and given us a one-eyed glance before going back to sleep, no longer afraid Geoff was going to insist he sleep in his kennel. He'd probably still be in the same place when we got home.

Geoff handed his menu to the waitress wearing a T-shirt decorated with a smiley face made of egg eyes and a bacon smile, having ordered his breakfast tacos. "I'm glad you suggested this, Jill. I can't remember the last time we had breakfast here."

"It was probably back when I had long hair." I offered him a half smile and tried to raise my nonexistent eyebrow at him. "What? It was a joke, Geoff."

"O-kay." His grin was hesitant. "I just wasn't expecting that."

"I know. I'm trying some different things—like ordering huevos rancheros. Besides, whatever I don't eat, I know you'll finish off."

I sipped my Boulder Breakfast tea—another "let me try something new" decision that I wasn't so sure I'd continue. I was too much of a coffee girl. "I was also thinking about the New Year and how everyone makes resolutions . . . even I do. I did." I pulled a folded piece of paper from my purse sitting next to me in the booth. Unfolded it, smoothing it out on the top of the table. "I've written down a list of at least ten items I want to accomplish this year. And then I realized how silly it was."

"What do you mean? Making goals is a good thing."

"Not for me. I have a difficult time keeping track of things from one day to the next—from one hour to the next, sometimes. I'm thankful I remembered to put this list in my purse before we left the house this morning."

"Then make multiple copies of it. Tape it up on the bathroom mirror. Or put it in Evernote."

I held up my hand to stop all the suggestions. "I appreciate you helping me. Really, I do."

This was what Geoff did—he always tried to help me. But he didn't understand, not really. He wasn't home during the day when I was looking for the list, trying to remember what it looked like. Where I'd put it. Where I'd put the tape so I could tape it somewhere. When I tried to decide if I should tape it on the bathroom mirror or the bedroom mirror or somewhere in the kitchen. Decide if putting it in Evernote was better. And if I did, what virtual notebook I should use, what tags I should use so I could find it again.

Geoff unwrapped his silverware from his cloth napkin, setting his fork, knife, and spoon just so. How had I not noticed this habit during all our months together? Was this particularity something he'd picked up from his parents?

It didn't matter. He was Geoff. My Geoff. Not his parents.

"So what are you thinking of doing?"

"I know you're probably wondering why I even brought this list. It's so I can do this—" I folded the paper and tore it in half—"and tell you I'm choosing a word instead."

"A word? One word?"

"Yes. Just one word. I know—that was a little dramatic, right? But I'm starting something new, so I wanted to emphasize it."

"Okay. What made you decide to do this?"

"I read a few blog posts about people who choose one word to focus on for the year."

"It sounds simple enough."

"Sort of. But then again, some people said concentrating on a word like *kindness* or *gratitude* or *forgiveness* changed their lives. They filtered their decisions, their choices, through the word."

"You read a couple of blogs and you want to do this?"

"I found a book and a website, too." Maybe I should have

brought my laptop to show Geoff. "I like the simplicity of it—and the idea that it could change who I am in a year."

"I thought that's what God was for."

I stilled. "That bothers you, doesn't it?"

"What?"

"That I've decided to believe in God."

"No, it doesn't bother me, exactly. I just don't understand it. First there's God, then there's this one-word thing."

"The two are related."

"They are? How?"

As I prepared an answer, the waitress appeared with our breakfasts, interrupting our conversation to set our plates in front of us and ask if we needed anything else, then refilling Geoff's coffee and bringing me a fresh silver carafe of hot water. I took a moment to savor all the fragrant aromas.

"Have you chosen a word already?" Geoff posed the question, but his attention was on his food.

"Yes. I've been thinking about it . . . praying about it . . . for the last week."

Geoff stiffened when I mentioned praying. "So what's the word? Or do you want me to guess?"

"No, it's not a guessing game." I set my fork and knife on my plate. "I chose the word *hope*."

"Hope."

"I want more hope this year. For me. For you. For us."

"And this goes back to the God thing?"

"Why do you have to say 'the God thing'? Yes, believing in God is giving me more hope . . . and I want to build on that every day this year."

"*Hope* is a good word." Geoff raised his hand, offering me a grin. "Not that you need my approval."

"Geoff, stop it!"

"It was a joke. Really. A joke."

I took a bite of egg, avocado, and black beans to buy myself some time. "I was wondering if . . . if you wanted to pick a word for the year, too."

"Me?" Geoff glanced at me over the rim of his glasses. "I don't even do resolutions."

"I thought it'd be fun if we both picked a word."

"Fun." Geoff grinned again and then took a bite of his breakfast tacos.

"Yes—fun."

"No, that's my word—*fun*."

"You're picking your word that quickly?" I swallowed against the sting at the back of my throat. Why wasn't he being serious? "You don't want to think about it?"

"I don't have to think about it. You want more hope this year. I want more fun."

"More fun."

"Yes. With everything going on, with all the stress, we're forgetting to laugh. To have fun. I want more of that. It can be something as simple as this—going out for breakfast—or watching a movie that makes us laugh. Or how about you go to the cybersecurity conference in the spring with me?"

"What?"

"I've been thinking about it and I don't want to go by myself. Come with me. We'll have fun."

"But it's just in Denver—"

"Fine, so we save on airfare and splurge on a hotel room. Your parents can watch Winston—although your dad may never give him back. And we'll eat out at some nice restaurants. Maybe we can go see a show one night. Pretend like we're tourists, not Colorado natives."

"Geoff, that sounds—"

"Like fun? I know! So are you going to run away to Denver with me in the spring?"

A grin spread across Geoff's face, reminding me of the early days of our relationship. Before cancer. Before the children-or-no-children stress. I wanted to see this smile more often. I wanted to love Geoff for who he was.

My husband wanted more fun? Fine. I would help that happen.

"Absolutely." I raised my red coffee mug in the air, waiting for him to toast the decision with me. "Decision made. Denver in the spring, it is."

There were certain advantages to having twenty-four-hour access to the hospital.

Johanna welcomed how most of the hallways were still dimly lit at four o'clock in the morning. How, save for a few other early hour employees, the building was empty of personnel and visitors. She'd worn ballet flats, allowing herself to move almost without sound as if she were on some vital secret mission.

That wasn't exactly the case, but she'd rather accomplish what she came to do and leave unnoticed.

Behind the closed doors of the staff café came sounds of people preparing for the day. Laughter. Conversation. Footsteps. The clink of silverware and ceramic plates and glasses.

Nearby, the atrium was a play of light and shadow, the stately grand piano sitting in the muted glow of two overhead spotlights while the world outside the glass windows was still in predawn darkness.

Johanna stood for a moment, unable to move into the light. Doing so would negate a choice made years ago.

She unclenched her fists and took one slow step at a time until she stood by the padded piano bench. Pulled it out, easing the legs across the tile floor. Sat. Moved her purse from her shoulder to the floor. Inhaled a slow breath to steady her heartbeat. Rested her hands on the white keys.

Closed her eyes.

She needed to remember the music. The notes.

Wait.

She was forgetting one of the most important things.

Johanna bent and retrieved the digital voice recorder from her purse, then paused. Where should she place it? A quick scan of the area revealed several chairs near the alcove. Johanna retrieved one, setting it close to the piano and then balancing the recorder on the seat.

Now to settle her thoughts again. To try to remember what she'd forced herself to forget for so long.

For some reason, she'd resisted purchasing any music, unwilling to do anything more than was absolutely needed to accomplish her task. If she was going to do this, she would do it without help of any kind. She stumbled through a few practice scales before her hands found the rhythm, moving from simple to more complicated.

All she hoped was that she could do it once, instead of needing to try over and over. Having to push Stop. Erase. Record. Again and again.

Enough. The longer she stayed, the more of a chance someone would come along and find her here. Johanna rose, stepped over to the chair, and found the Record button. Pressed it. Moved back to the bench, intent on sitting so that she made no sound.

Now all she needed to do was remember a melody. A song. Something . . . something beautiful.

It had been years since she'd searched her mind, trying to remember a piano composition.

"She has an amazing ability to hear music and be able to play it. How old is she?"

"She's four."

"Four. Why, that's unheard of!"

The voices from her past entangled with her thoughts, confusing her, and her hands froze, hovering over the keyboard. Her fingers curled into fists again. She couldn't think of the past now. Not if she wanted to finish this.

At last, she heard the music calling to her, leading her where she needed to go, and she found her way, back to the music, but not so far back that she tripped over memories. Not so close to things lost that she longed for them too much. Her hands relaxed against the keys, remembering the path into a melody that spoke of promises fulfilled, the notes warming her heart.

When the last note faded away, she opened her eyes. The air seemed alive around her, seemed to be embracing her.

How had she forgotten that feeling . . . that moment when she seemed to breathe with the music?

She'd forgotten it because she had to. And she needed to forget it again.

It was best not to linger here any longer. She'd needed to do this, even though she'd lain awake several nights, trying to talk herself out of it. But the idea, foolish as it was, wouldn't let go of her.

Johanna clasped her hands together, pressing them against her heart. She rose and turned off the recorder before depositing it in her purse. Moved the bench back into position in front of the piano.

She'd not be revisiting this part of her past again.

Time to go to work.

34

Even the simplest of weddings required a lot of prepara-tion—more than she'd ever imagined.

"I can't believe we pulled this off in four weeks." Payton turned so Jillian could zip up the back of her dress. "You need to thank Geoff for suggesting you elope."

"He certainly did make things easy for me, including packing my suitcase. All I had to do was say yes again and then get dressed."

"I thought a family-only wedding would be the simplest thing," Payton continued as Johanna began pinning her hair up. "But we still had to decide on dresses and boots and coats—"

"And you finally agreed to carry a bouquet." Johanna secured another strand of hair in place.

"It seemed silly at first, but I admit I do feel a bit more like a bride now that I'm carrying flowers."

Jillian sat on the edge of the bed to put on her black leather boots. "For not having time to go shopping together, I think we did well coordinating our dresses."

"Have to thank Johanna for getting things started there. Without her mad online shopping skills, I might be wearing sweatpants and a volleyball T-shirt."

"That was my fear." Johanna stepped back, tilting her head to assess Payton's hairstyle. "And that was a joke."

"I've got no time and even less desire to argue with you today, Jo." She leaned forward and tossed a wink at her reflection. "I do believe I look pretty good today—so far. Thank you for doing my hair and makeup."

"You're welcome."

"Do you think Zach needs to get into his bedroom for anything? I feel bad for kicking him out and turning it into a bride's room." Payton opened her makeup bag, handing it to Johanna.

"You let him use it earlier to get dressed." Johanna came alongside her and double-checked her own hair, pinning a loose tendril into place. "It's your turn now—and our turn for a little privacy."

"Another Thatcher sister getting married in an unconventional way." Jillian finished putting on her second boot, zipping it closed.

"Poor Dad. Do you think he minds not walking me

down the aisle?" Payton refreshed the blush along her cheekbones.

"Like you said, there's no aisle." Johanna turned. "And we're all walking out to the area together."

"Besides, he still has one more chance to do the traditional walk down the aisle with you."

"I may decide to keep my role as the single Thatcher sister for a while. Maybe permanently." Johanna sat in a chair, one that Zach had crafted. "And before either of you say anything, no, I haven't heard from Beckett. There's no reason for me to have talked to him."

Payton used the mirror to make eye contact with her sister. "I'm sorry, Jo."

"Why are you sorry? I don't want to hear from him."

"You don't miss him at all? You were together for eight years—"

"And those eight years are done. I don't forgive something like that." She grimaced. Shook her head. "Why are we talking about this today? It's your wedding day."

"I'm fine. I just need to put in my earrings."

Johanna stood, hands on her hips. "Where's your necklace? I'll help you with it."

"No necklace—I'm not wearing one."

"Oh? I guess you wouldn't see it since you're wearing a coat anyway."

"People aren't going to see your dress, either. And I'll take a couple of photos without my coat on after the ceremony."

Jillian smoothed her ice-blue dress. "There's no photographer."

"The pastor's wife is going to take some photos."

Johanna almost dropped the statement necklace she was putting on. "You're putting that kind of pressure on that poor woman?"

"There's no pressure. She enjoys photography and I told her that I'll be happy with whatever she gets."

"Payton, you could end up without a single good photo of your wedding day! You should have bent the 'just family' rule and gotten a professional photographer—"

"Johanna, this is my wedding day. You are absolutely not allowed to boss me around today." Payton's smile was backed with a firm voice. "We'll go back to normal interaction tomorrow. Deal?"

When Payton turned and held her hand out to Johanna, she hesitated and then smiled. "Deal."

The two shook hands.

Jillian glanced back and forth between her sisters. "Maybe we should try that more often."

"What are you talking about?"

"You and Payton came through a confrontation, an honest moment, and you both survived. Maybe we all just need to be honest with each other more often in the future."

"Duly noted." Payton nodded, applying another bit of lipstick.

"I do have a gift for you, Payton." Johanna seemed to have difficulty making eye contact with her. "I mean, it's not exactly a wedding gift. And you don't have to accept it if you don't want to . . ."

"A gift . . . What is it, Johanna?"

Johanna pulled a small digital recorder from her purse and handed it to her. "It's this."

Payton stood, her palm open, unsure what to do. "I don't understand."

"You said you wished you could have music for your ceremony. There's a song on there . . . if you want to use it."

Payton pushed the Play button, and all three waited for just a few seconds before the first notes on a piano began and filled the silence in the room. After a moment, she turned it off.

"Where did you get this?"

"It doesn't matter. And I don't mind if you don't like it. If you don't want to use it. I understand. It was just an idea . . ."

"I love it." Payton pulled her hand back, preventing Johanna from taking the digital recorder from her. "The song is beautiful. Who did you get to do this?"

"No one. I mean . . . that's me. I'm playing the piano."

"You? But you don't—"

"I used to play. A long time ago." Johanna's skin turned pink. "I'm a little rusty . . . well, a lot rusty. Like I said, you don't have to use it."

"Johanna." Payton swept aside all of the excuses by stepping forward and daring to hug her sister, caught up in the fragrance of Coco perfume. "Thank you. This is such a wonderful gift. I only stopped listening because I want to hear the entire song for the first time during the ceremony— with Zach and everyone else."

"Really?"

"Yes. Will you turn it on for me when we start?"

"Yes. Of course. I'll tell the pastor."

A swift rap on the door interrupted the moment.

"You ladies ready to take a walk?" Dad's voice came through the door.

Jillian opened the door. "We're ready."

"Good. Your mother's been standing here holding Payton's bouquet for the past ten minutes. If you don't hurry up, I may just ask the pastor to remarry us."

When they exited the room, Zach stood outside, holding Payton's winter-white coat.

"Sorry to keep you waiting." Payton offered Zach a smile.

"You were worth waiting for." Zach's voice dropped low so that only she could hear him.

"I never really thought of myself as a lace kind of girl. . . ." Payton's fingertips skimmed the delicate neckline of her knee-length gown.

"You look beautiful. I'm just sorry you have to wear a coat, but I can't have you freezing before we say, 'I do,' can I?"

"No." She pressed a kiss to his cheek. "We wouldn't want that to happen."

"All right, you two. No more dillydallying." Her father's words were laced with laughter.

"Yes, sir."

Zach helped Payton into her coat, while Jillian and Johanna each slipped into coordinating pale-pink coats. All the women, including the two mothers, wore pink leather gloves. On the brief walk to Pepper's bench, the men fell into one group and the women into another, as the pastor's wife took photos.

"I have to admit, I wasn't too sure about this at first." Payton's mom linked arms with Zach's mother, coming alongside Payton.

"I am so glad to hear you say that." Zach's mom shivered, tucking her wool scarf more tightly around her neck. "I wasn't either—and it *is* cold like we expected—but there's something special about having the ceremony here. And the fresh snowfall is like its own kind of decoration, isn't it?"

"I like it, too—it's definitely a Colorado wedding." Mom's smile encompassed everyone in their group. "I can honestly say I'm glad you and Zach chose to do your wedding this way."

"Zach and I are so thankful you're here today—all of you. But especially you, Sharon, and Weston." No one else knew the painful history, the years of separation, between Zach and his parents—and how it was just beginning to heal. "I'm looking forward to getting to know both of you more in the future."

"Maybe once classes are out, you and Zach can come to California for a visit."

"Maybe we can."

"The guys are all getting along." Her mother pointed to the group of men, who were talking and laughing as if they were going to a casual get-together, not a wedding.

"They're probably talking football."

She and Zach would be balancing the expectations of two families now. But she wasn't going to worry about that today.

Today was a celebration.

They had the unlikeliest of beginnings for a marriage . . .

and all kinds of hopes to unpack for their future. The scent of her bouquet was lifted by a frosted winter breeze. White roses, pink ranunculus, and tulips. Was that the aroma of hope?

At Pepper's bench, their pastor called the group to order.

"We're informal here today—and a bit chilly. And we all know why we're here, to witness Payton and Zach's wedding." He motioned to Pepper's bench. "The parents are welcome to sit on the bench if they'd like to. Everyone else is welcome to come gather around it. Except for you, Payton and Zach. Will you two please come and stand here in front of me?"

Payton could only hope that a brief visit to Pepper's bench earlier that day made it easier for her parents to be here now—to sit next to Zach's mother and father. Whispers of "Huddle close" and soft laughter accompanied the few moments of people finding their places.

"The actual ceremony will be brief, but before we start, Payton's sister Johanna contributed some music to begin the ceremony."

At his announcement, murmurs of "What?" and "Johanna's doing music?" were hushed as Johanna stepped forward, her gaze focused on Payton. "This is a gift for my sister . . . and Zach, too, of course."

There was a pause . . . and then soft piano music floated into the air. The melody, faint as it was, seemed to slip into the clearing as if it belonged there. The unexpected interlude lasted two, maybe three minutes, lingering in the stillness, until Johanna stepped back next to Jillian and the pastor spoke again.

"And now, Payton and Zach asked for a few moments to share something before they exchange their wedding vows."

Payton handed her bouquet to Jillian, removed her gloves, and then unbelted her coat. "Will you hold this for me, Johanna?"

"You're taking photos now?"

"No."

Payton shivered as the wintry air touched her skin through the sheer lace of her long sleeves. Zach took her hand, offering her a smile before addressing their family.

"Thank you all for joining us today. We can't imagine this day without everyone being here. We promise not to keep you outside in the cold for too long."

When he squeezed Payton's hand, she knew it was her turn to talk.

"Unfortunately, not everyone can be here—and I'm sorry Pepper isn't with us. We all are. That's why we wanted to have the ceremony here, at the bench Zach made to honor her memory. And there's another way we wanted to honor Pepper . . ." Her voice faltered, and Zach stepped closer, wrapping his arm around her waist. "Pepper bought me a very special gift on our sixteenth birthday. A gift I've never worn because it came with a bit of a stipulation."

Zach slipped the necklace from his coat pocket and into her hand, and she closed her fingers around the chain.

"Pepper bought this for me to wear when I knew Jesus like she did." Payton held the delicate gold cross with diamonds up, letting it dangle from her fingers. "I can now say that I do know Jesus like my twin sister did. So, before Zach puts a wedding band on my finger, I've asked him to put this necklace on me."

Payton returned the precious gift from her twin sister to Zach. As he stepped behind her, she closed her eyes . . . waited . . . and then the delicate chain came to rest against her skin, the small cross lying above her heart.

There was a moment, a fleeting moment of completion . . . something she'd been waiting for, longing for, since Pepper had died almost twelve years ago. The emptiness, the loss, was gone. Now, like no other moment, because of their common faith, Payton knew she'd see her twin sister again.

She kept her eyes closed. She didn't want anyone else's reaction to intrude upon this moment. This time was for her. Her and Pepper.

Payton's fingertips brushed the chain. The cross. Stayed there.

She wasn't wearing the necklace for Pepper.

But she would wear it, and when people asked, she would tell them about her faith and about her sister. How much she loved her . . . and missed her still.

"Can we get down to the business of marrying the two of you?" The pastor's question, infused with laughter, disrupted the moment.

Payton pressed her fingertips against the cross. "Love you, Pepper."

The whisper evaporated into the air.

Now she was ready to get married. She didn't want to keep Zach waiting any longer.

"Absolutely!" Zach shouted his reply, turned her around, and kissed her.

The pastor chuckled. "I haven't said you may kiss your bride yet."

"I'm sorry." Zach didn't look apologetic at all. "I got carried away there for a moment."

"Payton." Johanna spoke in a loud whisper. "Take your coat or you'll freeze before you make it through the vows."

Laughter floated around them.

"Good advice, Johanna."

Zach helped her into her coat again, making a grand display of belting it as the pastor tapped his watch. When he did pronounce them man and wife several moments later, Zach asked, "May I kiss her now?"

"Yes, Zach. You may now officially kiss your wife."

Zach followed his "Amen!" by pulling her close and dipping her back over his arm with a flourish and a long, lingering, perfect kiss.

35

AFTER TAKING WEDDING PHOTOS and enjoying some simple appetizers at Zach's cabin, it was almost time for all of us to pile into our cars and caravan to Breckenridge for dinner. A final chance to celebrate Payton and Zach before the newlyweds waved good-bye and headed . . . where, they refused to say. Come Monday, Zach would be back at work at 3:17 Cabinets and Payton would once again be a college student and a volleyball coach.

But first, I needed to execute Payton's unexpected request. She was greeting Zach with a kiss as he and Geoff came in the cabin's back door. What had those two guys been doing—and how had I not noticed their absence? I had no time to figure that out, since I needed to interrupt Mom and Johanna and convince my sister to go outside. In the dark. And the cold. Without telling her why.

Not that I knew the reason why, either.

I eased my way between Mom and my older sister. "Johanna, would you come here, please?"

Johanna stopped midsentence. "Now? Where are we going?"

"Just come with me, okay?"

I answered Mom's raised eyebrows with a silent *"Sorry."*

I retrieved our coats from the closet as Payton joined us at the front door. "Here. We're going to need these, or so Payton says."

"Why do we need our coats?" Johanna refused to take hers.

"Because we have to do something." Payton grinned as Zach helped her into her coat.

"And we have to do whatever this 'something' is outside? Can't we stay inside, where it's warm?"

"Jo, just put your coat on." I held her coat out to her. "Please."

"Fine." She slipped it on with exaggerated motions, yanking her leather gloves out of her pocket and putting those on, too.

"Stay warm." Zach pulled the collar of Payton's coat up around her neck, giving her another kiss.

"We will. We won't be long."

"Take all the time you need."

My "What's going on?" look tossed at Geoff was met with a blank stare . . . and then a grin.

No help from him.

"Wait." Zach handed me a long-handled flashlight. "You'll need this."

"Okay . . . thanks."

Once we were ready, I waved to everyone in the room. "We'll be right back."

"Don't be too long. Dinner reservations—"

"We know, Dad." I opened the door and ushered my sisters ahead of me, ready to close the door on any other comments.

"Stay, Laz." Payton stopped, but Zach grabbed hold of Laz's collar, preventing his—*their*—dog from joining us. "Thank you."

"See you soon, Wife." He kissed her.

She returned the kiss. "I like the sound of that."

Johanna shook her head and gave a soft snort. "You two are going to be disgusting, aren't you?"

"It's the privilege of all newlyweds."

Once the door closed behind us, I slipped between Johanna and Payton, linking my arms with theirs. "Where to, Payton?"

"Pepper's bench." There was a smile in Payton's voice.

"To Pepper's bench it is, then." Johanna stepped out into the darkness.

We walked without speaking to one another, the sky an indigo blanket over us, woven with silver stars. The flashlight Zach had handed me lit a small path ahead, just enough for us to take the needed next steps.

But as we got closer to the bench, the area surrounding it seemed to be glowing, awash in soft light.

My steps slowed, causing Johanna and Payton to slow down, too. "What is going on?"

Payton moved forward. "Let's go see."

Several portable lights were set up in a wide semicircle, revealing three rocking chairs arranged facing the bench.

"What is this, Payton?" Johanna's question, spoken out loud, echoed the one in my head.

"These are your belated Christmas gifts from Zach . . . and mine, too. He said I could say these were from us, but truthfully, this was all his idea. He didn't have a chance to give them to us back in December because . . . well, you know how things were just getting settled between us then. And he'd already made plans to visit his parents. So . . . Merry Christmas."

"I can't believe Zach would do something like this." I didn't seem to be able to step inside the ring of light.

"He chopped down one of the trees in the clearing near here . . . kind of like he did . . ."

"To make Pepper's bench." Johanna finished Payton's sentence.

"Yes. So part of each rocking chair has that similarity to the bench. Zach realizes we can't get up here to Winter Park, to Pepper's bench, that often, so he made us rocking chairs."

I moved first. "I don't know about anyone else, but I want to try my chair out."

"I do, too."

Without thinking about it, we sat, maintaining our customary positions—Payton and Johanna bookending me.

I settled into the chair, and for just a moment, the fleeting image of me, rocking a baby to sleep, interrupted the moment. But I blinked, pushing the thought away. I needed to stay here, in the present, with my sisters.

"So . . . you're married." I broke the silence.

"I am." Payton's words were carried on a sigh.

"Are you happy?" It was a silly question, but I found myself asking it anyway.

"I am that, too."

"In all this rush to get married in the past month, did you and Zach figure out where you're living? I mean, Winter Park and North Denver . . ." Johanna, ever the practical one, had to have been mulling that question over for a while. With everything else Payton and Zach had to do to get ready for the wedding, she'd shown remarkable restraint not asking about their living arrangements.

"Our own little long-distance dilemma, right?" Payton huffed a breath. "His boss is being gracious and letting Zach do more days remote so he can be at my place during the week, and we'll be up here on the weekends."

"A bit of a hodgepodge living situation, then." As Johanna rocked back and forth, pebbles and sticks crunched beneath her chair.

"For now, yes. And . . . keep this between us, but Zach may decide to start his own business."

"That's a big step."

"We know, and we're still talking about it. So, early stages yet, but it's something he's always wanted to do. Until then, we're just going to enjoy being married."

"It's kind of amazing, isn't it . . . you and Zach? I mean, almost eighteen months ago, when Zach showed up at Festivities . . . did you ever imagine . . . ?" My voice trailed off into the darkness.

"No. Never. I didn't even like the guy." Payton laughed. "And now I couldn't think of life without him. I think Pepper would like how things turned out."

"We've all changed so much, just in the last six months, haven't we?" I tucked my hands in my coat pockets. "I'm unemployed. I don't know if I'll ever have children. Yet I know my husband better than ever before."

We allowed the conversation to lag for a moment. Despite the cold wrapping around us, none of us were ready to go back to the cabin. The warmth. All the people waiting for us.

"What do you think Pepper would say if she were here?" Payton's question didn't surprise me—and I doubt it caught Johanna off guard, either.

"In some ways, I feel closer to her out here." I tilted my head back, watching the stars overhead that sparkled like a jeweler's precious gems. "I suppose she'd be happy you're wearing the necklace."

"I wonder if I would be—if she were here. If she were alive, the time capsule would still be closed. I might not be married to Zach . . ."

"We can't what-if our lives, Payton—always wondering what life might be like if things were different."

"Easier said than done some days, Jilly."

"Agreed." Johanna sounded as if her thoughts were someplace else.

I paused for a moment, debating on whether to speak out loud the thought lingering inside my mind. "I think . . . I think the last six months have been good for all of us."

Johanna stopped rocking. Shifted, half-turning to look at

me. "Good for all of us? How can you say that with every-thing we've all dealt with, everything we're still dealing with?"

"I'm not forgetting any of it, believe me." I wouldn't go so far as to admit there were nights that I battled both hot flashes and unrelenting memories of all that had happened—and thoughts of all that might or might not happen in the future. "We even failed at the book club, if we're going to be technical about it. But we didn't give up on each other . . . and that's something, isn't it?"

"It is." Payton's voice was a whisper.

"I hadn't considered that." Johanna's voice carried into the night.

"Oh, we're still the Thatcher sisters—minus one. And we all still tend to take our assigned places—oldest, middle, youngest. We spark off each other, like we always have."

"And like we always will." Johanna stated the truth like the fact it was.

"But so far, we haven't quit on each other."

Johanna gave a small laugh. "We haven't . . . so far."

"That's why I wanted to come here, just the three of us." Payton spoke up. "Last year? It was like we declared some kind of truce in Pepper's memory after all that stuff happened. I'm hoping that we can do better in the future. Maybe . . . maybe we've learned to trust each other a little more."

"I think we know each other better." I reached out my hands to Johanna and Payton.

"Agreed." Johanna squeezed my hand.

"I don't know what's up ahead for any of us." Payton continued. "But right this minute—even knowing we don't agree on everything and that we won't always understand each other—can't we just be thankful we're sisters? Not for Pepper's sake—although I think she'd agree with me if she were still alive—but for our sakes."

"Yes."

"Yes."

The winter air frosted our words. We held on to one another, refusing to let go.

I struggled to put my thoughts in order. "It's funny . . . To get here, to this moment, it's taken an odd mix of forgetting and remembering, hasn't it?"

"Forgetting and remembering . . . is that how we manage to be sisters?" Johanna seemed skeptical about my theory.

"Pepper would say there are moments to remember . . . and yet, you're right, Jilly. There are moments to forget, too." Payton's voice linked us all together.

"What's one thing you're going to remember, Joey?"

"Me? I'm going to remember how things didn't go like I planned, no matter how much I tried to control them . . . and I'm going to remember that you two stood by me."

"I would have to say that I'll remember that, too." Payton spoke next.

"That would make three of us." My words rounded out our agreement.

"Look at that." Johanna's words seemed woven with a mixture of laughter and tears. "The Thatcher sisters have found common ground again."

I held on to my sisters' hands. "We have at that—and it's a good place to be."

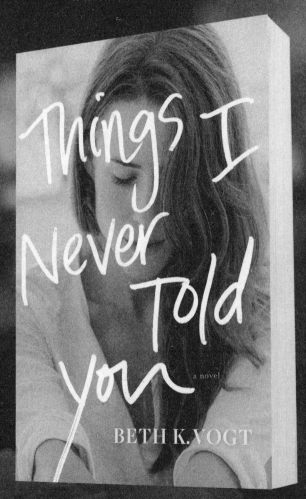

THE WHAT-IFS TAUNTED ME every time I visited my parents, but any hope of beginning again had vanished years ago— if there'd ever been one.

What would have happened if my parents had gone through with selling the house in Colorado Springs my sisters and I had grown up in? If they'd labeled and taped up all the boxes—the clothes, the books, the dishes, the photographs, the awards, and the trophies—and unpacked them in a different house?

A change of location. A chance to start over.

But unexpected loss held my parents captive.

For the most part, our family seemed unchanged. The

kitchen clock—a porcelain plate decorated with bright red-and-yellow flowers but lacking any numerals to designate the passing of time—hung in the same place it had since a dozen Mother's Days ago. The same white wooden shutters hid the bay windows in the breakfast nook. The same worn round table in the middle, surrounded by four chairs adorned with nondescript blue cushions our mother changed out every few years—whenever Johanna reminded her to do so.

I pushed the Start button on the once-new dishwasher. My parents had installed it at the Realtor's recommendation when they'd planned to move into the larger house that offered a coveted view of Pikes Peak.

Time to focus on the cheesecakes—the engagement party dessert finale. The hum of the dishwasher blended with garbled conversation as the door between the kitchen and dining room opened, the sound of Jillian's fiancé's booming laughter sneaking in. Geoff and his corny jokes.

"Just getting the dessert, Kim—"

"I'm not your timekeeper, little sister." Johanna's no-nonsense voice interrupted my concentration.

I stiffened, gripping the handles of the fridge. Why hadn't I posted a Do Not Enter sign on the door? Maybe I should have caved to Nash's insistence to attend the party, even though tonight was more work than play for me. Why not have my boyfriend act as bouncer outside the kitchen? Flex his muscles and run interference?

I had no time for my oldest sister. Any minute now, Kimberlee would return from setting up the silver carafes of coffee and hot water for tea, along with cream, sugar, spoons, and other necessities. She'd expect the trio of cheesecakes to be arranged on their individual stands—my job tonight, since we'd only had the caterers deliver the food for such a small gathering.

"Do you need something, Johanna?" I pulled the first cheesecake from the fridge, my mouth watering at the thought of key lime and dollops of whipped cream. Being the party planner for tonight meant I'd had no chance to indulge in the hors d'oeuvres or cocktails, despite this being my other sister's engagement party. And vegan or not, I could appreciate a decadent dessert—and postpone interacting with Johanna.

"You and Kimberlee are pretty good at this event-planning business." Johanna leaned against the kitchen counter.

"Mom and Jillian seem happy. That's the important thing." I settled the cheesecake on its stand, the plastic wrap clinging to my fingers as I uncovered it. "It's all about finding out what people want and then making it happen."

"Festivities is making enough to pay the bills, apparently."

"Yes."

Not that I was going to produce an Excel spreadsheet of our accounts payable and receivable for my oldest sister.

"You two didn't charge Mom and Dad full price—"

"Really, Johanna?" Not sparing my sister a glance, I shoved the fridge door closed with my hip, a turtle cheesecake balanced in my hands.

"Oh, don't get in a huff, Payton. Honestly, how do you manage your customers if you're so touchy?"

And this . . . this was yet another reason why I didn't

come home unless absolutely necessary. I concentrated on transporting the second cheesecake from the fridge to the island, refusing to square off with my sister. Best to change the subject and prep the desserts.

"Jillian and Geoff seem perfect for one another, don't they?"

Johanna took the bait. "Of course they do. They enjoy the same foods. The same movies. He makes her laugh. They're content with a typical version of happily ever after."

And now my question had set Johanna's sights on Jillian. Should I ignore the unspoken criticism or not? "You don't approve of Geoff?"

"I wouldn't marry him. They remind me of that old nursery rhyme. 'Jack Sprat could eat no fat, his wife could eat no lean . . .'"

"And I suppose one of the reasons you're marrying Beckett is because you make such a good-looking couple?"

"You've got to admit he's easy on the eyes."

Easy on the eyes? Who said stuff like that anymore? "Not that he's around very often for anyone to get a look at him."

"If I don't mind being in a long-distance relationship, I don't see why you should be so critical." Johanna's stilettos tapped a sharp staccato on the wood floor, her platinum-blonde hair caught up in a tight ponytail that swished down between her shoulder blades.

"I'm not criticizing. Just mentioning that Beckett plays the role of the Invisible Man quite well."

"You're almost as funny as Geoff." Ice frosted Johanna's words.

Time to change the subject again unless I wanted a full-blown argument with one sister during my other sister's party. Not that I could think of a topic Johanna and I agreed on. "Isn't it odd? You and Beckett have been engaged for over two years now. Shouldn't we be planning your wedding so Jillian and Geoff don't beat you two down the aisle?"

"It's not a race. Beckett's stationed in Wyoming and I don't want to give up my job to move there—"

"Did I know Beckett was in Wyoming?"

"Honestly, Payton, he's been there for a year." Johanna sniffed. "But then, it's not like we chat every other day, is it? You and Pepper were the close ones—"

Heat flushed my neck. My face. "There's no need to bring Pepper into the conversation, is there?"

"Why, after all this time, are you still so sensitive about talking about her?"

"I'm not sensitive. I just don't see why you had to mention Pepper when we were talking about you and Beckett—"

The sound of voices rose once again as the kitchen door opened. Poor Kimberlee. She didn't know she'd have to assume Jillian's usual position as the neutral zone between Johanna and me.

"Have you seen Jillian?"

Not Kimberlee. Mom, who was also an expert human buffer.

"Isn't she with Geoff?" I removed the cling wrap from the cheesecake.

"She was a few moments ago, but now I can't find her." Mom circled the island as if she expected to find her middle daughter crouching down hiding from her. "Isn't it almost time for dessert? And aren't we supposed to open gifts after that? They certainly received a lot of presents, didn't they?"

"Yes. It's a great turnout." If only the kitchen didn't feel like a revolving three-ring circus. How would Johanna like it if our family showed up at the hospital pharmacy where she was in charge?

Before I could say anything else, Kimberlee, the one person I'd been waiting for, joined the crowd. "Are we all set in here, Payton?"

"Just about." I swallowed back the words *if people would stay out of my kitchen.* This wasn't my kitchen. And family or not, Mom was a client, at least for tonight, and needed to be treated like one. And I'd been dealing with Johanna for years. If I wanted tonight to be a success, the less said, the better.

"Mom, why don't you and Johanna join the guests?" I removed the classic cheesecake from the fridge. "I'll find Jillian while Kimberlee makes the announcement about dessert and Jillian and Geoff opening their gifts."

As Johanna and Mom left, I faced my business partner, shook my head, and sighed. "Family. And before that, a longtime family friend wandered in, asking for the crab dip recipe."

"It comes with working for relatives." Kimberlee took the cheesecake from me, the eclectic assortment of rings on her fingers sparkling under the kitchen lights. "But honestly, everything has gone beautifully. There's hardly any food left."

"That's because I know how to plan portions."

"It's because we know how to throw a good party."

"Well, let's keep things going and get this dessert set up."

Once the trio of cheesecakes was arranged on the table in my parents' dining room, I nodded to Kimberlee. "I've got to go find our bride-to-be."

"No problem. I can handle this." Kimberlee smoothed a wrinkle from the white tablecloth and repositioned the vase filled with bright-red poppies, my mother's favorite flowers.

"It's not like she wandered far. She's probably in the bathroom touching up her makeup."

Not that Jillian was a "refresh her makeup" kind of gal. Mascara and a little bit of basic eyeliner was her usual routine. Lipstick was reserved for fancier affairs. She'd probably be cajoled by the photographer into wearing some on her wedding day.

The upstairs bathroom was empty, lit only by the flickering flame of a cinnamon-scented candle. Where could Jillian be? A thin band of light shone out from beneath the door of Johanna and Jillian's former bedroom at the far end of the darkened hallway. Why would my sister be in there? As I moved past my old bedroom, my fingertips brushed the doorknob for a second. I pulled my hand away, balling my fingers into a fist.

I paused outside the bedroom and then rapped my knuckles against the door. "Jillian?"

Nothing . . . and then, "Payton? Do you need me for something?"

Just for her party. I eased the door open, stepping inside. "What are you doing up here? It's time to open your gifts."

What had once been Johanna and Jillian's room was now a generic guest room. At the moment, the only light came from the slender glass lamp on the bedside table. My sisters' beds had been replaced by a single larger bed covered in a gray-and-white paisley comforter. An idyllic outdoor scene adorned the wall across from the dark oak dresser.

Jillian, who'd been hunched over on the corner of the bed, straightened her shoulders. "I, um, got a phone call and decided to take it in here away from all the noise."

"Is everything okay?"

"Yes. Absolutely." Jillian's smile seemed to wobble for the briefest second. "Did you need me for something?"

"Your engagement party? It's time to dismantle that Jenga tower of gifts in the family room." I shook my head. "*Tsk*. And after all the hard work I put in arranging it."

"Right." Jillian smoothed her yellow empire-waist sundress down over her hips. "It's been a wonderful party, Payton."

"Thank you for saying so, but it's not over yet." I touched Jillian's shoulder. "You're really okay?"

She nodded so that the ends of her hair brushed against the back of my hand. "Yes. Nothing that won't wait until Monday."

I didn't know why I'd asked. It wasn't like Jillian would confide in me. We weren't the "Will you keep a secret?" kind of sisters. "All right then. Why don't you go find Geoff and I'll bring you both some dessert? Do you want key lime, classic, or turtle cheesecake?"

Now it was my sister's turn to shake her head. "I should skip it altogether. We're going wedding dress shopping soon enough, and I know I'm going to look awful—"

"Oh, stop! Don't become a weight-conscious bridezilla."

My comment earned the ghost of a laugh from my sister. "What's wrong?"

"You know Mrs. Kenton?"

"Of course—the family friend who can get away with saying, 'Oh, Payton, I knew you when . . .' and does. Every time she sees me. She pull that on you tonight?"

Red stained my sister's face. "No. She just said—in the nicest way possible, of course—that she hoped I'd lose a few pounds before the wedding."

"And what did you say?"

"Nothing."

Of course she didn't. "Jillian—"

She waved away my words. "Forget I said anything."

"It was rude." And Mrs. Kenton, family friend or not, could forget about ever seeing the recipe she'd requested. "How about I bring you a small slice of each cheesecake? Calories don't count at engagement parties, you know."

"Really small slices?"

"I promise. This is a celebration. Your one and only engagement party."

"You're right." Jillian stood, brushing her straight hair away from her face. "Tonight, we celebrate. Tomorrow . . . well, we're not thinking about that, are we?"

"No, because tomorrow means playing catch-up for me. And prepping for next week."

And Saturday morning breakfast with my family.

Something else I wasn't thinking about.

ACKNOWLEDGMENTS

THIS IS ONE OF THE FUN PARTS of writing a book: thanking everyone who helped *Moments We Forget* transition from the initial idea to the finished product. I'm blessed to be living my dream of being a writer, which began back in grade school. And I value all the help I've had along the way as I wrote this book.

Research experts: I always write stories about things I don't know, and *Moments We Forget* was no different. And so I sought out people in the know to help me get it right. Any errors are my own. Many thanks to

Barb Straker, a pharmacist who first fielded my questions as I tried to figure out just what exactly Johanna Thatcher does.

My writing friend Daphne Woodall and her husband, Gene Woodall, a hospital director of pharmacy, who helped clarify questions about Johanna's profession.

Bart Swan, a longtime family friend and a mortgage loan officer who helped me figure out how to create a work problem for Jillian. (Poor Jillian.)

Terry Kehr, my husband's former officer manager, who is also a breast cancer survivor. We sat together one morning and talked through some of the more personal aspects of her journey and how they paralleled Jillian's journey. Her choice to trust God as she battled cancer—and the repercussions of her treatment—challenges me to trust Him when I face challenges, too.

Rob Vogt, MD—that name looks familiar, doesn't it?—who helped me with the medical aspects of this book.

Publishing staff: I'm so thankful to be part of the Tyndale House Publishers family. It's both an honor and a blessing. Jan Stob (acquisitions director) and Sarah Rische (editor) helped refine my initial idea and challenged me to write a better story. And Sharon Leavitt, while no longer with Tyndale, encouraged me until the day she retired. The marketing and publicity team, including Cassidy Gage (senior marketing manager), Emily Bonga (associate marketing manager), and Katie Dodillet (director of public relations), are a wonderful support. Elizabeth Jackson (acquisitions editor) stepped in whenever needed. Julie Chen (senior designer) once again created the perfect cover for *Moments We Forget*, capturing the essence of Jillian.

Writing community:
Rachel Hauck, my dear friend and mentor, not to mention a bestselling author: You continue to help me brainstorm my novels and to be a phone call, text, or instant message away. You listen, you pray . . . and you always, always, always tell me, "You can do this."

Angie Arndt, Jeanne Takenaka, and Shari Hamlin, my Preferred Readers: You each make a difference because you see the book first and give me oh-so-crucial first feedback. You let me know what's working. What's not working. Your questions and insights helped me improve *Moments We Forget*.

Mary Agius: You walk with me and brainstorm with me, helping me to keep the story flowing and to keep me mentally on keel.

My Dream Team: You'll be assembled by the time this book goes to print. Thanks for telling others about Jillian's story. I can't do it all by myself. A special thank-you to Gail Hollingsworth, whose question "What's going to happen with the necklace Pepper left Payton?" helped me refine that story thread.

Casey Herringshaw and Lisa Jordan: I needed not one but two VAs while writing *Moments We Forget*. But what was I supposed to do when you, Casey, fell in love with Nathan and got married in four whirlwind months? (We all love a great romance, right?) But then you, Lisa, stepped in and made certain I didn't lose my mind when I released book one in the Thatcher Sisters series and turned in book two!

Rachelle Gardner, my agent: It was fun to reminisce during the past year about how it all began. How Beth Jusino introduced us back when I wrote nonfiction and then I transitioned to the "dark side" to write fiction. And through it all you've been my voice of reason, my voice of truth—someone I trust without hesitation. And you're my friend, too. Can it get any better than that? Let's find out.

Susie May Warren: friend and mentor and founder of the My Book Therapy writing community. I always go back to what you taught me when writing fiction was like deciphering hieroglyphics. (I can still hear you asking, "Are you okay, Beth?" at that first writers' retreat. I wasn't, but you stuck with me and turned me into a novelist.)

My family: My husband, Rob, and our children and their spouses: Josh and Meagan, Katie Beth and Nate, Amy and David, Christa, and yes, my GRANDkiddos. You all are, simply put, the best. You hear the words *"I'm on deadline"* and you get it. You know the imaginary characters are back in the building—back in our lives—and that I'm going to be up early and stay up late. I'll be distracted. Exhausted. Elated. Frustrated. And every emotion in between. You remind me to eat. To sleep. And yes, to get back to the computer and put words on the page.

ABOUT THE AUTHOR

BETH K. VOGT is a nonfiction author and editor who said she'd never write fiction. She's the wife of an Air Force family physician (now in solo practice) who said she'd never marry a doctor—or anyone in the military. She's a mom of four who said she'd never have kids. Now Beth believes God's best often waits behind doors marked *Never*. The Thatcher Sisters novels are her women's fiction series with Tyndale.

Beth is a 2016 Christy Award winner, a 2016 ACFW Carol Award winner, and a 2015 RITA finalist. Her 2014 novel, *Somebody Like You*, was one of *Publishers Weekly*'s Best Books of 2014. *A November Bride* was part of the Year of Weddings series published by Zondervan. Having authored ten contemporary romance novels or novellas, Beth believes there's more to happily ever after than the fairy tales tell us.

An established magazine writer and former editor of the leadership magazine for MOPS International, Beth blogs for Novel Rocket and also enjoys speaking to writers' groups and mentoring other writers. She lives in Colorado with her husband, Rob, who has adjusted to discussing the lives of imaginary people, and their youngest daughter, Christa, who loves to play volleyball and enjoys writing her own stories. Connect with Beth at www.bethvogt.com.

DISCUSSION QUESTIONS

1. Payton decides to start a book club with her sisters in the hope that it will draw them closer together. Have you ever participated in a book club with family or friends? What kind of relationships developed?

2. Jillian has come through her treatment for breast cancer but finds herself struggling with the aftermath of her chemotherapy: forgetfulness, fatigue, loss of appetite, and discouragement. Have you experienced an illness that left you unable to function day to day? How did you cope?

3. Johanna is shocked when Dr. Axton Miller gets the promotion she's worked so hard for, especially after she's been interim pharmacy director for six months. What would you have done if you'd been in Johanna's place? Would you have stayed and tried to work with your new boss, or would you have decided it was time

to look for a new job where you would be appreciated? When have you found yourself in a situation where you and your boss or a coworker had very different approaches to work?

4. Johanna and Beckett have been in a long-distance relationship for eight years. What's your take on long-distance romances? If you've been in one, do you have any tips for success?

5. Jillian and Geoff decide to renovate their kitchen but discover one problem after another. If you've watched home renovation shows like *Flip or Flop* or *Property Brothers*, you know that happens all the time. Have you ever undertaken a major house project like theirs? It's time to share your house reno horror stories!

6. Jillian discovers Geoff has kept a huge secret from her—that he had two brothers and that his younger brother died, leaving him unwilling to have children— ever. Where do your sympathies lie: with Geoff and his grief or with Jillian? How do you think they should handle the issue of whether to adopt or not? Has infertility or childlessness touched your life in any way?

7. Jillian feels like she is stuck as the middle Thatcher sister—like she is "just Jillian." Does your birth order— your position in your family—define who you are? How so?

8. Payton is still questioning what she believes about God—and also why she believes in God, afraid that she's choosing Him because of Pepper and Zach. Has your faith ever been tripped up by others' expectations for you?

9. In *Moments We Forget*, both Payton and Jillian choose to believe in Jesus. Stop for a moment and think about your own faith journey. Maybe you don't believe there's a God who loves you, who created you. Or maybe you're searching for answers . . . or are in a season of doubt. Maybe you can remember when you chose to believe in the sacrificial gift of mercy and grace God offers through His Son, Jesus. Share your stories with one another.

10. At the end of the book, Jillian decides to choose one word to focus on for the next year, instead of doing New Year's resolutions. She asks Geoff if he'd like to pick a word for the year, too. What did you think of the words they chose? Which do you prefer: resolutions or theme words—or neither? If you did choose one word to focus on for a year, what would it be?

Keep an eye out for the next Thatcher Sisters novel.

VISIT WWW.BETHVOGT.COM FOR UPDATES.